A star sleuth, Father Blackie Ryan probes the brutal
assault on a star actress...in the most stunning
dram

Y0-DOV-434

HAPPY ARE THE CLEAN OF HEART

Her smoldering combination of innocence and sensuality had captivated the world. Now, on the eve of the most electrifying breakthrough of her life, Lisa Malone is ruthlessly struck down by an incensed, unknown attacker.

For her old and intimate friend, Father Blackie Ryan, the plentiful list of suspects includes her Mob-connected charity consultant, a pair of con-artist actors on the downsides of their careers, her envious biographer, an angry radical nun, her lovesick agent.

Father Ryan must find the culprit quickly. Because the would-be killer's work is not yet finished...

Will the killer strike again?

NOVELS BY ANDREW M. GREELEY

The Cardinal Sins

The Passover Trilogy

Thy Brother's Wife
Ascent Into Hell
Lord of the Dance

Time Between the Stars

Virgin and Martyr
Angels of September

Father Blackie Ryan Mysteries

Happy Are the Meek
Happy Are the Clean of Heart

HAPPY ARE THE CLEAN OF HEART

A FATHER BLACKIE RYAN STORY

Andrew M. Greeley

WARNER BOOKS

A Warner Communications Company

WARNER BOOKS EDITION

Map by Heidi Hornaday

The six-line refrain from *Catch a Falling Star* is reprinted by permission
of Emily Music Corporation and Paul Vance Publishing.

Warner Books, Inc.
666 Fifth Avenue
New York, N.Y. 10103

 A Warner Communications Company

Printed in the United States of America

First Printing: August, 1986
10 9 8 7 6 5 4 3 2 1

For June and Marvin

Catch a falling star
Put it in your pocket
Save it for a rainy day
Catch a falling star
Put it in your pocket
Never let it fade away.

—Lee Pockriss and
Paul Vance

How oft, amid those overflowing streets,
Have I gone forward with the crowd, and said
Unto myself, "The face of every one
That passes by me is a mystery!"

—William Wordsworth

Life is like an artist studio, filled with half finished scenes
that are quickly forgotten.

—Marcel Proust

Monsignor John Blackwood Ryan, Ph.D., is far too wise and far too gentle to be like any existing rector of Holy Name Cathedral. Sean Cronin is too courageous and outspoken to be like any known archbishop of Chicago. All the other characters in the book, Ryan clan or not, are imaginary, fictitious, made-up and otherwise products of my fantasy. Anyone thinking differently is wrong, that's all.

The account of naval action off Samar Island on the third day of the battle of Leyte Gulf is accurate, though Ned Ryan's participation in it is fictional.

THE BEATITUDES

This series of stories, featuring Monsignor John Blackwood Ryan, is based on the Beatitudes from Jesus's Sermon on the Mount. A variant form is found in Luke's so-called Sermon on the Plain which is accompanied by parallel Woes. I choose Matthew's version, which is probably later and derivative, because it is so much better known.

The Sermon on the Mount is not, according to the scripture scholars, an actual sermon Jesus preached, but rather a compendium of His sayings and teachings edited by the author of St. Matthew's Gospel, almost certainly from a preexisting source compendium.

The Beatitudes represent, if not in His exact words, an important component of the teachings of Jesus, but they should not be interpreted as a new list of rules. Jesus came to teach that rules are of little use in our relationship with God. We do not constrain God's love by keeping rules, since that love is a freely given starting point of our relationship (a passionate love affair) with God. We may keep rules because all communities need rules to stay together and because as ethical beings we should behave ethically, but that, according to Jesus, is a minor part of our relationship with God.

Nonetheless, some Christians, early on, went back to the rule game. It attempted to bind us so that our proper behavior would bind God. Often religion was pictured as a sort of contract: we keep rules, and God keeps His promise to us—sort of like giving a professor back in our tests the material we have transferred from his notebook to our notebook.

In such a framework the Beatitudes were converted into

new rules much tougher than those revealed on Sinai. All right, some Christians said, ours is a much tougher religion. Jesus and the Father, one might imagine, are not amused.

In fact, the Beatitudes are descriptive, not normative. They are a portrait of the Christian life as it becomes possible for those who believe in the love of God as disclosed by Jesus. If we trust in God, we are then able to take the risks the Beatitudes imply, never living them perfectly, of course, but growing and developing in their radiant goodness and experiencing the happiness of life that comes from such goodness.

"Cleanliness" or "purity of heart" does not mean, despite the sermons we all may have heard in our various churches in ages past, immunity to erotic images or longings. That sort of purity of heart belongs, perhaps, to angels and, perhaps, to us after we are dead. Moreover, it is not at all clear that very many people would opt for such purity of heart. Life without erotic longings might be easier, but it would certainly be much more dull.

"Cleanliness of heart" in the sense of St. Matthew's Gospel, means, rather, integrity of motivation, clear-headedness about the reasons for our behavior, honesty to ourselves about the purposes of our actions, a vigorous resistance to self-deception and, especially, resolute refusal to succumb to the insidious, demoralizing, and pervasive vice of envy or to be intimidated by those who have succumbed to that vice.

DRAMATIS PERSONAE

Lisa Malone, the famous singer
Roderick Malone, M.D., her brother
George Quinn, her husband
Kenneth Woods, her agent
Kerry Randall, her biographer
Tad Thomas, her co-star
Dina King, her protégée
Sister Winifred Murray, her conscience
Francis Leonard, her almoner
Monsignor John Blackwood Ryan, Ph.D., her sometime priest
Sean Cronin, cardinal archbishop of Chicago
Michael Patrick Vincent Casey, sometime acting superinten-
    dent of police, city of Chicago
Edward J. "Ned" Ryan, father to Monsignor Ryan
Various and sundry members of the Ryan Clan

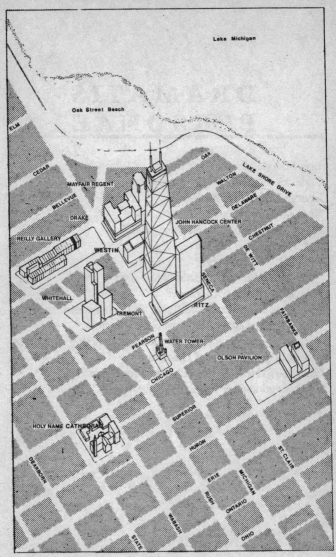

1
ALIQUIS

Murder, I thought with a wry smile, is as delicious as the taste of white chocolate mousse.

Mentally I savored the picture of the lovely face collapsing under the impact of my angry attack, coming apart like the face of a statue being devastated by a hammer and chisel. Or the mound of delectable white chocolate mousse being sliced up with a spoon. Human bones cracked more easily than did marble statues. The fog, rolling in rapidly from the dark, grim-faced lake, became blood red in my mind's eye. Tonight was the final chance, the last opportunity to discharge the hatred of so many years. I turned away from the lake and walked slowly up Delaware Street. The fog drifted ahead, leading the way.

Many times the image of her face shattering had brought cleansing peace at the end of a bitter and anxious day. It had been a fantasy at first, harmless if hateful daydreaming. As my sense of outrage and injustice grew and festered, the fantasy became richer and more demanding. In dreams I often did destroy that offensively lovely face, having first brutally beaten and tormented the victim's body. In the morning, before full consciousness, I was often not certain whether it had been only a dream.

What had been a pleasant fantasy gradually became an emotional and physical necessity. Lisa must die if I was to survive. That ought to have been clear long ago. Now it was so obvious that I wondered how there could ever have been any doubt.

Moreover, tonight murder was absolutely safe. They would never know. The door would open, a quick blow of the black-

1

jack to her jaw to stun, a jab with a hypodermic syringe to render her silent but not unconscious, then a leisurely but savage beating and sexual desecration and, even more pleasurable, the final destruction of that hated face. A few quick blows to the head, and all would be finished. I could slip out of the hotel room, ride down the elevator, dispose of the disguise, and walk freely away in the fog-shrouded streets of the city.

It was all so easy once you had the courage and the imagination.

God, I thought, licking saliva, how sweet revenge would be.

Most of the John Hancock Center was hiding in the fog, neither seeing nor seen. Across the street, in front of the white brick Westin Hotel, tongues of fog licking at its cream logo and gray awnings, long lines of travelers waited patiently for taxis and buses to take them to O'Hare, like concentration camp victims waiting for the gas chambers. Still encased in the fog (warm and protective it seemed) I avoided the main entrance of the hotel, a falsely glittering blur of yellow lights. How like Lisa to try to hide incognito in an inexpensive hotel instead of staying at the Whitehall down the street, where she belonged. Or the Mayfair Regent over on the lake. In either she would have been as safe as a cloistered Carmelite behind her double grill.

I crossed Michigan Avenue and walked half a block towards Rush Street before turning around and strolling along the construction site where the 900 North Michigan building used to be. Typical of the city to destroy such a landmark. Whore city.

Should anyone see the dark-clad figure slipping through the fog, it would be thought that perhaps I was some pervert drifting over from Old Town. My disguise, easy and simple, would confirm such a suspicion.

I hesitated at the Michigan Avenue entrance of the hotel. Stupid fool, don't go in that way. Why walk the whole length of the lobby? Walk by the main entrance and go to the second entrance on Delaware, across from the door to the Hancock condo. How dumb can you get?

Shaken by the near mistake, I breathed deeply before entering the revolving door. Take it easy, relax. This is fun, not work.

Lots of fun.

Inside, the hotel was a mix of chandeliers, mirrors, and

marble—fake Versailles—with a curved, free-standing stair-case to the second floor. A long line of exhausted travelers was waiting, like kids in a rock concert ticket line, to check in.

I ducked into a washroom and quickly adjusted the final details of a disguise—no longer a pervert, now a person of mystery but completely respectable. Before leaving the security provided by the door of the stall, I caressed the cosh lovingly, solid oak covered with hand-tooled leather. It would do its savage and brutal work efficiently—first the nose, then the cheek-bones, then the jaw, then the eyes, and then the final crushing blows into the temples and the forehead.

The excitement of vengeance and execution heightened my sensations, particularly the sense of smell—liquor in the bar, human sweat crowded around the registration desk, cigarette smoke hanging in the lobby, the undefinable aroma of illicit sex that seemed to flourish in all hotels.

Often I had imagined slashing her face with a razor-sharp little knife, but crushing it seemed somehow more satisfactory, although the knife was still available underneath the belt of my black slacks. Obliterate it, wipe it out, crush forever her offensively piquant eyes, her marvelous cheekbones, her pert nose, her lightly smiling mouth, her cute little chin, eliminate Lisa's hateful beauty forever from the face of the earth with savage, brutal, pitiless blows.

Thinking about it was like imagining sex a few moments before you met your lover.

Lisa finally had gone too far. All else might have been forgiven. What she had done now deserved death, clamored for death, insisted on death.

My mouth jammed shut, fingers clenched, teeth gritted. No, I must not lose control now. Save the pleasure for afterward, when the job is done. Body-wrenching pleasure should occur at the end of sex, not at the start of foreplay.

In the lobby I looked around and smiled. Anonymity was easy in the busy rush of the middle-range executive and convention hotel. I picked up the phone and softly whispered Lisa's room number. There was no answer. Where could she be? She had not gone out, of that I was sure. Why was she taking so long? Typical of the woman's stupidity and incompetence.

"Ms. Malone." The bright, cheerful voice, loved by tens of millions of Americans.

I spoke softly.

"Oh, sorry to have kept you waiting." A giggle. *"I was in the shower, singing in the shower, if you can imagine that. Come on up. I'll mix you a drink."*

That would be useful, I thought, permitting myself a faint smile. Sip the drink slowly and luxuriously, describing to the temporarily paralyzed woman exactly what you were going to do to her, amusing yourself sexually and inflicting delicious pain as a prelude to even more terrible agony.

Again I fought to regain self-control.

I boarded the elevator as quietly as a cat slips into a kitchen and lightly touched the button. Two fat, tipsy businessmen shoved the doors open just as they were closing, raucous Willy Loman caricatures from a New Yorker cartoon. At first I paid them no attention. Then with dismay I realized they had not pressed a button. They were going to the same floor. It did not matter, of course, it did not matter. No one would know what had happened until tomorrow morning, and the businessmen would perhaps be on planes flying home before the news reached the papers. They were sufficiently inebriated that they would not remember their companion on the ride to the fourth floor. Even if they did, my disguise was brilliantly effective for all its simplicity.

Nevertheless, I hesitated, an airline pilot inspecting a dubious weather report. The risks were higher now; not very high, but still, higher than they had been. The probability that others would get off on the fourth floor had been considered, weighed, evaluated, and then dismissed as not important; theoretical probabilities, I was discovering, are not as disturbing as actual dangers.

The businessmen turned in the direction of Lisa's room. I turned in the opposite direction, walking the full length of the corridor until the sound of their noisy laughter was shut out abruptly by the harsh clang of a slamming door. I hesitated. Facing the wall at the end of the corridor, heart beating rapidly, mouth now parched, nerves as tense as the strings on a harp. To the left were the exit stairs. I need only follow the *carefully conceived escape plan. Step out into the stairwell, quickly shed my disguise, stuff it into the small carrying bag, walk down the stairs to the third floor, board the elevator, descend to the lobby. Perhaps it would be satisfaction enough to dream tonight once again of what might have happened, revel again in the fantasies of make-believe pleasure, pretend for a few hours, at any rate, that Lisa had been destroyed.*

If they ever found out . . .

Most journalists hated Lisa so much that they wanted to do to her what I intended to do. They were merely less honest with themselves about their feelings. But if Lisa was killed, brutally, savagely, mercilessly, the media would have no pity on her murderer—no bail, no psychiatric excuses from standing trial, no favorable coverage of last-minute vigils at Cook County jail before the switch was thrown on the electric chair. Lisa Malone's killer would be hounded into the grave, even if they secretly felt that the destruction of that evil woman was utterly appropriate.

I considered very carefully. The chances of exposure had been increased only minimally by the two businessmen on the elevator. Indeed, that possibility had already been considered, had it not, and been discounted? Why hesitate now, when it might be weeks or months or even years before there was another similar opportunity?

Finally, so what? A world in which Lisa Malone continued to exist was by no means to be preferred to death. It was intolerable that Lisa should live. If her death meant my death, then so be it.

I turned and walked calmly, confidently down the empty corridor to room 403 and knocked on the door, the smooth feel of the cosh providing strength and vigor to the knock.

There was a wait, almost as long as in the lobby. The fool had gone back into the shower.

Finally the door opened slightly and Lisa's eyes and nose appeared, freckled with drops of water.

"Well, hello." She threw the door open. "What are you doing dressed up like that? Come in, come in!" She threw her arms around me. "It's wonderful to see you!"

I was filled with love for my victim, the same sweet, soft, mellow affection that Lisa always produced in me, melting away anger and tension and frustration. Destroying Lisa would be an act of hatred, but also an act of love.

She was wearing a white terrycloth robe hastily thrown around her slim, elegant body. Her midnight-black hair was pasted against her head, framing her ethereally delicate face. She smelled of soap and shampoo. I worshiped her, adored her, loved her.

Lisa, sensing the passion of the embrace, tried to ease gracefully away. My love would not be denied. Ever so delicately the cosh banged into the side of Lisa's head.

Her eyes widened in surprise and then in stunned disorientation. I lowered her gently to the floor, peeled back the shoulder of her robe, removed the hypodermic syringe from the bag while Lisa shook her head as though to clear her vision and struggled for consciousness and articulation.

I jabbed the needle into her arm and pushed the plunger.

Lisa cried out, not loudly, but enough to frighten me; I stifled the scream with a firm, gloved hand.

The drug took effect quickly, as it was supposed to. Lisa's body relaxed. Her eyes became glazed. She lay on the floor confused, tranquil, and helpless.

I picked up the drink that had been prepared from where it sat on the coffee table. Yes, of course, Lisa would remember what kind of drink it would be at this hour of the day. I was exhilarated, sky-high. Murder was the most powerful aphrodisiac. Slowly, for now there was all the time in the world, I sipped the drink and then placed it on the coffee table.

"Don't go away," I said to Lisa with a snicker and went into the bathroom and turned on the shower, adjusting the temperature so the water was the hottest possible.

"Scalding water." I returned to the parlor of Lisa's suite, and picked up the drink again. "That comes later."

I drained the glass and then filled it up again with the materials that Lisa had thoughtfully prepared. Then I sat down on the sofa, beside which Lisa was lying, passive, beautiful, powerless. Slowly, gently, tenderly I removed her terrycloth robe, loving preparation by a pagan pirate for the ravishing of a frightened Christian matron.

Such a lovely body, slim, lithe, yet intensely erotic. Marvelous breasts, full yet neatly sculpted. Perhaps eventually the knife should be used. All in good time.

I lit a cigarette, puffed on it leisurely, and then delicately pressed the glowing tip to the smooth skin on Lisa's belly, savoring the sweet smell of burning human flesh.

Lisa tried to scream. All that emerged from her lips was a soft whimper.

Her eyes dulled with pain and then looked at me with a mute plea for mercy, a plea that faded into resignation. Almost as though she had expected her death sentence and was resigned to it. A single tear appeared in each eye.

I willed hardness of heart. Now was no time for pity.

"Timelessly beautiful." I laughed. "Just as they say in the papers. You and I are going to have ourselves a very interesting evening, Lisa Malone."

Drink in one hand, I began to fondle Lisa with the other, caressing and hurting at the same time. "Do I see a touch of fear in those lovely if glazed blue eyes of yours?" I kissed her lightly on the lips. "Well, there's nothing to be afraid about, Lisa, dear, not for a while anyway. Let me go through the agenda and tell you exactly what I'm going to do to you. The nice thing about scopolamine is that you will know exactly what I'm doing and enjoy every second of it."

I twisted one of her beautiful breasts viciously. Lisa's attempt to shriek with pain was only a faint sigh, a dying puppy.

"And let me tell you the ending first. After everything else is over, and after I've had all the fun I possibly can with you"—I held up the cosh—"I'm going to smash your brains out!"

2
GEORGE

There were mixed emotions in the neighborhood at the news that Lisa was coming home for Christmas in 1970. "Yeah," said Blackie Ryan, who had gone to school with her and dated her occasionally, "a mixture of envy and resentment. The neighborhood doesn't need a star at Christmas time."

I, George Quinn, dubbed by her—not without a smile which, God help me, could have been interpreted as hinting at affection—George the Bean Counter, didn't need this particular Christmas star either. I would pull out of my files the dusty copies of the unfinished poems I once wrote about her and indulge again in foolish fantasies, fantasies that still are foolish as I write this memoir for Kerry's research project.

Blackie, a cherubic little man with kindly blue eyes blinking endlessly behind thick glasses and a "Father Brown" manner that is not altogether accidental, was being uncharacteristically imprecise. In fact, most of the people in the neighborhood couldn't have cared one way or another. Way behind in their Christmas shopping and uninterested in stars anyway, they had only the dimmest idea who Lisa Malone was or that she had once lived in the neighborhood. Some of the quiet people were kind of happy that our own celebrity would be home again. The rest of us, the self-anointed arbiters of the taste and the keepers of the conscience of the parish (people like my mother), were outraged.

Either Lisa would come home as a movie and TV superstar and would be denounced as "putting on airs"; or she would reappear as the same old Lisa and be condemned for trying once more to win our affection and respect, something that we would never give her.

"She has three strikes already," Blackie went on dourly. "She had the effrontery to pursue a career, the shamelessness to choose a career in Hollywood, and, worst of all, the unforgivable audacity to be an enormous success. The woman is intolerable, there is nothing else to be said about it."

There were those who would have said that the neighborhood was none of Blackie's business, since he had been ordained and assigned to a working class neighborhood in Jefferson Park. "That's the end of him," the Ryan haters in the neighborhood had said with a sigh of relief (premature as it turned out). In any event, his assessment was correct: our shooting star blazed a dazzling trail across the Christmas sky over the neighborhood, flicking out sparks of light that touched a lot of us, and then streaked away for Los Angeles, her brightness undimmed but some of the luster of her innocence forever lost.

It might have been better, all things considered, if she had descended on the neighborhood with a limo, a chauffeur, a maid, a mink coat, two French poodles, a press agent, and several trunks full of clothes. Even my mother would have been impressed, although offended. Lisa elected to return as the same old Lisa, riding the Rock Island (still called that even if it is owned by the RTA) in brown slacks, sweater, scarf, and beige cloth coat, wearing no makeup and carrying her own garment bag, a pretty young woman returning for Christmas, perhaps from graduate school. We met at the end of the car as we prepared to exit at the 91st Street station. I had seen her as soon as she boarded the car, of course, and knew that I wouldn't open my book of Paul Claudel's plays on that ride.

Blackie would have said of me that I was twenty years ahead of my time: I was thinking the thoughts of the 1950s about the books of the 1930s.

"You can't hide from me behind those horn-rimmed glasses, George." A brush of lips against my cheek. "Not married, I see. Wouldn't be working on Saturday if you were. Poor Lou

Anne. You look very proper and conservative and successful.
And nice." Second quick kiss.

One of the troubles with Lisa was that you didn't expect
someone that pretty to be so intelligent. One quick scan of
me with her probing blue eyes, and she knew all there was
to know about me.

Somehow, while I was recapturing my breathing mechanisms, her garment bag was transferred to my custody. You've
seen her on TV, of course, so I don't have to go into many
of the details of what took my breath away. Lisa looked like
a young woman in an ad for the Irish Tourist Board, maybe
a little bit too sexy for Church-sponsored tours, but perfect
for attracting young American men to Irish universities: short
ebony hair, skim-milk skin (she hated suntans), dancing hazel
eyes, a glowing, impish smile that lighted a delicately sculpted
face, and a figure which, for all its obvious appeal, also hinted
at fragility that needed to be protected. "Chaste Irish Catholic
eroticism," said one of the reviews of her first TV special
(*Lisa!*) earlier that year. "Sugar-coated sexuality," sneered
another.

Those of us who knew her would not have argued with
either description, but we would have rejected any suggestion
that her screen image was different from her private image.
She could not pretend even if she wanted to. She stole her
first big feature film, *A Time Without Tears*, from the leads
simply by being Lisa for the audience—funny, cute, viva-
cious, and incorrigibly if subtly graceful. In the bedroom
scene, without most of her clothes (to the deep offense of
my mother and her friends, although Lisa was overdressed
by the standards of many films), Lisa as the ingenious if
innocent virgin blended grace and comedy into an irresistible
combination.

"Shameful," clucked the neighborhood.

"Lisa!" exclaimed those of us who knew her.

So to be kissed by such a person on a snowy Saturday
early-afternoon in December was an experience not lightly
to be dismissed. Twice.

"Lou Anne was tired of waiting. And I work for Arthur
Andersen, not my father. But I am an accountant and I still

live at home. So, unlike you, I've only partly broken with the neighborhood."

"I haven't broken with the neighborhood." She accepted my hand for help down the steps of the train. "Why would I want to do that? I've gone away for my education and career. This is still home and always will be. Why not?"

Indeed, the same old Lisa, blithely oblivious to the more mean and nasty human emotions. She was not coming home for this Christmas of 1970 either to impress us or to win our affections. She was coming home because it was home and because it was Christmas.

"I suppose you must find Los Angeles's Beverly Hills much more interesting than Chicago's?" I held her arm tightly, lest she slip on the ice of the station platform. Large flakes of snow were drifting lazily across the little park, touching the black hair escaped from her scarf.

"Oh, I don't know, there're a lot of cougars in those canyons, and I don't mean Mercury Cougars either. Mary Kate Ryan Murphy said she'd meet me"—the merry laugh that charmed her film and TV audiences—"as if I didn't know where the Ryan clan lives." She glanced around the station.

A small girl child, perhaps ten, with a blonde ponytail, a piquant face, and vast blue eyes appeared.

"Good afternoon, Miss Malone," she recited from memory, as if repeating an elocution class exercise. "I'm Caitlin Murphy and my mother said that I should meet you and that she had patients till three today because all the sick people are sicker at Christmas and that you're welcome home and that..." She sniggered as breath and memory failed her.

"That you should lead me home." She kissed the child on the forehead. "I remember you when you were two years old, Caitlin. My, you're so grown up. You know George? He's big because he played football, but he's nice. He kind of carries my garment bag and fights off cougars, middlewestern ones, that is. Can he walk home with us?"

Caitlin considered me dubiously and then sniggered again. "Okay, I guess."

Lisa took one little mittened hand and Caitlin took mine in the other. We walked the two blocks to the Murphys' house

(Joe Murphy, Mary Kate Ryan's husband, is a psychiatrist, too) singing that Santa Claus was coming to town and praising Rudolph, the Red-Nosed Reindeer.

"My mommy says your best carol is 'O Holy Night.'"

"All *right*, Caitlin." Hands on her hips in mock exasperation, with the snow falling harder and darkness descending rapidly on the tree-shrouded houses with Christmas tree lights already shining in the windows, a woman hailed recently as the hottest young actress in Hollywood sang Adolphe Adam's "Cantique de Noel" for a ten-year-old worshiper and a twenty-eight-year-old cougar fighter. At that magic moment the latter would have quite willingly taken on a pride of saber-toothed tigers for her.

I walked home from the Murphy house, the snow stinging my face, and remembered Lisa and Kerry Ann Mulloy on the beach at South Shore in the late years of grammar school as their bodies showed the first appealing signs of womanhood. Kerry used to run tirelessly from one end of the beach to the other. Lisa in a maroon (her favorite color, I was to learn later) swimsuit would keep up with her for a while and then sink into the sand and stretch sensuously, causing my poor heart to bang against my ribs. She seemed to me then to be an incredibly pretty little girl with a sweet smile and a lovely voice. I fell in love with her on the spot. Remove the word "little" from the last two sentences, and I don't suppose much has changed.

Her mother and mine did not particularly like each other. Both viewed themselves as staunch defenders of the social proprieties and defined the other as putting on airs and displaying improper pretensions.

I chased the pleasant pictures of Lisa out of my mind and entered our house, fifteen minutes later than planned. "I *certainly* hope that nonsense isn't starting again," my mother commented as soon as I arrived home—such is the speed at which scandalous news travels in our neighborhood. I had long ago learned simply not to reply to such comments.

When pressed with the accusation that I had once dated Lisa Malone, my mother would smugly reply, "I put a stop to that nonsense in a hurry." Lou Anne Sprague's father is my father's partner, and on the day Lou Anne was born, my mother began to make the plans for our wedding. It was possible that I might marry someone else but unthinkable that it could be "May Malone's affected little brat."

My mother is very good at taking credit for whatever happens. I did come home from Notre Dame to date Lisa occasionally in her senior year (I'm two years older) and we went out often both in the neighborhood and at Grand Beach the summer after she graduated. (Blackie was bound for the seminary by then.) No one ended it, however; Lisa and I simply drifted in different directions. I was a bookish, shy accountant in the making, with musical tastes that ran to the classical and the serious, and she was a comic opera comet already exploding toward her place in the starry firmament.

It occurred to me as I went up to my room and began to read a computer magazine (there were only a few in 1970) that she must have known that I did not marry Lou Anne. I was sure that she and Blackie Ryan kept in touch with each other. Indeed, there were vague hints among the Ryans that he had helped her with a drug problem four or five years before. The headlines had said, "Chicago Starlet in Drug and Sex Bust." But no drug charges were filed against her. "Where there's smoke, there's fire," my mother insisted.

Blackie had flown to Los Angeles during his summer vacation, and one had the impression that the Ryans all heaved a sigh of relief upon his return—not for Blackie, but for Lisa.

So why was she pretending to have only just discovered my bachelorhood?

I thought as I went to sleep the night she sang for me and Caitlin in the snow on Glenwood Drive, that our little scene would make a great setting for her next special. It would be pleasant, I admitted in my last conscious moment, to have a daughter like Caitlin.

From the second grade on, Lisa had had a circle of admirers and friends who were entranced by her enthusiasm and charm. When her mother pulled her out of St. Praxides (after a big fight with Sister Superior) and sent her to a private academy ("A talented child like my Lisa needs special training"), she continued to be friends with the others kids in the parish.

Finally after two years of high school, she persuaded her father—a defense attorney who worked mostly for the Outfit before he became a political judge and left the rearing of the children to his much younger wife—that she belonged in a Catholic school. She was an instant hit at Mother Macauley, carrying off leads in the school play and soloing in the choir's annual Christmas record both of the years she was there ("O Holy Night" both times, of course). Her circle of worshipers expanded dramatically—as did the circle of resentment.

Christmas was Lisa's special time above all others. She poured her energy and organizing skills—which were and are considerable, as evidenced by her recent success as a producer—into a round of parties, concerts, benefits, and sessions of strolling carolers. Was the temperature below zero? Dress warmly; there's only one Christmas every year. Was there a foot of snow? All the more fun to mix caroling with snowball fights. And heaven help you when Lisa decided that your face required washing.

There were many of us boys, of course, who could hardly wait to be dragged into a snowbank by Lisa.

None of us who adored Lisa expected her success—two platinum records and an Academy Award nomination before she was twenty-six. But neither were we surprised by Lisa on the screen. She was the way she'd always been. Her acting skills more polished, her voice in much better control (the voice teachers Mrs. Malone had hired turned out to be inept), her humor a little more deft. Otherwise it was an act we'd all seen before.

Her voice, as you know, is "sweet" rather than powerful, and limited in its range. She doesn't do much rock, and only the lightest of light opera. "Bridge Over Troubled Waters" and "Raindrops Keep Falling on My Head" were her favorites that year—that was before her annual Christmas special (*Lisa at Christmas!*) became almost as much a part of Christmas in America as the Wise Men.

One critic suggested she was born in the wrong era: she was designed to sing Victor Herbert. At a time of Altamont and Woodstock, she sang as though the Beatles didn't exist. "Nonrelevant music," sniffed *Time*. "A Singer for Escapists," said *Rolling Stone* contemptuously. "A Kathryn Grayson or an Ann Blyth for her generation," *The New York Times* said, perhaps more accurately.

There was no ideology in her music, not because she lacked political concerns ("Why should anyone care what I think about politics?" she asked one interviewer), but because as always she did what she could do and did not attempt anything else. She admitted that she hated the Viet Nam war but that did not prevent her from going to Viet Nam one Christmas with Bob Hope.

In Viet Nam I had not heard about her success in her first appearance at Las Vegas and hence could not believe it was the same Lisa Malone. Still I pulled all kinds of strings to get to the Bob Hope show, but I was so far back, I couldn't tell whether it was our Lisa or not until she started to sing.

I don't suppose I could have talked to her that night even if I had tried, but I didn't try.

An attractive, talented young woman from our own neighborhood, ideologically inoffensive, who managed in feature articles written about her to sound intelligent, pleasant, and even-tempered—why did we resent her instead of celebrating her?

Those who come from neighborhoods or small towns will understand why: "She could win the Oscar, the Emmy, the Tony, and the Nobel Prize to boot," Blackie Ryan observed, his eyes blinking rapidly. "And it wouldn't help. She's still May Malone's daughter. That means she is a reject by definition."

In communities like ours, some people are always in by definition, no matter what they do. The Ryan clan is loud, contentious, attractive, and dissident. Kate Collins Ryan (Ned's first wife and Blackie and Mary Kate's mother) was a radical always and at one time a Communist. After she died, Ned married a much younger woman (selected, it was said, by Kate on her death bed) and set about rearing a second family. The Ryans collect strays and rejects like Lisa—and me, if I'd let them—and defy the neighborhood arbiters of taste. Half the people in the parish bitterly resent them. Yet no one would dream of suggesting that they are outsiders. If you are a Ryan, you can do nothing wrong.

If you are May Malone's daughter, you can do nothing worthwhile—and TV specials, platinum records, even critical kudos for your first serious feature film (playing the songwriter's wife in *Melody in the Night*, a movie about World War II, a hint of the serious acting that later became the most important part of her work) are irrelevant.

As any community does for its rejects, we fashioned brief descriptions of her, which were applied from her sixth birthday to her twenty-sixth—"affected" (or "stuck up"), "spoiled," and "her mother pushes her too much." In 1970 the only change brought on by her success was that "push" was used in the past tense. Once, a community said, "Is this not the carpenter's son? How come he's working miracles?" We said, "Is this not May Malone's daughter? What difference does it make if she has her own TV special?"

May was, you see, a very pushy woman. There was nothing wrong with being a social climber in our neighborhood. In those days women whose children were in school often had little else to do. There were, however, unwritten but very important rules. May violated them left and right. She joined the Saddle and Cycle Club rather than the Beverly Country Club. She aspired to associate with Lake Forest elites. She went to polo matches in Oak Brook. She dressed her daughter in "daring" dresses (fashions of the year after next), intruded her in theatricals and weddings where she wasn't wanted, arranged her debut at the Passvant Cotillion instead of the Presentation Ball, tried to send her to Bryn Mawr instead of St. Mary's of Notre Dame, made a nuisance out of herself jabbering about Lisa's dates with South Shore and North Shore boys, and didn't show proper respect for her betters, women like my mother and Lucinda Sprague and Harriet Finch. None of them had to admit, as May did, that, despite her marriage to a distinguished if somewhat down-at-the-heels political family, her father had been a "saloon keeper."

In 1970 they would add that "poor" May got what she deserved. She did not expect that Lisa would break the deadlock of St. Mary's versus Bryn Mawr by opting for UCLA and Hollywood. Nor did she expect that as a sophomore she would appear in very minimal attire in a bit part (no more than thirty delicious seconds) as a young singer in the forgettable spy thriller *Bloodnet*, of which the critics said that hers was the only interesting part.

Her father had his third and last heart attack a week after he saw the film (about which he bragged to his colleagues at Cook County Superior Court the next day). Everyone in the neighborhood (except his cardiologist) blamed the attack on *Bloodnet*, including, it is to be feared, May Malone. At the wake Lisa was treated as though she were a leper even by her own family. Her mother went off to live with Lisa's brother Roderick, a hotshot surgeon in Connecticut, ten years older than Lisa, and neither mother nor daughter ever returned to the neighborhood. In interviews Lisa would say that she visits her mother whenever she is in New York and that they are "good friends."

I have a tape of the film; while Lisa's clothes may leave something to be desired, she was anything but lascivious. Truth to tell she could not be lascivious if she wanted to. If she were stark naked you'd still have chaste Irish Catholic eroticism—which, mind you, is not necessarily bad.

So why come back to the neighborhood for Christmas after all that? Why come back to a place where you have a thin network of friends and a highly organized public opinion against you?

The answer reveals the final secret about Lisa and the one that tarnished her innocence during the 1970 visit: immune to resentment and envy herself, she hardly noticed the vices in others. She could not help but realize that some people in the neighborhood didn't like her. Yet even at her father's funeral, she was utterly unaware of the smug satisfaction of those who had always detested her. She came home at Christmas in 1970 not for vindication, not for acceptance, not to impress, but because she thought, poor, gentle girl, that the neighborhood was home, a place where she loved and was loved.

She swept down on the community like a playful winter storm. On Sunday after the 11:15 Mass, she shook hands and hugged old friends in the back of the church like she was the pastor or a candidate for public office. She even shook hands with and hugged the pastor. That morning she agreed to sing at the parish Christmas dance, the country club Christmas dance, the High Club dance, the YCS program at the county infirmary, the High Club Christmas play, the grammar school Christmas pageant, and the Mother Macauley Christmas festival.

Everyone wanted her to sing "I Think I Love You" (which the Partridge Family was doing at the time), "White Christmas," and "O Holy Night." Although my mother and her friends complained that it was all a public relations gimmick, there was no PR person present and, except for a note in Kup's column in the *Sun Times*, no press notice of her visit.

Lisa was having the time of her life, not enjoying a happy girlhood she never had, but rather, re-enacting a girlhood whose happiness had not been tainted by her mother's silliness or her neighbors' resentment. The neighborhood loved it. As John O'Connor wrote some years later in his column in *The New York Times*, "Even if you are determined to resist Lisa Malone, her laughter and her innocent beauty force you to smile." A lot of us smiled the week before Christmas of 1970.

Much of this was reported to me secondhand and with considerable disapproval. I didn't follow Lisa around. I was, however, constrained to be her date for the country club Christmas dance. Mary Kate Murphy complained to me that she had run out of residents from Little Company of Mary Hospital and asked would I please take Lisa as a personal favor?

Run out of dates for someone who had been named by *Esquire* as one of the fifteen most beautiful women in America? I went along with the game, however.

Her wardrobe did indeed seem to be limited to the single garment bag—a wine-colored suit, a white knit mini-dress with a red belt, and a white formal also with red trim, which she wore to the country club dance. The last named was modest enough to satisfy the morals of the most finicky mother superior. Not that it mattered: Lisa's figure was (and is) so attractive that she is erotic in almost anything. Especially to a lonely twenty-eight-year-old bachelor.

Mary Kate insisted that I dig my tux out of mothballs and wear my contact lenses. The pair of us attracted a lot of attention on the dance floor.

Remember what kind of a year 1970 was. The sixties were over, but there was still plenty of trouble. It was the year after Altamont, the year of Woodstock, the "incursion" into Cambodia, the Kent State and Jackson State shootings, the "interim" in which college kids were supposed to work for "peace" candidates (and mostly played basketball), revelation of the My Lai massacre, the collapse of Biafra, the murder of the Black Panthers in Chicago, Bobby Seale's trial in New Haven, and airline hijackings almost every other week. We all needed a little light and a little laughter. And our own local Tinker Bell returning from the land of the stars showered us with both.

Her first words when I picked her up, radiant and glowing, at Mary Kate's were that the pastor had invited her to sing "O Holy Night" at the midnight Mass. "The first time I've sung in church since I left . . . I go to church, so don't look shocked."

I pleaded that I was dazzled, not shocked. Then, since it made her happy, I added my congratulations on the midnight Mass song, something which, in the past, had always been reserved for adults.

She was an adult, too, but it was hard to admit. She was still Lisa, our luminous teenage package of concentrated womanly energy.

"I never dated a movie star before," I said in self-defense.

"I'm just Lisa." She smiled affectionately. She then proved it for the rest of the evening by needling me, gently but tellingly, about being a conservative, stuffy accountant—a bean counter. I responded with the defense that I was not a conservative and that's why I didn't work for my father, who believed that computers would never be important in our profession.

She listened carefully to my explanations about the future of personal computers and nodded intelligently. I had no idea whether she understood me, but she was so gorgeous that I didn't much care.

I also realized that she was sexually available to me. Nothing so crude or lewd as a proposition; no one else on the glittering dance floor would have noticed. We were not even dancing all that close. The woman I held in my arms as we danced, pale skin linen smooth, smelling of Christmas evergreen, was subtly submissive, inviting me to accept her, willing to yield herself completely to me, offering herself as a gift with no strings, other than Christmas ribbons, attached.

One of the fifteen most beautiful women in America in red and white wrapping as a Christmas present for you, George the Bean Counter. Are you going to accept the gift package? What are you going to do?

Her sparkling hazel eyes were amused by my mask—as she saw it—of the precise and dusty bean counter. She thought she saw something beneath the mask that she wanted, lightly, playfully, but definitely.

I love you, George the Bean Counter. Please love me in return.

All without a word being said. It's what happens when you find yourself dancing with an accomplished actress—more accomplished than her directors and critics realized then—in a white Christmas evening dress.

Lisa knew her target. She realized that she was in no danger of a one-night stand or anything of that sort. The invitation, however, contained no restrictions or limitations. It was a gift, pure and simple.

I was flattered and terrified and determined to run away as soon as I could escape from the club. How else would a sensible bean counter react?

That night, as I wrestled with fantasies, sure that her evergreen scent had come into my bedroom, and tried to sleep, I wondered if she had always danced with me that way when we were kids and I had never noticed. I also realized that she had returned to the neighborhood with an ulterior motive after all. Me. Doubtless it was a conspiracy set up by Blackie and Mary Kate. George the stray would be ministered to whether he wanted such attention or not.

I avoided her until midnight Mass. By then the luster of the shooting star had been snuffed out temporarily.

Our pastor at the time was an old-line Catholic liberal; he hated Nixon, denounced racism, and invited Dan Berrigan to speak in the parish hall. But he was pathologically afraid of complaints from parishioners. An anonymous letter or two, a few phone calls, a suggestion that "people" were criticizing him were enough to cause him to make a quick and arbitrary—and undiscussable—decision.

Harriet Finch, the chairman of the local Christian Family Movement group, called him the day before Christmas Eve to report that there was "talk all over the parish" about Lisa. "What's the point in keeping our kiddies away from R-rated movies and restricting their TV programs when you permit a woman who is not much better than a harlot to sing at midnight Mass? People are saying that they don't see why they should contribute to the Christmas collection when there is such hypocrisy in the Church."

That was that. A call went to the Murphy house five minutes later. Lisa was not home. Joe Murphy was told that "it has been decided" there would be no soloists at midnight Mass—the implication of the language being that the choir director or the curate in charge of the liturgy or maybe even the liturgy committee had made the decision. Joe, who is a quiet man compared to his in-laws, said that it was a very regrettable decision and hung up.

Worse was yet to come. Someone, my former fiancée Lou Anne Sprague O'Neill, to be exact, cornered Lisa at the Rock Island station, on the way home from Christmas shopping in the Loop on the morning of Christmas Eve and chortled about the cancellation of "O Holy Night."

It was a marvelous opportunity for the neighborhood to pour out its hatred, an auto-da-fé, a defenseless woman tied to the stake and slowly set on fire.

Her crime? My fists still clench to think of it. Her crime was that she was Lisa. That the neighborhood could never forgive. My Lisa.

"You're an evil woman." I still hear in my imagination Lou Anne's shrill, hateful voice. "You act in dirty films, you

wear filthy clothes. You flaunt your vulgar body. You lead a
scandalous life. You sing obscene songs. You're a drug ad-
dict. You killed your own father. How dare you come back
here and shock our innocent children? Thank God the Monsignor has finally come to his senses and thrown you out of
the midnight Mass. No one here ever liked you. You were
always a spoiled, stuck-up brat."

"Stuck up" was the kind of term Lou Anne would use.

God rest ye, merry gentlepersons!

"I'm sorry you don't like me, Lou Anne." She turned away,
tears in her eyes, and slipped away through the falling snow,
I'm sure with dignity and grace.

I learned all of this from Blackie, who called me before
confessions (there were still a lot on Christmas Eve in those
days).

"Bitches!" I exploded.

"She cougars," he replied. "The males of the species, however, do not disagree."

There was a dig at me in the cougar crack. What, I asked
myself after the conversation, could I possibly do to heal the
hurt, to wipe away the tears, to restore the innocence?

Nothing, I replied to myself. Not a darn thing.

No shooting star this Christmas.

Still, she was at midnight Mass. I saw her, as I was returning from the altar rail. She was walking down the aisle
to communion in her beige coat and wine suit with a red and
green Christmas scarf, the hurt only in her eyes.

Midnight Mass is the most spectacular of our Catholic
services—lighted candles, poinsettias and evergreens, carols,
bells ringing, feet crunching on snow perhaps on a crisp,
starry night, young people home from college, excited chatter
and laughter as everyone wishes each other "Merry Christmas." Through the years St. Prax's has learned how to do
midnight Mass with style and taste and authentic Christmas
joy.

For me that night there was no joy.

I slipped out of my pew and waited in the back of the
church because I was sure she would leave before the end.

"Merry Christmas, Lisa." I shook hands with her, realizing that there was nothing I could say that would help.

"And to you, George." She shook my hand firmly in return. Consummate actress that she was, she exorcised the hurt from her eyes.

"Where's the Ryan and Murphy clan?" I was reduced to making small talk.

"Father Blackie is going to say Mass at his dad's this afternoon. A few people are coming over. I'm sure he would want you to join us."

"I'll be there." Christmas was beginning to look merry again. The pastor's Christmas collection would be dangerously lower this year. The Ryans were the most generous contributors in the parish. Moreover Ned Ryan and Mary Kate and Joe and Packy and Tim and Nancy and their spouses would all make it clear to the pastor over the next two weeks why they were not throwing envelopes into the collection.

There must have been fifty people in Ned Ryan's house when I arrived. Ned and Helen and Chantal, the oldest child of the second family, greeted us at the door, the gentry admitting the rest of the village.

Blackie was fumbling around at the temporary altar next to his late mother's grand piano. Eileen, who is a lawyer married to Red Kane, the columnist, and is the official family musician, was thumbing through sheet music.

Caitlin materialized next to me. "Know what, George? Chantal Ryan is my aunt, and she's only a year older than I am."

"No!"

"Yes?" Giggle. "Do you love Lisa?" Another conspirator.

"Everyone does, Caitlin."

Lisa stood at the far corner of the room in her white knit minidress, fighting back the tears. By the time Blackie had himself organized, there must have been two hundred people crowded into the house, including the two curates, half a dozen of the nuns, and, with her usual ability to adjust to the inevitable, my mother.

"Now, let's see," Eileen said in her best courtroom voice. "We should keep the carols simple. " 'Adeste'—slowly please—at the beginning. 'The First Noel' at the offertory. 'Silent Night' at the end. And . . . hmmn . . ." A small smile. "How about 'O Holy Night' at Communion? Could you lead us in that, Lisa, dear?"

The poor child could only nod.

Blackie never fumbles and bumbles when he preaches. "Today is the feast of light. We celebrate the return of the sun. The coming of the son of God, the light of the world, which the darkness can never put out. We also rejoice that in His love we, too, have our own light to shine on the lives of others, each in our own way, light essential, light indispensable, light glorious. In the power of God's love and in the power of our own love for one another, our light, too, will never be put out. We celebrate especially the light of those whom God has given extraordinary gifts for bringing light and laughter and love to others. We promise that we will cheerfully cooperate in God's efforts to see that their special light is never put out."

So there. Lisa surrendered finally to tears. Caitlin, standing next to her, held her hand in mute adoration.

At Communion time she sang "Cantique de Noel" like she had never sung it before:

> O Holy Night, the stars are brightly shining
> It is the night of the dear savior's birth.
> Long lay the world in sin and error pining
> Till He appeared and the soul felt His worth.
> A thrill of hope, the weary world rejoices,
> For yonder beams a new and glorious morn.
> Fall on your knees, O hear the angel voices
> O night divine, O night when Christ was born
> O night divine, O night divine!
> Led by the light of faith serenely beaming,
> With glowing hearts by His cradle we stand;
> And led by light of star so sweetly gleaming,
> Here come the wise men, from the orient land.
> The King of Kings thus lay in lowly manger,

In all our trials born to be our friend.
He knows our needs; to our weakness, no stranger.
Behold your king! Before Him lowly bend.
Behold your king! Your king, before Him bend.

Need I say that there was hardly a dry eye in the room. Even Blackie had to polish off his thick lenses. Fortunately I was wearing my contacts still.

I didn't have a chance to talk to her after Mass because there were so many people wishing her well (my tearful mother, of course, among them). I did hear Lisa remark to Red Kane that there were a lot of cougars in the canyons of Los Angeles. I don't know whether I was supposed to hear that. Probably.

I am, as you have doubtless noted, a cautious, careful man. An assiduous, if computerized, bean counter. I did not reach a decision till New Year's Day, almost a week after our shooting star went away.

The decision was obvious. There was no room for George the Bean Counter in the life of a woman like Lisa. That, sadly, was that.

So on Twelfth Night I called Blackie from O'Hare to tell him I was flying to Los Angeles.

"I want to see," I told him ruefully, "what can be done about reducing the cougar population in those canyons."

3
BLACKIE

"Hard to believe he'd want to kill her, isn't it?" Mike Casey raised the Jameson's bottle questioningly.

"I'll forgo all quotes about love and hate and a razor's edge." I gently returned George the Bean Counter's manuscript to the pile on the coffee table in front of me. "No thanks, Mike, I never drink when I'm sad."

We were sitting in the parlor of my modest suite in the cathedral rectory, a room that had been constructed long ago with the smell of musty prints implanted in the walls—there being no musty prints within it, only a musty papal broom sweeper. From the wall we were viewed cheerfully by the three Johns of my late adolescence—Kennedy, XXIII, and Unitas.

Mike nodded sympathetically. He was a tall, lean man with silver hair, silver-blue eyes, a boyishly pink face—an Irish Catholic Basil Rathbone, a central casting design for a sophisticated big city cop, which is what he is, or was, Michael Patrick Vincent Casey, attorney at law, author of two books on detection, a sometime acting superintendent of police of the city of Chicago, now a successful painter of urban landscapes, happily married to his childhood sweetheart of forty years ago, Anne Marie Reilly, owner of the Reilly Gallery, according to the *Chicago Tribune* Magazine Section one of the most beautiful "over forties" in the city. Some people say that Mike Casey the Cop is Blackie Ryan's Doctor Watson. My niece Caitlin, who has read the Father Brown stories, claims that he is my Flambeau. His gorgeous wife may be closer to the mark. She claims that I am his Tonto.

"He wanted you to read all of the chapters." Mike poured

himself a good strong shot of my Jameson's. God knows he'd earned it today. "They're memos that he put together in Australia for the biography Kerry Randall was writing about Lisa."

"I'll read them, of course." I shuffled over to the icebox in the corner of my room, a Charles Dickens design of what an appropriate suite would be for the rector of Holy Name Cathedral parish, and withdrew from the icebox a large bottle of Perrier water. "Can Rich get a conviction?"

I felt like I had been in bed with the flu for two weeks—I almost said like I was in the grip of a monumental hangover, except that, much to the dismay of my siblings, I don't get hangovers.

Mike Casey and I are both cousins and good friends (his mother and my father, Ned Ryan, were brother and sister). He grew up on the west side and I on the south side. Having read George Quinn's manuscript, he probably knew I felt strongly about Lisa Malone. And since my father is the first lawyer that George called from the Chicago Avenue police station, Mike Casey had doubtless been informed by him that I cared deeply about her. But no one, not even my father or my sister Mary Kate, knew how much I loved her. As befits a priest, I have been in love with many women (never violating my celibate commitment in the process, by the way), but I have loved only two of them, my cousin Catherine Collins and my teenage date Lisa Malone. On this warm, foggy, pre-Halloween evening in Chicago, I was a heartsick, inarticulate blob of pain.

And fury.

Mike Casey was aware of my emotions and treaded very carefully. "They're talking murder one over at the State's attorney's office," he said, clipping his consonants like a real cop should. "Look at it from their viewpoint. Security at the Westin gets an incoherent, panicked call from Lisa Malone's suite. They rush up to it and discover her naked and unconscious body on the floor. Her husband, her estranged husband, mind you, is standing over her, swaying like he's drunk, the cosh in his hand. Lisa has been savagely beaten and burned with cigarette butts. There are two shattered vodka bottles on the floor. They call an ambulance to take her to Northwestern. Then they call Chicago's finest, who take one look and arrest George Quinn.

"Our Chicago cops are not dumb. They have read in the papers that a couple of months ago Quinn assaulted Lisa publicly in Morton's restaurant on Melrose in Beverly Hills. The situation looks obvious, doesn't it? Quinn decided to torture his wife to death. Played around with her for an hour and a half or so and then changed his mind. Or maybe he got too drunk to finish it up."

"Indeed."

"Everyone in America loves Lisa Malone." Mike crossed his legs, careful to protect the razor-sharp crease in his dark blue double-breasted Pierre Cardin suit. "Why would anyone want to kill her except her estranged and jealousy-crazed husband?"

It occurred to me that what I had just read of George Quinn's memoir of Lisa suggested that perhaps many others might wish to destroy her, too.

"Ah."

Mike tugged at one of the silver Celtic-cross cuff links on his blue and white striped shirt. "With all the evidence they have, a jury of Chicagoans would convict Quinn in fifteen minutes."

"Indeed."

I wanted to cry or get drunk or strangle someone. Instead I took a long drink of Perrier water.

"Quinn denies it, of course." Mike sipped thoughtfully on his Jameson's. "You've read his story in the paper: he knocked on the door of Lisa's room; someone pulled it open and slugged him in the jaw. He regained consciousness a few moments later and staggered over and turned on the light, saw what had happened to Lisa, stumbled to the phone, and summoned help."

"With the blackjack still in his hand?"

"He said he didn't realize he was holding it until the security men took it away from him."

"The Chicago Avenue police were alert enough to test for intoxication?" I pushed the Perrier bottle aside listlessly. That wasn't much of a help either. "I will have some of your Jameson's if you don't mind."

Mike filled my glass. "Marvelous to say, yes. They also examined the side of his face for contusions."

"And?"

"He was telling the truth." Mike shrugged slightly. "Not that it would matter in court. He was not intoxicated, and he had been struck a moderately severe blow to the side of his face, enough to render him unconscious for a couple of minutes. Of course, he might have done that to himself."

"Indeed."

Lisa! Lisa! Lisa! I've always loved you and I always will!

Tonight I was not Blackie Ryan, monsignor, student of Alfred North Whitehead and William James, éminence grise to the archbishop of Chicago, rector of the Cathedral of the Holy Name, sometime solver of mysteries, protector of the poor and the oppressed (most of whom had long since departed my parish), wise man, character, master of a wide variety of skillful personae. Tonight I was Blackie Ryan, a heartsick lover. What's more, this very clever cop across the coffee table from me knew that, and I didn't want him to know it. If I was to be heartsick, I wanted to be heartsick by myself.

"Your father tried to get him released on bail. Anybody but Ned Ryan and the judge would have laughed in his face."

Tonight, perhaps for the first time, I understood what my father must have suffered when my mother, Kate Collins Ryan, had died.

"Dad thinks he's innocent?"

"He didn't say," Mike observed lightly. "For what it's worth, however, my wife is convinced that your friend George is too sweet and gentle a man to have laid a finger on Lisa."

"And their contretemps at the restaurant in California?"

The Jameson's tasted terrible. If that nectar of the gods (Celtic gods, of course) offends the tongue of Blackie Ryan the Priest, he is in bad shape.

"Annie says that maybe Lisa brought that on herself."

"Indeed."

George the Bean Counter and Lisa the Singer, two damnable innocents messing around in a world in which finally neither of them belonged, a world of envy and viciousness, of sexual perverts and psychopaths, of serial rapists and muggers who will kill you for fifty cents; a world in which women are more in jeopardy than ever because society, granting them equality, protects them less and, granting us all mobility, exercises less social control over its crazies.

"Rich wondered if I would ask you a couple of questions, kind of off the record." Mike's silver-blue eyes considered me very tentatively. "We don't want to intrude on any professional relationship you might have had with her."

The State's attorney of the county of Cook would be the last man in the world to suggest a violation of the seal of confession. What better way to avoid that possibility than a discreet and indirect question?

"If the line of questioning has anything to do with events transpiring within the last year," I said wearily, "I could answer with very little difficulty."

"Fine." Mike placed his Lismore whiskey tumbler on the table at a safe distance from George Quinn's manuscript. "You were not aware that Lisa Malone was in Chicago, staying at the Westin incognito, were you?"

"Yes, indeed, I was. She called me here at the cathedral late yesterday afternoon. She refused to tell me where she was, but she said that she had some 'special' business to take care of and that she and George would be over to see me today. She even said that she would smuggle into the rectory a bottle of Jameson's so George and I wouldn't deplete the Cardinal's stock—as though the Cardinal had a stock other than my liquor cabinet."

"She seemed unhappy?"

"No." How does one convey the nuances of a conversation with a woman one has always loved who has suffered acutely in recent months? "On the contrary, she seemed quite cheerful. She told me that I shouldn't believe everything I read in the newspapers, that life was much better now, and that she and George would have some wonderful news to tell me."

"Was she pregnant?" Mike's thin white eyebrows leapt in astonishment.

"That thought had occurred to me. I asked them at the hospital. They said no."

"That tends to support Quinn's story. They had reconciled on the telephone, and he was coming to Chicago to seal that reconciliation."

"And stumbled on a psychopathic assailant in her hotel room." I concluded George's unpersuasive story to the police. Unpersuasive, but not necessarily untrue. A woman by herself in a busy hotel in a large city was easy prey for the psychopaths who roam our streets.

"Did she by any chance say what time Quinn was arriving last night?"

"She did." I struggled reluctantly to my feet and trudged over to the huge rolltop desk, which had belonged to a turn-of-the-century cathedral rector (who may have been murdered in a poker game in this very room). "I don't know why I wrote it down." Of course I knew why I wrote it down. Lisa's voice on the telephone reduces me to a state of stumbling incompetency. If I don't write everything down, I will remember nothing that was said. I shuffled through several stacks of paper, mail that was a couple of months old, notes for an article on G. K. Chesterton and William James, and finally, my telephone messages from the day before. "George arrives seven-twenty this evening on American flight six-sixty."

"If you count walking in from the gate, collecting bags, finding a cab, and driving from O'Hare, it would take about an hour to get to the hotel, if everything went right, which it often doesn't at that madhouse. Let's say he arrives at the hotel, then, at eight-thirty. That's two hours before security types at the Westin hear from him. Right?"

"They found him in her room, standing over her body at ten-thirty-seven, two hours and seven minutes by your scenario." A niggling objection tried to form itself in my preconscious. There was something wrong with the argument, but I wasn't quite sure what.

"A rather limited number of people knew she was in town." Mike picked up a sheet of lined yellow paper. Her husband, George Quinn; Ken Woods, her agent; Kerry Randall, her friend and biographer; Tad Thomas, who does the Christmas special with her every year; Dina King, the young woman singer she's taken under her wing; Sister Winifred, whose work Lisa funds; Francis Leonard, who is the head of her foundation . . ."

"And Monsignor John Blackwood Ryan, rector of the Cathedral of the Holy Name and her sometime priest."

"Well, yes . . ." Mike replaced the yellow sheet in his hand-tooled maroon Florentine leather briefcase. "Possibly, too, her brother, Roderick Malone, M.D., though I gather he denies it."

"Speak not about that bastard to me." The thought occurred to me that even if Roderick was not responsible for what had happened to his sister, I might still be constrained to strangle him during the next few days.

"Sister Winifred and Mr. Leonard," Mike continued, now elaborately casual, "work in Chicago, of course. Mr. Woods and Ms. Randall were themselves in Chicago, just down the street at the Whitehall Hotel. Ms. King and Mr. Thomas were apparently in Los Angeles but due to fly in this morning."

"Ah." I was not sure where Mike was permitting the conversation to drift. Perhaps I should reread the pertinent chapter in *Principles of Detection*—"Preliminary Interview," as I remember, was the title.

"And where were you last night, Blackie?" he asked lightly.

Indeed! I was a suspect. Marvelous, even under the present circumstances, marvelous. I've always wanted to be a suspect, one with an alibi of the sort that I had.

"I was in the front row center at the Lyric Opera of Chicago." I did my best not to look like a cat who had consumed a canary. "On my left was Signora Rossana Bartoletti, the wife of the musical director of the Lyric. That distinguished gentleman, Maestro Bruno Bartoletti, was, at that very moment, conducting the final performance of the season of *Eugene Onegin*. On my right was Sean Cronin, cardinal priest of the Church of St. Domitila and by the grace of God and inattention of the Apostolic See, Archbishop of Chicago."

It was from Sean Cronin that I first learned that Lisa was in the hospital. Not only does he insist on living in a curate's room in the cathedral rectory (I forbear to call it my rectory, because then I would be responsible for the losing battle fought in the rectory against pervasive dust and grime and deteriorating plumbing and electricity), he also insists on taking night calls twice a month, as though he were a simple parish priest and not a cardinal archbishop. It gets great media coverage, and my Lord Cronin does have some skills in ministering to the sick. With twenty years of practice, he might make a decent curate.

Wondrous, sad Russian music, without a single memorable tune, I must confess, but it does go on. It was after 11:30 by the time the Cardinal and I had returned to the rectory. I went to my study and he to the room of the curate who was "covering" for him while he was at the opera—since this was one of my Lord Cronin's much-heralded nights on call.

An hour or so later, fortified by plain soda water (I only do Perrier when there's someone else in the room because I want them to know that I am, indeed, a member of the elite), I was plugging away on my paper "Criteria of Truth in William James," when the Cardinal appeared, silver-blond hair awry, thin face ashen, hooded brown eyes blazing, as though he were a berserk Celtic warrior charging into battle. "Blackie..."

"What's wrong?" I asked. Something happen to my father? Or to his sister-in-law, Nora Hurley (the most important person in Sean Cronin's life)?

"Lisa...." he said hoarsely. "I just anointed her over at Northwestern. Somebody tried to kill her in the Westin earlier this evening. Most likely her husband. Right now it looks like the attempt is going to be successful. You'd better go over there."

Automatically I fumbled for the roman collar that accompanies my clerical shirt. It was nowhere to be seen. Not on the desk or the coffee table or in my shirt pocket or on my favorite easy chair. Oh, well, what mattered a clerical collar when the woman you loved was dying?

"Here." The Cardinal removed the collar from his shirt and gave it to me. "Get over there. Wait, hadn't you better call your sister first?"

Joe and Mary Kate and Caitlin had already left for the hospital, according to my niece Brigid, who answered the phone. I raced down the fog-shrouded Superior Street canyon, which looked an avenue in a Dali illustration for Dante's hell, elbowed my way through a mass of television cameras and reporters, overawed the security guard at the entrance to the emergency room of the Olson Pavilion with the announcement that I was the rector of the cathedral parish, and stumbled into the swarm of green clad doctors and nurses, surrounded by beeping and sparking equipment, who fluttered around the ivory face on the table. She didn't even look like Lisa.

Mary Kate's strong arms pulled me back into the corner. "Rodriquez is in charge. He's the best. Done a CAT scan. Doesn't look good, but no immediate surgery."

The next morning Roddy Malone wanted to fire Rodriquez on the grounds that not only was he "a sawed-off little Spick who can't even speak good English," but also he was not yet ready to do surgery to relieve pressure caused by hemorrhages in the brain. Roddy retreated rather quickly when my brother-in-law Joe Murphy, ordinarily the mildest of men, said in his thick Boston Irish accent (reserved for times when he's angry—twice every half century, more or less), "You get out of here and leave us alone or I'll break your neck."

"How is she?" Mike Casey interrupted my reverie, dragging my imagination from that terrible hospital room back to my study in the cathedral rectory. "The newspapers say her condition is 'serious.' I suppose the hospital isn't telling the whole truth."

"Serious is an understatement. Thirty-eight cigarette burns, multiple internal injuries, two hairline fractures of the skull, brain hemorrhages caused by a very severe contusion. The patient is in a coma and"—my voice choked—"close to death."

"Prognosis?" Mike asked crisply, like Mr. Spock in *Star Trek*.

"Not very good. It's the brain that's the problem, of course. Everything else can be fixed. The blow was meant to kill, according to Rodriquez, probably delivered in haste, and hence not too accurate—which kind of confirms George the Bean Counter's story, doesn't it? He may eventually have to operate if the hemorrhaging continues, to relieve internal pressures of the brain. Lisa could come out of the coma in five minutes or five days or five weeks or never, and she could die at almost any time, too. Moreover, if she does live and does come out of the coma, she may or may not be permanently impaired. The best guess—and Mary Kate was candid about it to me—is that Lisa will be a vegetable, one way or the other, for the rest of her life."

(Mary Kate and Joe are both psychiatrists. Joe is on the staff of Northwestern Medical Center, Mary Kate at Little Company of Mary out in Evergreen Park.)

Mike winced. "No hope at all?"

"Sure, there's always hope. Rodriquez keeps saying we know very little about how the brain works. By tomorrow afternoon she might be as good as new. She could open her eyes any time and be the same old Lisa with virtually no ill effects. The odds are against that, but it could happen, and, of course, the odds against it increase with time."

"When is the turning point?" Mike stood up, as though to leave my room. "I mean, how long does the coma have to last before maybe it's better if she doesn't wake up?"

"Mary Kate says that if she's not out of the coma by Thanksgiving, we're moving in the direction of a Karen Quinlan situation—somebody has to decide whether to pull the plugs on all the life-support mechanisms."

"My God!" Mike exclaimed. "Such a wonderful woman, too. How could anybody hate her that much . . . ?"

"Indeed."

"I'll pass on your responses to Rich, strictly background and off the record."

"They're not going to seek an indictment right away?"

"The charges now are attempted murder." Mike locked his briefcase. "That, of course, can always be changed to murder if . . ."

"If Lisa dies."

"Precisely. There's no point in seeking an indictment right away if you're going to change the charges in a few days."

"How economical of them . . ." Hey, wait a minute, I thought, something doesn't fit. "Why is the State's attorney interested in the alibis of other people if it would be so easy to get a conviction against George the Bean Counter?"

Mike sat down again at the coffee table and opened his briefcase. "That's the old Blackie Ryan, thank God," he sighed with relief. My sighs are artificial West-of-Ireland sighs, indistinguishable from the first onslaught of a serious asthma attack, and are usually employed for rhetorical purposes. Mike's sigh, sort of like a brief burst from an automatic weapon, is, on the contrary, always real. "I said Rich could get a conviction. I didn't say he had a case. The sticky point, as your father pointed out to him this morning, is the fog last night."

"Precisely." I began to feel like myself again. "George's plane was late."

"American six-sixty landed at O'Hare at nine-forty-five."

"So," I observed, urging my mind, which had gone into temporary retirement the night before, to start operating again, "even if they parked at gate K-one and he rushed to the taxi stand and made it to the Westin in half an hour, he couldn't have arrived much before he was discovered in her room, ten-twenty, ten-twenty-five."

"I suppose," Mike thumped his fingers on the coffee table, "that everything that was done to Lisa might have physically taken place in five or ten minutes. One might argue it in court, perhaps, but it doesn't seem very plausible. Rather, it had the look of a leisurely torture session, interrupted by an unexpected arrival."

"Aha! If we can document George's progress from Los Angeles to the hotel with witnesses, and if he is telling the truth about the time of his arrival at Lisa's room, Rich would hesitate before seeking an indictment. And search for someone else? Perhaps only a random psychopath?"

"Or perhaps one of those who knew where she was hiding for a few days to prepare for whatever business she spoke to you about."

My mind cleared sufficiently to understand what this meeting was all about. "And what you and Rich and the old fella want, is for me to make a few discreet inquiries of my own among that latter group? Blackie Ryan, in other words, is

supposed to find out who tried to kill his childhood sweetheart?"

Michael Patrick Vincent Casey nodded his head solemnly.
"Indeed," he said, "to use one of your favorite words."

"It will be a pleasure," I said, turning to my half-empty
glass of Jameson's, which now tasted much better. "A real
pleasure."

"And, Monsignor John Blackwood Ryan," he said, poking
his finger in my direction, "when you find who did it, always
assuming it wasn't George, you should leave both divine and
human justice to the appropriate powers responsible for such
matters, do you understand?"

"Happy are the merciful," I said in response.

"Ah," Mike replied.

It would be several days before I would be able to think
clearly, not because Lisa would improve, but rather because
time makes even grief irrelevant.

I missed two critically important aspects of the case that
ought to have been clear at the very beginning, one of them
that impinged on the honesty of George Quinn's story, the
other about the terrible danger for Lisa.

There were other threats to that poor unconscious woman's
life besides the hemorrhages that were devastating her brain.

4
BLACKIE

"Listen to this shit, Blackie!" Kerry Randall
slammed the newspaper in disgust on the desk in my office
on the first floor of the cathedral rectory, a somewhat more
formal-looking place than the parlor on the second floor—
and also somewhat more dingy. But even the best of the rooms
in the cathedral rectory are dingy, by definition. Outside the

window (upon which window-washing never seemed to have any effect) Wabash Avenue glistened darkly in faint light reflected on the rain-soaked street. The fog that hung over the city, some sort of meteorological accident accompanying the dastardly injustice worked by Steve Garvey and his friends in taking the National League championship away from our Cubs, was closing in again. If it wasn't a case for Sherlock Holmes, it was, perhaps, a setting for him.

"Lisa Malone was asking for it." She picked up the paper and began to read Farley Strangler's column in the next morning's newspaper. "'If you ask me, Lisa Malone was asking for it the other night in the Westin Hotel. What was she doing in a disguise in a medium-class hotel in Chicago while her husband was in Australia and her children were in the charge of a baby-sitter in Los Angeles? Waiting for a lover? Anyone who arranges a tryst in a North Michigan Avenue hotel is inviting trouble.

"'It's an unpleasant truth that women do get beat up in our society, particularly when they go around pretending to be someone they're not. What kind of game was Lisa Malone playing in the Westin the other night? If you ask me, it looks like a cheap, second-hand imitation of one of her cheap, second-hand films.

"'For the last several years, after it became clear that Lisa Malone was over the hill physically, no longer capable of dragging horny teenage boys into movie theaters of the country to pant as she pranced around naked on the screen, she has pretended to be America's sweetheart, just a plain old American wife and mother who sings Christmas carols with Tad Thomas on television during the holiday season: a sweet, wholesome, devout Irish Catholic, that was the Lisa Malone scam, a sexually appealing president of the Women's Altar Society.

"'So her husband walks out on her because he's fed up with the scam, then takes a poke at her in a chi-chi Beverly Hills restaurant because she's having a fling with that aging boy wonder, Tad Thomas.

"'Lisa Malone, it turns out, has been working a scam on all of us, apparently her husband included: not sweet and not innocent and not devout and not dedicated. She is, rather, an aging high-class whore, the sort that all the Hollywood sex goddesses become if they live long enough. That's the real Lisa Malone, and that's the woman who managed to get herself pushed around the other night in the Westin.

"'I don't know whether her husband did it or not. The case against him seems to me to be a little bit too much Hollywood cliché to be taken seriously: the bespectacled, balding accountant who can't keep up with his glamorous movie-star wife. It's all just a little bit too good to be true.

"'But if he did do it, while most of us might not approve, a lot of us would still understand. The person who's had to live with a consummate phony for fifteen years, and to cooperate in that phoniness, isn't always responsible for what finally happens.

"'So my guess is that the angelic Lisa has been into kinky sex for a long time and she holed up in the Westin for a few days of fun and games that got a little out of hand.

"'There's one aspect of this sordid business that depresses me: in years gone by, one of my great pleasures at Christmastime was erasing her sickeningly sweet Irish Catholic face from the TV screen and replacing it with a pro football game. Now I won't be able to blot out her face. Somebody else has beaten me to it.'"

"Fucking bastard!" Kerry Randall was pacing back and forth in front of the desk, unable to contain her rage while sitting down. "Goddamned fucking bastard asshole!"

I sighed—my West-of-Ireland sigh was in working order again. "It's said by those of the journalistic profession, or so I'm told, that Farley Strangler once noted that some of Chicago's best journalists were fat, loudmouthed drunks. He decided that if he became a fat, loudmouthed drunk, he would therefore be one of Chicago's best journalists."

"They all hate her!" Kerry turned on me, frowning furiously. "You can see the satisfaction oozing from that asshole's column. They're glad she's in a coma over at Northwestern Hospital."

"George isn't balding," I said mildly. "And save for one

burn, which apparently will not leave any scar tissue, Lisa's face looks fine."

Kerry Randall, or, to be precise, Kerry Ann Malloy Randall, is exactly the same age as Lisa and I and had sat in the same schoolroom with us through grammar school and with Lisa in high school. In truth, Lisa's face, even framed by masses of bandages, looked much better, and at least ten years younger, than Kerry Randall's. During the grammar school years, at any rate, Kerry was thought to be the prettiest girl in the class, a position from which I dissented, not for objective reasons, but rather because of clan loyalty to my cousin Catherine Collins and adoration for my beloved Lisa Malone. Nevertheless, although her tense, tiny figure was still trim and lithe, in a brown corduroy designer suit and beige sweater, something had happened to her once undeniably pretty face—too much cocaine, too much sun, too much anger, too much suffering. Life had not been kind to Kerry Ann—a bitterly unhappy marriage (no children) to a local TV news anchorman in Los Angeles and a string of disastrous love affairs dutifully and sympathetically reported to me by Lisa on her annual visit. Then she became disillusioned with the radical political causes she had supported in her twenties. Near successes in her career as an investigative reporter turned into messy and controversial failures.

All these disappointments had etched their lines on Kerry's face—totally and aggressively innocent of makeup, making her seem haggard, brittle, pinched. She spoke in harsh, explosive bursts, almost like a caricature of journalists in second-rate films, bitter, knowing, sarcastic. While she talked, her fingers jabbed at you as if she were a prosecutor with a murder suspect on the stand before a hostile jury. Except she used language that would never be tolerated in court or even in a rectory parlor, save on the lips of a liberated woman. And that only because one discounted the language as nothing more than a symbol of revolution.

Like many women of her generation who were converted to feminism the early 1970s, Kerry had fought valiantly to appear tough and masculine. In the process she had lost much of her femininity but had acquired little masculinity. She did not look tough, determined, cynical, as she might have wished; merely tired and discouraged and angry.

Yet, when she had smiled with delight as I came into the office—women, particularly women who have known me for a long time, tend to do that when I appear, for reasons that escape me save that they must find me comic—I thought her rather appealing. She smiled rarely during our conversation, but when she did, the smile erased the harsh lines on her face and she was once more the winsome little tyke who enthusiastically directed the St. Praxides cheerleaders in ecstatic support of our brave young warriors on the gridiron (in whose numbers I was decidedly not counted).

Throughout our conversation she alternated between the sweet and lively kid I'd grown up with and the hurt and angry woman she had become. The former still had her cheerleader's smile, the latter, a twisted sneer.

"It's all envy." She kicked one of the battered old hardwood chairs in which visitors to the rector's first floor office were constrained to uncomfortably squirm, doubtless a gesture that would have pleased many previous occupants of the chair. "They all envy her because she is so good, that's why they want to destroy her! And because she does it without any effort. They hate her because she is a natural!"

"Envy is a very powerful and insidious emotion," I rested my jaw on crossed fingers, trying to create the impression of being a serious philosopher. "Helmut Schoeck, a German sociologist of whom you've probably never heard, says it is the third most powerful human motivation, after survival and reproduction."

"I don't understand it, Blackie." She sighed and seemed to release all the anger inside her with the sigh, like air escaping from a child's balloon. "Why can't they just love her the way you and I do?"

"Indeed."

"She's a consummate professional and a wonderful human being." Kerry leaned her head against my desk like she was about to fall asleep in front of a television set. "That's why I wanted to write her biography. I've had it with this investigative shit, exposing all the squalor and the ugliness and the evil in society. I thought it was time to write something about someone who was genuinely good. I didn't think she'd be dead...." She began to weep quietly, without any touch of hysteria, mourning a lost playmate.

"She's not dead yet." I tried to generate the appearance of professional hopefulness, expected of a cleric, that I did not feel myself. "We may still have her back with us in a few days."

"Isn't Rodriquez going to operate sometime tonight?" She sniffled and continued to cry. "That sounds like a desperation measure."

"Let me get you a drink." I struggled rather heavily to my feet. "The operation is merely to permit some of the blood that's been released in her brain to drain off so that the pressure that was building up won't do any more damage. He doesn't think he'll have to cut into the brain tissue, at least not very much. What would you like to drink?"

"Oh..." She looked up at me, face twisted with pain. "I don't know. Vodka and water, I guess. Sorry, Blackie."

"Not at all. I know how you feel."

I went up to my room, mixed the vodka and water, put a few ice cubes into it, and phoned the nursing station at the hospital. Caitlin Murphy, soon to be Caitlin Maher, answered. "She's in surgery now, Uncle Punk," she said, using the normally affectionate diminutive popular among the women members of my family. "Dad is up there in surgery with Dr. Rodriquez. Mom's gone to the airport to bring the three children to our house. They're going to stay with us."

Beth, age thirteen, Georgia Anne, ten, Ned, four and a half—there never had been a moment's doubt that my sister would wrangle temporary custody of those attractive, wide-eyed little innocents. Farley Strangler was wrong about one thing, at any rate: whatever failures there may have been in Lisa's life, she had been a good mother.

"I'll keep you posted." Even the wondrous Caitlin had lost some of her verve.

Back in my office Kerry Ann was dabbing at her eyes with a rumpled sheet of tissue. "Thanks much, Blackie." She reached eagerly for the drink. "I'm afraid I need this."

She drained half the drink in one gulp and then, with trembling fingers, put it down on my stained and pockmarked desk, of a design that I believe is called Scandinavian Decrepit. "I guess I can't do much damage to this desk, huh?" Once more her dazzling smile brought back the old Kerry Ann and made her the kind of woman of whom a man would not be instinctively afraid.

"Why do we envy others? I don't know why I say 'we.' Not everybody envies. I don't think Lisa ever knew what envy meant from the inside. That's why she was so astonished and hurt when she was a victim of envy."

"She is one of the few of us who are clean of heart." I rested my chin on my crossed fingers again. "That doesn't mean people who don't feel sexual emotions. When Jesus said 'happy are the clean of heart,' he meant happy are those who have purity of motivation, whose purposes and aspirations are transparent and whose characters and goodness are simple and unaffected. It is precisely that simplicity of goodness which is the absence of envy and is one of the things most offensive to the rest of us for whom envy comes at least as naturally as breathing."

"The media are filled with envious people." Absently she stirred the ice cubes in her drink. "When I did that exposé of the hospital in San Francisco, it was the income of the doctors that attracted all the attention from my colleagues. Look at the way we went after poor Patty Hearst because she was rich; and Geraldine Ferraro, attractive, successful, with a good husband and fine kids—and rich besides. Goddamn it, we had to destroy her, didn't we?"

"And Italian, too," I said mildly.

"It's four letters, Blackie." She was becoming angry again. "R, I, C, H—we hate rich people, don't we?"

"And when they're not only rich, but successful and happy and good, then we really have to destroy them. Envy is the stuff of which assassins are made."

"I've known her since we were toddlers in the St. Praxides playground." She finished her drink in another single gulp. "And I probably know her better than anybody else in the world but you and maybe poor George. I've done most of the research for her biography, and I tell my colleagues what she's really like and they say I'm crazy. They've never met her, never seen any of her films, probably never even watched her on television, yet they know she's a phony and a fake and a scheming little bitch."

"A collective neurosis..." I suggested tentatively while wishing that Kerry would get over her anger and confusion and begin to tell me more about Lisa, who, despite all the love I felt for her, had been a stranger now for many years. "And like all collective neuroses, seamless, impermeable, irrefutable."

She shook her head in sad dejection. "You know, Blackie, none of us were ever satisfied with Lisa the way she was. We all wanted to remake her. I wanted her to be more militantly feminist and more aware of the political uses of beauty, George wanted her to be more of a wife like his mother was a wife, Ken Woods wanted her to be the helpless little girl he thought she was when she came to California. . . . Why did we all want to change her?"

I wondered tentatively whether I had wanted to change Lisa. I didn't think so. Yet if she had been around Chicago for the last fifteen years, I probably would have had my own remodeling plans. "Perhaps because she was a challenge, demanding that we change. No one likes to do that."

"I challenged her," Kerry said fiercely. "She didn't seem to mind. It didn't do much good, but she didn't seem to mind."

"What did you challenge her about?"

"The politics of beauty. You know, how it's unfair that some women should be better looking than others because it gives them so much more political power in dealing with men. I'm not an ideologue about that anymore, Blackie. Not like I used to be. But I still believe that every woman is equally valuable and that we should be admired for our political and spiritual actions, instead of our faces and bodies. Women with beauty should be careful not to take advantage of it if they want to be fair to other women."

"Ah."

"I told her that often."

"And she said in effect 'both'?"

"Yeah. How did you know?"

That was one of Lisa's favorite words. "No one would kill her because she was attractive, would they?"

"I don't know. You'd be surprised how terribly inferior someone like her makes other women feel." She sipped from the dregs of her drink. "God knows all of us probably had some reason to want to kill her, not just poor George."

"Oh?" Finally we were getting down to cases; indeed, to the case of Lisa Malone, one of the clean of heart, one of those of whom Jesus said that they shall see God. "What do you mean?"

Before Kerry Randall could begin her answer, the phone rang. It was Caitlin again. "Dad just phoned down from surgery. The operation went all right, I guess, but Dr. Rodriquez says there was even more damage inside than he thought. He told Dad the chances of her lasting more than twenty-four hours are not very great."

5

KERRY RANDALL

Okay, Blackie, I'll tell you what I think happened. It shouldn't be hard to find someone who hated her enough to kill her.

Take her brother, Roddy, for example.

Remember what it was like when we used to go over to their house—you didn't come much because Mrs. Malone didn't think much of the Ryan family, did she? Anyway, Roderick, as Mrs. Malone always called him, was about ten years older than us, and he wouldn't give us the time of day, always arrogant and supercilious, looking down his goddamn intellectual nose at two giddy little girls. We didn't know anything about books or music or art. We weren't very bright, not by his standards anyway, though we both got good marks in school, and we weren't destined to be world-famous heart surgeons. I suppose he envied the poor little kid even then. He'd been around ten years before Lisa showed up, and figured he had a monopoly on family affection and attention, especially because he was teacher's pet and everybody knew he was going to be a great surgeon. Remember?

Well, then what happens? Lisa is born and is terribly, terribly pretty and also has a sweet, wonderful voice, as the nuns discover when we're in the first grade. Their father, first, and then their mother, too, switch to Lisa and make her the family favorite. By the time we were in the eighth grade and Lisa was singing at wedding Masses it didn't much matter that her brother was at Harvard Medical School. Nobody in the family paid any attention to Roddy, nobody except Lisa, who adored him and who used to bore us stiff bragging about her brother, who had such high marks at Notre Dame and then in med school. I hate doctors, especially surgeons. They're the worst goddamn male chauvinist pigs in the world. I wouldn't let a male doctor put a finger on me. Even now I resent that little runt Rodriquez messing around with Lisa. Anyway, Roderick was and is the most arrogant M.D. I've ever known. He used to sit there and lecture us about how good it was to wake up in the morning and know that you're going to do something fine in the course of a day. By fine, of course, he meant stitching up some defect in human plumbing, not singing a song that makes people happy or writing a newspaper story that tells the truth.

So he marries that rich little bitch from Scarsdale and settles down in Connecticut, becomes a famous cardiologist, saving lives and doing fine things all over the place, patron of the Metropolitan Museum, patron of the Philharmonic, associate editor of the *New England Journal of Medicine*, member of National Science Foundation review committees, you know, the whole bit. Maybe just the best Irish Catholic cardiologist in the Northeast. "If you're in doubt," an M.D. I slept with for a while said, "see Malone."

He didn't mean Lisa either. He meant her goddamn asshole

brother. And so what happens? He's making money hand over fist putting hearts back together, and he's spending even more rapidly than it comes in. His wife is into horses, strings of horses, European thoroughbreds, big fox hunts, you know the scene. Because he's a smart asshole surgeon, he thinks he knows everything about everything, he begins to play foreign exchange markets—precious metals and European currency. The Hunts and their Arab friend goose up the silver market a couple of years ago, he's convinced it's going to go to fifty, so he buys in with just about everything he has at thirty, and of course the bottom drops out on him. To make his margin calls, he will have to sell his wife's racehorses and their three homes and make his kids go to work and cut back on his big prestige contributions to museums and concerts and that sort of shit.

He's been avoiding Lisa like she has leprosy ever since their father died. Almost twenty years, not even a Christmas card. Without a word of warning, he and his bitchy wife and a couple of his degenerate brats show up in Beverly Hills, and he announces that, because of family loyalty to her, he's willing to accept a huge, interest-free loan until he can dig himself out of the hole. He ignores George, he has no time for her kids, treats the rest of us, her friends and colleagues, like we're animals in a zoo, and departs, the check in his greedy little fingers.

No, I don't know how much. A *lot*. If he said thank you to her, I didn't hear it. And Lisa is absolutely sweet and gentle and kind, like she and her brother have been lifelong buddies. Not a word. I tell you, Blackie, not a single word about where he'd been these last fifteen years. When we drove him to the airport, I never saw such a look of venomous hatred in any man's face as when he said good-bye to her. A fat, bald, arrogant little man who has been humiliated by his sister's generosity and will never, never forgive her for it.

Like they say, no good deed goes unpunished. If he could have killed her and escaped that afternoon at LAX, he would certainly have done it. Lisa knew the great cardiologist didn't like her and was exploiting her. I don't care, she said as we drove back to Beverly Hills in her BMW, he's my brother and I love him.

"If I'm generous with him, maybe he'll love me back. But that doesn't matter, does it, Kerry Ann? Love is not a commodity that you can speculate on in the foreign exchange markets."

"What happens when he comes back a second time?" I asked her. "He'll never have enough money. That bitch he's married to will make him buy two houses for every one of their daughters on their wedding days, one near the family mansion in Connecticut and the other up at the summer resort on the island in Maine. Sweet old Roderick is going to take a bath every couple of years for the rest of his life. Are you going to bail him out every time?"

"As long as I have the money," she says quietly and firmly, "I'll help him whenever he needs help. He is, after all, my brother."

"So you would have noticed the last twenty years," I sneered.

"That doesn't matter," she says serenely.

If she had made him eat shit, it would have been much better. If he'd had to pay the price of humiliation for the money, he wouldn't have hated her so much because then he'd have known that she was not better than he was. It was the gracefulness of her generosity that infuriated him.

I was right. He did get in over his head again, in gold this time. Last spring he decides that the dollar is too high and that gold is too low, so, brilliant cardiologist that he is, that nerd sells dollars and buys gold. What happens? You read the newspapers, you know what happens. The dollar stays sky-high and gold keeps slipping. He's busted again, his third daughter is being married at Christmastime and he needs lots of money, so he pays another visit to California, this time without his wife and kids, and tells Lisa she can bail him out again.

Only this time she can't because Lisa has turned movie producer and sunk all the free money that she had into *The Friendship Factor*. You know the story, about a singer who fights her way back from alcoholism and mental illness. It's the most serious film she's done. If she's successful as a producer, she figures, she'll step down gracefully from acting, of which, to tell the truth, she's tired. Everybody in Hollywood has their own version of what the film is like. Two directors and three writers quit while it was being made and it came in exactly two times higher than budget. Lisa's friends will tell you the guys who quit were male chauvinists who couldn't tolerate a gentle but determined woman. Lisa's enemies will say that they couldn't work for a castrating bitch. From what I hear, I think it's a surefire Academy Award for her and for the film. She wouldn't let anybody see it until the final cuts were made—and that came in way over budget, too—but I know a couple of reporters who sneaked into a private screening in order to ridicule it and came away saying that if she doesn't win the Academy Award it will be the biggest scandal in the history of the film industry.

So she's broke, or just about, and she can't help poor Roderick. He lost his temper completely, screamed, ranted, beat his head against the wall, called her every name in the book and some I'd never heard before—and he had a few choice ones for me, too, of which female faggot was one of the milder. Lisa nodded sympathetically, told him she understood, and offered to help him when the money came in for *The Friendship Factor*.

"I won't take money from such pornographic crap," he yells and storms out of the house.

Lisa wants to drive him back to LAX, but I talk her out of it. Let him yell at me, I say. I'm immune, and you have work to do.

You can take my word for it, Blackie: the scenes are not pornographic. They may just be the best and most artistic nude scenes ever done in a film. Lisa is not much good on feminist theory, but she sure is fed up with soft-core films. She tells me that she figures the only way to stop that is to do erotic scenes that aren't exploitative and increase rather than diminish respect for women's bodies. "Kind of reversing *Penthouse*," she says to me with that impish little grin.

Those reporters I was telling you about came out dazzled. One of them even wrote that anyone who went to see *The Friendship Factor* for prurient reasons would be sadly disappointed. They'd see a lot of Lisa all right, he said, but a transcendent Lisa rather than a pornographic Lisa.

Are you ready for it, Blackwood? Our little Lisa a sign of the transcendent, and with her clothes off, yet?

What's transcendent eroticism? You tell me, Blackie. I suppose its eroticism that points toward God.

Anyway, to get back to the point. That's the pornographic crap from which Roderick Malone, M.D., won't take money. You better believe it, when March comes around and the film wins an Academy Award, he'll find it in his conscience to be able to take her money. And to keep taking it.

Funny thing. I suppose this accident, or murder attempt, or whatever will guarantee the movie will make an enormous amount of money. Ironic, isn't it? If Lisa dies, Roderick stands to inherit a hell of a lot of money. You didn't know that? Sure. In her will, she's left a quarter of her wealth to that old fart and his bitchy wife and his vile little children. If *Friendship* flies like I think it will, that could be fifteen or twenty million dollars before taxes.

A lot of people morally superior to him would kill for much less.

6

BLACKIE

The telephone at my elbow jangled nervously. They would not have disturbed me unless it was important. Dear God, don't let it be...

"Father Ryan."

"Mike Casey, Blackie. You were right, as usual. Tad Thomas and Dina King did come in a day early. They were both put up at the Mayfair Regent, no less. In separate rooms, on separate floors, by the way, and of course, on Lisa Malone's tab. Nothing but the best when she's paying for it. Moreover, despite what her brother says, he didn't come in Tuesday morning after he heard about it on the radio. He had checked into the Drake at noon on Monday. That's right, the Drake— right around the corner from the Westin. But, hell, that doesn't mean anything. Woods and Randall are down the street at the Whitehall, so five of our suspects are within walking distance and as far as I've been able to find out by asking a few discreet questions, neither the out-of-towners nor Leonard nor Sister Winifred have much in the way of an alibi. It could have been anyone. Sister Winifred is a nurse, by the way. Think about that. She might be pretty quick with a hypodermic. The Randall woman has had a serious drug problem on and off for the last ten years. I wouldn't be surprised if she was pretty good with a hypodermic needle, too. She's been clean the last couple of years, as far as we can tell."

"Indeed."

"I'll be back to you later. I gather the news from the hospital is none too good. Joe Murphy phoned me."

"Not really." I tried to sound smooth and self-possessed, the pastor at the sickbed of a parishioner who has left all his wealth to the Church. "Dr. Rodriquez succeeded in easing some of the pressure on Lisa's brain. He's not especially sanguine, but then, he never has been."

By now the reader will have doubtless noted the unconscionable oversight of which we'd all been guilty. Perhaps because none of us really expected that Lisa would ever open her eyes and identify the person who had savaged her, we had not calculated the possible impact of the guardedly hopeful press releases from Northwestern University Hospital on the person who had tried to kill her.

If Lisa should recover, and if, in time, she should come to remember who it was she had admitted to the hotel room that night—and there was every appearance from the room that the killer was someone she knew and admitted without concern—then the investigations that the State's attorney and my father and Mike Casey and I were doing, each for our own reasons, would become academic exercises.

We would all know who it was that Kerry and I and a lot of others wanted to strangle.

Somehow none of us thought of that scenario. None of us pictured Lisa's clear hazel eyes opening in recognition, and hence none of us realized how grave was the danger that the killer might strike again to finish a work so well begun.

7
KERRY RANDALL

Why might I have wanted to kill her, Blackie? That's a hell of a question. No, I don't mean that you haven't the right to ask it. Of course you do, because you're playing your old Sherlock Holmes—or is it now Father Brown?—game. Remember the time in grammar school when you figured out who stole Mrs. Cahill's notebook? And where the eighth graders had hidden the St. Patrick's statue? After a while, I think people deliberately created mysteries just for the fun of watching crazy little Blackie Ryan solve them.

Anyway, sure it's a fair question. Didn't I say myself that we all had some reason to kill her? With me, I guess, it's a little less specific than for the others. For instance, Sister Winifred has been sending some of Lisa's money to the guerrillas in El Salvador, kind of trading off with Frank Leonard, who has got some kind of complicated scam in which he's been using the Malone Foundation to launder Outfit funds. Yeah, mostly cocaine funds—lots of money. It's pretty kinky, and while the feds have sniffed what's going on, they don't have any hard evidence yet. But Lisa knew it was true; she knew that both Frank Leonard and Sister Winifred were cheating her. I wouldn't be surprised if that's why she came to Chicago.

Would she have dumped either one of them? No, of course

not, but she would have drawn the line, the way Lisa draws the line—you know what I mean—quietly, gently, and firmly, the kind of thing that made those asshole directors quit on her. Look what happens: Sister Winifred loses her role as Central American messiah—God, she's come a long way since she was teaching drama in high school, hasn't she? And that asshole Frank Leonard, who is probably in hock to the Mob for something or the other, could get himself real dead one night when he climbs out of his car in Lake Forest, or maybe merely indicted by a federal grand jury which finally catches up with him after Lisa stops him from laundering their money.

Sister Winifred capable of murder?

Would you believe revolutionary justice?

And doesn't what happened to Lisa have some of the earmarks of a Mob torture hit job? Yeah, I know they normally don't cut up women, but for the drug business the Mob has become an equal opportunity organization.

Dina, of course, becomes the new Lisa Malone if Lisa dies. That means she doesn't sing just one carol on the Christmas special, but all of them. She is the most ravenously ambitious little bitch I've ever known. I could never understand what Lisa saw in her. She doesn't have a tenth of Lisa's talent either. But she's tired of waiting, a crown princess who wants to become a queen. After all, she tells me, Lisa was doing Christmas specials when she was two years younger than Dina is now. So Lisa's death is a real boon for Dina.

For Tad Thomas, too, who is kind of Dina's ally. Look, between you and me, and whatever that dummy George Quinn thought, Lisa never went to bed with Thomas. I mean, she's just not a highly sexed woman. She doesn't need it. The whole problem in that relationship is that George needed it all the time, Lisa needed it hardly ever. Thomas is kind of a switch hitter, but he really likes men, and especially little boys, more than he likes women. It was his PR person who planted the rumors in the press that he and Lisa were having a grand old time with one another in bed. Yeah, there might have been a little kissy face some of the time, and he might have felt her up when she was discouraged. Like I say, Lisa has always been a sponge for affection. Remember how she used to hug us in grammar school days? Sure you do. I can tell by the way you're blushing. You liked it, too, didn't you?

All the guys had a crush on Lisa.

But I can guarantee she wasn't sleeping with Tad or with anyone else either. That whole business is a combination of press-agent garbage and idiot Quinn's congenital jealousy. Lisa found out that Tad had spread the story. Why? To keep his name in the papers, that's why. He was tired of playing second fiddle to Lisa after all these years, too. If, when the Christmas Special comes up, people see Lisa singing with a guy that, like, maybe is her lover, then that guy gets a lot more attention. You know what I mean?

Sure it's sick. You've been to Hollywood, haven't you? What else do you expect?

So Lisa had begun to believe that Tad was trying to ruin her marriage. I was there when she told him off, always a calm, well-behaved young lady from a Catholic girls' high school: "You must understand, Tad, that I've been in this city long enough to know what press agents and media consultants can do. I can accept anything happening once. If it ever happens again, it will be the last time. I don't like to sound unpleasant, but I hope you understand."

Yeah, you're right. A sort of new Lisa—not taking shit from anybody. But would you have expected her to fire those directors and writers and even supervise every fucking cut herself? To tell the truth, I was proud of her. She'd become a goddamn feisty woman. Still a lot of false consciousness, if you know what I mean, but tough when she had to be.

Her public image? Believe me, Blackie Ryan, when *The Friendship Factor* appears, her public image is going to change. Sweet and lovely and graceful and witty little Lisa will also show up as one tough and fierce and very sexy broad. Sure, she took a big risk, but, what the hell, that's what life's about, isn't it?

At least she's found out that she has some other currency to use than beauty. Sure, looks are power, everyone knows that. For some of us the only power we have. When we lose our looks, we're broke. Thank God Lisa has stopped using her beauty like it was cash. She has not learned that beauty is political, but she's never been much good on theory. At least she's not trading on her looks anymore.

No, I don't see any sign that she's fading. Not at all. She's not like me. Her good looks could last forever. That's not the point.

What is the point? The point is that she's not exploiting her beauty anymore. That means that men can't exploit it either.

I don't know whether she really would have dumped Tad. If you take that Christmas special away from him, there's nothing much left to his career. But he was afraid she might. Yeah, he overreacted. The little freak is so petrified that he thought she said she was going to fire him. I tried to calm him down, but I think he was still terrified that he'd get that phone call in the middle of the morning how come John Denver was going to be in the Christmas special with Lisa? Or Michael Jackson? Wouldn't that be a great Christmas gig? Lisa and Michael?

Are you ready for it!

Yeah, I saw in the papers that Michael said he was going to pray for her. Hell, at this stage of the game, Blackie, we'll take prayers from anyone, won't we? Even media consultants!

Who told her that Tad was the one planted the rumors about their love affair? Well, I suppose I was the one. I smelled Tad's Christian Dior cologne on that from day one, so I did a little checking. I figured Lisa ought to know.

But to get back to your first question. She wasn't threatening my career or my income or my self-image; nor, like Ken Woods, am I a perennially rejected lover. Just like Lisa, I don't need much sex, and I pretty much gave up on it a long time ago. Friendship is what counts, and Lisa was my closest friend in all the world. . . .

No, I'll be all right. No, please: another drink would make me worse. Hell, Blackie, you've known us for thirty-five years. You remember how she infuriated me: always so god-damn sweet and pleasant and friendly and innocent. I used to tell her, especially when we were in high school, that she couldn't trust boys, that she shouldn't believe everything the nuns said, that her mother was exploiting her, and that the only reason so many of the other girls hated her was because she was pretty and talented. She just wouldn't listen to me. Then, when she finally decided to go to UCLA, she did it on her own, without asking me for advice or even telling me about it till after she'd enrolled, and there I was, all the way across the country at Columbia Journalism. Well, look what happened at UCLA. If it hadn't been for you, who knows where Lisa would be now?

Did you ever try to warn her about the creeps? I suppose not. Sure, it's her own business who her friends and advisers are, but I couldn't stand it, to see her permitting herself to be exploited by all those crapheads.

Why the fuck did she marry a drooling orangutan like George Quinn? I don't know whether he beat her up last night or not. No, it doesn't sound at all like George. He doesn't have enough imagination for S and M sex—all George can do is the good old slam-bang-thank-you-ma'am missionary position style. Counting beans and getting erections are what George's life is all about. In fact, sometimes I think George is nothing more than a walking erection.

You know what? I kind of suspect (Lisa would be too modest ever to admit it to anyone) good old George turned up impotent on her before they separated. He ran off to Australia, if you ask me, because he couldn't get it up anymore. I'm sure it didn't bother Lisa at all. Like I said, physical sex never did mean much to her. Even in high school, when we were all as horny as hell, Lisa could kiss a guy for three or four hours and be surprised that he'd get a little aroused. It had no effect on her at all—except the affection part, and, like I told you, she really is a sponge for affection. Poor dear woman.

So maybe while he's away in Australia, George tries some highly specialized Aussie whorehouses and discovers he can get it on again with leather boots and bondage and some whips, so maybe he comes back and experiments a little with Lisa. . . .

The goddamn fucking bastard!

I'm sorry, I really am. I have no reason to say that. I've

never liked George, not even when he used to hang around us at the High Club dances salivating over Lisa, but I have no reason to think he'd hurt her, not physically anyway. In his own dumb macho way, I guess he loved her. But he gave up a lot when he came to Los Angeles with her. Sure he's a power in their West Coast office, and apparently a whiz with computer programming, but he'll never be more than one of a horde of senior vice-presidents. If he'd stayed in Chicago, he might have made it to the top. One night when he was a little tuned—which is about all George ever does—he told me he was sure he could have been president of some big firm like Beatrice or Esmark or Inland Steel or even Continental Illinois Bank. Can you image that! Big fucking deal. It sounds to me like being disappointed that you don't make president of the bootblack union.

But that's George for you. Lisa, poor, sweet little bitch, married him because she felt sorry for him and has regretted it ever since.

God, we had fun in the old days, didn't we, Blackie? Remember the weekends at your mother's house at Grand Beach? And the parties after the proms? And necking in the parking lot in Ryan's Woods? Why did we ever have to grow up? Nineteen-sixty-two was a wonderful year to graduate from high school. Kids today are like we were, aren't they? Fun and games, sex and booze, and fuck political relevance. That used to infuriate the hell out of me until I stopped to realize that all the relevance of the late sixties and early seventies didn't change the world one goddamn bit. Sure feminism makes it a little easier to be a woman, but I don't see much difference between the phony liberal males who dominate the media now and the guys who tried to feel me up, maybe even score with me, when I was in high school and college, except maybe that the latter guys were a little bit more honest about what they wanted from a woman.

Oh, my God! No, I don't believe it! Let's get over there right away. I don't want her to die. God in heaven, I don't want her to die!

8
BLACKIE

We waited nervously at Lisa's bedside in the neurological intensive care unit, Kerry Randall, Joe Murphy (later joined by Mary Kate and Caitlin), and I watching Dr. Rodriquez—nervous, impatient, finally frantic—and his staff fluttering helplessly about the apparently dying woman.

Belatedly I remembered that I was a priest and said, "Gentlepersons, we are after all, Catholics. We should be praying for her. Let's say the rosary together."

Of course I hadn't brought my rosary, but I began tolling the decades on my fingers. Gently Caitlin slipped a lovely Connemara marble necklace of prayer into my fingers, doubtless a present from the inestimable Kevin Patrick Maher, her "one true love," as Caitlin (a recent Notre Dame grad and now a lavish blonde who could be, according to her mother, either a model photographer or a photographer's model) always referred to him.

I noticed, as we progressed from the joyful mysteries into the sorrowful mysteries, that Dr. Rodriquez was muttering the paters and aves with us. The ponderous machinery with which Lisa was surrounded beeped uncertainly, and the gloomy hospital smells—disinfectant, drugs, soap, and death—settled on us like a medicinal smog.

As one of the most distracted prayers in the history of humankind, I wondered about my bizarre interview with the tender/tough Kerry Ann Randall.

The first thing I wondered was whether Kerry Ann was one more of the creeps besetting Lisa's life. Her portrait of herself as the only sensible and reliable person in the coterie around Lisa was remarkably devoid of self-perception. It never seemed to have occurred to poor Kerry that Lisa was putting up, gently and patiently, with her, just as she was putting up with, for example, Sister Winifred or Ken Woods—out of memories of old friendship instead of for any comprehensible reasons in her present life.

From Kerry's description of Lisa's recent months, I concluded that Kerry was obnoxiously present in Lisa's life; indeed, never permitting the poor woman any peace or privacy. Lisa apparently had to tolerate her vulgarity, her cynicism, her simplistic ideology all the time. While Kerry didn't actually live in the Malone house, her own townhouse apartment was only five minutes' drive away (and in Beverly Hills, nobody walks). Poor George the Bean Counter—small wonder he would leave for Australia, with that woman poking her nose around the door to peer at his marriage bed.

Moreover, Roddy Malone wasn't the only one who had disappeared from Lisa's life when she went to Hollywood. As I remember the story, Kerry, already into relevance and radical activism substantially ahead of much of the rest of the country, was furious when Lisa decided to attend UCLA and try to be a movie actress. The rumor in the neighborhood was that Kerry's letter denouncing this decision was incredibly vicious. Lisa, who found it difficult to be unkind about anyone, admitted to me with an amused little grin, "Kay Kay" —our not particularly affectionate nickname for Kerry—"is a little angry with me."

"One of the reasons you chose UCLA was to get away from her," I insisted, "and Philadelphia is too close to New York."

"Well." She kissed me, as she was wont to do on almost any possible occasion. "Some people think I'm going to California to get away from my mother, and others think I'm going there to get away from Kay Kay"—yet another kiss—"while you and I both know that the real reason is to escape from *you!*"

"I'll be locked up in a seminary for seven years," I said helplessly.

"That's not much protection for me." She laughed. "Not even in Southern California."

This was the woman who, Kerry Randall assured me a few moments before we were to huddle around what seemed to be her deathbed, was not much interested in sex.

I wondered what kind of distorted biography Kerry "Kay Kay" Randall would produce. Lisa was an ink blot. What purported to be a biography would, in fact, be Kerry's own autobiography.

Lisa ought to have known better. She told me, in one of her rare visits to Chicago after she was married, that Kay Kay had surfaced again after the failure of her marriage and a couple of professional disasters.

"The poor girl has this terrible reputation among journalists," Lisa said sadly, "of cultivating someone's confidence and affection, falling in love with him, even going to bed with him, and then turning against him and stabbing him in the back. I suppose it's all right to do that if you're a journalist, so long as you're not too obvious. But they say that poor Kay Kay is too obvious about it."

"Stay away from her," I said, as forcefully as I could.

"Don't be mean, Blackie. You never *did* like her. But she's an old friend from the neighborhood, and I can't let her down when she needs help."

An old friend from the neighborhood. I almost told her, even then, that it would be old friends from the neighborhood who might do her in. I thought better of it because she'd married an old friend from the neighborhood and was deeply in love with him.

The problem with Kay Kay as a grammar school child was that, while no one hated her as much as some of us and some of our parents hated Lisa, no one loved her as much as a few of us and our parents loved Lisa. Everyone *liked* Kerry Ann, but practically no one loved her. I suppose the reason was that she lacked the sort of character that stirred up powerful emotions either way. She was popular, she was energetic, she was admired, and she was, alas, easily forgotten. A typical neighborhood mother would be horrified to learn that my cousin, Catherine Collins, was painting nudes at her "studio" at Grand Beach, even when she was in the seventh grade. The same mother would be appalled to hear that Lisa Malone was going to sing at *another* wedding, even though she was only in the eighth grade. Then that very same mother would remark, in passing, that Kerry Ann was very cute cheerleading last Sunday.

Who the hell cared about cheerleaders?

So she became, even in those days, upper 1950s, a bit of a leech, following Lisa around avidly. "The poor little girl," my mother said. "She's not satisfied with the admiration she gets on her own; she wants to share in some of Lisa's. Isn't it sweet of Lisa not to mind?"

"The Punk minds!" Mary Kate (in those days, an often obnoxious bobby-sox-, saddle-shoe-, and bermuda-short-wearing teenager) proclaimed triumphantly. "He's in *love* with Lisa!"

"A changeling, definitely." My mother had a knack of agreeing with something that no one had said. "I certainly can assume no responsibility for him at all. Changeling or not, if he's in love with Lisa, he shows good taste."

"I never said that he didn't," Mary Kate responded, even in those days insisting on the last word.

Sometimes when I am discouraged in the priesthood (which is usually several times each morning before 11:30), I tell myself ironically that instead of presiding over a totally impossible parish like Holy Name Cathedral, I could be happily married and living the life of luxurious ease in California as Lisa Malone's husband.

By lunchtime, however, it is clear to me that the fantasy is absurd. Admittedly, if I had not entered the seminary, Lisa and I would have dated during college years. Admittedly, too, she did not marry until after I was ordained. But in truth, the latter was a romantic conceit on her part, and the former would never have led to the altar. Lisa and I were designed to love each other in grammar school, then again, briefly, at the end of high school. We were not, heaven forfend, designed to live together in marriage. While I don't normally accept the judgment of my sister Nancy O'Connor that God was awfully good to some woman when he gave me a vocation to the priesthood, I'm prepared to acknowledge that Lisa and I would have been a singularly ill-matched couple in the canyons of Beverly Hills. As I knelt at her deathbed, I told myself that realistically this was not the woman who might have been my wife.

At least not for long anyway.

Nonetheless, she was my first and in a way my only love.

"Hi, I'm Lisa!" the five-year-old girl child announced, one foot on the pedal of her red and white tricycle and the other planted tentatively on the sidewalk of Glenwood Drive. "What's *your* name?"

"I'm Blackie," I said, rather proud that I had graduated to a bicycle.

"That's a *funny* name." Lisa's snub nose crinkled upward. "You don't *look* black!"

"Some people call me Johnny," I observed tentatively.

"I like Blackie better." She grinned cheerfully. "It's a *nice* name, even if it is *funny*."

"Can't you ride a bicycle?" I demanded, tiring of this conversation over names.

"You're a *funny* boy, too." She giggled. "But I guess I like you. Can I try to ride your bicycle?"

It was a birthday present from my father, whom I then, as now, worshiped. No one in the world, I had solemnly promised myself, would ever touch that bicycle.

"Sure."

Already I was in love.

Most adults refuse to take seriously love affairs of children that age. After all, they don't know anything about sex then, do they?

Well, Dr. Freud might have had something to say on the subject. The loves of a kid whose age is still in the single digits are fleeting, but the kid doesn't know that. If, when the kid grows up, he denies or forgets about his single-digit love affairs, the reason is not that they didn't exist and not that they weren't awesomely important at the time, but rather that the sweetness and the pain of being loved by someone outside your family who doesn't have to love you—at just about that age in life when you learn that love isn't automatic—is almost unbearable.

Lisa liked me. I didn't know why, but it didn't matter. My

response to her affection was total surrender. She could have my bicycle or anything else she wanted, even my vocation to the priesthood, which, fortunately for her, she didn't want. For two years we were inseparable on Glenwood Drive, riding our bicycles together and calmly ignoring the rest of the world. Then, as we grew older, the boys and the girls divided into wolf packs of their own. Lisa and I had to pretend that we were unaware of each other's existence. We still found ways to smile at one another, serving notice that later on we'd take up where we had left off.

My mother's thesis that I was a changeling was not unsupported by the data. Indeed, it fit all of William James's three criteria for truth. The Ryans are handsome, athletic, and, with the exception of my father, tall and rangy. I was short, clumsy, unathletic, and—to put the best possible face on the matter—quaint.

Some of these characteristics later on in life would turn out to be most useful and, indeed, provide me with many effective masks behind which I could lurk to deal with reality.

The role of the elf or the imp or the leprechaun or the goblin or the changeling or, as Eileen once remarked, the "white sheep" in the Ryan clan might have been a bit much for a little boy who, beneath it all, was also extraordinarily sensitive; at least, it might have been too much if, on those occasions when he began to wonder whether he really was "kinda weird," he had not been able to tell himself—usually implicitly—well, anyway, Lisa thinks I'm all right.

I wonder, reflecting back on those years in the forties and the fifties, if I overestimate her importance. God knows she was on my mind almost every day from five until she kissed me good-bye for the last time before I left for the seminary and she for UCLA. I don't think we ever quarreled or disagreed, mostly because, when I tried to start a fight (quintessential Ryan clan behavior), Lisa simply laughed at me.

Come to think of it, the last time she and George visited me at the cathedral rectory, she also laughed at me. Maybe I could have matured into a moderately functional human adult (which is all that I claim for myself) without Lisa's admiration and love. Maybe, but I wouldn't bet on it.

There was nothing self-conscious about our relationship, not even on that day in 1962 when she and Catherine Collins together arrived at the Ryan house on Glenwood Drive to kiss me good-bye. They were allies in this event, as they cheerfully admitted, to protect one another from disgraceful tears.

I would miss them both as the years went on, but, God forgive me for it, as I tried to fall asleep in the uncomfortable bed at Mundelein that night, I congratulated myself on having reduced two such lovely young persons to the brink of tears.

This dying woman in the hospital bed in Northwestern's intensive care unit—she can't be the five-year-old on the tricycle who told me her name was Lisa, can she? What connection could there be between this woman, who will probably never open her eyes again, and the passionate girl whose kisses and fresh young breasts almost smothered me in the old family Cadillac in the Ryan's Woods (no relation) parking lot on the night of her senior prom?

I'm still not clear how I survived that night.

And how can she be the same hazel-eyed star who splashed across our sky at Christmas in 1970 and dazzled us singing "O Holy Night" in the Ryan family parlor because she was banished from the parish church by envy?

No, that can't possibly be Lisa who is breathing her last breaths as we ineffectually pray for her recovery. There was too much vitality, too much energy, too much laughter, too much hope in Lisa. She can't be dying.

Not interested in sex? What an absurd notion. Modest and chaste? Yes, genetically and by definition. But sexless? Devoid of erotic interest? Innocent of passion? Surely not the young woman whose salty skin tasted so good against my lips twenty-two years before. No way!

Yet Kerry Randall insisted that sex was no longer important in Lisa's life; it had been left behind, along with the horniness of our adolescence.

I guess maybe you're still an adolescent, Blackie Ryan, I told myself as we began the glorious mysteries of the rosary. If sex turns Lisa off now, something must have gone profoundly wrong with her marriage. She certainly pursued poor

George the Bean Counter with passionate intensity, once I'd been tucked safely out of the way. What went wrong between those two?

I felt guilty because, God knows, I'd had a part in aiding and abetting her capture of George. I was too young then to realize that most human relationships, even those that seem to be the best, given sufficient time, go bad.

Dear God in heaven, please don't let her die. Give her another chance. Give George another chance and give me another chance to help them. All my life I have been receiving from Lisa. Now is my chance to give something back. Please help me do it.

The Lord God promptly pointed out, in the ears of my memory, that I was engaging in a rare exaggeration.

Lisa hadn't particularly needed me to bring down George the Bean Counter in mid-flight. A couple of years before that, she was in deep trouble and did need me. My contribution was trivial. The point is that there was no one else around to make it.

I came home from Mass at St. Praxides to the house on Glenwood Drive on a Monday morning in the first week of June vacation after the first year in the seminary—marveling that indeed, the human race was half female, a proposition the seminary authorities seemed to have rejected on the grounds that it was aesthetically unsatisfying.

"Lisa phoned," Helen, my stepmother, said, becomingly pregnant with what would turn out to be Trish, as she placed in front of me my usual breakfast of grapefruit, bacon and eggs, pancakes, strawberries and cream, freshly brewed Earl Grey, and a side order of steak, the kind of breakfast seminary authorities seemed to think exceeded my nutritional needs.

I've always been charged by my siblings with being a metabolic freak; indeed, according to my brother Packy, a human garbage scow. Packy sometimes has trouble with his nouns: he meant scoop, not scow, I suspect. There is no relationship between my intake of food and drink and my physical shape. No matter how much I eat or don't eat (and I still keep the traditional Lenten fast merely to cause consternation among my curates), my weight fluctuates not in the slightest.

Lisa!

Even if my vocation to the priesthood was now definitive and irrevocable, her name could still cause my heart to do flip-flops. "It's only six o'clock in California."

"She's in Our Lady of Angels Hospital. You know, that's the one on the expressway." Helen had had a brief acting career of her own, terminated, as she would ruefully put it, because of an unfair distribution of talent in the world—she didn't have any. "She said she was all right, poor little thing, but she certainly sounded under the weather to me."

I finished my breakfast and phoned back. "Please, Blackie," the timid and frightened little voice said, "help!"

I checked with my father to learn the names of his legal cronies in Los Angeles and departed for O'Hare, Helen at the wheel of Dad's perennially reconditioned gull-winged Mercedes. By noontime I was on a United Airlines DC8— new in those days—on my way to Los Angeles. A few hours later I was standing at Lisa's bedside in a four-room ward in the hospital. She had two black eyes, a broken arm, and a large bandage on the side of her head, looking like a refugee from an urban riot. She began to cry as soon as I came into the hospital room.

"What the hell happened to you?" I exclaimed. Blackie Ryan wasn't always cool.

"I had an accident!" she wailed. "Please, *please* don't be angry with me!"

"All right, Lisa." She could still get from me whatever she wanted. "But tell me what happened."

"You'll get mad again," she sobbed.

"No, but I might laugh."

"Oh, that'll be all right." She tried to grin and winced with pain. "I had a *terrible* accident."

You'd better believe it was a terrible accident, a fall from a window on the second floor of a house in Malibu. "I'm lucky not to be dead."

Why had she fallen out the second-floor window of a house in Malibu? Because she had been on a very bad LSD trip.

This was back in the days when LSD was as fashionable among our more advanced and self-defined "progressive" elites as cocaine is now.

"I thought it would help me to be an actress," Lisa moaned. "At first it was fun, my world filled with the most wonderful lavender elephants, and then there were terrible monsters, huge fairie demons that looked like my brother Roderick."

"You sure the elephants weren't pink?"

We both laughed, and Lisa regained some of her composure. But the story she had to tell was no laughing matter.

It was the story of a genteel and casual drug and sex ring, amateur, not professional, run for the benefit of some middle-management studio executives with a string of beach houses just outside Malibu. Lisa was a recent recruit, a naive Irish Catholic kid from Chicago who, over the last several weekends, had offered considerable amusement to men who promised they could "do a lot" for her career. It was a not unfamiliar story; indeed, almost a cliché: the innocent starlet corrupted by evil studio executives—evil and dishonest because they probably couldn't do much for her career.

It would be pleasant, I thought, to throw them in the piranha tank at the local aquarium, if Los Angeles was civilized enough to have an aquarium.

"I've been such a stupid little fool," Lisa said contritely. "I thought the whole world was like the neighborhood and I was as safe in this Beverly Hills as in our Beverly Hills."

"Maybe you were lucky to learn so early in life that that's not true," I said lamely.

"I sure did," she sighed. "I'll know better next time."

Lisa was a quick learner. I'm sure there were many other promises of career advancement in return for sexual favors as she climbed the ladder to success. They were sweetly and politely but definitely rejected. "I'll make it," she told one interviewer early in her career, "by talent and hard work, before the camera and in the recording studio—not in some-one's bedroom."

The picture next to the quote showed a young woman whose wide-eyed modesty had earned her a place on the front page of the local Catholic newspaper, as the Irish Catholic teenager of the year.

The innocence, which Lisa was able to cling to for twenty more years, would no longer be purchased at the price of ignorance. She understood, after the Lord God had eased her quietly off that windowsill in Malibu and deposited her unceremoniously on the beach, that what had passed as virtue until then in her life was merely the social controls of a very tightly structured and conservative community. In tinsel town her virtue had to come from the inside.

Lisa would continue to be sensitive and fragile, but whatever softness seemed to remain about her was illusory. Kerry Randall misunderstood Lisa completely if she thought that the toughness Lisa displayed during the production of *The Friendship Factor* was a recent addition to her character. It was a very tough young woman who shook hands gravely with me in the United Airlines terminal in the old Los Angeles International Airport later in the week. "I've learned my lesson, Blackie," she said somberly. "I really have."

"I believe you, Lisa," I said with equal gravity, while wondering if her heart was as heavy as mine was.

She was wearing a simple white sleeveless dress, sunglasses to cover her still spectacularly blackened eyes. I thought of bundling her into my arms and bringing her home to the neighborhood and to the family. It was a very appealing thought. Just at that moment, I was sure she would come.

The Lord God presumably had different plans for both of us, but just then I wasn't thinking much of Her.

"I'm good at what I do; all my teachers say that." She sounded like she believed it, at least partially. "And I'm going to get better. No more fun and games."

"God bless," I said as my flight was called, an almost direct intervention of the Lord God. "I'll see ya."

"If I don't see ya, I'll see ya," she grinned impishly. "God bless, Blackie."

The next time I saw her in person was in the front room of my family's home in 1970 when she sang "O Holy Night" for a couple of hundred of us.

Seven years, I told myself as I parked in front of the

sprawling old heap on Glenwood Drive. Her dreams have come true. She's a successful actress and singer, a polished, sophisticated woman of the world. She'll have nothing in common with the frightened little girl I left behind at LAX after bailing her out of trouble with the Los Angeles fuzz.

I was wrong. Lisa had not changed—still fragile, still tough, still easily hurt by the rejection of her own people, and still overwhelmed by the love and admiration of her loyal friends.

She steered clear of romantic involvements, or so I read in the papers, between her stay at Our Lady of Angels Hospital and her determined and skillful assault on poor George the Bean Counter at Christmastime of 1970. I'm still not quite sure how she managed to remain celibate for seven years. Lisa loved men more than most women do and I think needed a man around her more than most women. "Sometimes I think I ought to have been a nun," she jokingly told one of the interviewers. "I'm not ready for marriage yet and I'm not going to let myself fall in love until I'm ready for marriage."

She certainly managed to fall in love quickly enough after I was ordained—or perhaps I should say she managed to activate quickly enough one of her old loves.

I helped her, and the bastard killed her!

I was suddenly furious at George the Bean Counter, so furious that I wanted to see him roast in the electric chair, scarcely a proper emotion during the third glorious mystery of the rosary, when one was supposed to be contemplating the descent of the Holy Spirit, Spirit of wind and fire and love, upon the Apostles.

It was awfully late in the game to be feeling jealous of poor George Quinn. My anger at him quickly subsided. After all, he'd done a fine job for ten or eleven years, hadn't he?

Catherine and Nick Curran had visited the Quinns in their Beverly Hills palace in 1980, when a Los Angeles gallery was doing an exhibition of Catherine's work (a curious mixture of nudes and sunbursts). Catherine and Lisa had kept each other at cautious arm's length during grammar school and high school, too clever to permit their rivalry ever to become a fight. Lisa was expecting Ned at the time, and, according to my cousin and her husband—who, in combination, make a pretty perceptive reporting team—Lisa and George seemed content and pleased with one another.

"Like mellow, you know what I mean?" Cathy had said.

"Like you and Nick?" I rolled my eyes suggestively.

"Don't be silly," Catherine fired back. "Nick and I aren't the mellow type."

"Thank God!"

"You'd better believe it," Cathy said fervently.

Looking back on that conversation, I wondered, as we moved into the fourth decade of the rosary's glorious mysteries, whether George and Lisa were the mellow type either. I would have thought not. Perhaps there were signs on the horizon, no bigger than a man's hand even then, of the trouble that was to come.

I feel partly responsible for George the Bean Counter and also greatly responsible for Ken Woods, who, everyone agreed, had engineered Lisa's rise to stardom.

Woods was the finest agent in the Hollywood of his generation. His greatest triumph, it was said, was the creation of Lisa Malone. Now, career virtually at an end, Kenneth A. Woods had been so shunted out of the limelight, it seemed as though he were Lisa Malone's creation instead of vice versa.

Grounds for murder? If you were as proud and sensitive a man as Kenneth Woods, and if you had fallen as deeply in love with Lisa as he did on that first visit to her hospital room, yes, it might be grounds for murder.

Had I not brought Ken Woods into her life, Lisa Malone would never have "made it" in Hollywood. In all likelihood she would have come back to the neighborhood, married a local boy, perhaps George Quinn, settled down, and raised a family in an environment of economic and social irrelevancy. She would suffer from vague and nameless frustrations, complain that she was fifteen pounds overweight, and drink far too much. She might still sing at an occasional wedding in St. Praxides—though *Panis Angelicus* and Schubert's *Ave Maria* were now out of fashion—but no one beyond the boundaries of the neighborhood would ever have heard of her.

And she would still be alive.

Kenneth Arthur Woods had been a young ensign fresh out of Harvard, a ninety-day wonder trained only a block away from Lisa's bed at Northwestern's Abbott Hall, who was assigned to my father's destroyer escort (improbably named the *Charles Morton Stedman*) in 1944, only a couple of months before the old fella led a charge of such fragile craft against a squadron of Japanese battleships at the north end of Leyte Gulf and saved the lives of tens of thousands of Americans waiting offshore in troop transports. For reasons that no one could ever quite figure out, the Japanese Admiral turned tail and ran.

"He was daunted by the steely light of my blue eyes," the old fella claimed on occasion.

And on other occasions, "The poor man was more drunk than I was."

My father came home, participated in my conception, moved to the south side, and resumed his legal career and his passionate love affair with my mother. Kenneth Arthur Woods, rigidly uptight Ivy League grad that he was, settled "temporarily" in Los Angeles, tried law school for a year, and then drifted into the movie industry. Eighteen years later, a month after the Cuban missile crisis, he sat across from me in the Polo Lounge Bar in the Beverly Hills Hotel, the hottest agent in Hollywood.

That was in the day when the hot agents did indeed have lunch in the Polo Lounge and not in places like the Hermitage, where the hot agents eat and drink today. Ken Woods, of course, still can be found at his regular table in the Polo Lounge, determined to maintain the past now just as he was to shatter it forty years ago.

The Beverly Hills Hotel appeared in a bean field in 1912, six years after a subdivision was laid out between Santa Monica and Wilshire boulevards. The Los Angeles Beverly is younger than our own by a good decade, if now larger and more affluent (though not nearly as fascinating). In 1920, when the boom started, there were only 674 people living in the community. Douglas Fairbanks, Sr., and Mary Pickford moved in first, and then the world seemed to follow them. The Beverly Hills Hotel suddenly became the center of social life for the new celebrity caste. The Polo Lounge, green and pink and white and sun drenched (no polo field in sight), was the place to see and be seen.

Native of the Chicago Beverly Hills, I was not impressed.

Ken Woods, however, expected me to be impressed. In 1963 he was a short, broad-shouldered, square-jawed, crew-cut, black-haired man with just a tinge of distinguished gray at his temples, wearing white slacks and a double-breasted navy blazer with a rough-stitched white turtleneck, as though he was planning an excursion on his yacht that afternoon (which, it turned out, was exactly what was on his agenda). I went along just to see how the other half lives and decided that I, too, wouldn't mind owning a forty-five-foot cabin cruiser, were it in Marina Del Rey.

At first glance you would have thought that Ken Woods might be a third-generation member of the New York Yacht Club, a cigarillo-smoking member of the monied Yankee aristocracy, who had not done an honest day's work in his life because he had never had to. In fact, Ken was the son of an unemployed (during the Depression) coal mine foreman from Pennsylvania. His elite New England demeanor, highly marketable in Hollywood at that time, was carefully culti-vated. There was enough cold ruthlessness in his grim brown eyes to air condition the Beverly Hills Hotel for a whole season.

Through most of the meal, he sang my father's praises, entertainment for which I have been a willing chorus most of my life. As much admiration as I have for the old fella (who once admitted to me, "All the rest of them are change-lings, Blackie—you're the only one like me"), I never could make sense of the hymn to the heroic and popular destroyer escort captain. The old fella had far too much sense to take on a Japanese battleship by himself.

Nevertheless, I always joined in enthusiastically in the chorus.

Ken Woods, then in his middle-forties, seemed authentically healthy and happy, a vigorous, successful hard-driving man content with his work and with great plans for his future. He matched my single glass of Jameson's (all right, so I was under age, but who was going to deny a drink to Ken Woods's guest in the Polo Lounge Bar?) with three old-fashioneds and puffed compulsively on a cigarillo, jutting at an FDR angle from his thin lips. I suspected he'd had one or two drinks before he came to lunch. His two marriages, my father had told me, had both ended in dramatic divorces. "Too many young women available in that business," the old fella had sighed, whether out of sympathy or envy was not altogether clear.

The fast track on which Ken Woods was racing was not tolerable, I concluded, without a considerable number of preprandial old-fashioneds. Was this the world in which Lisa wanted to be a success?

I had second thoughts during the meal as he entertained me with anecdotes about the film industry, allegedly comic anecdotes but, in fact, always stories in which he was the hero; indeed, the only one with intelligence. Maybe my head was turned by the Polo Lounge Bar of the Beverly Hills Hotel, however, because my hesitations did not prevent me from finally raising the subject of Lisa.

"Well, Father." He leaned back and stretched his hands expansively. "I owe my life to your dad, the old fella, as you call him. We all would have died that day off Samar Island if it hadn't been for him. I'll do anything that you or he asks me to do. But I have to be candid and say that this town is filled with beautiful young women who think they can act and sing."

Call me Blackie.

Not Ishmael, just Blackie.

"I can't call a priest by his first name, Father"; his dry, rasping voice reminded me of a lawn mower motor that needed lubrication. "What do you think I am?"

He favored me with his most carefully practiced personable smile. It had done no good at all to tell him that my black suit and black tie did not mean that I was a priest and that I would not be a priest for seven more years and that at my age seven more years seemed a lifetime. "Anyway, I'll see the kid, visit her in the hospital even, and have a good heart-to-heart talk with her. The best advice I could give would be for her to go back home to Chicago, find a nice Irish Catholic husband, and settle down and raise a big family. Right now this city doesn't need any more Marilyn Monroes."

"That's not quite the nature of her appeal...." I said tentatively.

"I'm sure, Father, I'm sure." He held up his hands as though to stop traffic. "Look, I'll talk to her, I'll listen to her sing, and I'll give her the best advice I possibly can. Okay?"

"Okay."

You know what, Kenneth A. Woods, I thought to myself, you are in for one hell of a surprise!

Lisa will have a nice family and she'll also have a successful career. She's the kind of person who says "both" as easily as she breathes.

I went back to my room at the Beverly Wilshire—the old fella insisted any son of his who went to Los Angeles to salvage a girl from the neighborhood should stay in a "decent" hotel—phoned said old fella with Woods's greetings, and then called Lisa to tell her that Ken Woods would be over to see her the next morning.

If he was unimpressed and told her to come home, she would either be on the plane with me or fly back to Chicago a few days later. That would be the end of her screen career and would create certain problems in my life. It would be a lot easier to live through seven years of hell in the seminary of those days with Lisa in Los Angeles instead of Chicago.

Oh ye of little faith!

"Ken Woods, Father," said the voice on my phone just before lunch the next day. "My God, why didn't you tell me what she was like!"

"I tried to say that she was talented...."

"Talented? Hell, Father, you should excuse my expression, the city is crawling with talented women and beautiful women, but only occasionally in a lifetime do you meet one with star quality. That poor little kid has it! She's luminous, transparent, radiant. In five years America will worship her."

Welcome, America, I thought, into the club!

And so the die was cast, the flight of the swallow begun, a flight that would bring her eventually to the neurological intensive care unit at Northwestern Hospital, bringing me and my family to her bedside to finish the fifth glorious mystery of the rosary, the crowning of Mary as Queen of Heaven.

Dr. Rodriquez's team stopped fluttering. They gathered around the bed upon which Lisa rested, watching intently. The room was calm and peaceful. Was it the silence of a tomb?

9

BLACKIE

"I can't remember when Lisa wasn't an embarrassment." Roderick Powers Malone spoke through a mouthful of scrambled eggs, wolfing down an early morning breakfast in the dining room of the cathedral rectory. "I sometimes am astonished at the durability of my wife and children in surviving our Lisa problem."

As a trencherman Roddy Malone put me to shame. He was on his third helping of bacon and eggs and was awaiting his fourth stack of buttermilk pancakes. His gluttony had ruined my appetite, no small achievement.

I glanced at one of the morning newspapers. Farley Strangler's thesis today was that the attempted murder of Lisa Malone was, in fact, a publicity stunt gone wrong. Or maybe, after all, not gone wrong.

"Wait till the advance hype begins to roll on Lisa's little stinker, *The Friendship Factor*. Nobody who values money would bet against Ms. Malone making a miraculous recovery just the way her heroine, who spends most of the film waltzing around in the nude, makes a miraculous recovery. Being biffed on the noggin is a small price for an aging sex goddess to pay to maintain her box-office numbers."

That did not improve my appetite any.

"Mind you," he said as he emptied a maple syrup jug on a newly arrived stack of pancakes, "I didn't want her to die. That would be even more of an embarrassment."

The blubbering sounds behind us during the last couple of minutes of the glorious mysteries of the rosary were not the noise of a malfunctioning computer but of Roderick Malone having an emotional collapse.

An authentic emotional collapse? If Kerry Randall was to be believed, Dr. Malone would be a rich man after Lisa's death, and, as I remembered, Roddy had tried his hand at college dramatics, Hasty Pudding, Lisa had said proudly.

It was hard to believe that this disgusting little man sitting across the table from me was Lisa's brother. He looked like an overweight, undersized Kojak, not bloated fat so much as bubbly fat—thick flesh restrained not merely by a hand-made brown suit (at least a thousand dollars) but a tailor-made shirt as well. As we walked back from the hospital, leaning against the solid wall of wind that the high rises of my parish funneled into the the lower canyons, his obesity was further concealed by a deftly designed trenchcoat. His excess weight was distributed all over his body and not merely in his belly, solidly packed meat pressing against the skin of a frankfurter. Mistakenly I had offered him a drink when we emerged from the hospital, just as the sun was investigating the possibilities of rising once again on Lake Michigan.

"I have confidence in the team at Northwestern," he said, with a mouthful of buttermilk pancakes, "Rodriquez knows his business. My colleague Howard, who owes me a lot of favors, was ready to fly in from Mass General. Howard," in a tone we Chicagoans normally reserve for the late Mayor Daley, "is the best there is. When I told him Rodriquez was in attendance, he said there was no point in his coming, because Rodriquez was every bit as good."

"Some of these Puerto Ricans are surprisingly gifted," I murmured ironically.

"You can tell he has a lot of white blood in him," Roddy

said, wolfing down three pancakes in a single swallow. "That's what counts in the long run, isn't it?"

He had missed my irony. I was not inclined to explain it to him. Roddy Malone had been born into the world and lived fifty years totally innocent of a sense of the ironic. When I had offered him a drink, he had said, "No, no, I never drink," waving his hands nervously. "I owe it to my patients to keep my bloodstream clean of chemicals. It might impair the effectiveness of my judgment or the steadiness of my hands."

I am too kind a soul to have said that a bloated stomach draws a considerable amount of blood away from the brain.

"If I might have breakfast at your rectory?" He glanced suggestively at his watch. "I'm sure the restaurant at the Drake isn't open yet. And then a call to my wife?"

Sure. Doesn't the Bible say I was hungry and you fed me? That hungry?

Rodriquez had looked like a Puerto Rican padre, his green hospital gown almost a liturgical vestment, when he had turned to us, his hands folded on his belly, and said, "Perhaps our prayers have been heard. This danger is over. We must continue to pray, pray very hard. Most of it now is in the hands of God."

"The next danger, Miguel?" my sister Mary Kate asked.

He shrugged, the padre trying to explain the inscrutable ways of the Lord God. "This evening? Tomorrow? I cannot say. Her condition is somewhere between grave and critical—whatever those words may mean. I will not deceive you about the medical grounds for hope. That she is alive and breathing regularly and with sensation in most parts of her body is miracle enough for the moment."

With considerable guilt I watched the wonderful little man, not only shorter than Roderick Malone but even shorter than me, preach his ferverino. I ought to be preaching the homily because after all, not only was I a priest, I was also the pastor of the parish. Well, clergy, the Lord be praised, have no monopoly on Christianity.

It was precisely Christianity that I had forgotten. Lisa's life was in the hands of God as all our lives are all the time. I could imagine the Lady God saying to me impatiently, "You have your work to do, Blackie Ryan—find out who tried to kill her, and let me worry about what's next for Lisa. After all, I love her even more than you do."

Thirty hours it had taken me to arrive at that fundamental truth. Well, better than thirty days, I suppose.

So my marching orders from Himself were to cease worrying about my responsibilities for the past and to begin worrying about my responsibilities for the future. There was a vague, half-formed, profoundly disturbing image lurking in my preconscious, still pretty deep in the preconscious, but there. If I could force it out into the open or, to be more precise, facilitate the development of that image, I would have the solution. I knew something already, or perhaps only part of something, that was critically important. As Michael Polyani would have said, the image required faith, works, and grace. I had to believe it was there, I had to work like hell to find out what it was, and then I had to wait for the burst of illumination.

I made a note on the front page of the *Chicago Tribune*: Polyani's criteria were not unlike those of William James. A good point for my article.

If I was thinking of my William James piece again, it must follow that the tide was turning against grief and shock and anger.

Better late than never.

For a moment I almost saw the picture, then it faded back behind the smoke screens in my brain. What about it disturbed me so much? The image itself? No, not that. Rather, the implication in the image, whatever it was, of worse dangers ahead for Lisa.

I poured myself a second cup of tea, Earl Grey for breakfast, of course. What was there about the act of pouring tea which seemed to jab at the sore spot in my memory?

"Wonderful pancakes," said my guest, in a tone of voice that would have been more appropriate had he said, "Wonderful sex!"

"I'm glad you liked them."

"It is an enormous relief to me," he said, reaching for a last croissant on the plate in front of him, "that my sister didn't die last night and it will be an enormous relief for my wife and children."

"Ah."

"You can imagine how terrible it would be for them to have to live with the fact that their sister-in-law and aunt had been savagely murdered by an unknown assailant in a cheap hotel room in downtown Chicago. It would be an acute embarrassment for them for the rest of their lives."

"It would be pretty hard on Lisa, too."

10
RODERICK
MALONE, M.D.

You must remember, Monsignor Ryan, our family was not typical: we are hardly south side Irish post—World War II vulgar new rich. My grandfather was one of the directors of the 1892 World's Fair and was later president of the South Park Board. My father graduated from St. Ignatius College—which later became Loyola University, as I'm sure you know—and then Loyola Law School. He earned an immense reputation for wisdom and wit in his very distinguished career as a judge before his untimely death, a death which, I hardly need remind you, came after the release of Lisa's first salacious film. My mother, God be good to her, attended the Convent of the Sacred Heart and was in one of the first classes that graduated from Mundelein College. She went to Mundelein because it was Depression time and her parents couldn't afford anything better. That's why she so very much wanted Lisa to go to a distinguished higher educational institution, preferably Bryn Mawr, of course, but

St. Mary's at Notre Dame, if Lisa insisted on a Catholic school. My mother was a refined, genteel woman, Monsignor. I'm sure there must be many like her in your parish—cultivated, civilized, sensitive. She survived my father's death by ten years, as you know, but she never recovered from the shock of Lisa's betrayal. It is true, in the very literal sense, that Lisa killed both my parents.

Through the years I have found it in my heart to forgive her for her base ingratitude and for her callous indifference to my mother and father, but I have not been able to forgive her for the constant embarrassment that my wife and children have suffered because of her sleazy career.

Can I explain to you, Monsignor Ryan, how important good music, good art, and good literature were to the family in which I was raised and are to the family I am endeavoring to raise? I often think we were the only ones in the neighborhood who knew where Orchestra Hall or the Art Institute was. When we were little children my father often read us Dickens, before we went to bed at night. My mother used to play a movement from Mozart or Bach or Haydn after supper while the other children in the neighborhood were rushing to their television sets. My wife and I happen to agree that a similar atmosphere is important for our children. She, too, Monsignor, comes from a very distinguished old New York Catholic family dating back to the 1830s. Her father and her grandfather and her great-grandfather were all in the investment business, and her brother today is a senior partner of the firm into which her father's company merged after reorganization. If anything, her family background is even more distinguished than mine. You can picture, I suspect, how acutely she suffered when our children would come home from school saying that their little friends wanted to know when Aunt Lisa was going to be a centerfold in *Playboy*.

Lisa was fundamentally a spoiled little brat. I suppose it's not altogether her fault. My mother and father indulged her shamelessly because she was so attractive and so charming. Even as a baby Lisa knew how to manipulate others through her physical appearance. Her power to control easily the behavior of others was shallow and heedless and inconsiderate. Physical attractiveness is a dangerous and potentially evil force. I have come to despise it because of our suffering at Lisa's hands.

I once discussed her with my colleague Warren, who is, as I'm sure you know, the nation's most distinguished specialist in character disorders. He said that Lisa clearly suffers from an antisocial personality disorder called the screen goddess syndrome, a form of acute narcissism in which all behaviors other than self-exhibition become unimportant and all persons other than the self-exhibited are devoid of value. It seemed to me that it was a very perceptive diagnosis.

Let me assure you, Monsignor Ryan, that I am not unaware of the artistic possibility of the cinema. Quite the contrary, my wife and I are generous patrons of a contemporary film festival in the area of our summer home in Maine. Truffaut, Godard, Bergman, these men are great artists. Their work is completely different from the slovenly, sentimental kitsch from which Lisa has earned her millions.

No, we do not normally attend her films. The reviews are quite enough to embarrass us, thank you.

I will confess to acute anxiety about this new film of hers, *The Friendship Fashion*, or whatever it is called. It sounds rather like a title for one of those spy stories, doesn't it? No, of course I don't read such trash! When I have fulfilled my obligations to my medical journals, I would sooner reread a classic—Dickens, or Scott, or Thackeray, or perhaps even Virgil or Homer. My father, as you doubtless remember, read the Latin and Greek poets in the original for recreation at the end of a hard day in court. He used to say that he much preferred Virgil to golf at the Beverly Country Club. I try to sustain that family tradition, as do my sons, though I will confess that I am not as literate in either Latin or Greek as my father. Nonetheless, I do take pride in seeing my teenage boy curling up with Horace when other boys his age are playing foolish games with their computers.

This new film, which causes me to shudder whenever I think about it, sounds as though it will be hard-core pornography. I am doubly humiliated that a sister of mine would sink so low merely to preserve, for another year or two, a reputation as a sex goddess.

Let us be candid with one another, Monsignor Ryan. None of us is as young as we used to be. Lisa is losing her physical attractiveness. The only talent, if you want to call it that, that she has ever possessed is deteriorating. She is making a shameful display of an aging, sagging body in one more final attempt to win the acclaim of the vulgar crowds. Such behavior is by definition pornographic. I do not know how my wife and children and the grandchildren we soon expect will be able to bear it. I would not blame them if they demanded that we change our family name.

Several times I've had the occasion to present major and important papers on cardiac surgery before the most distinguished medical bodies in the world and then be asked to answer, as the first question, whether I am really Lisa Malone's brother, a question that is always, need I say, accompanied by a knowing wink or leer.

I fear that this trouble Lisa caused for herself here in Chicago, in addition to that film, will make it impossible for me ever to appear on a responsible medical academic platform again. Even now, to be perfectly candid with you, Monsignor, on those rare occasions when I have no choice but to read a paper, I take it for granted that the audience is thinking more about her than about me.

How do I answer the question? I say simply that any statement about my sister will have to come from her public relations consultant.

Do you know, Monsignor, how many men and women are alive and walking the streets today who would be in their graves if it weren't for these hands of mine? Thousands. I am certainly among the best cardiac surgeons of my generation; I will make no claim to be the very best. Yet I am not known for the extraordinary recovery rate of my patients, I am known as Lisa Malone's brother, the brother of a cheap little music hall tart.

Yes, I have had occasion to visit her several times since her unfortunate marriage to that flabby little man. Pardon my candor, Monsignor, but I fail to understand how any man whose gonads are still secreting hormones into his bloodstream can possibly accept his emasculated role. I firmly believe in equality between the marriage partners. I consider my wife to be a full partner in all our joint activities, but I would not tolerate, and my wife would not want, a situation in which she becomes, if you will, the managing partner. It is patent that George Quinn exists merely to service Lisa's sexual needs when no one else is available. Otherwise he is of no importance to the zoo that she dignifies with the name of family.

I am appalled at the thought of what will certainly happen to those poor little children. Bad enough that they must be raised in a godless California subculture. What must it be like, however, to go to a school in which all your little playmates tease you endlessly that your mother is a porn queen?

My sister, Monsignor, is obsessed with sex, not the healthy, normal sex that binds a husband and wife together in conjugal love, but kinky, hot-tub, California sex. I am quite confident that she has had sex on occasion with all those in her entourage. In particular, that crude Randall person, whom she maintains on a full salary on the pretext that she is a publicist, is nothing more than her lesbian lover. Sexual narcissism, as my colleague Warren informs me, imposes the need to revert to the polymorphous perversity of childhood. While I myself don't subscribe to a rigidly Freudian approach to personality development, I can see how Lisa fits the paradigm very nicely. She must have physical sex with as many people as possible to reassure herself that she is the center of their universe as well as of her own. I find that also a useful explanation for her film career, and Warren agrees with me that it is a quite plausible theory—Lisa imagines herself engaged in physical sex with all those who see her films or listen to her songs.

Why, even my wife, who, if I may say so, is extremely attractive for a woman of her age, has remarked that she felt that Lisa's behavior when we were visiting them in California was, in effect, a sexual proposition. Needless to say, my wife simply ignored it.

And those two singers, King and Thomas, are both obviously heavy users of cocaine. I would not have them in the same block much less the same house with my children. No, they don't actually *live* in her house but they seem to be around it all the time. And that pathetic old alcoholic fool, her agent—I forget his name, I cannot imagine a more perfect example of a dirty old man. I warned my own daughter, who accompanied us to California, to avoid all conversation with him.

The purpose of our visits? Well, of course, to renew friendships. And to hint to Lisa that she ought to consider her family as well as herself in planning her public behavior. There were some small family financial matters that needed straightening out. Our parents did not leave us very much money, but on occasion there are minor difficulties in the estate settlement that have to be adjusted.

I suppose one could say that Lisa is not difficult to deal with in these matters. The reason actually is that she has little sense of financial responsibility. Why should she be responsible about money when she is responsible about nothing else?

As a matter of fact, yes, one of those minor problems has arisen again. I visited Lisa in Los Angeles a few months ago, but there still were some small details to be ironed out. I had hoped we might be able to do it on the phone, but she said she was going to be in Chicago this week and suggested we meet here to talk about it. I was loath to make the trip because it meant postponing scheduled surgeries—sometimes I operate for fifteen hours in a row—with the attendant inconvenience and heartache for the families of my patients. As I say, Lisa never thinks of anyone but herself. We had an appointment to meet in her room at the Westin, let me see, when was it? I'm confused. . . . It would've been yesterday afternoon. So much has happened. . . .

Well, in fact, I did fly in a day early. I had hoped to visit briefly with my colleagues at the St. Luke's cardiology center, but the fog delayed my plane so that the consultation became impossible. Actually I detest flying, especially at night, so even if it means a night away from my family, I normally attempt to arrive a day early for an appointment. Lisa knows I detest flying. As is probably patent to you by now, the feelings of other human beings are of no importance to my sister.

What arrangements has she made for me in her will? Candidly, Monsignor, I have no idea. I have not given the matter any thought. I pray fervently that the issue may not arise and that she will recover fully, for reasons which I trust I have made clear. I may be permitted to hope, though not expect, that this tragic experience will cause her to realize how short life is and how, ultimately, selfishness and heedlessness are destructive of our emotional well-being. It is not a likely outcome, but as that ugly little neurosurgeon said, we can pray for miracles, can't we?

In point of fact, Lisa may have mentioned to me that both my children and I would benefit from a substantial inheritance. I did not take her promise seriously, and I sternly advised my wife and children not to take it seriously either. Lisa would promise anything for a few moments of limelight. Moreover, I had been led to believe from colleagues of mine with contacts in the investment world that her financial situation is rather awkward just now. Apparently those investors who usually back her cinematic escapades were quite properly wary of this *Friendship* business, which, I presume, is about lesbian love. It is one thing, I suppose, to fund sleaze and quite something else altogether to fund hard-core pornography. Even in that world, I would assume, there are people who are capable of making some crude distinctions.

Yes, of course, she will now make an enormous amount of money on that film. In all candor, Monsignor, it would be money so soiled that I could not bear to touch it even if some of it were given to me.

I am too much of a Christian—did I tell you that I am president of our parish council?—to say I would be glad if Lisa did not recover. I must, however, tell you honestly, Monsignor Ryan, for my parents and myself and my wife and children, it would have been much better if she had never been born.

11
BLACKIE

The Lord God will have to assign me a fairly large share of whatever points She is granting these days for my restraint in dealing with Roderick Malone, M.D. I listened politely and sympathetically, I did not argue, I did not even mention that his father-in-law had done four months in a minimum security federal prison for stock market manipulation. Nor did I—and this should excuse me from considerable amounts of purgatory—strangle the miserable, lousy son-of-a-bitch.

He had reasons enough to want Lisa dead—his murderous envy of her and the financial profit he would earn from her death. He had the opportunity—the Drake Hotel was right around the corner, and he had the weapon—access to the hypodermic needle and the drug with which it was filled, though in these days you don't have to be a cardiologist to know how to work a hypodermic needle.

Moreover, he knew enough about the human body to know, at least crudely, what sort of blow to the head would effectively dispose of his hated sibling. He did not even attempt to provide an alibi. I suspected a phone call to St. Luke's hospital might reveal that he had no appointment with the cardiologists there—unless he got to them before Mike Casey did. Doctors, like priests and Mafia dons, are nothing if not loyal to one another when under assault by outsiders.

Moreover, he was sufficiently obsessed by his own overwhelming self-importance to be able to persuade himself that disposing of Lisa was at least as fine an action as patching up battered human hearts. When he spoke of her, Roddy Malone displayed the darting eyes, the dancing fingers, the little jerky motions of shoulders and chest that characterize a monomaniac. I suspected that his colleague Warren would have shrugged his shoulders after a conversation with Roddy and perhaps remarked to his wife that night that his "colleague Malone" had gone "round the bend" over his sister the film star. Indeed, Warren might have added to the worthy woman, "Of course, he always has been an obsessive-compulsive little nut: you know what surgeons are like. . . ."

However twisted by envy and hatred he might have been on the subject of his sister, I could not quite imagine Roderick engaging in preliminary tortures. Murder for him would be like surgery—clean, neat, decisive. You get in, do what you have to do, and get out. There was little reason for him to surface the next morning at the hospital, not unless someone else knew he was in Chicago. Could he not have slipped out to O'Hare, flown back to LaGuardia, and been innocent of all suspicion? To show up at the Olson Pavilion of Northwestern Hospital might have provided him with a new stage for self-dramatization, but if he were the would-be murderer, such an appearance would've been a dangerous blunder.

Still, on the subject of Lisa, it seemed to me Roderick Malone was sufficiently off-the-wall that he might blunder dangerously. I would have to check to determine whether any of the others knew that Roderick was in Chicago. If they did, the quick escape to LaGuardia would have been damning rather than ingenious.

I sort of hoped he was the one who beat up my Lisa. It would be fun to watch him squirm on the witness stand.

Thoughts unworthy of the rector of Holy Name Cathedral? Doubtless.

I wandered up to the room of my senior associate and informed him that he was in charge for the next couple of days, a needless ritual because the senior associate was always in charge. In the new Church a pastor or a rector is merely a canonical figurehead, existing to legitimate what his staff has decided to do.

"You're working on the case?" asked this seasoned, mature veteran of four years in the priesthood.

"Bungling along."

"Okay. Let me know if there's anything we can do?"

"Indeed."

As I wandered back to my own suite, his voice trailed behind me. "Go get 'em, Blackie!"

Indeed.

I donned my World War II aviator's jacket and a fake navy commander's cap, which had "BOSS" emblazoned on it in gold letters, and, with George Quinn's manuscript under my arm, sallied forth from the rectory down Wabash and turned on Chicago Avenue toward the lake. October is the finest month in the year for our city, which, together with Florence and Hong Kong and San Francisco, is one of the four most beautiful cities in the world. In rapid succession, as though racing to finish their performance before the cold of winter comes, there follow foggy, humid days with no wind; brisk, clear, cloudless days with the northeast wind stirring up nervous whitecaps on the lake and driving crystalline air across the city; and then the most magical interlude of all, Indian summer, when a golden haze settles on the city and paints everything elegiac. On those days the poets in Chicago (of which I am not one) do half their work of the year and the philosophers in Chicago (of which I am one) do half their thinking of the year. That morning, however, was of the second rather than the third variety: a brisk, clean, deep-blue autumn morning of the sort on which even professional cynics have a hard time not being happy. Should Chicago weather be like that every day of the year, no one in the world would live anyplace else.

I parked myself in one of my favorite places for philosophical reflection, a little park across from the Water Tower, surrounded by the giant canyon walls of the John Hancock Center, Water Tower Place, the partially finished Olympia Center ("Needless Mark-up Building" my nieces call it, taunting Neiman-Marcus's prices) and—substantially less tall— Loyola University. It's an arena of pure privacy, despite the rushing traffic, human and nonhuman, surging back and forth on Michigan Avenue. The pedestrians who see a funny little man hunched over a manuscript on a park bench have two choices: if they don't know who he is, they leave him alone because he looks, as the teenagers say, "like, kinda weird, right?" And if they do know him, they dismiss him with a laugh, "Oh, Monsignor Blackie is thinking again!"

I permit them that illusion.

After listening to her brother, it was a relief to turn to Lisa's husband. Roderick had never loved her, not since the first day the adorable little mite had been brought home from Little Company of Mary Hospital. George Quinn, gentle, soft-spoken, self-effacing pillar of strength, had loved her—both tenderly and passionately—since they were kids on the beach at the South Shore Country Club. Unless I missed my guess, he still did.

To which it did not follow, alas, that he had not tried to kill her.

12
GEORGE

      I parked my maroon rented Chevy in the driveway and waited. I had required three weeks of building up my courage before I was ready to just drive by her house. Would it take three more before I would acquire the fortitude to ring her doorbell?

During a brief exploration of the canyons of this Beverly Hills, I had seen no cougars, nor panthers, nor tigers. A number of Jaguars, but of the automotive variety. I suspect I had seen every top-of-the-line model of every foreign car in the world, counting five Porsches and one Ferrari. I kind of hoped that Lisa had a Porsche: a Ferrari would be a bit excessive, or so it seemed to me.

Later I'd change my mind.

The sky was blue, the windless air a warm lazy seventy, healing for a Chicagoan in February, and the silence both profound and absolute. This neighborhood of California's Beverly might well be a cemetery, devoid of noise and people.

Lisa's house, on a quiet, palm-lined side street just off the 9500 block on Sunset Boulevard, was imitation Spanish Colonial—tasteful imitation, the kind of white house that said to a passerby, "Look, you and I both know that this town is a colony of New York and not of Madrid or Barcelona and that I'm no more Spanish than you are, but I do look kind of attractive in the California sunlight, don't I?"

With systematic planning I had burned my bridges. If one was journeying to the canyons of Southern California to protect one's woman from predators (no matter what kind of cars they drove) and perhaps in the process persuade her that she didn't need to be protected from you, then one had to burn bridges. In this particular change of life-plan one didn't build bridges to cross canyons, one burned them.

So I had reported to our firm's Los Angeles office and was greeted with considerable enthusiasm because of the advance rumors that I knew something about computers. Afraid to phone Lisa and learn that she did not want to see me, I had worked in the office for three days and had begun to think that perhaps my room at the Century Plaza was a bit too expensive and that I should find myself an apartment somewhere.

Before burning the sort of bridge that would be put to the flames when I paid a deposit on a year's rental of an apartment, it would probably be a good idea to see if the woman still wanted protection.

I was afraid to telephone her.

Thus, a little after noon on a sunny, early February Saturday, I was waiting in Lisa's driveway.

She didn't keep me waiting long.

A white Porsche convertible pulled in behind my Hertz Chevy (George the Bean Counter does not buy a car until he's sure he'll stay in lotus land) and a lovely young woman in a maroon minidress with a white sweater over it emerged from the car. The sight of her took my breath away, as it has done ever since.

"Yes?" she said, a large package of groceries held protectively against her chest, keys to the Porsche in her other hand.

"I'm a cougar administrator, lady." I walked slowly towards her so as not to frighten her. "And I wonder if there's any of them critters that's been botherin' you lately?"

"George," she said softly, depositing the grocery bag on the hood of the Porsche. "Is it really you?"

She was far more afraid of me than she would've been of some threatening stranger. Or a home-grown cougar.

"I think so." I reached in the jacket of my dark-blue suit, removed my wallet, and checked my identity. "Sure enough, here's my name, and it says that I am George James Quinn, an employee of the Los Angeles office of Arthur Andersen and Company."

"George!" She leaped across the driveway and embraced me enthusiastically. "I can't believe it!"

"Neither can I," I said in all honesty.

"Come in, come in, don't stand there. Have you really come to California to stay? No, I can carry the groceries, oh, all right if you want . . . are you really working in the Los Angeles office now? How wonderful!"

The house was as tasteful and as opulent inside as it was on the outside. If there were any servants attached, they didn't work on Saturday.

"May I make you a drink?" She was rushing around the house in frantic confusion, "Why didn't you tell me you were in town? I would've had the house cleaned . . . now isn't that a ridiculous thing to say? . . . Sit down—no, go out on the sun deck by the pool. I'll bring the drink out to you." She cast aside her sweater with a quick, unintentionally seductive gesture that made my heart pause in excited dismay. "And oh, George, you look so funny in that sober suit . . . if you're really going to stay in California, we'll have to dress you up like a Californian. . . ."

A few minutes later she emerged with two Waterford crystal tumblers and a full bottle of Jameson's. "Have you had lunch? I have two steaks thawing. We'll have to go out for supper. I know the most wonderful Italian restaurants and Mary Kate

told me that you simply *adore* Italian food! George, I still
can't believe it!"

The two of us were shy and nervous. We both knew damn
well what the stakes were in the game we were playing, a
game that would affect the rest of our lives, and we weren't
quite sure of the next moves.

"How did you know I liked Jameson's?"

"Oh." She smiled mysteriously. "I have my sources. You
and Blackie Ryan and, of course, Mr. Ryan, the old fella. I
keep the bottle in the house just in case you or Blackie should
pay me a visit." She lowered her eyes and blushed. "That's
a terrible thing for me to say, isn't it?"

"I think this Blackie character threatens me," I said, raising
the Jameson's to my lips. Irish courage, I suppose.

She looked up at me, her marvelous, wondrous, hazel eyes
glowing. "Oh, George, don't be silly. Blackie's a priest. I
love both of you, but I don't want Blackie and I do want
you."

I gulped down a considerable amount of the Jameson's.
"And do you think you have me?"

She considered me thoughtfully, carefully, for a moment
before answering. "Yes." She grinned impishly, then said,
"Yes, George the Bean Counter, I think I just about have
you!"

Her lip was trembling, whether now with nervousness or
delight I wasn't sure. How, I found myself wondering, could
a woman, especially this woman, possibly want me that much?

"I may still run," I warned her.

"You won't get very far," she said confidently. "Incidentally, how long have you been in Los Angeles and where are
you staying?"

"I'm staying at the Century Plaza."

"Blackie," she said, a look of mock-horror on her face,
"stayed at the Beverly Wilshire."

"I'm sorry, ma'am, George the Bean Counter has no class.
I will confess it."

"He does, too," she said tersely. "It's just an Arthur Andersen kind of class."

"And I've been here for four days now, working the last three of them."

"Why did you wait so long to let me know? Why didn't you call me the day you came to town?"

"Scared stiff, Lisa. Simply scared stiff."

"Oh," she sighed with infinite tenderness, "George, never be scared of me."

"Ha."

A few moments later she burst in on me again, determined chin cocked at a dangerous angle, a steak in her right hand. "Why scared?"

I gulped. "I'm not sure I'm good enough for you."

"Is *that* all?" She waved the steak at me with a dismissive gesture, a judge overruling a ridiculous objection from defense counsel. "This is no time for your low self-esteem, George."

"Oh?" It was my low self-esteem and I didn't like it being dismissed.

"No way." She darted towards me and teased my lips briefly. "What counts hereinafter is not what you think of you, but what I think of you. Clear?"

"Yes, ma'am."

Clear and scary. I was trapped in what she thought of me, deliciously but frighteningly trapped.

She reappeared wearing a red checked apron and this time carrying a bottle of steak sauce.

"You are the finest man I have ever known, good and true and loyal. Now, is *that* clear?"

Kitchen-stained hands held at arms' length, she bent over me and pressed her body against mine in unmistakable demand.

"Yes, ma'am." I gulped again. "Now go back to the kitchen. I like my steaks rare."

She flounced away with a haughty sniff.

"I like my women rare, too." The words could not have come from the mouth of George the Bean Counter, could they?

I really had not spoken them, had I?

Bell-like laughter from the kitchen said that I had. I loosened my tie. It had become much warmer. Suddenly.

It would not be a long engagement, I told myself.

The steaks were quickly cooked on an outdoor grill, and I was instructed to remove my jacket. Eating in shirtsleeves in the sunlight (I in the sunlight, she in the shade to protect her fair skin) on a February afternoon was a new experience for me, one that I didn't mind at all, not as long as Lisa was cooking the steaks and watching me with adoring eyes.

The Jameson's was set aside to be replaced by a bottle of California Cabernet Sauvignon in Waterford red wine goblets.

"I did snare you at Christmastime, didn't I?" She put aside her half-eaten steak, a gesture I would see many times in the future.

"You sure as hell tried hard enough," I said, continuing on my slab of steak. If she didn't want to finish hers, I would do it for her—an offer that would be made and accepted many times in the years to come.

"George Quinn," she said impatiently, "George James Quinn of the Arthur Andersen Los Angeles office, stop eating your steak and kiss me, kiss me like you're the man who's going to make me happy for the rest of my life." Large tears formed in her eyes, slow, gentle, happy tears.

At the moment, it seemed an excellent idea. I put aside my steak knife, made sure that the red wine goblet was secure on the poolside table, took her into my arms, and kissed her, at first very lightly, exploring what was still an unknown territory, a region tasting of spicy steak sauce. She responded eagerly, intensely, indeed, passionately. This woman really does want me, I thought to myself, astonished that such an observation could possibly be true. Her passion ignited my own like charcoal starter fluid thrown on a match. If the woman wanted to be kissed, then, goddamnit, I would kiss her properly.

I caressed her bare arms slowly and gently, then the back of her neck. She rested her head against my chest. Our lips searched for one another's face again, probing cheeks and eyes and nose and forehead and chin and throat on a delightfully delayed pilgrimage to the other's lips.

Finally we found them and our mouths merged in a sustained kiss that both of us wanted to last forever.

Reluctantly we parted, both of us shaken by the torrent of emotion we had unleashed.

"Wow," Lisa murmured, picking up our steak plates with trembling hands. "You don't fool around, do you, George? You get right down to business.... Don't bother with the steak sauce and the ketchup, I'll make a second trip."

"I was under the impression," I said as I picked up the bottles and followed her inside the house and into the kitchen, "that someone else was getting down to business, too."

"Poor defenseless girl." She laughed pleasantly. "Overwhelmed by the heat of male passion."

"Sure." I put the sauces on the kitchen sink and took her into my arms again. "Poor girl without any passion of her own."

Our two bodies pressed violently against each other and we used our hands to explore one another with dedicated fervor. Lisa groaned softly and went limp in my arms, making herself a complete gift. "We should eat dessert," she sighed.

"I like this dessert." I pushed her back against the sink and kissed her neck and throat. Frantically Lisa's fingers clawed at the buttons on my shirt, and her lips nibbled the flesh of my chest as though she would devour me. I realized that I was supposed to make love to her, not weeks or months down the line, but today, now, this moment. That was the way they did things in California, I told myself, realizing that it wasn't true. That was the way Lisa did things when she finally had the man she wanted. With clumsy fingers I removed her dress and dropped it on the kitchen floor next to my shirt. We went into another desperate clinch, kissing, caressing, exploring, loving, pushing each other toward the point of no return.

Just short of that point, Lisa slipped away and held me at a distance, hands on my naked shoulders, her lovely chest moving rapidly with deep, gasping breaths. She considered me carefully, as if making a decision. Or perhaps ratifying a decision already made.

"Outside, George." She laughed between gasps. "This is Southern California. When in Rome." Another gasp. "Do you think you could carry me out? I mean, you wouldn't mind, would you?"

I couldn't imagine anything I would rather do. "Your fantasy, ma'am." I picked up my lace-clad woman, who was, to tell the truth, not an especially light burden, and lugged her out the sliding door to the sundeck.

"Take off the rest of my clothes," she sighed with satisfaction as I deposited her on a chaise longue next to the pool.

Awkwardly I removed her maroon undergarments and then paused in astonishment as I looked, for the first time, on her full, womanly splendor.

"What's the matter, George the Bean Counter?" she giggled. "Never seen a naked woman before?"

"Not one like you."

"You're juvenile!" Quite pleased by my praise despite her protests, she rose from the lounge, turned away blushing, and picked up our wineglasses and offered one to me. "As the Irish would say, George James Quinn, slainte!"

As gravely as I could under the circumstances, marveling at the desire for me in her eyes, I toasted her solemnly in return, a buttermilk-skinned, sinuous Irish Venus with jet black hair and firm, full breasts. "Slainte, Lisa Anne Mary Malone!"

"You even know my middle name." She laughed. "You know everything about me, don't you, George?"

"I'll never know everything about you, Lisa," I replied, taking the wineglass out of her hand. "But it's going to be fun learning what I can." And so we made love for the first time. For many years I had thought that I was too shy and inept ever to be a good lover, perhaps ever to be a lover at all. With Lisa I was easily, effortlessly spectacular. Neither of us had had much sexual experience, Lisa a little bit more than I (a fact that would later cause me great emotional anguish as I wrestled with jealousy), but she was a natural lover and a natural teacher of lovemaking. She explored the path to ecstasy for herself and guided me down the path at the same time.

"Dear God, I thought you'd never appear in Los Angeles.

I prayed so hard . . ." she murmured just before we celebrated on the summit of our mountain of joy.

Lisa is the kind of sexual partner about which the adolescent in every man fantasizes—unselfconscious, intense, reckless, unashamed of her own body, and honest about her needs and hungers. Yet even at the peak of passion, the label of the *Time* magazine article still stuck: chaste, Irish Catholic eroticism. Lisa may have been outrageous in lovemaking, but she never seemed lascivious or even undignified. Later she would flaunt her body at me, driving me wild with desire and still keeping me at bay until I thought I would lose my mind, yet in all her naked dancing for me, she managed somehow never to be immodest or crude. I don't know how she did it. I guess it's part of what Ken Woods would call her "luminosity."

After our first union she dragged me into the heated swimming pool. We swam and drank wine and ate chocolate ice cream and huddled together under an enormous towel to protect Lisa's pale skin from the sun, and then we made love again. And again. And again.

When I wanted to return to the Century Plaza, Lisa swore that she would follow me in her Porsche and run naked through the lobby in pursuit of me. I decided it would be imprudent to put that challenge to the test. We spent our first night together, peaceful and contented in our physical love.

The next morning she carried me off to Mass and Holy Communion. "You don't really think we were sinning, do you?" she demanded cheerfully. "We have to receive Communion to thank God for one another."

I did indeed thank God for Lisa, for the intense and enormous joy I had experienced with her and for the beauty of the experience.

The last is worth dwelling on. Loving and being loved by Lisa had been not only pleasurable physically and emotionally, but exquisite aesthetically. It was the most important experience in my life both because I had found or had been found by my woman and because it transformed my attitude toward my own body. Somehow Lisa's grace was contagious. My tentative interests in art and music soared in the warmth of physical union with her. My sense of elegance in computer programs took a quantum leap, and even my golf game improved notably as I realized that I was not necessarily a big awkward goof.

"You're such a wonderful mystery, George," Lisa squealed happily when I explained this result many years later. "You are always a new surprise."

"I'm supposed to say that to you."

She resolutely refused to accept her own mysteriousness. "Now you understand why I had to seduce you on the spot. If we'd waited even a day or two, you would have become tense and self-analytic and tied up in knots. . . . Does it hurt your male ego that I did the seducing?"

"It flatters and frightens me that a woman would want to seduce me." I felt my face grow warm with pleasure and embarrassment.

"Don't be ridiculous." She began to prove once again that she could still do it.

Love with Lisa, while always graceful, was never passive. She is a solidly muscled woman with athletic enthusiasm and strong fingers and hands. When you wrestle with her, you know that you are not involved with a weak and retiring Victorian maiden.

To put it mildly.

On that Sunday after Mass, we were hopelessly in love. We were lovers, but we were still strangers. Except for the Christmas interlude a few weeks before, Lisa and I had not seen each other for years. There was much exploration still to be done. "Don't worry, George the Bean Counter." She threw aside her dress when we came home after our post-Mass brunch in the Polo Lounge at the Beverly Hills Hotel ("This is where the *real* stars eat brunch"). "We have lots of time to explore, and the best place to do the exploration is in bed. C'mon, we have to make up for lost time."

"Lisa," I pleaded.

"Don't be a prude." She threw her bra at me. "We're not really living in sin, dear Bean Counter." She stepped out of her panties, rolled them up into a ball, and threw them at me too. "I'll marry you, I'll even marry you next week if you

want, but you don't have to marry me if you don't want.
Let's forget about those things now and love one another."

"Lisa," I gulped again, grabbing her naked shoulders.

"Oh, all right." She laughed. "Admire me. That's what
I'm for, I guess. Admire me all you want," she sighed as
desire clutched at her voice. "Anything you enjoy makes me
happy."

Lisa naked was and is (as, I am told, those who see *The
Friendship Factor* will be able to judge for themselves) quite
overwhelming. When you see her at first you think, well,
she's certainly not voluptuous, not a centerfold type, not even
really all that sexy. Then the subtle perfection of line and
curve, of fullness and hollow, of innocence and challenge has
captured you. Before you've even realized what has happened, as when you mistakenly gaze at a powerful light, her
image is burned into your brain for hours to come.

She is not an exhibitionist. In her films she is rigorously
professional about nudity and sex. Whatever is required by
the nature of the story will be done coolly and unself-
consciously. If the director wants it to go beyond the require-
ments of the story, Lisa draws her own quiet and effective
line, and that is that. On the other hand, if the director, for
reasons of his own prudishness, does not want to go as far
as Lisa thinks appropriate, then he loses, too. She brusquely
rejected, and several times, a Hefner invitation from *Playboy*,
even when the *Playboy* empire was prepared to concede that
she could keep virtually all her clothes on. "No way!" she
said crisply, and that was that.

More clearly and confidently than anyone I've ever known,
Lisa thinks of her body as herself; with her lover, poor,
bedazzled, astonished, slack-jawed, wide-eyed George the
Bean Counter, she revels in the splendor of her naked self.

"I am not going to put on a stitch of clothing for twenty-
four hours," she announced one morning on our honeymoon
in Grand Cayman Island. "What do you think of *that*, George
the Bean Counter?"

"I'll need a Seeing Eye dog by tomorrow morning."

"I *bet*. Men only want one thing on honeymoons, I *know*

that. You could never get enough of *that*, silly, goggle-eyed husband mine!"

"I guess not," I agreed, wrapping my arms around her and drawing her as tightly against myself as I could.

"Oh, George," she whimpered, tears streaming down her cheeks. "I love you so."

Sex and tears. If there was anything else in the month of our life after she pulled off my clothes at the side of her swimming pool, I can't remember it.

The candid ferocity of Lisa's sexual energies troubled me, when I had time out for breath and reflection. Women, in my world at any rate, were simply not supposed to act that way, especially women who ordinarily exuded an aura of modest chastity. Even then I worried about what she had done for a man before I appeared in her driveway. I worried even more at those times later in our marriage, all too frequent as the years went on, when the two of us were separated.

"Don't be juvenile, George," she would respond with mild asperity whenever I asked that question in one of its many forms. "It's not any man, and it's certainly not every man, who sets me on fire. It's only one man, and that"—she grinned—"all the time!"

Never look a gift horse in the mouth, they say. To my eternal shame, I did indeed look a bare-assed, bare-breasted gift goddess in the mouth. And, unlike Othello, I didn't have an Iago around poisoning my mind and trying to kill my love.

Often, at deadly dull Hollywood cocktail parties, she would catch my eye and wink, and her own hazel eyes would glitter fiercely for a moment and then turn wide and soft. Her lips would open, and then she would bite them closed and turn away, only to glance back in a moment with a look of pathetic invitation.

Usually we'd make it back to our bedroom before I totally accepted that invitation. But by no means always.

I understand now, too late perhaps, that my problem was never with Lisa's fidelity. Of course she would remain committed to, indeed, fixated on, me. The problem was with me. How could any woman, and how especially could this astonishing woman, see anything in me to merit such ferocious commitment?

We were married before February was over at St. Praxides Church, with an impishly cheerful Blackie Ryan presiding at the services, Mary Kate and Joe Murphy acting as the principal witnesses, and Caitlin Murphy effectively stealing the show as the grinning little flower girl. My family was there in full splendor, as usual making a virtue out of necessity. "This is the happiest day since my own marriage," my mother told everybody with pious conviction. Neither May nor Roderick Malone nor his Edith came or sent word. I was just as happy not to see them, and Lisa never mentioned them. Somehow in the few weeks we had to prepare for the wedding, Lisa managed to find a spectacular wedding dress that occasioned "ah's" from the men as well as the women in the church—the whole parish came to the Mass even though it was supposed to be a "quiet" and "private" ceremony. "You look wonderful in that dress," I whispered in her ear, while Blackie fumbled through the pages of the ritual.

"And almost nothing on under it, as you'll find out before the day is over," she whispered back, beginning a wedding day which, for her, and eventually for me, was pure, giddy delirium.

After our honeymoon on Grand Cayman, we returned to the California Beverly Hills where Lisa began the filming of *Night of the Half Moon*. It would have been one of her more forgettable films if the critics had not noticed what one of them called "the astonishing radiance of Lisa Malone's beauty" in that picture.

"See what sex every day does for a woman," she crowed enthusiastically after she'd read that passage to me. "With the right man, of course." She put Bethie back in the crib and embraced me enthusiastically. "Oh, George, if I really am luminous now like Kenny Woods says, it's because of you."

"Motherhood," I murmured, when her lips permitted me to speak again.

"Silly." She returned to her assault on me, and automatically my fingers began their familiar pilgrimage to her breasts, fuller than ever with milk to feed Bethie.

Oh, yes, we were substantially on our way to producing that fey and enigmatic little teenager when we came back from Grand Cayman. They had to shoot *Night of the Half Moon* pretty quickly, even though Lisa thought of an ingenious twist of the plot that permitted the heroine to be pregnant in the final scenes. According to Lisa's calculations, we had indeed conceived Beth that afternoon by the side of the swimming pool.

"Which time do you think it was?" she taunted me. "C'mon, super-potent male, was it on the chaise longue or on the float or on the carpet, or maybe even in the water?"

"I don't think that matters much, does it?" I felt my face grow furiously warm.

"You shouldn't be ashamed of being so virile, George." She laughed merrily. "Most men would be proud of it."

I would then attempt—it was part of the act—to explain to her that a man who was not sterile would normally be fertile all the time, while a woman would be fertile only occasionally, so that any credit for starting Bethie on her way toward birth on that particular day should be given to Bethie's mother and not her father. That would send Lisa off into peals of laughter, the exact reason for which I never did comprehend, even though I enjoyed the laughter and the lovemaking that almost always followed.

Her laughter was a mystery to me, as was so much else in this passionate lover of mine. When the mood was upon her, she would laugh at anything and everything, even my pathetic puns. When she thought she had not laughed enough in the last several weeks, she would make me take her to one of her "laughing places"—in recent years we would drive over to the Metromedia Center at Sunset and the Freeway to gaze at John David Mooney's "Star Steps," a massive and yet ethereal mixture of metal and light that always produced in Lisa fits of laughter.

She never did succeed in explaining why it amused her, beyond saying, "Don't you see, George, it is supposed to make you happy? It's an angel of laughter." She would clutch at my arm. "Doesn't it look like an angel of laughter?"

Sometimes a visit to Metromedia would be followed by a sudden decision that we had to "go out to the beach," to our beach house at Malibu. The children would be handed over to appropriate protectors and Lisa would lead me to one of our "orgy" days or weekends—food, drink, laughter, and sex. She threw her diet out the window, became mildly tuned on champagne, consumed prodigious amounts of steak and chocolate ice cream, frolicked on the sands by moonlight—clad usually only in jeans or shorts—and loved me with skillful and determined passion.

The sharp smell of sea water, the restless beat of the surf, the ooze of wet sand between our toes, the taste of salt water as we dunked each other, the demanding energies of our hungry bodies—such were the remedies that renewed us body and soul on these adventures, which Lisa called, not altogether jokingly, "retreats."

We have not done that lately, not, I fear, in a couple of years. What a terrible judgment on me that is.

Chocolate is one of her great vices. When Cathy Curran was here a year ago, she and Lisa slipped off to a new chocolate shop Lisa had uncovered in Brentwood with conspiratorial delight appropriate for a pilgrimage to a newly discovered house of assignation (the two of them lamenting that "Blackie isn't here").

We also had to eat supper that night at La Toque on Sunset because, according to Lisa, Ken (the chef) made the best chocolate pastries in the world—a judgment with which Cathy concurred after long thought and experimentation.

I once accused Lisa of assaulting chocolate with the same passion with which she assaulted me.

She considered the charge thoughtfully. "The big difference is that you don't create a weight problem. Still"—she grinned wickedly—"I see the point. When I pig out on either, I don't feel guilty."

Her standards for chocolate were like all her other standards, precise and uncompromising—only dark chocolate and only when it was fresh. Lisa was a sensualist, alternating between intense professional dedication and indulgent hedonism. Both interludes of the cycle had to be well done; she demanded of me in bed the same standards she demanded of her professional colleagues at work. For many years I had no trouble living up to her demands. On the contrary, I loved it. When our lovemaking deteriorated finally, it was for other reasons.

"Blackie says," she informed me one morning over breakfast at the beach house, "that the Irish oscillate back and forth between hedonism and mortification."

"If Blackie says so, it must be true. Tell me, which side of the cycle is a breakfast of raisin bran and Diet Pepsi?"

"You know what I mean." She tugged at the shoulder of her T-shirt, which, together with bikini panty, was her standard morning garb at the beach.

"What if Blackie leaves the priesthood?" It was during the years when men were exiting en masse.

"He won't." She reached for the Pepsi can. "No way. Do you think it is too cold to swim in the ocean today?"

"It might be the only way to cool off."

"From what?" She cocked an eyebrow. "You don't think you turn me on that much, do you, George the Bean Counter?"

I reached across the table for her T-shirt. It was one of those times I would be the aggressor, just to prove that I could. She protested at first that her raisin bran would grow soggy.

When she appeared on the cover of *Vogue*, the article inside was a breathlessly admiring description of how Lisa combined her wife/mother and actress/singer roles. She was in one of her indolent, sensuous interludes, lying all day on the chaise by poolside, not dressing till supper, if then, sipping champagne, and reading novels. She laughed for weeks at the "Supergirl" article as she called it.

"If they could only see me now, huh, beloved Bean Counter? An absolutely slovenly Irish whore. Good thing they didn't do research for their silly old article when I wasn't working."

Despite the intensity of her episodes of sensuality, Lisa was disgusted by the California "coke and hot tub" culture, as she called it. There were no drugs provided at our parties, and there was no hot tub at the side of our pool. It soon was understood that anyone who brought drugs into our house would not be invited back. "I'd love to spend all day in a hot tub with you, Georgie Porgie," she told me, "but we'll have to settle for swimming naked in the pool. I won't share myself with anyone else."

I didn't particularly want a hot tub. Yet there was a certain lack of logic in her argument. However, I had learned through the years not to question such illogic, but to understand the message behind it. Lisa was a sensualist, but a private sensualist, and the latter for reasons of taste and instinct that were so profound as to escape articulation.

I saw no reason to debate her stand. Especially since I agreed with her completely, even if her private sensuality often frightened me, despite my conquering male act on occasional raisin bran and Pepsi mornings at the beach.

The girls seem to have inherited her propensity to cycle between fervor and laziness. She usually plays the role of big sister/co-conspirator with them, the leader of a group of women with sense and sensibility plotting against the foolish man with whom they put up, as with a silly little boy. It was not clear, when our marriage fell apart, which side would be assigned to Ned.

In the first year of our marriage, we marveled at how well two such different people, strangers more or less to one another, could adjust so quickly to a common life, I hunched over my computer terminal and Lisa fighting off morning sickness gamely, going before the camera on the California desert, which was supposed to be, I guess, the Sahara. Two nights a week she went off to Chinese cooking school because I had remarked once that I liked Mandarin food. I tried to talk her out of it, as she wearied toward the end of her pregnancy. No luck. Her man liked Mandarin food. Lisa would learn to prepare it. That was that.

We were still strangers, though surely lovers, and beginning to become friends. We had made almost no plans as to how we would organize our lives. We told one another that we would each respect the independence of the other's career and that she would no more mix in my accounting than I would mix in her filmmaking. "I might want to be an accountant." She reached for my belt as she said it. "But I'm sure you'd never want to be a movie star. You'd be a good one though. You're such a gorgeous, handsome, wonderful male sex object."

I doubted the truth of any of those things but in a few moments was beyond arguing with her.

It was not as easy as that, however. Especially when Georgia Anne followed Bethie a couple of years later and both our careers began to demand that we be away from home for long periods of time. We'd always fly back on weekends, however, sustaining our protestations and actions of love, no matter how weary we were. We would recommit ourselves solemnly to our mutual faith that nothing, nothing was going to interfere with the joys and the happiness and the peace and the contentment of our marriage.

There was much for me to learn about Lisa. First of all, and I suppose most importantly, she was a totally committed professional. We accountants are meticulous types: only someone with a fastidious character and personality would be attracted to the field to begin with. I am even more compulsive than most accountants, but, believe me, I am a sloppy and irresponsible bean counter compared with Lisa's professional diligence as an actress and a singer. Even though she was already a superstar, she still took acting and singing lessons every day—right up until the beginning of birth pangs—and worked with astonishing care at her roles and at her songs, sometimes staying awake until five in the morning acting out the scenes that would be staged before the camera later in the day.

"Does any other Hollywood star do that?" I asked her sleepily one morning as I placed a coffee cup in her hand.

"I don't care what anyone else does," she said firmly. "I only care what I do."

Exercise, diet, makeup, clothes, public relations, all were the subject of the same fierce professional dedication. "It goes with the territory, George. It's part of my job." She paused in her weight-lifting exertions, the sweat rolling off her body. "If I were not an actress, I wouldn't be doing this, but if you weren't an accountant, you wouldn't be worrying about debugging your programs. Same thing."

"The body looks perfect to me," I said appreciatively.

"Thanks." She blushed as though she were still a virgin and I had just propositioned her. "I'm glad you like it, but I'm the one who has to be satisfied. I can't let the effect of carrying around poor little Bethie for nine months change my effect on those who see me in seventy-millimeter Technicolor."

"And Dolby four-channel sound!"

"Of course!" She started lifting the weights again.

Despite what some of the Hollywood reporters will tell you, Lisa is not vain or ambitious or hungry for money or on a power kick. We've always lived well within our joint income. Lisa can't stand adulation and is quite content to put on her glasses, wrap a scarf around her head, and push a stroller down Sunset Boulevard, becoming quite indistinguishable from any other attractive Beverly Hills matron.

Ordinarily she was content with nondesigner jeans and T-shirts or, in hot weather, shorts (very short) and a halter (very skimpy). She found clotheshorse women "vulgar." On the other hand, when she visited Holly's Harp "to do the boutique thing," she emerged looking like someone who might be on the cover of *Vogue* every month. Her taste in fashion was both natural and impeccable. Lisa at a formal dinner with a strapless gown—maroon, white, or red, in the order of her favorites—would steal the show from everyone else at the party and seem to be quite unaware that she had done so.

I never was sure whether such coups were accidental or the result of very shrewd planning. I didn't ask. Enjoy.

For reasons about which I also did not inquire, golf courses brought out the fashion model in her. The day Jack Nicklaus and I won the LA pro-am at the Riviera, Lisa appeared in a willowy blue pastel Givenchy dress (with vast matching hat, no less) that upstaged me and my handsome blond partner completely.

As one of the directors said to me, "Look, she has less ego than almost anybody in this city. She's responsible, punctual, a joy to work with. There are no temper tantrums from

Lisa and no production-set power struggles. Most of the time you'd think she was a diffident starlet making her first feature film. She's wonderful to work with. *Until* you threaten one of those quirky standards she's set for herself. *Then*, let me tell you, brother George, it's either today or a year from today, but there's only one way it's going to be done—your good wife's way, and that's that."

"So I've noticed," I murmured above my glass of Jameson's straight up.

"An absolute perfectionist," he went on. "Gentle and sweet about it—have you ever noticed how she always knows, even after the first time you've been into her house, what your favorite drink is? Like I say, sweet and gentle and charming about it, but unless we do it right with your lovely wife, we don't do it at all."

"No kidding?" I asked wryly.

"Do you realize what a lucky man you are, brother George?" He was not, I think, changing the subject.

"I sure do."

But, in fact, I don't think that I did.

On the screen and on television and on her records, Lisa sounds easy, relaxed, laid back. But, looking back on the good and the bad in our years together, I have to say that the single most striking characteristic of my wife is her intensity—in bed, in mothering our, on the whole, happy and healthy children, and in the professionalism of her career. "The point, George," she said to me after a two-hour recording session in which she had not succeeded in getting a single chorus down on tape the way she wanted it, "is not to be relaxed but to give the illusion of being relaxed."

And on another occasion she said, after an all-night practice session with a script that had reduced her to hysterical tears, "The secret in this business, beloved mine, is sincerity." Faintly manic chortle. "Once you've learned to fake that, everything else is easy!"

On my 747 flight to California to claim Lisa, I told myself repeatedly that it would be terribly difficult for a free spirit like her to be married to such a demanding husband. I could not have been more incorrect in my projections. Lisa was the partner with the truly demanding character. That only made me love her more.

She was not, God knows, an intellectual. Acting and singing were her life. Well, they were her professional life. Her husband and her daughters and then, eventually, Ned were her personal life. She was desperately determined that she would be good at both, and heaven knows she gave both lives all the energies she had. If, finally, things have not worked out between us, the reason is not that Lisa didn't try.

Her favorite word was "both." If I tried to force a choice on her, she would impishly insist that we could do both if we wanted to—Christmas both at the house and at the beach, chocolate ice cream and raspberries both for dessert, career and family both for both of us.

I understood the power of the word for her only a few years ago, when Jane Pauley was interviewing her on the *Today* show.

"Which is more important, your family or your career?" Jane, serious and intense.

"Both." Lisa, bright and cheerful.

"Your husband's career or yours?" Jane, even more intense.

"You mean my husband the accountant who can't add?" A wide-eyed reference to the comedy skit she had done in her one—highly successful—escapade in Las Vegas. "Actually that's only arithmetic. You can be a wonderful accountant and not be able to add. Computers do it before you. I'm very proud of my husband's skill with computers. The machines will own Hollywood in five years!"

"But which is more important?"

"Both." Lisa, giggly and silly.

"Music or acting for you?" Jane was fitting into the spirit of things.

"Both!"

"You think you can do everything?" Jane, giggling now, too.

"Only the important things—and both of them!" Lisa now solemn and serious.

Afterward, down the street from NBC, in front of St. Patrick's Cathedral, where Lisa had decreed we would go to

Mass, I told her that I finally understood what "both" meant. "You don't mean that you combine two things that are separate, you mean that they are already combined, like two flowers on one stem."

"George!" Vast embrace. "How wonderful, my magic accountant. You *do* understand!"

I hate to say this. Yet I must. At the end I think Lisa permitted one flower to wilt on the stem.

But in the first decade of our marriage, both marriage and career bloomed vigorously. With those two passionate commitments, there was room for little else. She listened to popular music carefully and monitored the rise and fall of rock groups, but she scarcely listened to serious music. But when I played Mozart or Haydn, she would unconsciously tap out the beat with her foot. Of the newspapers, after a quick glance at the headlines, she read only the entertainment sections (but devoured every word of those in the Sunday *Times* and *New York Times*—"See what a Californian I have become!"). While many of her friends in the industry campaigned enthusiastically for George McGovern and then celebrated enthusiastically when Richard Nixon was turned out of office, Lisa paid practically no attention to these events. "I don't have to read the papers to know how to vote," she told me bluntly when I tried to discuss the McGovern campaign with her. "I'm a Democrat and always have been. And what's more"— raising her voice in mock ire—"we're going to raise our daughters to be Democrats, too. Do you hear that, George? Arthur Andersen or not."

You can, if you live in Beverly Hills, have an intense cultural life: art, music, literature, academic lectures, intensely serious discussions. Lisa went to an occasional art exhibit with me because I wanted her to and because, after a while, I began to serve on the boards of a couple of galleries. "They're kinda cute, George, but I wouldn't want to wake up at night with one of them staring down at my bed," was the most serious comment of which she was capable after those visits, so I discontinued them.

"Don't try to educate me, George Quinn!" she railed in one of her rare temper tantrums. "I am what I am. And I'm not going to become one of your goddamn Beverly Hills intellectual snobs!"

"Can I say a word?" I shouted back.

"Only one!" she yelled, unable to control a grin—even when she was bitterly angry, Lisa rarely lost her wit.

"You want to be not just a good actress, a great actress—"

"More than one word..." Her grin became wider. "But go on, you interest me. I never said I wanted to be great. That's your interpretation—"

"To be a great actress," I cut in, "you have to be a fully rounded human being, and that means appreciating the value of high culture, art, music, ideas...."

"When there's time, George," she sighed, the angry wind going out of her sails and the spinnaker flapping listlessly at the mast. "Anyway, most of the great actors and actresses I know are pretty limited human beings. They concentrate so much on one thing that their personalities don't develop much in other directions."

"That's not you, Lisa."

"I suppose not." She sank back into the low-slung modular couch in our parlor. "If there were only more time."

I sat down next to her and put my arm around her shoulders. "I'm sorry, Lisa. I really wasn't trying to remake you. I like you the way you are. I was only..."

"Trying to help." She brushed her lips against mine. "No, George, you were trying to remake me a little bit, but only for my own good. That's all right, lovers do that to one another. But I guess I have to decide what really is for my own good, don't I?"

"Of course." No way this session was not going to end in lovemaking. Not that I objected.

"If only there were more time," she sighed again.

Those words might be a fitting epitaph for our marriage.

When the dinner party conversations turned to serious matters, Lisa's eyes glazed over. As a matter of fact, they also glazed over when the conversation turned to entertainment industry gossip. At most such parties, indeed, she was a silent and demure if breathtakingly attractive young woman. The heavier the intellectualism of the conversation became, the more likely her hazel eyes were to wander tauntingly in my direction and offer startling hints and promises of what was in store for me as soon as we returned home or perhaps as soon as we entered her Ferrari.

Oh, yes, though Lisa indulged herself in neither food nor drink nor relaxation much of the time, she indulged herself in cars. "That red Ferrari is a paramour, young woman," I accused her one day, only half joking.

"Of course," she said calmly. "Enzio's not as good in bed though, George, darling. He's still fun to ride, though!"

I didn't even have the grace to laugh at that crack.

The first night she proposed that we make love in the front seat of the Ferrari, she said, "I really do want to see whether you're more fun to ride than Enzio."

At the end of that particular session, she whispered in my ear, "Enzio's good, but he loses by a mile."

When the dinner table conversation turned, however, to serious films or to the history or the philosophy or the development of the motion picture industry, Lisa would charge into the thick of the discussion and eventually dominate it with wit and charm and erudition and cleanly articulated opinions. Eric Rohmer was one of her favorites. *Ma Nuit chez Maude* she hailed as one of the greatest films ever made, and the scene in the snowstorm on the hills above Clermont just before the end of the film, her favorite scene in all the world. More recently she was absolutely ecstatic over Rohmer's *Pauline at the Beach* and insisted vigorously that *none* of the critics understood what the film was about. She also admired Bresson, Buñuel, and Bergman "some of the time." *Lancelot du Lac* and *Silent Spring* and *Wild Strawberries* were among her all-time favorites. She also "simply adored" *Belle du Jour*. "I wish I looked as good in my underwear as Catherine Deneuve did in that film," she told an astonished audience at the dinner party of an extremely powerful studio president.

Everyone laughed.

"Did I say something outrageous?" She glanced around the table with a smile, but her eyes probed at us. "I mean, that's

a *very, very* important part of the film. Isn't it? Anyway, I
am convinced that the second ending is the one that poor old
Luis prefers, the one in which the woman recovers from her
paralysis."

Riding home that night in the Ferrari—I always drove
home from parties in which Lisa became wound up because
she was then much too tense to handle the manic Enzio—
"I mean, you saw the film. Wasn't it obvious that her beauty,
with just a little bit of white lace covering her, was a crucial
symbol?"

"I hadn't quite thought of it that way," I said—stupidly,
of course, but that's what my accountant's integrity would
make me do in these conversations. "Anyway, I think you're
much more lovely than Catherine Deneuve in similar garments."

"Darling George, that's not the point!" She slapped my
arm in half-serious anger. "I suppose maybe I am, but I've
never been that kind of symbol in a movie. Someday, maybe."

"It's religious filmmakers who really attract you, isn't it?"
a very sophisticated and well-educated British novelist asked
her one night while we were sipping cocktails under a starry
sky on our own sun deck. "I suspect you're a very God-
obsessed woman, isn't she, George?"

"Of course I'm interested in religious films." She put her
champagne glass on a table and folded her hands intently as
she always did when beginning a serious conversation. "The
film is the most religious of all art forms, though you have
to be very subtle about how you use it. Men like Buñuel—
even when he's being antireligious, or trying to be—and
Bergman sometimes, are obsessed with God. That's why they
make their pictures."

"Are you obsessed by God?" the Englishman persisted in
his question.

"Of course I am!" she said impatiently. "Isn't that true,
George?"

"Just as you're obsessed by having precisely the same kind
of champagne for me tonight as you did at your so very
gracious supper last year?" The Englishman tilted his champagne glass in respect towards her.

"No." She tapped her foot dangerously. "They're two entirely different kinds of obsession. And, George, you haven't answered the question."

"Well," I began cautiously, "we accountants are accused of being obsessive, perhaps not without reason. I wouldn't say you felt about God the way I do about my numbers."

"George." She kissed my cheek. "You're wonderful. I'm not obsessive about God the way you are about numbers, I'm obsessive about Him the way I am about you." I was rewarded with yet another kiss on my cheek.

Well, I escaped that particular confrontation neatly, but the answer to the Englishman's question, if I were honest, would've been that I did not think that my wife was a very religious person at all. She was devout, heaven knows. She attended Mass every Sunday and often several days during the week. She said her night and morning prayers no matter how tired she was nor how much sex came before or after. (Kneeling beside your sexual partner, both of you quite naked, and reciting the Our Father and the Hail Mary in blissful contentment is an intriguing experience, to put it mildly.) She carried a rosary in her purse, contributed generously to Catholic causes, and treated the clergy with more respect than they deserve (save for Blackie Ryan, whom she treated with affectionate disrespect, on which he seemed to dote), but I would have thought that her religious commitment was like her political commitment. She didn't vote for Nixon because she was a Democrat, and she didn't approve of abortion because she was a Catholic. Beyond that, the issue was not God or religion, but the next screenplay.

All of which goes to show that you can live intimately and intensely with a woman for almost fourteen years and be quite ignorant of who she really is.

Dangerously ignorant, as it turns out.

13
BLACKIE

Angry at the stupidities of married people—stupidities of which I would doubtless be guilty in spades if I were married—I jammed George's manuscript into the pocket of my aviator's jacket, resolved in my head that I would shortly purchase a Chicago Cubs jacket out of respect for the team's valiant, if finally unsuccessful, efforts this season, and plunged into the flow of pedestrian traffic down the canyon toward Oak Street Beach. Across from the Westin, the 900 North Michigan building, where Annie Reilly had her tussle with the devil, had vanished, neatly excised from my parish by a most responsible wrecking company the way a skilled oral surgeon would extract a perfectly good tooth in the name of improving the bite in one's mouth.

Where the lovely old matron had been, a strange, raw, open space changed the perspective of the Magnificent Mile, however briefly, until William Pederson's new building tried to duplicate the genius of his green glass miracle on Wacker and Wacker (a building that had proved, the previous year, to be the undoing of my brother-in-law Redmond Peter Kane). They would not leave my parish alone; it had become a playground for the world's greatest architects.

I tuned out the noise of Michigan Avenue—beep, bustle, bluster—and avoided looking at the Westin as I passed it by. Nor did I pay any attention to the Drake, where, doubtless, Lisa's brother was nursing his foolish little ego. Rather, the gracefully dancing whitecaps of Lake Michigan, lightly teasing the empty beach, were what I wanted to see because, somehow, they would have promise of life triumphing over

115

death, of Lisa walking the path back to recovery from a savage beating, as Catherine Deneuve had in *Belle du Jour*.

I pondered the lake for a long time, listening to the protesting murmurs of the waves and feeling the sting of the northeast wind as it tried to invigorate my face—a vain task at best. I strove to absorb and digest and integrate the waves of information that had leapt up from George's memoir. I would not have guessed the link between Lisa as woman with star quality and Lisa as perfectionist professional, not in a thousand years. Once it was pointed out to me, it seemed, for reasons that were still too obscure to articulate, terribly important. The image of Lisa Malone as a sweet but essentially superficial black-haired Irish Catholic sex goddess was enough to infuriate, perhaps to the point of murder, many of those who hated her. It did not seem likely that the additional overlay of serious, indeed, God-obsessed professional, would mitigate their anger.

Dear God, poor Lisa.

Clues, hints, half-formed notions, maddeningly imprecise images whirled around in my brain, misshapen pictures in a Picasso nightmare. Instead of telling me not enough about his wife, George had told me too much. Like him I was dazzled by the richness and complexity of her personality. If I was to find out who wanted her dead badly enough to beat her savagely, I couldn't afford to be dazzled.

It would never have occurred to me, either, that she was a God-haunted woman. Devout, as George had said? Unquestionably. Pious? Indeed. Loyal to the Church? Certainly. Respectful to all clergy but me? Of course. But God-haunted? Like, wow! as my fourteen-year-old niece Biddy Murphy would say.

I wandered back to the rectory, prepared myself a late-afternoon snack of pastrami and cole slaw on rye washed down with a double chocolate sundae with chocolate sauce and a large bottle of Diet Pepsi, and withdrew for further contemplation to my room.

After I woke up from such contemplation, I flipped on the television set for the 4:30 news on channel seven.

The attractive Italian-American woman, her brown eyes

flashing, was telling the world that Lisa Malone's doctors had issued a statement to the press indicating that her condition had substantially improved. We were switched live to the Olson Pavilion at Northwestern Hospital and a smooth, articulate "spokesperson" for the hospital, an attendant at a mass-production funeral home on the way up in the world. I sat up straight and leaned forward eagerly. Had she truly improved?

I was destined to be disappointed. All the young woman from the hospital had to say was that some of the immediate danger of the last twenty-four hours had diminished, nothing really beyond Dr. Rodriquez's sermon of early morning. Back in the channel seven studio, Ms. Esposito observed that everybody in Chicago would certainly be happy that Lisa Malone was getting better and would be looking forward eagerly to her Christmas television spectacular on ABC.

It was only a slight misunderstanding, I suppose. Indeed, not so much a failure of accuracy as a failure of precise emphasis.

A failure which, it would turn out, could be deadly for Lisa.

14
ALIQUIS

I watched the television screen with frozen eyes. The program continued. The foolish man and woman babbled happily about the tragedies and disasters that were the routine of daily life. I wasn't interested in either their babble or the fools about whom they were babbling. So . . . she was recovering, was she?

It had been a terrible mistake to panic in the hotel room.

A little more coolness, a little more iciness of intention and steadiness of nerve, and it would all be over now. That the stupid police thought George had bashed in the head of his wife was a happy accident I had not anticipated. However, it ought to have been anticipated. Who else would they blame but poor, stupid, worthless George? A few more seconds, a half-minute at the most, and everything would have been wrapped up nicely, tied with a silver ribbon. Now that Lisa was alive and recovering, George would be cleared, and unless her brains had been so badly scrambled that she did not remember, Lisa would point an accusing finger at me. My hands gripped the chair with feverish hatred.

How characteristic of Lisa to spoil everything. She could not even die with class. No, she had to struggle back to life, a broken vegetable—a broken vegetable with an accusing finger.

I was physically exhausted from the strain of the past two days. It was one thing to see clearly the wasted opportunity and quite another to try to seize a new opportunity. It would be better to sit here comfortably and continue to drink. Too much drink, that was the problem, too much vodka in the hotel room. It had dulled my reactions, blotted out common sense, asphyxiated instincts. I pushed the bottle away, as though dismissing a powerful temptation to serious sin, and struggled out of the chair.

"I've got to do something," I screamed, pushing fists against temples. "I have to kill her again!"

Then I collapsed to the side of a chair, kneeling on the floor, beating hands against the soft cushion, sobbing hysterically.

And saw clearly, as though in a vision in church, how it might be done again.

15
BLACKIE

The Pump Room at the Ambassador East is maintained in a state of permanent semidarkness, doubtless to recall London during the Blitz in 1941. This elegant gloom is not a measure necessitated by the quality of the food, which is excellent, though perhaps not quite as excellent as it used to be.

Back in London during the Blitz of 1941, that is.

However, the darkness of the room made it difficult for me to search out Ken Woods twenty years later. He had aged, while patently I had not.

Neither the State's attorney nor the judge was quite ready yet to release George Quinn, even on bail. The airlines had been badly confused the night before last. Indeed, George was on American flight 660, but American flight 660 had been merged with American 192, which had arrived at 9:09— two hours later than its scheduled arrival. Some of the passengers of American 660, also still holding 660 tickets, had in fact been put on a United DC10 flight 108, which arrived at 8:30—an hour and fifteen minutes late. So George could have been on any one of those three planes, the last two of which would have brought him to Chicago in time easily to have worked mayhem on his wife. Unfortunately, so far no one could be found to identify him on any of the three flights, and the airlines paperwork was still a mess. All my father had been able to obtain was permission for George to leave the lockup to visit his wife in the hospital, not that such a visit would do either him or Lisa much good.

The three children at Mary Kate's house were in a state of

shock and confusion, trying to be brave but desperately missing their mother.

"Father Ryan?" I blinked in the dark. Could this little old man really be Ken Woods? "Great to see you again, Father. You haven't changed a bit." He pumped my hand enthusiastically.

"Neither have you, Ken," I lied shamefully.

Ken Woods, who was eight years younger than my father, now looked ten years older. Not only had his hair turned white, but he drooped. His shoulders, which had been square twenty years ago, were huddled protectively over his chest. His back, which had been straight and erect, was bent, a reed shaken by a powerful wind. His head was bowed as though in mourning. The pressures and the burdens, the struggles and the responsibilities of the last twenty years, had weighed so heavily on Ken Woods that he could no longer carry them without stooping. He was an Atlas, running out of strength and energy.

"How's the Admiral?" he said as his clammy hand pulled me to a table in the corner, where the light was roughly equivalent to that at eight o'clock on a cold winter evening.

"The Admiral?"

"Your father." His hand, trembling uncertainly, reached for a half-empty old-fashioned glass.

"Oh, we don't really call him that much around the family, except when we're angry at him, and there's no point in getting angry at the old fella. Never was."

I was prepared, by long experience, to spend the first part of every conversation with someone who knew my father reminiscing about his past. I personally preferred to discuss Ned Ryan's present, which I thought was far more impressive, but others didn't quite seem to think of him that way.

He'd come out of the navy after the war as a captain, and somehow or the other had been promoted twenty years later, doubtless by one of the Annapolis men who had served under him and had become big navy brass, to the rank of a rear admiral in the reserves. For the Ryan family it had been a subject of great hilarity.

I told an eager Ken Woods, as he struggled with quivering

fingers to light a cigarillo, that the Admiral and his lady had
sailed to Europe the previous summer on the *QE2* and that
Helen had made him pack the navy white formal dinner jacket.
They weren't exactly invited to sit at the captain's table, but
when the captain heard the name of the distinguished little
man in the sailor suit and that he had been the captain of the
legendary *Charles Morton Stedman, he* came to my father's
table.

Helen had been greatly impressed when the handsome jun-
ior officers of the *QE2* also swarmed around his table and
told her that the achievement of the *Charlie M* was now
standard textbook material in the courses they had studied at
Dartmouth. While we listened to the old fella's occasional
yarns with fascination—because they always were different
in the telling—we had never taken him too seriously as a
great naval hero because he never took himself very seriously
in that role either. In our inner selves, however, we were
proudly convinced that it was no mean achievement to emerge
as the textbook hero of the greatest naval engagement in
history.

"Next week is the anniversary, Father," Ken Woods exclaimed. "Forty years ago next week. For most of us it's been
downhill ever since. I'm glad that's not true of Ned."

"No, I don't think he would say that his life has been
downhill since then."

Ken Woods began to retell the story. It was the morning
of October 25, 1944, off Samar Island at the north end of
Leyte Gulf. The Japanese, brilliant strategists as always, were
coming at the American invasion armada—with 130,000 men
in transport ships—from three sides. A battleship squadron
was steaming up from the south toward the Seliban Sea. An
aircraft carrier squadron was steaming down from the north.
A third group, composed of the best battleships and cruisers
of the Japanese fleet, was sneaking in between the islands,
hiding in the tropic rain until the northern and southern forces
had lured away from Leyte Gulf the Seventh Fleet on the
south and the Third Fleet on the north. Then they would
swing around Samar Island, plunge into Leyte Gulf, and
destroy Douglas MacArthur and the American infantrymen

waiting helplessly on their transports and landing craft. The
first two plans worked—the northern and southern pincers
were sacrificed the way they were designed to be. The Seventh Fleet, for the only time in naval history, performed the
classic maneuver of crossing the enemy's T and wiped out
the southern Japanese force. Bill Halsey's Third Fleet raced
far to the north. Obsessed with Japanese aircraft carriers,
Halsey sunk four of them, scarcely paying any attention to
the fact that there seemed to be no Japanese planes flying off
those carriers. (After the war it would be revealed that the
Japanese air crews had been so devastated in previous battles
that there was no one to fly the planes and that the sunken
carriers were worthless to the Imperial Navy.)

When the Japanese battleships, headed by the world's biggest and most dangerous battleship, the *Musashi*, steamed
around the corner of Samar Island and into the entrance of
Leyte Gulf, they were met by a handful of American destroyer
escorts and escort carriers, a weak line of pickets hampered
all the more by the fact that their communication systems,
as was typical at that time, did not function during battle.

"Our division commander had been transferred to a cruiser
just a few days before. Your father was not only captain of
the *Charlie M*, he was also commander of the four-ship division. He was the senior captain on the four ships, with two
weeks of seniority over a furious Annapolis grad. We were
standing there on the bridge, McConnell, a kid who had just
graduated from Annapolis, the old man, and I.

"'We have visitors,' your father said calmly. I looked up
and saw this massive line of Japanese battleships, big enough
to be invaders from another planet. I was so scared, I couldn't
say a word. McConnell was jibbering. Your father didn't bat
an eye. 'Kenny,' he said, as though he were opening with a
one no-trump in bridge, 'make a signal to the others. I don't
care how.'

"'What signal sir?'

"He cocked one of those ice-blue eyes at me. 'DE DIV
39, follow me.'"

"I've heard about that signal," I murmured respectfully.
Whenever the Ryan family wanted the old fella, they called

him up and gave him that signal. Such respect for an authentic hero!

"So we charged the Japanese battle line, laying down a smoke screen as we came, zigging and zagging, ducking their shells, and barreling on toward them. McConnell whispered in my ear, 'The old man thinks we're the fucking Light Brigade!'"

"Helen said that one of the young British officers on the *QE2* remarked that it was as though the Light Brigade had won instead of lost."

His eyes shining with delight in a treasured memory of his youth, Ken Woods didn't hear me.

"'Prepare to launch torpedoes.' Hell, we had practically no experience firing torpedoes on that old bucket of bolts. The V-12 kid that was our torpedo control officer ground out the tubes. I glanced back and saw the same thing was happening on our other ships. We made a sharp left turn, and Nedie says, calm as ever, 'Fire port torpedoes.'

"Then we heeled over in the opposite direction, and he says, 'Fire starboard torpedoes!' In the space of maybe a minute or two, we put sixty-four torpedoes in the water and sent them racing toward the Japanese ships. You wouldn't believe, Father, how bad our torpedoes were through the whole war. It was lucky that some of them didn't blow up in the tubes as we were trying to launch them. Some of them sank, some of them broached, some of them were duds, God help us, some of them turned around and headed back toward us. Not a single one of them came anywhere near one of the Japanese battleships. And we kept charging on. Later McConnell said maybe the Japs thought that our torpedoes were as good as theirs."

Ken Woods had shed not merely the twenty years since I had seen him in the Polo Lounge Bar; he was now a twenty-one-year-old kid, just out of Abbott Hall, on the deck of the *Charles Morton Stedman,* enacting Balaklava, Pickett's Charge, and the Little Big Horn. Only with a very different ending.

"I don't know what happened, though I've read all the books. Maybe it was all those torpedo wakes bubbling crazily through the water that panicked the Japanese admiral. He turned tail and ran. Your father broke off the engagement, kinda reluctantly, I think, by the look of him, because our job was not to chase the Japanese battleships but to protect the landing fleet. McConnell whispers in my ear, 'The bastard wanted to sail right up to Tokyo Bay!'"

I couldn't deny poor Ken Woods his moments of youth returned. "The Old Fella has always said that the Japanese were incredibly brave warriors, brilliant strategists, and terrible tacticians. They tended to become hysterical when things went wrong. When he saw all those battle wagons steaming towards you folks, he remembered that Spruance and Frank Jack Fletcher beat them at Midway because the Japanese admiral, the same one who engineered Pearl Harbor, blew his cool when the Americans didn't react the way they were supposed to react. So the old fella figured that the safest thing to do was the last thing the Japanese expected. That's why he charged the Japanese battleships."

His exact words to me were, "It was a coward's way out, Johnny." He said it with a glint in his icy blue eyes. "A shanty Irish gombeen man's cowardice."

"Then he turns to McConnell," Woods rushed on, fists clenched, eyes radiant, face flushed, glowing, "and says, 'Well, Mr. McConnell, it looks like the Light Brigade wins this one.'"

"Damn the torpedoes, full steam ahead," I murmured subaudibly, wondering about the parallel between Mobile Bay and Samar Island.

"We didn't lose a single man in DE DIV 39," Woods began to relax, the memory fading, "and there were thirty thousand American families that didn't get next of kin telegrams that week. DE DIV 39, follow me...."

"A dramatic moment," I said, quite unnecessarily.

"The high point of my life," Ken Woods agreed sadly.

The old fella's reaction had been somewhat different. "Everything after that, Johnny, was gravy, pure blessing. I figured I ought to enjoy it."

Apparently, as far as my calculations can be trusted in this matter, the first thing he did upon returning home—to receive the Medal of Honor from President Roosevelt in the Oval Office—was to do his part in my conception, whether, indeed, after Kate Collins Ryan had made a Blackwood Convention at bridge or not is a matter better left to family mythology than to accurate family history.

Maybe the fact that I was conceived after the Battle of Samar Island explains a lot about me. I should like to think so, at any rate.

"Well, Father." Ken Woods had now shriveled back to his 1984 self, hunched down in his youthful blue tweed sport coat. "We aren't here to talk about victories, are we?"

"Indeed."

"That was a story with a happy ending. There are not very many stories with happy endings in life, Father."

"Ah?"

"Lisa's story ends tragically, doesn't it?" He lighted another cigarillo.

"Do you think this is the end of Lisa's story, Ken?" I studied the muscle twitching under his right eye carefully. "Do you think there isn't any hope?"

He ran his hand over his face, his thumb and index finger over his eyelids, and shook his head, as though to clear out confusion. "I don't know. I suppose there's some chance she'll come out of it, but she'll be a vegetable, won't she? Not the Lisa we used to know?"

"Dr. Rodriquez says that's one scenario, not necessarily the only one." I tried to keep my voice and my gaze even and steady.

16
KENNETH WOODS

     It happens to all of them, Father. They forget who they are and where they come from and who made them and what they can do.

I understand how it happens. The whole world is at your feet. You're rich, attractive, powerful, in demand for more scripts than twenty people could make in their lifetimes, pursued by directors and producers and studio presidents, the toast of the world—not the whole world, of course, not even the real world, but the world of Hollywood. You begin to think, particularly if you are an unsophisticated woman, that you deserve all this, that you've won it by your own hard work, that you're entitled to it, and that you can do whatever you goddamn please. You know what I mean?

I used to kid myself into thinking that it would be different for Lisa. She had more sense and more taste and more professionalism and more, well, emotional stability. I never would have made her a superstar unless I believed that. I loved her too much to let her destroy herself that way.

Maybe it was my love that deceived me, too. Maybe I saw more character in Lisa than was really there. Maybe I imagined that she was strong enough and honest enough to turn away from the path that leads to shriveled old woman alcoholics walking their dogs down Sunset Boulevard.

The handwriting was on the wall to read, if I had wanted to, when she married poor, dumb George. I can't help it if I sound contemptuous of him, Father. I realize he's a friend of yours. He's probably a good man in his own world; in Hollywood, and for Lisa, he was a dud. A woman who has "star quality" needs a strong, vigorous, even domineering

man to keep her in line. George isn't strong or vigorous or
domineering; all he is is a pigheaded little jerk. He doesn't
understand luminosity and never realized what a precious
prize he had in Lisa. He's responsible for what happened in
the hotel the other night, even if he didn't do it. As soon as
she married him, I ought to have pulled out. At my age in
life, I don't need to go through another tragedy. I should have
realized that once George got into bed with her, it would be
all downhill for Lisa and there was nothing that I or anyone
else could do to stop it.

Luminosity is a given. You don't earn it, you can't create
it, you can't even hang on to it after a while. It's simply
there. It's my business to spot it, develop it, reveal it, sustain
it, promote it, protect it. I'm indispensable. Most of the
radiant kids who come to Hollywood blow it early because
there isn't a Ken Woods around to point them in the right
direction. I'm not the one with luminosity; I'm not the one
who causes theater audiences to glow. Yet without me, the
luminous people are dead. And I mean dead.

If you have star quality and any sense to go along with
it—and most of them don't have much sense—you play out
your string, do the kind of films you can do while you can
do them, invest your money wisely, don't reach too high,
and get out while you can, before you're hooked on Hollywood and glamour and adulation—an addiction a lot worse
than heroin or cocaine. I thought I could protect Lisa from
addiction. God help me. I was wrong.

She was better than most. After that brush with the hop-
heads out in Malibu, she got her moral act together. She
didn't need a different man in bed with her every night to
persuade herself she was still lovable. If anything, she went
in the opposite direction and became some sort of a puritan.
A lot of them are frigid, Father. In time Lisa went that route,
too. Know what I mean?

She wasn't as good-looking as some of the sex goddesses
who have been around. As far as that goes, Marilyn Monroe
wasn't all that good looking either. Lisa had a sweet little
voice and was a decent enough actress. She worked hard, I'll
give her that.

Like most of them, she had no sense of loyalty. She didn't realize that Ken Woods was the one who made her—not the one who created her luminosity: God did that, I suppose—but the one who polished it and sold it to the world. It's strange, Father: if you look at the careers of the great stars, the turning point always comes when they break with the one who discovered them. Oh, they may last ten or even fifteen more years, but they're finished. They end up suicides, or nymphomaniacs, or drug addicts, or alcoholics, or bitter, psychopathic old men and women. The few who do stand by their original friends somehow manage to survive—like Jennifer Jones with Dave Selznick, for example. They're one in a thousand, maybe one in a million.

God, Father, I remember that day we had lunch at the Polo Lounge. Do you remember, too? I knew, as we sat there talking, that I'd stumbled on one of the greats. I could hardly wait to get over to Our Lady of Angels Hospital to see her. I felt in my bones that this would be the magic one who was more magic than any of the rest. When I walked into the hospital room, at first I said to myself, Ken Woods, you're a damn fool. She's just a pretty kid from Chicago who should go back to Chicago and forget about this goddamned septic tank called Southern California. Then she smiled at me, a shy, slow, sunrise smile, and I knew that my original instincts were right, this kid was pure magic. The sky was the limit. There wasn't anything we couldn't do together.

Then a funny thing happened, Father. You won't believe it because she was such a shy, shallow little nonentity at the time, a nonentity with glow, but a nonentity just the same. I fell for her. Ken Woods, veteran Hollywood cynic, fell head-over-heels in love with a shallow, late-adolescent female. A kid, a girl, so dumb, so naive, and so innocent that she thought the guys who were fucking her and shooting her up on week-ends could help her career. Maybe, looking back on it, I should have thrown her to the wolves for a few more week-ends and then sent her home. It would have been a lot better than what finally did happen, wouldn't it?

No, I didn't fall in love with her later, I fell in love with her that afternoon in the hospital. I've been in love with her ever since. I didn't tell her at first. There were a lot of things that had to be done before we could talk about love. I figured maybe my emotional reaction was transient, like a kind of passing fancy, you know what I mean?

Well, I got her out of the hospital and into a decent apartment and found her a voice instructor and an acting coach and arranged for a few interviews and finally, on a long shot, got her a screen test. She wasn't much of an actress then, Father, a little bit of talent, you know what I mean, and the willingness to work hard, I'll give her that, but still, not much. Then we put her in front of a camera in a basement in that old studio in Culver City, gave her a script to read, and said, "Come on, honey, make with the sex appeal." I've never seen anything like it, before or since, in all my life. She absolutely came alive.

"Little bitch can't act worth a damn," said the producer, who was one of the great queens of his era in Southern California.

"Who cares?" said the director. "As far as I'm concerned, she has the part and almost any other part she wants. Kenny, where do you find 'em? This one has it all."

I knew it was all magic, Father, nothing to do with intelligence or ability or brains or taste or sensitivity. Nothing like that. The same kind of grace that a tiger has, slipping through a forest with those gorgeous stripes. Know what I mean? The tiger doesn't earn it, doesn't deserve it, shouldn't really be praised for it, and is, finally, a terribly destructive creature. But you don't pay attention to any of those things while you're watching her.

Sex appeal? God, yes. Not your ordinary kind of sex appeal, not your typical love goddess. They're all special. But Lisa was special in a special way. She was the girl down the street turned glowing and radiant. You could bring her home to mother and still enjoy her in bed. She suggested a kind of erotic intensity mixed with overwhelming sweetness that you would like to fantasize about in the girl down the street, even if you know that the girl down the street is probably clumsy in bed and a little frigid. Lisa was the ordinary pretty girl with extraordinary erotic grace. Know what I mean?

Look, she could barely read and write. She doesn't read much, she doesn't think much, she doesn't even talk much in a serious conversation. I've known women who are better than her in every possible way, but I never fell in love with any of them. Knowing how ephemeral it all was and that there was no depth behind her grace, knowing that as well as I know my own name, I still fell for her, totally, completely, and, I'm afraid, God help me, irrevocably.

I took her to supper the night of the screen test and congratulated her on her success. She was sort of dazed, hardly believing what had happened, quite incapable of understanding what her secret was. She never did learn. None of them do. Anyway, I acted like a goddamn fool high school kid. I told her I loved her and I wanted to marry her eventually and suggested we return to my house and go to bed to celebrate.

I suppose you're shocked, Father. I mean, you have to disapprove of sin and all that, don't you? She sure as hell hopped into bed with George Quinn quickly enough, didn't she? That first kid of theirs was born eight and a half months after they were married, and they were married two weeks after he came to California, so she wasn't all that chaste and hesitant with him, know what I mean?

Well, she was embarrassed and shy and awkward, and said no, thank you, not tonight, she had a headache. I had told her that she was the great love of my life, and she told me she had a headache.

Well, so it went. One part of me—that part of me that's made me the best agent in the business—kept saying quietly, Ken Woods, you're a lucky son-of-a-bitch that she's turning you down. Another part of me, I suppose the kid on the bridge when Nedie Ryan was charging the Japanese admiral's tea cups, said to hell with rationality, I want her. And I'm going to have her.

Well, I never did get her. She kept having headaches. I even proposed marriage to her in 1970, seven years after that first screen test. Hell, I had always intended to marry her anyway. She said no, she wasn't quite ready for marriage yet. Six months later she calls me on Thursday afternoon and tells me she's gonna marry this George Quinn shit in Chicago on Saturday and would I like to come.

Excuse my emotional outburst, Father. I'm tired, I'm over-wrought, I'm shattered by what has happened. I still love her, you see. Maybe one of the reasons I hope she dies is that I'll finally get the stupid little tart out of my system.

Because you get a lot of fan mail and they write you up every couple of months in the *National Enquirer* it does not follow that you have the kind of talent necessary to make a film classic. That's precisely what that stupid little nitwit has tried to do. Hey, Father, what did the critics do to Bill Murray when he tried to put aside the comedian role and be a serious actor in *The Razor's Edge*? They ate him alive, and most people like Bill Murray. What do you think they will do to Lisa, whom they already resent, when she tries to be not only a great dramatic artist, but a director and a producer and a screenwriter, too? The bigger they come, the harder they fall. Know what I mean?

Sure, I've seen the film. I have a video tape of it back at the Whitehall. You can see for yourself how bad a clunker it is. No one in Hollywood thinks she could have carried it off.

I'll be the sacrificial lamb, the scapegoat. The critics and the columnists will say, why didn't Ken Woods stop Lisa Malone before she destroyed herself? I pleaded with her, I begged her, I threatened. I gave her every argument in the books. She listened politely, smiled sweetly, and then went ahead as though I hadn't said a word. I'm going to be blamed for it, Father, even more than she is. Lisa is finished in the film industry, and they're all going to say that it was Ken Woods's fault.

The film is a stinker. It will smell up every movie house in the country. Sure, some people are gonna go see it simply because Lisa's in it. The dirty-old-man types will flock in because the word is around that she doesn't have her clothes on for part of the film. Even the most stupid high school sophomore—and he's the one we're making films for these days—is gonna know after the first ten minutes that Lisa has had it. It's an unintentional comedy, a great big pretentious bore. Poor Lisa's put all her money into it, and she's not gonna get a penny of it back. I hear that the distributors are so scared by the reaction at some of the sneak previews that they may withdraw it. Even as arrogant as she is these days, Lisa isn't going to be able to distribute it on her own.

I forgot. The poor woman is unconscious in a hospital bed, isn't she? Well, like I say, better that way than the shame and the humiliation. I suppose if she doesn't pull out of it, and I hear there's not much chance of that, the distributors will forget about the film and it'll be locked up in cans for the historians. That's probably the best way out.

Anyway, who wants to see a film when the leading actress is a vegetable in a hospital? Know what I mean?

Who do I think did it? Hell, I don't know. Probably poor dumb George, fed up with being the weak partner in their marriage. George is so stupid, he probably actually believes that Lisa went to bed with a faggot like Tad Thomas.

Where was I the night that it happened? Aw, c'mon, Father. You don't think I'd do something like that, do ya? I've been around too long. I've been there and back a dozen times. That's not the way Ken Woods acts. Anybody in Hollywood will tell you that. I mean, I was here in my room in the hotel all night. I was supposed to have breakfast with her in the morning. I phoned her from LA and said that I'd heard this rumor about the distributors and I wanted to come to Chicago to plead with her one last time to drop the whole project. I told her that if she did, I might be able to get her a part next year so she could make some of the money back, not a lead maybe, but a decent part. A kind of "comeback" for Lisa Malone, know what I mean?

She gives me that patient little sigh and says, "Why, of course, Kenneth, I'll be happy to talk to you."

I asked her if she's heard the rumor, and she says no, that she hasn't heard it, that the distributors seem quite happy with the sneak previews. "Jesus Christ, Lisa!" I shout at her. "Everybody out here is telling me that it's a crock of shit."

"Well, let's talk about it at breakfast, Kenneth," she says, sweet as ever, and then hangs up on me.

I made her a success, Father, and she hangs up on me. No

agent worth a damn expects gratitude, but why the hell can't
they listen to you when you know what you're talking about
and they don't?

Sorry I broke down again, Father.

But ya see what I mean?

I'm glad that she's dead.

17
ALIQUIS

*It is all too absurdly simple. Doctors and nurses
are fools, I have always known that, but I am nonetheless
astonished at how easy it is to deceive them. Inside the hospital room I hesitate; there's been some mistake. That woman
on the bed is not Lisa, it can't be.*

*Nostrils twitching in revulsion at the hideous smells of a
hospital, I approach more closely. It is Lisa. The bandages
and the oxygen mask over her pale, lifeless face disguised
her. She is almost a vegetable. My heart twists with anguish.
Did I do that to her?*

*I didn't want to, Lisa, my dearest. Please forgive me.
Understand that I had to do it. Just like that man who killed
Robert Kennedy had to do it. It will be a grace to finish you
off, end your agony once and for all.*

*Again I am filled with love for the victim, poor, dear Lisa.
I love you so much, what I do now is an act of love. I've
always loved you. Why ... ? But enough. I will snuff out the
last breath of life in you in order that I may love you all the
more. And then perhaps you will love me in return.*

A doctor!

No, merely an orderly. He nods at me and checks the dials

on the oxygen unit. He makes a minor adjustment. Then he looks at me again. Does he suspect?

I shake my head disconsolately, as though I don't believe there is much hope for the woman. He shrugs in agreement, hesitates again, then leaves the room.

He has given me an excellent idea.

I consider the complex mechanism that is keeping Lisa alive. A ventilator, I believe it is called. There is not one plug to pull; there are many plugs. Which ones are the most important?

There is not much time; a nurse or a doctor may appear any moment, someone not as easy to bluff as a technician.

I tug desperately at the tubes and the lines that link the massive equipment surrounding her bed to Lisa. Nothing moves.

I pray to God for strength to finish my work of love. Please help me finish what must be done.

I gather the network of cords in both my hands and pull with all my strength. Some come easily out of their sockets, some do not.

I lose my balance and fall back against the window, knocking over a plant. Dear God, they must have heard that!

I'm pushing my luck. One more chance and then I must run.

Which line is the most important? The oxygen, of course. I ought to know that. If I could only calm down for a few moments, I'd recognize the appropriate cable. What's the matter with me? Why has my mind stopped working?

Of course. That's the one. How stupid not to have pulled it in the first place. I tried brawn instead of brains. This time I will do it right.

I pull on the line linking the oxygen tank to the ventilator. It won't move. Desperately I yank again. The line breaks, oxygen flows uselessly into the room.

There, that will finish you.

I turn and walk calmly and serenely out of the hospital room and into the corridor. Mustn't panic now. I will stroll slowly to the staircase, open the door gently, slip down the

*stairs, and catch the elevator on the next floor. A few people
smile and greet me. I nod graciously in return; my exhausted
brain sings for joy.*

   That is the end of Lisa Malone.

18

BLACKIE

   "It's the worst October in years, isn't it, Monsignor?" The doorman at the Whitehall bowed respectfully to
me as I walked out into the chill rainstorm. "Could we lend
you a raincoat or an umbrella?"

   "No," I said, hunching down to make myself as small a
target as possible for the wind ripping in off the lake. "I've
got a clean suit back in my room. I think."

   The worst October in years, huh? Tell me about it.

   There was a fourth kind of October weather, which I didn't
mention before. It anticipates March: cold, mean, ugly rain,
the meaner and the uglier because it comes during what is
supposed to be our golden month. Whatever happened to
Indian summer? Something went wrong when the Cubs lost
that fourth game of the playoffs.

   I wandered down the street, lost in reflection about winter
and death, leaving my return to the cathedral to my frequently
unreliable automatic pilot.

   Next month was the month of the Holy Souls. Whatever
happened to the Holy Souls? We had dumped them sometime
after the Vatican Council as an act of ecumenical goodwill.
Maybe older people still prayed for them. A historian I had
read a couple of weeks ago had neatly demonstrated how
purgatory as a place had emerged around 1200 and that the
first really good description of it had been written by an
English monk named H (for what, no one knows) of Seltray.

It was a description of Station Island, as we call it now, or St. Patrick's purgatory on Loch Derg in County Donegal, another great Irish contribution to the human imagination! Indeed, despite the abandonment of purgatory as an ecumenical encumbrance by our better theological thinkers, it had been celebrated again in a lyrically quirky way, by Seamus Heaney in a marvelous poem, published this year, called "Station Island" (featuring a cameo appearance, if you please, by your man Jimmy Joyce).

Nor did D. M. Thomas in *The White Hotel* think purgatory was outmoded. Like Heaney and Chateaubriand, he realized that purgatory produces better poetry than heaven or hell because purgatory has future.

If you're a disciple of Lord Whitehead, as am I, you believe that heaven has future, too. How absurd to think it would not. As Dr. James would have put it—I'm a disciple of his, too—the notion has congruence, luminosity, and fruitfulness.

When Blackie Ryan takes consolation in philosophy, it is a good sign that he's up a tree.

How absurd of me to be thinking about future in heaven when I had an all too earthly problem unsolved; and a woman in a hospital bed who perhaps was already in her purgatory.

I looked up from the rain-drenched street. The massive buildings looming ahead of me did not look like the cathedral. They were, in all probability, Cabrini Green.

"Lost, Father Ryan?" A black teenager grinned at me.

"My automatic pilot apparently is not working."

"Hey, man, that's great. Automatic pilot? Wait till I tell S'ter!"

A student of Cathedral High, beyond doubt.

"She says that I don't know whether I'm coming or going?"

"No, Father, she says you can't tell the river from the lake. Turn left and hurry home 'fore you come down with pneumonia!"

I dutifully obeyed air traffic control and returned to my reflections.

Nonetheless, I kind of miss the Souls in purgatory. They stand for two things that our activist, socially committed clergy and religious seem to have forgotten: hope and vicarious suffering.

What the hell do you tell kids in a dentist's chair these days?

I thought I had liberated millions from purgatory when I was forced, as a small child, to wear braces on my teeth. All that suffering in vain.

What do you tell cancer victims?

Or what do you tell poor, damned souls like Kenneth A. Woods?

He faded rather quickly after the Chateaubriand with mashed potatoes, broccoli, carrots, green beans and béarnaise sauce, plus rum raisin ice cream with chocolate sauce for dessert and a couple of glasses of Bailey's Irish Cream for me.

He drank cognac.

I shepherded him from the Pump Room back to the Whitehall, helped him to his door, opened it, and eased him into a couch in the parlor of his suite.

For a washed-up agent, rejected by the goddess he had created, Ken Woods was still leading the good life.

While still in the elevator, he suggested the Pygmalion metaphor to me. "What was the name of that man who brought a statue to life, you know, Leslie Howard played him in the movie, and one of those musicals was based on the story?"

"Pygmalion," I said, proud of my classical learning.

"Yeah, I'm a Pygmalion. Did Pygmalion kill the girl?"

"No, I don't believe so."

"Did she kill him?"

"No, the story didn't end that way either."

"Well, then, how did it end?" He swayed as the elevator door opened.

"In the Greek myth, I believe, Pygmalion gets to keep the girl. In George Bernard Shaw's play, he loses her. Shaw seems to think that it was his good fortune. In the Leslie Howard film to which you referred, as well as *My Fair Lady*, we have the conventional happy ending."

"No happy ending to this story, Father." He sighed, with something not unlike satisfaction, as I lowered him to the couch. "Know what I mean?"

Oh, yes.

Had he tried to kill the goddess he had created and with whom he had fallen in love? Maybe. There was just enough despair in his character for him to do that and enough hatred to want to torture her before he killed her. Money wouldn't be a motive, at least I didn't think so, though it might be that Lisa had left him some money in her will, for old times' sake. The professional humiliation... ? Well, it was not inconceivable. Lisa, I feared, was in a no-win situation with the man who claimed to be her creator. If *The Friendship Factor* was a success, then the obvious implication would be that she did not need him and had never needed him. Perhaps it might even be said by some of those in the know—and it was those in the know who were the relevant audience for Kenneth A. Woods—that she might've achieved greatness much earlier if she hadn't been saddled with such an incompetent agent. On the other hand, if the film were a disaster, as he apparently believed and hoped it would be, he would be blamed for not talking her out of it.

I didn't think Ken Woods was Pygmalion. It seemed to me he had more in common with Dr. Frankenstein.

I deftly and discreetly removed the tape of *The Friendship Factor* from his briefcase in the Whitehall suite while he snored blissfully in the other room. Well, my movements were not all that deft. I dropped it twice, with considerable clatter, as I was trying to tuck it into my jacket pocket. In due course, and with proper advisers, I would review the film—perhaps Lisa herself could give me some clues.

There were two very different opinions about the film. Kerry Randall would have persuaded me that it was a work approaching genius; Ken Woods was convinced that it was a crock of shit. Biased opinions both, and both from personalities whose equilibrium was sufficiently distorted on the subject of my Lisa as to make them untrustworthy witnesses.

In both versions, however, there were portraits of Lisa that astonished me. Nowhere in my memory of her was there room for a picture of Lisa reaching defiantly for greatness. Nor any image of her summarily dismissing writers and directors. All very interesting.

Indeed.

I struggled through the rain in search of the cathedral, becoming lost in my own parish only twice. As Joe Murphy said to one of his patients, I am more confused than I appear to be, not less. Joe, gentle Bostonian saint that he is to put up with the daft Ryans, promptly added that "it doesn't matter."

God bless him.

One of the reasons that I became befuddled at the deceptive intersection of State, Rush, and Division (and began to walk in the general direction of Seattle, if the truth is to be told) was that I was thinking about the other possible killers—Tad Thomas and Dina King, professional allies of Lisa and also, I was sure, professional rivals; Frank Leonard, the smooth, bent bank vice-president on whose dishonesty Lisa had stumbled (as she herself had reported to me); and Sister Winifred Murray, a radical nun who was the beneficiary of Lisa's charity, but was probably about to be driven away from the trough of Lisa's money.

All had reason and all had opportunity. Sister Winnie was into revolutionary rhetoric, but that did not make her a killer. Frank Leonard, as the liaison between First Illinois and the Outfit, was familiar enough with both murder and murderers. Thomas and King? I did not know them yet.

If I had to choose, it would be Leonard. Sheer prejudice. I saw in him a slick, handsome Irishman gone wrong. The flip side of my brother Packy.

Or, if you eliminate the word "handsome," even the flip side of Cardinal Cronin's gray eminence.

Bedraggled physically and emotionally, I finally arrived at the warmth and comfort of the cathedral rectory, shivering both from the cold and at the thought of what all of the womenfolk in my family would have said if they knew about this escapade.

I could have taken a cab, a thought which, in all truth, had never occurred to me.

"Blackie, what the hell?" my senior curate exploded, as I trailed a path of water up the steps to the switchboard. "You look like a Labrador that's been chasing birds in the lake. Did someone throw you in?"

"It is a day," I said dully, "for Sherlock Holmes."

"It's a day," he said, "for a raincoat."

"That's what I so admire about the younger generation of clergy. Their ability to incisively diagnose a situation and prescribe for it."

"Have you been over to the hospital?"

"No, not the hospital."

"You'd better get upstairs and pour yourself some of that Irish jet fuel that you keep stored there."

"I am an abstemious man," I replied.

"Hey," he shouted as I slopped my way into the first floor corridor, "you heard what happened at the hospital, didn't you? It was three-and-a-half hours ago . . ."

"No." I felt my heart sinking. "What happened?"

"Some damn-fool nun pulled the plug out of Lisa Malone's life-support systems. The cops are out hunting for Sister Winifred. They think she's the killer."

19

BLACKIE

"Well, John." She stared at me balefully. "I must say it's typical of what one would expect from a male-dominated Church."

No one, you may have noticed, calls me John. To my father I am, on occasion, Johnny. To my siblings and my stepmother I am either Blackie or Punk. To my nieces and nephews, Uncle Blackie or, in circumstances when they wish to ask for a favor (chocolate ice cream or a half-day driving their water ski boats for them), Uncle Punk. To the people of the parish I am Father Blackie or, if they're being formal,

Monsignor Blackie—the latter is favored by the children in the grammar school, not, I might remark, without a tendency to giggle when they give me that medieval title. To virtually everyone else, on the earth, under the earth, or above the earth—including, of course, the Lord God Herself in Her various manifestations—I am Blackie. Only radical feminist nuns call me "John."

Proud of the revolutionary politics of referring to the rector of the Holy Name Cathedral by his first name—like so many other Catholic radicals, arriving a little breathless and a little late.

I retaliated by calling her, with infinite courtesy, Sister Winifred (an elegant Anglo-Saxon name never, I repeat never, to be contracted to the vulgar Winnie, as in Winnie the Pooh—at least not to her face).

"Indeed?"

I have, contrary to rumors you may have heard, nothing against nuns, not even anything necessarily against radical nuns. My opposition is rather to man-hating women, whether they be in the religious life or out of it. I can deal with the most radical of radical feminists provided they have not defined me automatically as the enemy simply because of the way my chromosomes happen to be arranged.

"Are you going to deny that you sent the police to arrest me?" she demanded with flashing eyes appropriate for a Dominican friar in fourteenth-century Spain insisting that a tortured heretic must repent before being granted the merciful end of an auto-da-fé.

"Of course I'm going to deny it, Sister," I said meekly. "I was having dinner with Mr. Woods, whom you may know, at the Ambassador East all evening. I had no idea what had happened until I returned to the rectory."

"I suppose," she said with triumphant skepticism, "that you didn't suggest that they drag me over to Northwestern Hospital to see if the nurses could identify me?"

Come to think of it, Sister Winifred did look a bit like Winnie the Pooh, though that may be a bit of an unfair judgment on the appearance of Mr. Milne's classic storybook character (to whom the real Christopher Robin has apparently recently vigorously objected as a sibling rival). In earlier days Sister's badly arranged body would have been covered with the voluminous robes of her religious order. Bulges in all the wrong places would not have been noticed. One would not have said that her thin hawklike face and nervously darting black eyes permitted the adjective "attractive" to be predicated of her—but then one never thought in such terms with regard to nuns in the old days anyway.

Indeed, one might have said of her, clad in black with the white wimple, that she looked like a possibly dangerous bird of prey, a condor or something of the sort, but, I would have thought, a smooth, graceful condor, a dean of discipline or someone with that kind of title in a Catholic women's high school (we would have said "girls'" high school in that benighted era). The young women in her charge would have been in mortal terror of her.

Her physical unattractiveness—an ill-fitting polyester trouser suit, hair cut short, quite possibly in a male barbershop, and a heavily jowled face as well as the inevitable "nunny" shoes, which would have, by themselves, been the giveaway—had become a political statement that said to the observer, "I am a radical activist nun. Don't you dare even think of me as a sex object."

Not much chance of that.

"I'm sorry if you were inconvenienced," I said, as though I were in mortal terror of her (which I surely was not). "Obviously they didn't identify you as the sister who ripped the cable from Lisa's oxygen tank."

"Male stereotyping," she screeched, not unlike, I think, a condor would screech. "I haven't worn full religious habit in ten years. I burned my habit. I'll never wear it again. Those nurses dared to look me in the eye and say they were not sure whether I was the one or not. Outrageous!"

I rearranged the stack of letters on my desk that represented this morning's mail, composed entirely, if truth be told, of advertisements and form letters from the Chancery Office— "How fortunate for you that the other sisters in your apartment were able to assure the police that you had been there all evening."

"It's outrageous! One of the women in my collective is a practicing attorney, an expert in civil litigation. We are going to sue *everyone*, including you and Cardinal Cronin!"

"That is, of course, your privilege, Sister," I said formally. "By the way, I realize it's still morning, but you are, and quite properly, shaken by the events of last night. Might I offer you something to drink?"

"I will not be bought off by liquor or smooth clerical charm!" A little stream of saliva was slipping down the left corner of her chin. "Anyway, I don't drink. It's a filthy and disgusting habit. If you males, who dominate the Church, drank less and worked more, the Church would not be in the shambles that it is."

An undebatable point, to give the devil her due.

It had been a disastrous evening. The police, who had picked up Sister Winifred, had more or less acted on their own initiative, knowing that she was on the technical list of suspects, before either my father or Mike Casey or the State's attorney found out what was going on. The headlines in this morning's papers about her outraged annunciations ("Nun hits Daley, Cops, Cardinal!") obscured two facts that did not seem to worry either Sister Winifred or the press: someone had brutally cut off Lisa's oxygen supply, and for a brief period of time, Lisa had stopped breathing. Brain damage? "It is hard to say whether there is any more," Dr. Rodriquez had said with a shrug. "There has been so much already."

Any one of the suspects might have donned a religious habit and walked down the corridor of the Olson Pavilion. The men were all short enough, and the women, save for Kerry Randall, all tall enough to fit the vague description of a nun in a black habit and a black raincoat (an old-fashioned black habit at that) who entered Lisa's room and vanished a minute or two later.

Kerry could have worn high heels. I wondered if she owned any.

You would think that nurses and residents would find old-fashioned religious garb sufficiently noteworthy to have more carefully examined her face. To make matters worse, none of the interns or residents was able to say with confidence that Sister Winifred was not the woman—if it was a woman—they saw in the hospital corridor. All of the other nuns—or women, as I should be calling them—in her collective were prepared to swear that she'd been with them since 5:45 in the afternoon. There was no way in rush hour traffic she could have traveled that quickly up Lake Shore Drive and Sheridan Road to their residence. I did not necessarily accept this alibi. Winifred's collective was so angry at all men that I'm sure they would have viewed a lie to the Chicago police department as an act of high virtue, not unlike being thrown to the lions in the days of ancient Christianity.

Moreover, although I was in the Pump Room shortly after six drinking my Jameson's with Ken Woods, and while he *seemed* to have been there for some time, he might have arrived from the Olson Pavilion shortly before my appearance. It would be worth a few discreet inquiries at the Ambassador East. I had suggested to Mike Casey that he request that one of the clever artists at the police department draw nun's habits around the faces of all our suspects and see if one or two of the brighter hospital staff on Lisa's floor might identify one of them.

"Even your face, Blackie?"

"If you wish," I replied imperturbably. "Though I should think that the last thing I will ever be confused with is a nun."

"What they will say, of course, is that it's Monsignor Blackie in drag."

Farley Strangler, who was receiving a lot of publicity because of his skepticism about the authenticity of the attack on Lisa, was on the *Mert Rosenblum Show* later in the evening. Rosenblum is a mathematics professor from the University of Illinois at Chicago Circle, who runs a talk show on WLS as a sort of genteel sideline. He and Farley called upon the mayor of Chicago to end "this unholy charade" about Lisa Malone.

They would have to find the mayor of Chicago before that message could be delivered.

Somewhat to my surprise, and in support of my conviction that human nature, even as manifested in those who listened to radio talk programs, is basically good and decent, the phone calls were overwhelmingly against Farley Strangler and Merton Rosenblum.

My niece Caitlin, I am sure, was one of the callers, faking her middle-European intellectual accent, pretending to be a Marxist supporter of the Hapsburg monarchy. "Ya." She sounded like a woman in a Maximilian Schell film. "You both are nothing but capitalist parasite pigs!"

None of which was bringing us any closer to solving the murder, or still, thank God, the attempted murder, of my beloved Lisa.

All of us knew, as the dreadfully cold rain continued to drench Chicago that morning, that no one at the hospital had been criminally negligent and that the killer had struck again with the same reckless, almost lunatic cleverness as in the first attempt. "We're dealing with a brilliant and dangerous madman," my father had said on the phone. "He'll try again, Blackie, mark my words. He'll try again."

"Or she."

"That's right, I should have said madperson."

The old fella is an equal opportunity crime hunter.

Normally we would have both laughed when he corrected the sexist mistakes in his vocabulary. Now neither of us was in a mood for laughter.

One slight streak of silver lining in the rain-soaked clouds: some of the suspicion would be lifted from the head of poor George Quinn. The State's attorney would tell the superior court justice at eleven o'clock this morning (only fifteen minutes away) that he had no objection to bail being granted to Lisa's husband.

"Why would I want to kill Lisa?" Sister Winifred bent toward me. "Me of all people?" She looked, now, no longer like a condor but only like a crow, a crow with a very sharp beak, however. "I've been her spiritual adviser since she was in high school. Lisa never trusted your male-monopoly capitalistic priesthood!"

"Neither did she approve of the money she gave you being spent to buy guns for revolutionaries in Central America!" I fired back quickly.

It was difficult to listen to Sister Winifred on the subject of Lisa Malone without the clean, brisk, boglike smell of Jameson's in my nostrils to kill the smell of Sister Winifred's ideology. My duties as the puzzle solver required that I trick her into a lengthy diatribe. If she'd had the slightest suspicion that I was actually interviewing her for one of my investigations, she would have stormed out of the rectory and phoned the woman from her collective (practicing civil law, such are the vocations of brides of Christ these days) to file yet another suit against me, Sean Cronin, and, in all likelihood, John Paul II.

Quite possibly the Holy Spirit, too.

"The money is going to the cause of liberation theology!" she shouted at me. "To liberate the poor and the oppressed in South America from enslavement by North American multinational corporations!"

Twenty-five years ago, when Lisa was a sophomore in high school, Sister Mary Winifred, as she was known then, was drama and chorus director of the high school, an appealing, energetic young nun on whom the young women with dramatic or musical aspirations all had the slight crush that comes with going to a single-sex high school. She was only a few years older than the students, and they identified with her and she with them. I fear that she spent much of her time on religious indoctrination instead of music and acting, though apparently she was not without some talents in these latter areas. She was an enthusiast for SDS, a decent "dress crusade" which adhered to a measuring stick approach to women's clothes—a perspective which implied that the Lord God had made an artistic mistake in ordaining that women should have breasts and thighs (ironically the three letters so combined would stand for something very different a few years later); devotion to Our Lady of Fatima; and fierce opposition to "obscene" records, which included *all* of the efforts of a certain Elvis Presley. She also was plugged into the private revelation grapevine and knew every dire prediction from Padre Pio about the forthcoming end of the world before the Italian stigmatic himself had uttered them.

Sister Winifred was still crusading. The substance had

changed, but not the style. Liberation had replaced Our Lady of Fatima, and Marxist revolutionaries occupied the pedestal once reserved for Padre Pio.

"I'm afraid I have to disagree, Sister," I said apologetically, trying my best to look like Father Brown. "Lisa has given you tens of thousands of dollars every year, in addition to the monies distributed by her foundation. She thought the money was going to missionaries, to hospitals, and to schools. She didn't know that it was going to revolutionary guerrillas. She told a number of her friends that there would be no more contributions. It's not altogether impossible, Sister Winifred, that you might become very angry at her under such circumstances."

"If I did," she spat back at me, "it would be a simple exercise of revolutionary justice!"

20

SISTER WINIFRED

Certainly not! I didn't hit her over the head. That's the sort of suspicion I'd expect from a chauvinist cleric in a male-dominated Church. There were many times when I would have enjoyed boxing her ears to knock some sense into her thick skull. Even in high school she never seemed to understand what I was trying to say; her mind was too filled with dreams of glory in Hollywood. She should have been a nun, John, you know that. She almost went to the novitiate when you went to the seminary. I'm convinced that if we hadn't lived under such oppressive rules in those days, if we'd had as much freedom as you had, in other words, she would've become a nun and would now be part of our crusade for justice for the oppressed women of the world.

She'd even be a member of our collective instead of making a public display of herself in those exploitative, male-chauvinist films. I never tried so hard with anybody to break through false consciousness as I have with Lisa. Wasn't I the one to persuade her that her voice was a good deal more talented than her mother realized and that she should have higher ambitions than merely singing at midnight Mass and at weddings and at parish luncheons? I wanted her to study voice and drama at our college. She would have had a fine education there and developed her talents before she entered the novitiate.

She had already made a preliminary application to the Hill. You were probably too concerned with your own seminary plans to pay any attention. Oh, yes, I knew that you were sweet on her. She told me all about your little romance. You were exploiting her even then. Typical male, typical priest.

She told me that she wanted a year in college before she made up her mind about entering the order. Her mother and father insisted that she go away to school partly because they wanted to destroy my influence over her. Well, I showed them!

Her parents thought the music and drama interest was getting out of hand. May Malone wanted her pretty daughter to have a "nice" voice, but not a voice that was so good as to give her a "big head." She used those very words to me, John. Can you imagine a woman actually thinking that it would be bad for her daughter to be too talented?

In neither of the schools where they made her register was she going to be able to take any music or drama. Her mother screamed at me that they were very disappointed with her high school education because we were encouraging Lisa to "put on airs." "She doesn't know her place, Sister, and it's all your fault. If Lisa hadn't listened to you, she wouldn't be reaching beyond herself."

"What's the matter with reaching beyond yourself?" I spoke right up to her. "She's a very gifted young woman. I don't approve of her going to UCLA either. You paid for her voice lessons. You put her on public display. Now you're blaming me because she liked it."

"I just wanted to be proud of her," the foolish woman blubbered, "when she sang sweetly at wedding Masses."

I was as horrified as everyone else when that first film appeared. Here was Lisa, whom we'd all pictured as a docile little novice, cavorting around the screen with very little clothing on and pretending to act. I wouldn't have used the words then, but she was the victim of objectification. Her false consciousness made her eager to permit men to objectify her for the profit motive.

I prayed for her every night. I wrote her letters pleading that she protect her virtue in that sinful world. Now I know better; you don't pray and you don't plead and you don't write young women urging them to protect their virtue. You challenge them to rise out of their false consciousness and realize that they are being objectified and exploited by men. When I understood how men have exploited women in the Church for centuries, I realized how badly the Church had failed Lisa and felt that I was bound in conscience to make up for that failure. I committed myself to the struggle to raise her consciousness. Lisa and I, I realized, were sisters; we shared our women's experience of male oppression. I had failed her two decades before because I did not understand clearly enough the structures of male and capitalistic domination. Now, I understood them, it was my sacred duty to try to save Lisa.

Did she respond to the letters I wrote?

Certainly she responded, with the pious drivel that the male-dominated Church had forced us to teach her: she prayed for me every night, she hoped I was praying for her, Hollywood was really a very interesting place, there were many good men and women there who were being very kind to her, and she was grateful to me and to the other sisters for giving her confidence in herself and in her talents.

She was saying that we had been the unconscious tools of the capitalistic oppression that forced her into the white slave trade of which she'd become a part. She was doing all this in the name of Christianity!

That's what your male-dominated Church does to young women.

Most of the girls from St. Praxides were spoiled rotten. Their parents had too much money, and the girls thought that they were better than everyone else. There were a few of them in every class. They became the class leaders, of course, because they were so pushy and self-confident.

We dreaded each new crop of them because we knew they would be troublemakers—young women who thought they could run the school better than we could. Lisa Malone and little Kerry Ann Mulloy were not as bad as some of the others. They were docile little girls, eager to help and ready to learn from us. It was hard not to like them. The two of them were inseparable, and little Kerry Ann was *so* loyal to Lisa. She was almost as talented as Lisa but never got the attention or the praise. Still, it didn't bother her at all. When Lisa was praised, Kerry Ann was as happy as if she were being praised herself. Lisa was more selfish and self-centered, but in her own shallow and superficial way, she was loyal to Kerry Ann, too, and helped her with her lines and her songs for the school play.

Although they were from St. Praxides, I thought they might learn something in my Young Christian Students group. Girls from St. Praxides knew nothing about what was going on in the world. They had no experience of poverty or suffering or misery or loneliness. In Young Christian Students—YCS, you must remember it, John—we taught them how to observe, judge, and act: to look closely at what was going on in the world around them, a world that girls from St. Praxides had never critically examined, to judge the selfishness and the cruelty and the exploitation in the world in terms of what Jesus said in the Gospel; and then to act, perhaps only in small ways, but to act just the same, the way Jesus would've acted if he were alive today and had observed the immoralities and the false values and the injustices in the world.

It was all very democratic; the sister in charge of the YCS group wasn't even permitted to say anything at the meetings. The girls did it all themselves. Kerry Ann was very docile. She came up with the right answers all the time. She saw what was wrong with women watching soap operas all day and judged that waste of time very quickly and brightly in the light of the Gospels. Lisa was slower and more stubborn. "If they like the stories in the soap operas and if they don't fail in their responsibilities to their husbands and children," she would try to argue, "what's wrong with watching one or two of them every day?"

The discussion leader—the one I had prepared beforehand—would argue and argue and argue with Lisa. Sometimes it would take a whole meeting to persuade her to concede one point—that the soap operas were trash, for example. I used to think that she'd agree finally just so we could go on with the meeting but she really wasn't convinced. That's the way Lisa has always been, sweet and agreeable on the outside, but terribly stubborn inside.

I remember the day she told me that she was going to UCLA. "Can't I have a vocation to be a singer and an actress?" she said with that sweet simple little smile that I had learned to hate. "Couldn't I serve God in Hollywood almost as well as I would in the convent?"

I'm afraid I lost my temper and screamed at her. My consciousness hadn't been raised then. I didn't realize how exploitative commercialized sex in the movies is. I saw everything then in the moral categories of the male-dominated Church.

"You'll lose your immortal soul in that sinful place!" I yelled at her. "You're turning your back on God! You're deliberately and maliciously turning your back on God!"

"I don't think I am, Sister," she said, tears in her eyes. "Might not God want me to be an actress?"

"That's blasphemy! God wants you to enter our order, Lisa Malone, you know that. You're rejecting a vocation."

"I'm sorry, Sister," she murmured through her sobs. "I just have to try. Maybe after I fail I'll come home and be a nun like you want me to."

Like I wanted her to. Can you imagine that for stubbornness, John? It was God who wanted her, not I.

Well, if that's what she has chosen, I told myself, that's what she has chosen. There was nothing more that I could do. I didn't even bother answering her letters. There were always other young women who were less stubborn than she was. Those seemed to be happy times. Lisa graduated in 1962, you remember. The Council had just begun. We were all confident there were going to be great changes in the Church. So we were enthusiastic about the future. The enthusiasm spread to many of the young women, even though vocations were already beginning to fall off. We didn't realize then how many changes there were going to be—probably because we didn't understand how deep was our false consciousness and how much we were being oppressed by the males who dominate the Church.

Well, it was eighteen years later that I read in the paper that her mother had died and that Lisa had flown home to the funeral—that was four years ago. I hadn't seen any of her films, of course. I didn't even watch those awful television specials. I realized that she'd been estranged from her mother, and I wrote her a letter of sympathy. I told her I was sorry about her mother's death. Then I asked her if now she understood the passages from scripture that we had studied in the YCS group—what does it profit a person to gain the whole world and suffer the loss of their soul?

She wrote back, her typical sweet, empty letter, thanking me for my sympathy and enclosing two tickets to a benefit concert she was giving in the Rosemont Horizon which that terrible male chauvinist, Francis Leonard, had organized. Well, at first I threw them in the wastebasket. Then I decided that I would ask one of the other members of our collective to go with me to the concert. Maybe we could help Lisa realize that she was a prisoner of false consciousness.

Her voice had improved a lot, I'll give her that. And she did look as young and sweet as she ever had—she must have spent hours and hours every day on her physical appearance. The audience was mostly rich, well-dressed, middle-aged men and women. Every one of them the kind of capitalistic fat cats that I suppose Lisa would've been if she had stayed in St. Praxides parish. All you had to do was look at the expression on the men's faces while they listened to her sing to know that it wasn't music they came to that concert for. Men only see one thing in a woman, especially when she's wasted hours of her time trying to make herself look attractive to them.

After the concert was over, Sister and I went straight up to her and told her what we thought. She was pleasant and charming—nothing seemed to have changed since high school days—but I could see a haunted expression in her eyes. Lisa knew that all the acclaim and adulation were worthless and that her life was slipping through her fingers.

"Why don't you make something of yourself, Lisa?" I asked her.

She looked at me in a funny, puzzled sort of way and said, "That's a good question, Sister. I ask it of myself often. Maybe I should reach higher."

Well, she also gave us a check—a thousand dollars as I remember—for our work in South America, the money our collective sends off to help the People down there. I never told her it was for missionaries. I said it was for the priests and sisters who were working in the cause of the People.

Frank Leonard told her last month that the money was going to Communists. What's wrong with it going to Communists if they're the only ones who are trying to liberate the People? If Jesus were alive in Central America today, he would be a Communist.

I've kept in touch with her ever since. I even went out to Los Angeles last spring at Easter to see if I could be any help to her. I took her to a charismatic renewal ceremony because that's often a first step in consciousness-raising. Lisa was very nervous at the prayer group, afraid to let go, afraid to face her own experiences of exploitation and oppression. "I *am* trying to do more, Sister," she said. "I *am* trying to reach for the stars. They seem so far away..."—and her eyes turned vague and misty—"so far, far away."

Her stupid husband was away in Australia. I don't know why she ever married him, John. He was unworthy of her. I said to myself, if that's what she gave up the religious life for, she certainly regrets it now.

Certainly she gave us a check at the end of that visit. Why shouldn't we ask money to help the People in their fight against Gulf and Western?

Well, I suppose reaching for the stars meant this terrible new film. I can't bear to think of it. After all my work with her, her consciousness is as false as it ever was. Twenty years ago, I would've said that all I can do is pray for her. Now I'm not even sure that prayers will help her. Oh, I don't think she'll lose her soul or go to hell. I've abandoned that kind of mythological religion. Lisa is having her own hell here on earth and will have it for the rest of her life.

Certainly I was the one that told her that Francis Leonard was giving her money over to the organized crime syndicate. One of my collective sisters works for the United States Attorney's Office as a paralegal aid. What if it was a secret? In the collective we keep nothing secret from one another. The government knows that Leonard is laundering Mafia drug money through his bank. They don't have the evidence they need for an indictment yet, but they're going to get it. He's using the money of the Lisa Malone Foundation, money that's supposed to go to schools and hospitals and churches and missionaries, as part of his scheme—I'm too busy to bother learning the details. I was bound in conscience to report him to Lisa. Then he told her not to pay any attention to me. He said I was trying to cover myself—he used a more vulgar word than that, the male chauvinist pig—because I was giving her money to Communist revolutionaries.

Lisa called and asked me if what he said was true. "I thought the money was going to missionaries, Sister," she said in that naive, innocent voice of hers—as though you could be naive and innocent in Hollywood. "I didn't think you were giving it to Communists."

"You say 'Communist' like it's a dirty word, Lisa," I said right back to her. I refuse to grovel to people who have money. "Our Lord Jesus would be a Communist in some of those countries in Latin America. The Communists are the only ones who fight against the American multinational corporations. You've made films for Paramount, haven't you? Well, do you know what Gulf and Western is doing in Central America? It's restitution to send money down there to help the people resist multinationals like Gulf and Western."

"Yes, Sister," she says meekly. "I have to come out to

Chicago in a few weeks. Maybe we can talk about it then. I don't want my money going to Communists."

I had *no* intention of giving in on the point. My collective sisters voted unanimously to support me. I wrote Lisa and invited her to come to a session at the collective. We would be direct and blunt with her. Sometimes that's the only way to begin the consciousness-raising process. Occasionally it is necessary to use some salutary physical violence to shake women out of their false consciousness. Such violence is not wrong so long as it is done with sisterly love.

She phoned me three days ago and said she would try to come visit us late in the afternoon the next day. Well, you know what happened. I suppose it would've been a waste of time anyway. I'd have shouted at her all afternoon. She may have shed a few tears; she would've smiled sweetly and left.

The money? Oh, I'm sure with a false consciousness like hers, she would've cut off the funds. We would have voted to refuse to accept her decision.

"I don't want my money going to Communists, Sister." That's what she said at the beginning of the phone conversation, that's what she said at the end, and I'm sure that's what she would've said after our shock session at the commune. She always was a stubborn little chit.

So, John, what happened to Lisa is exactly what she deserved. She made her own bed, and she gets no sympathy from me if she has to lie in it.

Of course I'm storming heaven that she recover. She was such a cute little thing. Well, I'll pray for you and the family, too, John. I know how close all of you were to her.

And you pray for me, too.

21
BLACKIE

I considered the chart I had prepared. I tilted it in a number of different directions and then read it from the bottom up. It still made no sense. Possibly I should stick to locked-room puzzles, such as the one I had wrestled with in the Transylvanian Gothic Quinlin home at Long Beach last summer.

I paused to reflect on Sister Winifred Murray, a distasteful subject for reflection if there ever was one. Yet at the end, in the promise of prayers and the request for same, she was a novice again, in the days before the Council. Marx had replaced Mary. Liberation had taken over from the Sorrowful Mother novena. But the style was still the same. And perhaps the substance, too.

Given long enough life and the rate at which fashions in the Church change these days, Winnie might be back with the Sorrowful Mother some day.

Was everything else merely talk? Revolutionary violence might sound wonderful in the pages of the *National Catholic Reporter* in a letter from some mildly deranged missionary. But could all the talk in the world make you do something so uncharacteristic for a nun as to actually try to kill someone?

The answer, I feared, was that enough talk, day in and day out, becomes a reality in itself, a landslide of words roaring down the side of a mountain with an independent momentum of its own.

Or, to change the metaphor, you can readily hypnotize yourself by the sound of your own words to follow the content, no matter how much the content is foreign to who you really are. We learned that in the late sixties, did we not?

So far there had been five different pictures of Lisa Malone—her husband's, her friend's, her agent's, and those of her teenage sweetheart (turned cathedral rector) and her high school teacher turned consciousness raiser.

For Kerry she was a beloved, if naive rival; for George, a magical, mysterious, ultimately frustrating wife; for Ken Woods, the star he had created who had turned on him; for Blackie Ryan . . . well, a memory that proved he did have other choices besides the priesthood. To Sister Winnie the Pooh, she was the faithless student who refused to respond to God's call time after time. Her stubborn consciousness resisted all efforts at transformation.

If Sister Winifred's Lisa was the least probable of all, there was still something to be learned from her story. There never had been a chance of Lisa joining the convent—all virtuous young Catholic women thought about it in the old days. From attendance at the YCS meetings, however authoritarian and manipulative they might have been, and from harassment about vocation from Sister Winifred, Lisa may have acquired her convictions about professional dedication and her impulse to "reach for the stars" as she approached her fortieth birthday. It was an intriguing possibility that Sister Winifred had far more effect than she realized. The vocabulary and the ideology she had taught Lisa in high school, and perhaps the shot in the arm from her reappearance twenty years later, might in the Lady God's scheme of drawing straight with crooked lines, be responsible for *The Friendship Factor*.

I put my ballpoint pen aside, phoned Jim Reardon at the seminary and Roger Ebert at the *Sun Times* to set up the time when we would play the videotape of the film in my study—presuming that Ken Woods could not quite remember who had borrowed the film from him. I was not going to try to view it without help.

And protection.

"I can hardly wait," said Roger.

"Sen*sational!*" responded the always effervescent Reardon, the local clerical expert on classic films.

Well, at least they had both heard about it.

Might Sister Winifred have battered and tried to kill Lisa

in her hotel suite as an exercise in revolutionary justice? I asked myself that question in just so many words as I hung up after my phone conversation with Reardon. Winifred's personality was a mixture of anger and absolute confidence in her own possession of the truth. In the early sixties her anger had been directed at the spoiled young women from Beverly, and her truth had mandated her various crusades for decent dress and decent records. Her mission then had been the recruitment of more young women to her religious order.

Now her anger was against men and capitalism and the oppression of the People and the "American multinationals" (a phrase of whose self-contradiction she was oblivious). Her crusade was for liberation and consciousness-raising and freedom from male domination. Her collective of radical nuns had replaced the religious order as the community of the elect. Under some circumstances, and with the right ideological support—revolutionary justice, or something of the sort— Sister Winifred might do almost anything. She lived now on a permanent emotional high of violently expressed outrage. In a moment of fury she could undoubtedly hit Lisa over the head with the nearest blunt instrument.

The sadism of the cigarette burns and the systematic battering of Lisa's body—that did not seem to fit Sister Winifred's personality. However, who could say what might fit the personality of other members of her collective? I didn't think that they had turned to terrorist actions yet. Like most other Catholic revolutionaries, their revolution was merely talk. Unlike their counterparts in the Islamic countries, they were not yet prepared to kill and be killed. Yet a group neurosis can easily, after a certain threshold of rage has been passed, slip into violence and destruction—I would have to check with Mike Casey to see what the police had learned about Sister Winifred's commune.

Back to my charts. From what I had learned, only Frank Leonard, who claimed to have been at his office in the First Illinois Bank building, and Sister Winifred, who claimed to have been at her commune in Rogers Park, were not in the neighborhood of the Westin Hotel at the time of the assault on Lisa. Indeed, they were all out walking in the fog, astonishingly not encountering one another. At nine o'clock, presumably about half an hour before the assault began, Kerry Ann Randall had walked from the Whitehall Hotel down Michigan Avenue to the river and then returned. Roderick Malone, M.D., had "taken a bit of fresh air," pacing up and down East Lake Shore Drive in front of the Drake and the Mayfair Regent and then returning for a "bite to eat" (probably half a steer). Ken Woods had left the Whitehall and walked down Rush Street, "for old times' sake—it was a place we used to escape to on the occasional weekend off when we were ninety-day wonders at Abbott Hall." Tad Thomas and Dina King, together if they were to be believed, had walked right by the Westin through the Delaware Canyon to Lake Michigan. I wondered what the odds were, even on a foggy night, of such explorers not encountering one another.

Blackie Ryan? Ah, he was in the front row of the opera house in the presence of the cardinal priest of St. Domitila's, etc., etc., etc.

George Quinn? Where was George at 9:30? On an airplane over O'Hare? In a bus riding down the Kennedy Expressway? Poor George was so confused by his long flight from Australia and by the time change that he apparently didn't really know where he was at 9:30 Chicago time because it was already, according to his body clock, tomorrow morning. All he knew was that he was not in Lisa's suite.

There was no particular reason to think that Sister Winifred's collective sisters would not cover for her against the male-dominated police force. We had only Frank Leonard's word that he was still in his office in the First Illinois building working late on the documents of the Lisa Malone Foundation, about which I would have to question him in further detail this evening.

Ergo, as we would have said in the seminary, Meathead!

I shoved the chart away in disgust and punched the number of the Reilly Gallery on the phone.

"Reilly Gallery," the beauteous Annie said at the other end of the line.

"Cathedral rectory, your ladyship. Is himself present?"

"I'll get him, Father Blackie. Any daylight yet?"

"So far a lot of murk and not much else."

"Dead ends everywhere," Mike began without preliminaries. "It is certainly true, however, that neither Sister Winifred nor any of her friends at the Liberation Collective wear the old-fashioned religious garb or apparently even own it."

"Ah. Liberation Collective."

"Sometimes, Blackie, I'm not sure all of these changes were a good thing."

"Tell me about it. Is there any evidence that those collective sisters are turning to 'revolutionary violence'?"

Mike hesitated. "The department is becoming a little uneasy about them," he said slowly. "They have turned to minor shoplifting in stores up there in Rogers Park—secondhand jackets, medicine, food—nothing very large or very valuable."

"For the People, of course."

"Small shopkeepers up there are not people? The thieves, if you can use the word, are not very skillful. It looks like impulsive or perhaps compulsive behavior rather than a systematic scheme."

"An outrage binge pushing potential kleptomaniacs a bit round the corner?"

"Perhaps. Anyway, none of the victims wants to press charges against nuns, even nuns in lay garb. We had a couple of women patrol officers visit the commune, and they report it's a shattering experience, verbal and even the beginnings of physical assault, not much willingness to accept gentle warnings about shoplifting."

"Physical violence?"

"They pushed around one of our patrol officers. The kid, a little Puerto Rican girl from Logan Square, spent a couple of hours in the emergency room of the hospital—mostly shock, I think, that nuns would hit her and shove her down the stairs."

"Shove her down the stairs?"

"She wouldn't press charges either," Mike went on implacably. "Everybody respects the clergy, even now. Incidentally, have you seen Sister Winifred on TV today?"

"Not so that I've noticed."

"Exactly." Mike used the specially clipped tones reserved for the discovery of clues.

"Like the barking dog?"

"Why would she suddenly vanish from TV when she has a chance for so much publicity?"

"Because she is afraid that someone might recognize her, not perhaps from the hospital corridor, but from Michigan Avenue the other night."

"Indeed, to coin a phrase."

"We might have two separate killers working together, or perhaps independently . . ." My voice trailed off at that nightmare thought.

"Not likely, but not impossible either."

"I trust, Michael, that Lisa is adequately guarded finally?"

"They could get at President Reagan more easily."

"Given the history of the past few years, I somehow don't find that reassuring."

"I'll only be reassured when you figure out who they should arrest."

"Indeed."

I shut my charts in the drawer of my faithful rolltop desk and closed it. I had lost the key to the desk, as best I could remember, the first day in the rectory. In any event, if I had locked it, I would have promptly lost the key again thereafter and would have had to open the desk with a hammer or a saw or some other such violent instrument.

I was to meet Tad Thomas in the grill of the Ritz Carlton Hotel at noon. In Chicago we do things differently. The Ritz Carlton is part of the Four Seasons chain of hotels (which means that it will be efficiently managed and effectively maintained), whereas the Tremont and the Whitehall are owned by the same chain that manages most of the other Ritz Carltons scattered around the country.

However, a Water Tower is a Water Tower is a Water Tower, to paraphrase Ms. Stein. Whereas Water Tower Place, the grotesque marble skyscraper across the street from our beloved gingerbread Water Tower, of whose upper floors the Ritz Carlton is composed, is an insult to the eye of all who must walk down the Magnificent Mile. A convenient insult,

I'll admit. The first six floors of the building are a monumental shopping plaza, space for urban teenagers to "mall crawl" —an apparently biologically programmed behavior of the species—and, with Lord & Taylor, Marshall Field, Kroch's and Brentano's, and F.A.O. Schwarz scattered conveniently about, an ideal locale for a cathedral cleric to do his last (and first) Christmas shopping on Christmas Eve.

I rode to the top floor of the shopping plaza and entered an Accent Chicago store, where I purchased a Chicago Cubs jacket that I thought might make an appropriate addition to the color of the "Monsignor Blackie" wardrobe. It would hang next to the Quigley Seminary jacket I had worn for twenty years and which, my female siblings claim, has never once been cleaned.

"Aren't you going to buy a Chicago Bears jacket, Monsignor Blackie?" asked the young person behind the counter, a red-haired, green-eyed little person whom I did not recognize.

"If they beat Tampa Bay next Sunday, they will certainly win their division," I temporized with her, "and then I might add one of their jackets to my collection, too."

"What if the Bulls and the Sting and the Blackhawks and Northwestern and even the University of Chicago win championships?"

"I will get down on my knees and pray because I will know that the Day is at hand!"

The redhead, and all the other young persons in the Accent Chicago shop, squealed merrily. As Mrs. Chesterton said of G.K., "If you cannot make him attractive, then at least make him colorful."

Or, in more modern parlance, there are various dimensions of "cute."

Outside the store I was accosted by two juvenile delinquents, of about eighteen and twenty-four—months that is. Of opposite sexes (the older female and very much in charge of the younger). They persisted in making grotesque faces at me—in response, I'm sure they would say, to the "funny" faces I made at them. Moreover, despite the fact that I hid around the corner from them, by an ice cream store, they pursued me with noisy gurgles, giggles, and pointing fingers.

In order to free myself from these little hellions, I asked their mother's permission to purchase two small ice cream cones, chocolate needless to remark.

"Oh, Monsignor Blackie, that's not necessary!" She permitted her eyes to go round in feigned dismay and giggled much like her children.

"All right." I sued for unconditional peace. "I'll buy for all three kids."

"You shouldn't, Monsignor Blackie," she protested insincerely.

I could not remember meeting her. However the children said, "Thank you, Senior Ackie," so they must all have been members of the parish.

Did I share a cone with them? Did I spoil my lunch in direct violation of all the orders the various women in my family would have issued under such circumstances?

Is the Pope Polish?

I'm sure that mother and daughter told Daddy that night that Monsignor Blackie was "so cute!"

Indeed.

Tad Thomas would certainly have been cute on some of the dimensions, though I think my little redheaded friend in Accent Chicago and the slightly older brown-eyed mother of the juvenile delinquents would not have found his neat gray perfection interesting after a first glance, especially if, in the first glance, they had noted that his face was discreetly and carefully, but nonetheless obviously, made up.

"Like, Monsignor Blackie," the young person in the store would have said, "a *man* with makeup on his face? Yucky! Right?"

I would have accused her of female chauvinism. Indeed, if I were true to my own more or less androgynous principles, I would have argued that cosmetics are legitimate for both sexes of the species. I would have fallen back on considerable amount of historical data to support such an argument.

Nonetheless, despite his diffident courtesy, his Bill Buckley articulation, and his impeccably tailored suit, tie, shirt and hair (flowing iron-gray waves), I was in basic agreement with the redhead's imagined evaluation of Tad Thomas: Yucky!

From a distance you would judge that he was forty-five; closer up, you might say he was perhaps fifty; and peering through the makeup, you might even guess fifty-five. Not ancient exactly—indeed, fifty-five seems progressively less old with each passing day—but the artificiality of his every studied sound and gesture and movement seemed somehow inappropriate in an aging idol like Tad Thomas.

"So good of you to come over to talk to me, Monsignor." He rose from his chair in the grill and shook my hand with both of his smooth, well-manicured hands emerging from starched French cuffs that extended precisely half an inch out of his jacket—no more and no less.

If you are able to ignore the sound of the fountain in its sprawling, terraced, glass-windowed lobby, a sound like Niagara and Iguaçu combined, you would conclude that in its Chicago effort, the Four Season's chain manages to come closer to real continental elegance (which means, of course, Disney World continental elegance) in its restaurants than do most of the other national hotel chains—waiters with French accents, elaborate menus and wine lists, thick maroon brocaded wall covers, plush Louis XVI chairs, lighted candles on the table, service that is both relaxed and prompt. Moreover, since most Chicagoans didn't see the point of riding forty-four stories into the air for a restaurant when there are so many to be found on the ground level of Michigan Avenue, there is never much of a crowd in the Ritz Carlton grill at noontime, heightening the impression that it is a suitable place for a midday assignation. Glancing around the room I concluded, with a notable lack of charity, that older men continued to be attracted into assignations with young women, some of them not much older than my teenaged nieces. Yucky! Right?

"May I invite you to share in a glass of Niersteiner Eiswein?" Tad Thomas bowed me into my chair, which was far too plush for one of my relatively diminutive stature. I almost asked the waiter to find me a telephone book.

"Why not?" I liked Eiswein as well as anyone did.

"I was really surprised to find such an elaborate wine list in a simple Chicago restaurant." Tad Thomas had a knack of bowing to you respectfully every time he began to speak. "You must forgive me for the indulgence. I limit myself these days to white wines, almost always sweet white wines. I simply adore this wine. The last time I was in Europe, I made, if I may use the word, a pilgrimage to the commune at Nierstein to watch the process of producing this delicate nectar."

"Ah."

"Poor, dear Lisa always has a bottle of it chilled for me when I stop by her marvelous home in Beverly Hills."

"The white Spanish modern place?" I said knowingly.

"You've been there, too." He lifted an eyebrow—the alternative motion to bowing his head. "She could afford a much more elaborate place. It has some sentimental attachment for her and poor George. Their romance began, I believe, at the side of the swimming pool."

"How impulsive of them."

His carefully watching gray eyes flickered for a moment, and then he laughed—after he had discovered on my face a sign that I was joking.

"This is a terrible event, isn't it, Monsignor?" He banished his practiced smile, lifted his wine goblet delicately, and savored the aroma, as though he were drinking a funeral toast to Lisa. "Poor, dear Lisa. I don't know how any of us will survive without her."

"It was your Christmas special, wasn't it, before she began to appear with you?"

He replaced the wine goblet on the table with equal delicacy. "This will be the twentieth year—the longest-running Christmas special in history. The first year I was the lead singer. Then the next year Lisa was given subordinate billing. The year after that we were equals, and then"—his laugh, like everything else about him, was wry and self-deprecating—"well, after that, it was all Lisa. I must say that I was not surprised. In recent years I sometimes was made to feel that if it were not for Lisa's indulgence, I would've been banished from what, after all, I might have some right to consider my own program."

I am not very good at interpreting the direction of someone else's sexuality—and to be honest, I am skeptical of those who make instantaneous judgments about such matters. I would not have decided on the basis of his practiced and precise affectations that this short, fading, handsome man across from me, with the carefully barbered eyebrows, might be a homosexual or a bisexual. I was, however, prejudiced into judging his sexuality because of what I had heard from others. The "switch hitter" hypothesis seemed to me to be most probable. Indeed, the sadness that clung to Tad Thomas the way the humidity on Michigan Avenue clung to pedestrians was the only aspect of him that did not seem studied. I suspected that for much of his life, he, too, had not been certain about his sexuality: enough to make anyone sad!

"Entertainment is a rough business, isn't it?"

"As Lisa herself will find out eventually," he said, his lips tightening dangerously. "As, I suppose we must say, she has found out already. Poor, dear woman."

Tad Thomas's voice was described once by a critic as "Perry Como with a sinus infection." It was a perfect background for the sweet purity of Lisa's tones.

"No matter how hard you work," I continued sympathetically.

"I never knew anyone to work harder than Lisa." Tears seemed to be forming in his eyes. "And she made all of us who worked with her labor with equal diligence. It was annoying, maddening, and, if I may say so, Monsignor," —another nod of his head as if seeking permission— "terribly impressive. Even when everyone in the room felt like murdering her, one could not help but respect her perfectionism. It was unnecessary, perhaps, and certainly overdone, yet you knew you were working with an artist who, despite rather small talents, was totally dedicated to her work and her career." Another bow. "And as much as I hate to say it, utterly dedicated to herself."

"Indeed."

"Such dedication leads, does it not, inevitably to self-destruction?"

22
TAD THOMAS

You must forgive me, Monsignor, for making that leap without explaining it. I don't know who assaulted Lisa the other night. I confess that I sympathize with your police force's suspicion that it was her husband. I was present at the unfortunate incident in which he slapped her—such a crude and uncouth man.

However, it need not have been him. He was not the only person to feel enormous ambivalence about the poor woman. On the one hand, as I say, we respected her dedication and also were flattered by her kindness and consideration. On the other hand, she was impossibly demanding to work with and concerned, totally and completely, about herself. As I have hinted, such self-focus is probably essential if you're going to be a success, particularly if you possess only the very limited talents with which Lisa was endowed.

I was, of course, deeply fond of her. She won my respect, which is more than most such women would have done. At no time did she ever scheme or conspire behind anyone's back. Neither did she ever attempt to do in someone who was perceived as a threat to her. That nasty little wench Dina King, who, as you may know, is also staying at the Mayfair—which is why I proposed lunch here—would not hesitate for a moment about putting a stiletto in the back of anyone she

thought was a threat to her career. She would not think twice
about hurting Lisa, though Lisa has been astonishingly kind
to the little bitch.

She would justify her actions on the grounds that Lisa had
enjoyed her success. "Now it's my turn."

La King is a classic entertainment industry type, the ruthlessly scheming young woman who will stop at nothing to
achieve success. I mention this not to incriminate her in what
happened, because, as you know, we were with one another
when the unfortunate assault occurred, but by way of contrast.

I want to emphasize that while Lisa was single-minded,
she was not unscrupulous in the ordinary Hollywood sense
of the word. She would face you up front rather than scheme
when your back was turned.

That approach, if I may say so, Monsignor, is even more
successful than the stiletto-between-the-rib gambit. When Lisa
would say to you, all calm and gentle and wide-eyed, "I
really don't think we should sing it that way, Tad," how could
one resist her? Not only did she have all the cards, at least
after the first few programs—we would sing it her way; she
was the star—but there was such an appealing charm in the
request that one could not possibly disagree.

It was only as the years progressed that one realized that
one's name appeared in ever-smaller letters in the advertising
and Lisa's name in ever-larger letters. That is the way of it
in our industry. Lisa is beginning to grow older, too, and
there are many like Dina King, waiting in the wings to edge
her offstage. They will be less gentle with Lisa than she is
with me. Nonetheless, if you can follow what must seem a
grotesque line of reasoning, Monsignor, it would be easy to
hate Dina King should she ever become a superstar—which
in my judgment is unlikely. Her ambition is coarse, her
ruthlessness is obvious, her personality, singularly unattrac-
tive. None of these comments could be made about Lisa. It is
very hard to hate her despite the fact that she is dedicated,
absolutely and obsessively, to the pursuit of her own self-
exaltation. Oh, yes, one of the most self-obsessed persons
I've ever known in a long career in the entertainment field.

And far more effective precisely because there's no scheming, no pretense, no dissembling.

I doubt that there are many more effective mothers in the whole of Southern California. She would not sacrifice her family for all the career success in the world. Nor would she do injury to her friends. Even taking inflation into account, I will make more money on this Christmas concert than I did on the ones when I was something more than a supernumerary for her face and voice. She takes good care of you, she provides for you, she even showers you with affection, but don't, whatever you do, ever permit yourself to be in her way because, Monsignor Ryan, you will lose. Depend on it.

Should you attempt to resist Lisa's charm and loving concern, you will be dismissed as abruptly as were those directors and writers in her most recent film. The whole industry was shocked to hear that gentle, sweet Lisa had actually fired five men. I said to my friends, "The reason you are shocked is that you don't know Lisa."

I would wager she sat down with them much like a novice with an archbishop and said, "Why don't we do the scene this way," and the director said, "No, we will not do it this way," and Lisa said, "I'm afraid we will" and he said, "Well, then, you can have my resignation," and Lisa, perhaps with tears in her lovely hazel eyes, murmured something like "I'm so very sorry."

That was that. I waste no sympathy, Monsignor, on those men. They all were gainfully employed in several weeks. I merely strive to illustrate my point. I am sure she will invite all of them to dinner and serve their favorite wine, their favorite spirit, their favorite liquor, their favorite meat, perhaps even their favorite dessert. Should the film be a success, and I am informed that the preliminary reactions indicate that it will be an enormous success, Lisa will insist on giving those men all the credit they deserve, more than they deserve and, to be candid, Monsignor, more than they want. Nonetheless, the film was done her way.

Everyone will eventually know that.

Yes, that presumes that she recovers. Pardon me. . . . It would be very difficult to imagine the world without Lisa.

No, there won't be a Christmas special if she does not recover. That would be too tasteless, even for ABC. Perhaps next year or the year after. No one with any sense would even try to take the place of a deceased or injured Lisa Malone.

The stupid King person is convinced that she and I will do the program ourselves. You can see the hunger for an audience of a hundred million people in that little bitch's eyes. It won't happen.

I don't know what I will do. In point of fact, I believe I'm approaching the end of my career. I'm sixty-two, Monsignor. Would you believe that?

Well, I try to stay in shape. In any event, the Christmas special is my only major performance in the season now. Oh, occasionally a few small concerts at Las Vegas. I am, how shall I say? reasonably well situated. Perhaps I should have been more cautious in my investments, but it seems to me that life is served appropriately if one lives with something more than caution in one's mind. I've never seen much reason for investing money when it can be enjoyed. I would not say, and I hope there's no question in your mind about this, Monsignor, that I desperately needed my little stipend from the Christmas special. It would have been nice, of course, but one is prepared always, particularly in the entertainment industry, for disappointments. Her marriage? I confess I was never very fond of George. A bit too much of the Chicago Irish-Catholic macho type—I hope I don't offend you. Nor have I any reason to suppose he was particularly fond of me. He was always perfectly civil, mind you, up until the last sad incident, but not exuberant in his friendship.

It is my impression that George Quinn was equally single-minded about his own career, which brought him much less fame than Lisa's brought to her. More recently he has traveled a good deal—as you know, he was in Australia for many months before this regrettable incident at the hotel down the street. Ardors cool, Monsignor. My own feeling is that when a relationship finally ends, one should be thankful that it has endured as long as it has and accept the inevitable with gratitude and gracefulness. If Lisa and George were of that mentality, there would have been no public display. Perhaps because of their Irish Catholic background—you must enlighten me about that—they were constrained to insist they were still in love, even though love really had long since ended. In that unwise self-deception, I firmly believe, is to be found the explanation for the lamentable contretemps at Morton's.

That is not to say that they would not come together again, should Lisa recover. If they do so, however—and there were rumors that such a reconciliation was in the offing—it would be for reasons of convenience and religious commitment, rather than because passion still burns. It is in the nature of love, Monsignor, to believe it is eternal, and it is also in the nature of love to deceive itself about its transiency.

Yes, of course. Surely you would want to know what was involved in that unfortunate incident in the restaurant.

Well, how can I explain it to you?

One finally has little direct control over what one's media adviser does. Obviously one hires a media adviser with the intent of maintaining the sort of public image that is appropriate for one's talent and one's career. The person, how shall I say it? who instigated the unfortunate rumors about the nature of my relationship with Lisa was a recent addition to my team. She had, ah, perhaps more energy than sense. Undoubtedly the rumors obtained for me considerable, if quite impermanent and undeserved, attention. Lisa never mentioned them before the unfortunate incident in the restaurant. Nor did she ever discuss them afterward. Well, with one exception.

I presumed that she dismissed them as the usual sorts of stories that appear about the great and the near-great in the *National Enquirer* and other similar trash. Sadly, these rumors appeared even in the *Los Angeles Times*.

Do I have to say to you, Monsignor, that there was absolutely no truth in them?

I must, in all honesty and charity, observe that if George Quinn had not been so exhausted from that frequent commute between Los Angeles and Sydney, he would not have been stirred to such provocative jealousy. It should have been clear to him that our relationship was as bland as discharged soda water.

He apparently phoned their home, spoke with Kerry Randall, who is one of Lisa's most loyal friends, and learned where Lisa and I were dining. It was a dinner party with a coproducer—thus far undismissed—of her most recent film. When she learned that George Quinn was unlikely to be able to fly from Sydney for the dinner, she asked me to replace him—it was, if I remember correctly, the producer's birthday.

There had been one round of drinks at the most when George Quinn came storming in, exhausted from the long jet flight across the Pacific. Both his behavior and his language were intemperate. He shouted at us, pushed me rather violently, and slapped Lisa when she said to him, erroneously as I recall, "George, you're drunk!"

He demanded that she return immediately to their home. She said, with the usual mixture of sweetness and firmness, of which, as you've doubtless realized, I have become rather weary through the years, "I'll be home, George, after dinner."

When I drove her home, he had left to return to Australia.

I am quite certain that there was no previous violence in their relationship. Lisa would not have tolerated it, and, to be fair to George, he was always so overwhelmed by her that I do not think it would have entered his head. Why he should have seen in me of all people a threat to his rights of possession of that woman's body, I will never understand.

Yes, it was unfortunate that the photographer happened to be there and captured the picture. It was not a very savage blow. In fact, I believe the marks of his fingers on her cheek faded almost at once. The picture on the front page of so many of America's newspapers the next morning will not fade, not ever, I dare say. Doubtless, in whatever jail cell he now languishes, George Quinn profoundly regrets that blow. I will give him the benefit of the doubt and say that he probably regretted it an hour after the Qantas jet left LAX.

My discussion of the matter with Lisa?

It was a matter of little importance, actually. Yet, if you wish to hear of it, I suppose I must be candid about the incident.

A few days after the episode she stopped by my home, all crisp and businesslike, the attractive woman movie producer, if you will, and asked me quite candidly whether I was responsible for the rumors of a romance between the two of us. I explained, I hope with equal candor, that my media consultant had, without my knowledge or consent and also without any wisdom or common sense, in a misguided and ill-advised moment, planted that story. I told her that I had already discharged the person responsible and that I was deeply and profoundly sorry if it had caused any troubles for her. "I could issue a denial," I offered.

Her hazel eyes considered me thoughtfully, now devoid of both charm and affection. "That will only make matters worse, Tad," she said. "You should know that."

"You're right, Lisa, my dear," I said, with all the sympathy I could muster. "Would it be any help if I tried to explain matters to George?"

Her face became quite red. For a moment I thought she was going to strike me just as George had struck her. I may have actually cringed. "That will hardly be necessary, Tad," she said, struggling to contain her emotions. "I think you've done quite enough so far, thank you!"

Chastened and sad but certainly not feeling any guilt, I showed her quietly to the door.

"I'm very sorry you feel this way," I said as I opened the door and saw her red Ferrari glowing in the sunshine. "I really am."

She turned to me now, quite serene again, and said in firm, self-possessed tones, "Don't ever endanger my marriage again, Tad. If you do, it will be the end of you."

Then, heels clicking authoritatively, she walked briskly down to the car and drove away.

I will not deny, Monsignor, that I was extremely upset. Why should I endanger her marriage? I suppose that when something goes wrong in our lives, we need a scapegoat. Something had gone gravely wrong in Lisa's relationship with George Quinn. I happened to be a convenient scapegoat. Since I do have some instinct for survival, I carefully instructed all my colleagues and associates that there was to be no hint of this sort of rumor ever again. I'm sure they understood me.

We were to meet in New York at the beginning of next week to finalize the plans for the Christmas special with network executives in that city. We were to "round-table it" with them, to use the terrible jargon currently popular in the industry. Lisa phoned us and suggested that we meet in Chicago to discuss the program beforehand. Both Dina and I were, quite properly I imagine you'd agree, upset, especially because Lisa would not discuss the subject on the phone with us.

One had heard rumors last week of a reconciliation between her and George Quinn. So one became anxious about the implications of this for one's career. Especially if Quinn was still angry at me. Miss King also felt she might be the target of his wrath. So we flew to Chicago the very next day, the day on which Lisa was assaulted. If we were to have our heads lopped off, we wanted to be informed of the execution before we read about it in the papers. We feared that it was altogether possible that we were to be the sacrificial victims who would be slaughtered to celebrate the reconciliation.

Might I have so lost my patience with her, Monsignor, as to have actually struck her? All I can say is that I am not a violent man and that, moreover, I had everything to lose. There was a possibility that I was going to be severed from the body of the Christmas special, only a possibility. In the present situation, there will be no Christmas special, so I had no motivation whatsoever for harming her.

Dina? She is a fiercely hotheaded young woman, as you will discover when you see her later in the afternoon in the lounge at the Mayfair. If it were not for my restraining influence, I would not hazard any guess as to the upper limits of that young woman's viciousness. I am not sure whether the rumors that her family is connected to the Mafia are true. If they were true, I suspect that her career would have been more meteoric than it has been. Nonetheless, I think in her saner moments she realizes that her career is as closely tied to Lisa's as mine. If Lisa should fail to recover, she will be as much a has-been as I am.

When I reflect on all of these sad phenomena, Monsignor, and then look back at my own career, I am moved by two conflicting thoughts. The first is that if I had wished to achieve the heights of success that my talent might have made possible, I would have had to be at least as single-minded as Lisa. Whenever I find myself regretting this final lack of driving energy, I consider that while it has its rewards, it also has its costs. He who acts ruthlessly, or she if that be the case, will be responded to ruthlessly.

As the Bible says, Monsignor, he who takes the sword shall perish by the sword.

23
BLACKIE

The old fella was waiting for me at the cathedral rectory, his John Paul II eyes twinkling, his ageless little face glowing like a handsome leprechaun cheerfully defending his pot of gold. Ned Ryan was enjoying one of the two or three most pleasurable activities in his life—fighting a legal battle.

"You should have helped yourself to the Jameson's." I swept yesterday's mail off the coffee table and removed the Twelve Year Special Reserve—for the old fella, nothing but the best—from my cabinet.

"Thought you would have rationed it," he said with the odd cocked head, amusement that seemed to be reserved for me alone of all his offspring. "I'm sure I would've consumed too much. That Twelve Year Special Reserve is very dear, I'm told."

"In every sense of the word." I poured him what might be considered one shot, hesitated, and added to it, then deliberately hesitated again. "You have a sore arm?" The old fella demanded.

"Better that than the heavy hand," I filled the tumbler halfway up. "Will that do?"

"Nicely, thank you." He beamed merrily, proud of his monsignorial son.

I think.

"The judge wouldn't let him out," he said flatly, after sipping the precious fluid. "This stuff gets better every year, Johnny. I hope you or your friend the Cardinal has a large supply down in the basement."

"The judge said there was no reason to believe that the assailant in the hospital was the same one as in the hotel?"

"Precisely." The old fella savored the taste of the Jameson's on his lips. "Theoretically, of course, he's right; psychologically," he said with a shrug, "it's absurd, and the judge knew it. The State's attorney made it clear he had no objections to bond being set. The judge gets some newspaper headlines, and that's the whole point of the American legal system, isn't it?"

"No, Admiral Ryan, the whole point of the American judicial system is that you go in tomorrow morning on appeal and spring George Quinn."

"How can they say you're the changeling?" He flickered his eyebrows in my general direction and returned for another sip of the Twelve Year Special Reserve. "It might not even be necessary. By tomorrow afternoon I confidently expect the airlines to have straightened out their paperwork mess, and the Chicago police department to find cabin attendants who remember which plane George was on."

"The kids?"

"I was over at the hospital with your sister and Joe Murphy when they brought the kids in to see their mother. Very brave little tykes. You know the Irish, hold it all in until forty years later and then see a therapist to work out your grief. Right?"

"Right. You're convinced George is innocent?"

The old fella looked surprised. "Why, of course. Aren't you? He loved her too much to hurt her."

"The slap in the restaurant in Beverly Hills?"

"Purely symbolic." The old fella shrugged. "What have you found?"

The reader will have divined by now that my father and I speak in a certain elliptical code. We both learned it from my mother, the late Kate Collins Ryan, God be good to her, who never believed in simple, straightforward dialogue.

"Almost everybody has a motive. They all loved her, one way or another. They all hated her, too."

"Not George." The old fella glanced at his watch. "I should put in a call to Mr. Daley to see what his people have come up with. No, George didn't hate her. He may have been angry at her, but there isn't much ambivalence there."

"Envy?"

"The worst of sins, Johnny. Everybody had a motive, like you say, but this is not a *crime rationnel* but a *crime passionnel*."

"Ken Woods is a pathetic bastard."

"He was a nice kid, should have stayed away from Hollywood."

"Lisa, too?"

"You're the expert on Lisa, Johnny.... All right, just another drop. Pete Murphy is driving me."

"If I didn't think so, I wouldn't have given you the first drop. Lisa? Before all this happened, I thought I knew my one true love perfectly. Now Lisa's the biggest mystery of all."

"Oh?" He took the Twelve Year Special Reserve bottle out of my hand and poured me an extra drop or two.

"She's one of the clean of heart, the single-minded, the souls who see God because God sees their transparent motivation. That's why she has star quality, the luminosity that your sometime ensign Ken Woods talks about."

The old fella reached for a phone and punched out a number. "Ned Ryan, Mr. Daley. I want to observe for the record that when Dick was mayor of Chicago we didn't have this kind of weather. Yeah, I know. Next time." He listened impassively. "Right.... Right.... Right.... Okay, it's a pleasure to do business with you. Give my best to Mrs. Daley and to Sis, too."

Note the titles. For most people "Mr. Daley" was the late mayor and Mrs. Daley was his wife. But the old fella always called the parents by their first name and the son and daughter-in-law "Mr." and "Mrs."—quite possibly the only person in Chicago to do so. I didn't get the way I am by chance.

"Twenty-four more hours and he'll be ready to drop charges?"

"Something like that. Wouldn't it be wonderful if she's out of the coma about the same time he's out of jail? Okay, what was her motivation?"

"I don't know."

"I thought you said it was transparent?"

"Transparent, but I don't see it. Not yet."

"When you do? You'll have solved the mystery?"

For just a fraction of a second, a critical picture that was still floating in my preconscious, like driftwood in the lake after a storm, almost shaped itself. I had it for a moment and then, I didn't have it.

"Maybe."

"Mr. Daley is counting on you, too. He said to tell you that he has a witness, a United flight attendant, who is prepared to say that she saw Ken Woods coming out of the Westin just as the cops were going in."

"The State's attorney wishes to put me on his payroll?"

"Not very likely when he can obtain your services for nothing. He also says that one of the bellmen saw Frank Leonard, in his usual dinner jacket—he must sleep in it—striding manfully through the lobby about the same time."

"A strange alliance, that."

He cocked his head again. "I'd say impossible. But I'm only a lawyer. . . ."

"And a retired rear admiral like Archbishop O'Connor."

". . . Like I say, I'm only a lawyer and not the Father Brown of North Wabash Avenue."

"Indeed." I poured a wee drop into both our tumblers. "Slainte to rear admirals and cathedral rectors."

"Slainte indeed."

"They still have guards in her room." I could not bring myself to another personal inspection, not until I had a better handle on the puzzle.

"A patrol officer in her room in neurosurgery intensive

care. Just as well, if you ask me. Kerry Randall and Roderick Malone and Ken Woods are hanging around all the time."

"You have reason to suspect any of them?"

The old fella, with obvious regret, placed the Powerscourt tumbler—reserved for his use alone—on my coffee table and stood up. "No particular reason. You're the detective anyway, Johnny. I'm the lawyer. Right?"

"Right."

I helped him on with his raincoat, and he removed his familiar battered beret from the London Fog pocket. I was prejudiced, but if I were the Japanese admiral and I saw those frosty John Paul II eyes, I think I might've turned tail and run around Samar Island, too. The American bombers that finally wiped him out in the channels among the Philippine Islands would've seemed less scary.

"Envy, Johnny, pushed to its ultimate logical conclusion means murder. Fortunately, most of us are not very logical or don't have the courage of our convictions. The mixture of love and hatred that constitutes envy demands that the other be driven from the face of the earth. When you figure out who tried to kill Lisa Malone, it'll be somebody for whom her continued existence had become intolerable. Sirhan. Oswald."

"Somebody who's crazy, you mean?"

"No." We were walking down the corridor toward the staircase to the first floor. "Just somebody who is logical and has the courage of his or her convictions, somebody willing to act on the voice in the head that says, 'Lisa must die!'"

"Then the murderer will try again?"

"Until you find out who it is, Johnny. Until then."

The rains had stopped, and there was a hint of sun in the sky—not the real sun, which we would probably never see again in Chicago, but a kind of a gray glow, as though the Lord God had turned on a searchlight behind the clouds to tease us a little bit. Wabash Avenue looked like it had become a tributary of the Chicago River.

"Helen dragged me off to see *Amadeus* the other night." The old fella tapped his umbrella on the stone steps of the rectory. It was a falsehood so blatant that it required no com-

ment. My father is one of the great all-time movie lovers of
the modern world.

"Ah?"

"It was about envy. The story has Salieri killing Mozart
because God had given Mozart talent to which Salieri thought
he was entitled. But Salieri, you see, was a geek."

"You're spending too much time with your grandchildren."

"Indeed. At the end of the story, Salieri is like, totally
spaced out. And as they wheel him through the madhouse in
his wheelchair, he announces that he is the patron saint of
all the mediocrities in the world. A good point. Mediocrity
can't stand talent. It is driven, whenever it can, to destroy
genius. Is Lisa a genius?"

"I'm not sure."

"Find out." He swept down the steps, swinging his umbrella back and forth like it was 1935 again.

I waved to Pete Murphy as he drove the old fella off in
the ancient, but every year refurbished, gull-wing Mercedes.
I murmured a prayer to the Lord God for Edward "Ned"
Ryan. His health was excellent for a man in his early seventies. We would lose him eventually, but please Lord God,
not yet.

The Lord God, of course, does not normally answer such
petitions directly. In my imagination I heard my father's remark from many years ago, "After Leyte Gulf, Johnny, it's
all been gravy."

A *crime passionnel*, not a *crime rationnel*. What about that
clever little liar, that smooth-talking, wine-sipping phony, Tad
Thomas?

No media consultant plants a story like that without clearing
it with her employer. Probably she doesn't even think of it
unless he thinks of it first. Tad wanted some attention for
himself and some embarrassment for Lisa. He got both. To
his surprise, Lisa fought back. Gentle, nonviolent man, huh?
If that isn't sadism, I'm not sure what is.

There would be no point in trying to kill her unless he
knew that she was finally dropping him down the sewer in
which he belonged. Maybe he knew that already. I would

have to ask Mike Casey to see if some of his friends in New York could check it out.

Did that shifty-eyed fraud really think he fooled me with his pretense of a balanced, judicious, wisdom-filled portrait of my Lisa? Single-minded she may be, one of the clean of heart. More power to her, says I. However, she was not the delicately ruthless person he tried to sell me at lunch, even if his Niersteiner Eiswein was a marvel to imbibe.

The real Lisa was to be found in his little vignette in which she warned him off her marriage, the transparent, luminous, clean-of-heart woman who had dragged me, not protesting very loudly, to her senior prom and assaulted me with kisses and caresses in the Forest Preserve parking lot.

I punched Mike Casey's number on the phone in my first-floor office. "Mike? Blackie. I have a hunch. Get pictures, good ones, of King and Thomas. Show them to the staff that was on duty at the Westin that night. I bet they were in Lisa's room sometime in the course of the evening. Together. Let me know as soon as you can. I have to meet King for a drink in the lounge at the Mayfair at six. Thanks."

That gave me enough time to read the final chapter in George Quinn's memoir of his wife and discover why their romance, so well begun, ended up in a ridiculous public fight about Tad Thomas.

George the Bean Counter would be in deep trouble if he did not provide a good explanation.

Not perhaps with the State's attorney.

But with me.

24
GEORGE

Time destroyed our marriage.

Weariness and distance, too. But they are functions of time. There was never enough time. As the decade, and then almost a decade and a half, passed, we seemed every year to have even less time. Then the two of us noticed, almost simultaneously, that time was running out on our lives and we wanted more than we'd had so far.

Lisa and I lived in a deadly *ménage à trois* with time.

Time became a silent partner in our marriage, a secret lover that made ever more insistent demands on both of us, a black-hooded hint of death that stalked us every day and cheated us of our passion and affection.

"Reach for the stars," Lisa said to me. Why reach for the stars? Because you're in your late thirties or early forties, in a classic mid-life crisis, when you look back and say to yourself, "God, I have accomplished absolutely nothing with my life so far, nothing that has any value or merit."

I became obsessed by an idea for a computer program I called "Smoke Alarms." There are two reasons in general why a business can find itself in trouble: one is an external factor like Saudi sheikhs or Iranian ayatollahs and skyrocketing oil prices. Braniff Airlines was done in by that sort of thing, and maybe, I repeat maybe, the Penn Square Bank. The other reason is that there's something wrong with the internal functioning of a company: productivity down, bad loans up, indebtedness ratio too high, inventories declining too rapidly, deliveries falling behind.

The latter type of problems should show up on your accounting sheets, which is to say, these days, on your computer output. They'll only appear, however, if somebody who knows what the right questions are is reading the printouts. In many companies the person who should be reading the printouts doesn't know what to look for or doesn't want to see it when it's there or is afraid to tell those higher up there are troubles deep down in the numbers or deliberately hides the problems. Afterward, when the new management comes in or the FDIC takes over or Congress runs an investigation, then swarms of accountants pore through the old printout and trace the mistakes back to their origins. The barn door, in other words, is locked far too late.

It seemed to me, and I began to say so with increasing confidence, that you could build in a program that would send out warning signals—smoke alarms—early rather than late. It was actually a theory of programming more than a program. You would have to determine from industry to industry and from company to company what the critical smoke alarms should be. Once they told you where the early warnings ought to be sounded, you could build into their system— write for them the program that would sound those warnings loud and clear—when they needed to be sounded.

A simple idea, you say? Sure, like a lot of other things in the world that seem simple and elementary after you hear about them. But, it takes a long time for somebody to think of them first.

I remember the first night I told Lisa about the idea. It was a hot early spring evening, with the sweet scent of the flowering bushes lingering in the air. We were sitting at the side of our pool. The children were in bed. Lisa had tied a maroon wraparound skirt that matched her bikini around her waist and refilled my Jameson's glass and her Diet Pepsi glass. The pool lights glowed underwater, a romantic orange radiance; a light breeze slipped across the water. Easy-listening music—almost essential background for Lisa, who could hum every tune—drifted on the night air.

Not quite paradise. But close enough. So what does George the Bean Counter say?

"Can I talk about accounting instead of love for a few minutes?"

"You can talk about both, George," she chortled, "in whatever order pleases you."

She didn't understand accounting and was not, for that matter, much interested in my work. However, she was interested in me. In any case, it was not a very elaborate theoretical concept.

"Darling!" She beamed proudly. "What a marvelous idea. It may take all the fun out of the motion picture industry, but so what? And you mean no one has ever thought of it before? I'm so proud of you!" And she dashed across the patio, arranged herself elegantly on my lap, and kissed me enthusiastically.

Automatically I shoved away the skirt and started my ingenious explorations.

"It's not fair, George," she sighed, "that you know so much about accounting and all my secrets, too."

"You taught them to me." I unhooked the top of her bikini.

"No, I didn't." She cuddled closer, her salty skin pressing against my lips. "You forced them out of me, right here at the side of the pool. I was young and innocent, and you took away all my secrets before I knew what had happened."

That was the end of our smoke signal conversation.

People often wondered what we talked about, since we seemed to have so few interests in common besides sex (which we didn't discuss much). Well, we talked about one another and about our kids and about our jobs. I didn't understand motion pictures and she didn't understand accounting, but, as I said, while we were not interested in each other's work, we were interested in each other. As the first decade of our marriage wound down, we enjoyed each other's company more than that of anyone else either of us knew. Lisa was fun in bed and fun out of bed. Her quick insights into absurdity made her a natural comic—hence her success on that single trip to Vegas. I was never so tired that Lisa could not make me laugh, never so discouraged that her smile, a woman leprechaun's mixture of amusement, affection, and impishness, could not renew my hope.

"Mommy's a real flake, isn't she?" Beth, a dark, elfin West Coast version of Caitlin at Christmas in 1970, said to me

soberly after Lisa had turned her tenth birthday party into a
riot of laughing prepubescent girls by an act in which she
played a group of Beverly Hills mothers talking about their
ten-year-old daughters.

"Does it embarrass you?" I asked anxiously.

My daughter's wide hazel eyes became even wider. "Uh,
nuh. I want to grow up just like her."

Talk about identification.

The conversations and the laughter died as gradually as the
days shorten in summer, a change that is noticed only after
it has happened.

I was the first one to whom she told her ambitious plans
for *The Friendship Factor*.

"I don't know, Lisa," I said, groping as I always did, and
always unnecessarily, for the most judicious phrase, "incredibly ambitious—but what the hell, run for daylight!"

On that evening she promptly bounced into my lap again.
As I remember it, we were down at the beach house and she
was clad in panties at the most.

There is a lot about sex in this story because there was a
lot of sex in our life in those days. My wife was a fiercely
passionate woman who doted on me, for reasons that were
beyond my comprehension. I often thought that I had the sort
of sex life of which most men can only fantasize.

How could I have lost it?

I give the impression that ours was a happy and mutually
supportive partnership in those days. It was for the most part,
for at least ten years and maybe a little longer. We were still
in love with one another. We had become good friends and
pleasant companions. Our sexual couplings were not quite as
frantic as they had been immediately after we were married,
but they were as satisfying as ever; we ached for one another
whenever we were separated. We promised each other that
we would always be together on weekends. We didn't always
keep that promise, but at first we honored it more often than
not, as I wandered around the country and then the world,
giving my seminars and consulting with ever more important
corporations, and she went on location and tours to almost
as many places as I traveled.

I am one of the world's all-time champion losers in the travel game. Jet lag, motion sickness, pressurization effects, travel fatigue—you name it and I have it. My body clocks and circulatory system and inner ears were not designed to fly from Burbank to San Jose, much less across the Pacific Ocean. Lisa, on the other hand, can take half-hour catnaps almost at will and emerges from the jetway looking and feeling fresh and alert. She would meet me at the international terminal of LAX with her typical gamine enthusiasm.

"Poor George. Worn out? I promise I won't be the lively, exhausting sprite who so depresses you when you come home. I'll act like a stolid, dull hausfrau who has forgotten what horniness is."

She didn't mean it. She couldn't mean it. She knew that I would be a prickly grouch. She wanted to play it low key until my nerves and my balance centers and my internal clocks rearranged themselves. Yet even when my demeanor sent up every warning signal possible, Lisa was irrepressible.

Should we eat dinner at Morton's or at the Westwood Hotel? Why not both? Main course at one, dessert at the other. Go to Mass on Christmas at our parish or at the mission? Both, of course. Watch the Bears play the Rams or see the latest Spielberg? Why choose? We could do both if we caught the late film. Take the kids down to the beach or have one of our orgies? Do both, of course, the orgy after the kids were in bed.

"It's good for them to see the glow on my face in the morning after you've done all those terribly obscene things to me."

"Which ones this time?"

"Both, of course, George. Unless you're too tired."

I might have been, but in the spirit of the moment, I forgot about being tired.

I told myself that I had to take the bad with the good, a churlish response to a beautiful and loving and horny wife.

You've noticed by now that I am, if not exactly a creep, at least somewhat slow moving. I drive slowly, talk slowly, think slowly, make decisions slowly.

"George, for heaven's sakes, hurry up," she would sometimes snap at me impatiently. "You're as slow as molasses in January."

"And you're as fast as quicksilver," I would reply, hiding my hurt feelings. The response was guaranteed to win me a kiss and another profession of her faith that my soundness and reliability (euphemisms for pokiness) were part of what made her love me.

Occasionally I felt I had to repress the irrepressible. "Lisa, you simply cannot do a Christmas special in Britain, too. You're tired as it is. It will interfere with our family Christmas. Let them replay the American special."

Thunderclouds would gather on that lovely brow. I was breaking one of the rules. The clouds would fade a little. Maybe she was breaking a rule. "All right, George," she'd say slowly. "I suppose you're right." Then the clouds would be exorcised by sunshine. "Of course you're right. You're *always* right. I didn't want to go anyway."

I rarely drew the line. When I did, never once did she fight back.

It might have become one of her rules: you should not argue with George the Bean Counter when he's really serious.

The rules were another of our personality . . . I won't say conflicts but differences. A sluggard I might be, and an honest accountant I surely was, but I followed my gut instincts most of the time. As in my decision to exterminate canyon cougars. Rules were not permitted to interfere with what was important.

Lisa, on the other hand, had rules for all situations. No, absolutely not, she would never return to Vegas (her comedy routine was about her husband, who was an accountant who could not add—a hilariously funny, nonlibelous, alas, and deeply flattering portrait of me). No, she did not want a mink coat for Christmas. She would never wear one of those things. Yes, she had to dress for bed every night even if she hadn't dressed for the day, and she didn't care whether she was the only woman in the world who did.

A dispensation was granted when we were at the beach. Nor did she attire herself carefully each evening for me. When I wasn't home, she did the same thing, she assured me.

"Naturally, George," she sniffed, "it's more fun when you're here to enjoy."

"Why dress up just to undress?"

"Come on, beloved Bean Counter, I don't have to answer that, do I?"

Yes, all Christmas cards had to be signed personally. No, we couldn't miss Georgie Anne's concerts, even if we had to fly from New York. No, we could not think of ignoring the pastor of our parish at our annual spring party. Yes, we had to go to Barbra Streisand's fete, even though she was one of the few people whom Lisa could not stand. (She asked Meryl Streep for her autograph and told Kathleen Turner that she wished she had a quarter of that young woman's talent, a compliment that made the lovely Ms. Turner blush with gratitude.)

Absolutely not! A TV sitcom series was unthinkable. Of course, she would do an album of spirituals with Stevie Wonder. There would be no negotiation about top billing: it would be called *Stevie and Lisa Sing Black Spirituals*.

The mundane as well as the mysterious was regulated by rules. Brunch was always at the Polo Lounge, even if the real people now went to the Westwood Marquis or the Hermitage. Because of Ken Woods? Don't be silly. Because that's where Blackie had stayed. Actually he'd stayed at the Wilshire, but I didn't argue.

Another rule said no more than one album a year—*Lisa in Ireland, Lisa Sings Religious Songs, Lisa's Old-Time Favorites, Lisa's Folk Favorites* (the last her most popular album, with its heartrending version of "Shenandoah" at the top of the lists for weeks). And only the "right" kind of film, almost always a romance or a comedy now, and often a romantic comedy. (After her first Academy Award nomination, before we were married, she shied away from "serious" parts. I did not think it appropriate to ask why.)

It was unthinkable, according to her rules, that we should not meet the Pope when we were in Rome, even though Lisa was convinced that he was a chauvinist. ("He sure is cute," she bubbled after our audience. "Not as cute as you, George.") It was equally unthinkable that we would attend a White

House reception for film stars. ("We *are* Democrats, George, or have you associated with rich people so long that you've forgotten?" Note that it was assumed that we were not rich.)

We absolutely had to see the tall ships on the Bicentennial Day, even if it meant flying across the country. We had to play tennis with Chris Evert (who mopped up the court with us, of course, but adored Lisa). We went to the dedication of the Viet Nam Memorial but ignored Irish Northern Aid, even though we thought the English had no right in Ireland.

All of Lisa's rules were simply stated, as though they were self-evident theorems that did not require and did not, indeed, admit of explanation.

At first in our marriage I thought these rules were morality, then I thought they were matters of propriety, then of taste. Finally I decided that, while they shared all three qualities, they were unique. Moreover, they applied only to Lisa. If I disagreed, she put no pressure on me to comply and did not even seem upset in the rare instance when I said, for example, "I won't go to that woman's party. Regardless."

"I don't blame you, George." She pursed her lips thoughtfully. "I wouldn't go if I were you."

The rules were infinitely flexible. She did not approve of mink coats but she adored jewels, not enough to buy them for herself, mind you, but enough to burst into tears when I bought them for her. A collection of rubies—earrings, bracelet, pendant—from Van Cleef and Arpels, spread over a year of Christmas, birthday, and anniversary presents, produced flash floods of tears.

So, as a matter of fact, did a single rose brought home at the end of an ordinary day, just because I loved her.

Or two pounds of dark chocolate to eat in bed when she was in one of her bed and bon bon moods.

Lisa wept incessantly, except in times of crisis, like when we thought we were going to lose Georgia Anne to convulsions one terrible night at the beach. Then she was crisp, dry eyed, and resourceful. She suffered from nightmares that seemed real even the next day, but never wept because of them either. Despite the rules she seemed relatively free from anxieties; despite the nightmares she slept soundly, save when she woke up and wanted to make love to exorcise the demons.

She would drift off into long periods of thoughtful silence, which she would explain to me when I asked as, "Thinking, George. Is there any law against it? I *do* think sometimes, you know. I'm not just a pretty face."

"Pretty body, too."

"Oh, shut up!" She would blush, pleased at the praise.

She absorbed praise and kisses like she was a brand-new sponge.

How could someone drift away from such a fascinating, lively, beautiful, and sexy wife?

I don't know. I'm writing this memoir to try to understand.

As I say, it seems now that the reasons are mostly time and jet travel. And, I guess, my fears of her.

After my world travels began, we promised one another solemnly that we would at least spend weekends together, even if it meant a trip from London or from Sydney. While we didn't keep that promise always, we were reasonably successful in honoring it most of the time.

Lisa's sexual energy continued to astonish me. It was, I told myself, part of the intensity of her personality. Yet the faint touches of jealousy that always threatened to contaminate my attitude toward her never disappeared completely. How could a woman with such powerful sexual longing go without a man for a week or two weeks or, on occasion, even three weeks?

Stated thus baldly my fears were absurd. I do not want to attribute to jealousy the terrible and perhaps fatal crisis that arose in our relationship. If, at the end, I made a fool out of myself because of jealousy, the explanation is that weariness and disappointment and frustration and, finally, my own impotency had put our love in great jeopardy, if not destroyed it altogether.

Impotency. Physiological? Of course not. Psychological? Surely. For a long period of time? Of course not, Doctor. How do you explain it? Not enough time? Not enough time for lovemaking? Not enough time for anything. Jet fatigue. Travel exhaustion. Not enough sleep. Too much worry. A classic case, then? That's right, Doctor. Then isn't the solution obvious? Yes, of course it is. We have to take some time off, relax, talk to one another, get to know each other again. When was the last time you had a vacation together? We try to get down to the beach house for a day or two every month. That's a vacation? We're terribly busy, Doctor. Counseling, perhaps? No time for that either. You really have to make time, you know that, don't you? Yes, Doctor.

In many of the consultantships I was taking on, I became, for a few days or a couple of weeks or even several months, the de facto CEO of the corporations, mostly because the men who were technically in charge of the firms were dunderheads. The only reason this is the greatest industrial nation in the world is that the people who run the firms in other nations are even worse dunderheads than ours. I discovered that I had the makings of a first-rate CEO and that, moreover, I enjoyed the power and the responsibility that went with it. Since the supply of qualified CEOs is always substantially under the demand, I began to receive flattering offers almost every week. I didn't want U.S. Steel or General Motors, but increasingly I wanted a place of my own—I suppose like an associate pastor who has waited twenty years for a parish of his own.

No, I didn't have to go to a therapist to think these things out. I did it all by myself, after I shattered our relationship on that stupid Saturday evening among the potted plants in Morton's. When you see your hand jarring your wife's face on the front page of every paper in Australia, you have the sort of experience that makes you think things through.

One of my Aussie friends, who knew more about the entertainment industry, I guess, than I did, asked me why, if I finally wanted a place of my own, I didn't become the chief executive officer of Lisa Malone Productions. "A bit speculative, old chap," he said, as I worked my way steadily through a bottle of Jameson's. "I should have thought that it would have been an interesting challenge. Independent and intelligently administered film production company? You could hire me for it, old chap. Why didn't you give it a whirl?"

The answer was that I had never even thought of it. The

business world was the real world, not the world of film-making. Oh, sure, I knew that was a business too, but not a real business—like selling life insurance, for example.

As much as I prided myself on the fact that I didn't have a taint of male chauvinism in my character, there was a lot more of that vice hidden inside me than I realized. While I was proud of my wife's professional success, I was not prepared to admit to myself that her world was as real as mine. I had pledged at the beginning of our marriage not to meddle in that world. It never occurred to me that later on the pledge could be renegotiated, much less that I would have been any good in that world or that she would have wanted my skills and training for her own film company as she set about to remake her world.

I don't know even today, if I had applied for the job of CEO of Lisa Malone Productions, whether I would have been hired.

That's a ridiculous statement if I've ever written one. I'm tempted to blot it off my word processor screen, but I'll leave it on disk as a judgment against my own stupidity. Of course she would have hired me.

Gossip columnists all over the world said that I resented the fact that Lisa was so much more successful in her career than I was in my own. I denied that vigorously to myself and to my Aussie friends at first, and then came to understand that in some deep and twisted way the accusation was true. I was being required, subtly, unconsciously, but nonetheless effectively, to make a bigger sacrifice than she was. My male ego didn't like it one bit.

So what did I do? I got even. What else does an Irish male do when he's angry at his wife? I took the job in Australia, a six months' consultancy in which I was, for all practical purposes, in charge of one of the largest corporations on the continent, partly to demonstrate to all the world that I was at the very top of my profession, partly to escape from Lisa Malone Productions, which was getting on my nerves because I was so dubious about it, and partly, God forgive me for it, because I had begun to resent Lisa and wanted to punish her.

Australia and impotency were very effective punishment

tools. I didn't even realize until later what I was doing, until it was too late.

How did I know that Lisa Malone Productions was a mess? I knew it because, by definition, my wife, the singer and actress, a hard-working and talented woman, could hardly be expected to be a successful businessperson, too. Indeed, that was unthinkable. Match me at my own game? Ridiculous. Define a situation as competitive and it becomes competitive, even if the other person in the situation has no idea that competition is going on.

I am not absolving Lisa from her share of responsibility. As I tell the people who hire me for advice, the first thing that a good CEO does is be honest about his own mistakes. If I did not think of applying for the job as CEO of Lisa Malone Productions, neither did she think of offering it to me. If I did not try to understand sensitively and sympathetically her sudden passion for something more than just entertainment, I don't think she ever really grasped why I wanted a firm of my own. She sympathized, of course, and worried about it. Yet she was too busy to understand.

Understanding takes time, and neither of us had any time.

I guess the turning point began when Lisa's mother died. Before she flew to Connecticut for the funeral, I offered to accompany her. She said that she thought it would be better if I did not. The two women had never actually been reconciled because her mother refused to forgive Lisa for her father's death. They spoke occasionally on the telephone, exchanged Christmas cards, and Lisa stopped by the Malone house in Stamford, Connecticut, once every few years, always at her initiative. The one time I was there with Lisa, her mother acted as though she were doing us an enormous favor by saying hello to us. My existence was ignored for most of the visit. I was given the very definite impression that Roddy and his wife felt their mother was a saint for letting us into the house. Mrs. Malone was explicitly not interested in meeting our kids: "My Connecticut grandchildren," she simpered, "are more than enough for me."

When the Irish don't forgive, they *really* don't forgive.

I met Lisa at the Pierre in New York after the funeral and

found her dry eyed and sad. I listened attentively at dinner while she described the details of the funeral, the sermon, and the burial in the cemetery.

Later, in our hotel suite, I lay in bed and watched her brush her hair. The wardrobe for that evening was a black nylon gown with thin straps, white trim, and a very low-cut bodice. Lisa was, understandably, in one of her faraway moods. My body and soul filled, like a river when winter snows melt, with tenderness, affection, love, desire. I knew I could cure, temporarily at least, some of her hurt. With other women, I would probably be a very poor lover. With Lisa, I had enormous power, power that frightened me. How was it possible for a nerd like me to mean so much to such a glamorous and wonderful woman?

What did she see in me? Why had she given herself so totally to me? The same questions that I had asked at the country club Christmas dance and had been asking ever since. Without finding an answer.

Sometimes she would gaze at me with almost hypnotized adoration, like she was a groupie and I was a rock star. It didn't seem right that a wife should stare at her husband that way, particularly a husband who was not all that wonderful anyway.

I didn't argue with her about the point because I knew, after a few attempts, that she would collapse into hysterical fits of laughter. And because the physical and emotional payoff for me in being loved intensely was so great—even if it was terrifying.

"Your hair looks fine, woman," I said.

"Does it?" She put the brush down, rose from the vanity bench, and turned toward me, causing my mind to melt with desire.

"It's a lovely gown. You're not planning to wear it all night, are you?"

"I certainly won't take it off myself." She walked toward me, shy and flushed and eager.

I took her hands and pulled her down on top of me. The straps came off her shoulders with an easy brush of my lips. "Lots of kisses tonight, my love."

"Unlimited, please, darling. I need to be healed."

"Maybe we can arrange that, too." I eased her away so that my teeth could find an available nipple.

"Both." She laughed and groaned at the same time, an expression of deep pleasure and expectation of even greater pleasure. In moments like that I could hardly believe that it was George Quinn who was mastering this incredibly luscious and eager woman.

I don't know. Maybe it wasn't. I was good at it, however.

Afterward, in bed, her body pressed close against mine, her breasts firm against my chest, Lisa said some strange things which, if I had had any sense at all, would have alerted me that there were troubled years ahead.

"My mother used to say, 'You make too much of yourself, Lisa; you reach too high.' Do you think that's true, George?"

"I think your mother resented your success."

"Maybe; but it was more than that. Mom believed that her parents and grandparents had earned respectability for the family and it was her responsibility to defend it, as if it were a precious jewel that could be easily lost. When I made too much of myself or reached too high, I was threatening that gem. Do I make any sense, darling?"

"Sure. You're not feeling any regrets, are you? You really didn't make too much of yourself."

"No, I don't think that at all." She shifted her position in my arms, brushing her lips against mine in the process. "I worried all through the funeral Mass whether maybe I haven't reached high enough."

"Oh?"

"I have been playing things safe, darling. I've been content to be a pleasant little actress and singer. Now I wonder if that's enough. Maybe I should reach higher still."

"For what?"

"For the stars."

We made love again. I forgot about the conversation the next morning. I'm sure that Lisa thought about the stars during our romp in the bedroom at the Pierre. She had the capacity to be lovingly attentive to me and enjoy lovemaking enormously and work out complex problems in her head at the same time.

As we were riding out to Kennedy Airport in the limousine, she said softly, "I want to try my hand at a great role. I even think I may want to be a producer and a director. Is that wrong, George?"

"More power to you, if that's what you want, Lisa," I said, with more fervor than I felt. You see, I didn't think she could do it, and she might get hurt in the process of trying. Fortunately, I told myself, it's one more enthusiasm will soon pass away.

I had no idea that her reaching for the stars would put our marriage in jeopardy.

Well, there's not much more to tell. We drifted apart. We hardly noticed that we were drifting. We ran out of time. We took on even more commitments. Our ambitions grew more passionate, and our love turned cold. What happened at the end was entirely my fault. I phoned from Sydney and said that I couldn't possibly make it the coming weekend. I would try for the following weekend, perhaps would stay several days into the next week. She mentioned the birthday party for her coproducer, a man whom I'd never even met. I don't know whether she'd told me about it before or not, but I hadn't remembered. I said I was sorry but it was too late now. She said she understood. A lifeless, disinterested conversation, and all the while I was aching with longing for her.

So the next morning I said to hell with it, went out to the airport, found an empty seat on a Qantas 747, and flew to Los Angeles. I was so exhausted and sick when I stumbled through customs at LAX that I could hardly walk a straight line.

I know that I do dumb things when I suffer from travel fatigue. I should have gone home to bed. Yet I was as surprised as anyone when my jealousy exploded at the restaurant, in the midst of potted plants, California nouvelle cuisine, and hordes of gay waiters in pink and beige. I didn't think I was jealous, and especially not of Tad Thomas, despite the nonsense in the newspapers. That shows you how self-aware I was.

I was on the same jet when it returned to Sydney a couple of hours later. We had hardly taken off before I realized what a fool I was. Then the harm had been done. I don't even know whether Lisa wants to be reconciled. We have spoken a couple of times on the phone the last few months. About the children. She seemed cold and unfriendly, and I can't blame her.

I was cold and unfriendly, too.

One of the problems, you see, with never learning how to quarrel with the woman you love is that you never learn how to be reconciled with her.

25

BLACKIE

The classic discretion of the lobby of the Mayfair Regént, with its Chinese prints, oak panels, marble fireplace, and arched window view of Lake Michigan, was not an appropriate setting for Dina King. Both the lobby and Ms. King radiated an aura of expensiveness, the former from an art deco coffee table book, the latter from a portrait in the latest issue of *Rolling Stone*.

Her fingers curled around a half-finished gin and tonic, Ms. King was tapping her foot impatiently against the vast Persian carpet to indicate that my ten-minute tardiness was unacceptable. One might feel impatience in the stately precincts of the Mayfair Regent, but it was definitely and obviously déclassé to manifest it so blatantly. I was prepared to dislike her, and my preparations were not in vain.

She reminded me of the kind of person you would see across the counter at the shooting gallery in a small-time

carnival. Thin, save for her oversized chest, sexy perhaps but
certainly not pretty, much less beautiful, silver hair in one of
those wild perms, and a thin, petulant face whose natural
sulk was created by a jaw that seemed too heavy for the rest
of her face to sustain—and the whole effect reinforced by a
perpetually sullen personality. Her makeup was skillful but
heavy. Her eyes stared dangerously under long artificial lashes.
The stack of partially smoked cigarettes in the ashtray by her
left hand was smeared with blood-red lipstick. When she
laughed, which was not often, it was with a snide cackle,
and her voice, which had a certain sharp prettiness to it,
reminded me of a ruler screeching against a blackboard.

"I thought you'd never come," she began the conversation,
with a glance at her watch. "I really don't have much time.
Would you care to join me in a gin and tonic?" With a
practiced hand she lit another cigarette and inhaled deeply.

I declined and ordered Perrier water instead. I would need
every bit of my wits about me for the rest of the day, and I
had yet to recover from the Twelve Year Special Reserve
(which is now almost twenty years old, in case you didn't
realize it) that I had sipped with the old fella.

I was distracted from her version of the story of Lisa Malone at first, because I was still dismayed by the final chapter
in George Quinn's memoir. Their marriage had tumbled into
a serious crisis, one aggravated, doubtless, by Lisa's status
as a celebrity, but it was a manageable crisis. They had de-
spaired all too easily and quickly. The dramatic confrontation
in the restaurant was not a happy event, and made their path
to reconciliation more difficult, yet it was certainly not an
impossible pilgrimage. George was too ashamed of himself
to take the initiative. Lisa, I suspect, was too preoccupied
with *The Friendship Factor* to pay any heed to the conflict
with her husband. I could imagine her saying, "After the
editing is over, I'll take off a week, fly down to Australia,
and win George back, just like I won him the first time. No
big deal."

Well, perhaps she wouldn't add the "no big deal," and
maybe she wouldn't even think those words explicitly. Still,
I was willing to bet that she thought something pretty much

along those lines; women, doubtless as a cultural response to their disadvantaged position, long ago developed a certain laid-back patronizing attitude toward their men's emotional crises. "Conceited vulnerability," was how one wise matron had dismissed men's worries.

God made women mothers, my sister Mary Kate the Shrink contends, more for their menfolk than for their children. Children grow up, she says; menfolk never do. Men hurt. Sometimes they break. Lisa deserved a good deal more of the responsibility for the contretemps with her husband than George was prepared to assign her, especially for permitting the silence between the two of them after their public quarrel to endure so long and then turn icy.

George was slow to respond to the crisis because it was in George's character to be slow. It was the flip side of the solid tenacity and determination that Lisa loved so much. She was the sprite, not George. Too busy with her film to be a sprite right now?

Poor, foolish woman.

Their love was in remission. So what? It didn't have to stay in remission. Your average rectory presides over several reconciliations per week to which there are a lot more serious obstacles than there were in this marital tiff.

Now it might be too late. George might have to go through the rest of his life with a powerful but finally unreconciled love. I shivered at what an Irish guilt complex would do with such a memory.

I mentally cursed the Roman Church for the way they/we failed our married laity. George and Lisa were the green wood—a well-balanced, compatible couple who genuinely enjoyed one another's company. Lisa was neither prudish nor frigid. George was neither macho nor timid. They knew how to take time off from the demands of life to rekindle their passion and love, to fall in love again. Neither had wandering eyes. They had demonstrated the capability of talking on occasion about the problems of the marriage. They were not candidates for family therapy, in the ordinary sense of that word, in any event.

Yet with all their resources, they had drifted apart at a

critical turning point in their life cycle—not an unusual nor incurable phenomenon. And what did their Church offer them in the way of warnings and skills and motivations and insights about the asceticism required to cope with this routine event in their marital history?

It warned them against birth control, infidelity, and unbridled passion. Nothing more. Granted the wisdom of such warnings, were they all we had to say to the Georges and Lisas of the world?

I thought not. But it was all we were saying. Someday Catholics of the future would denounce us for our insensitivity and cruelty on the subject of marital sex the same way we denounce the Inquisitions and the Crusades.

I dismissed George and Lisa from my mind temporarily and tried to concentrate on the noisy chirpings of Dina King. If Sister Winifred was an outraged, screeching crow, La Dina was an angry, squeaking canary of the sort whom one would cheerfully strangle and throw down the incinerator chute. I found myself hoping that she was the one who had brutalized Lisa.

26
DINA KING

I didn't want to come to Chicago. It was that dried up old faggot Tad Thomas who came up with the idea. I said to him, "Look, dummy is not going to toss us off the program. Her sweet little Lisa image has already been tarnished by that restaurant fight and all the people she's fired from her production. She is shrewd enough to know she can't take another black mark. Why get all shook up because she wants to talk to us beforehand? Tell her we'll meet her for coffee in New

York an hour before we round-table it with the network people."

Tad doesn't have the balls to call her bluff. He falls apart if he has to sit in his hot tub over in Westwood and stew and bite his fingernails waiting for Lady Bountiful to say that she's definitely going to need him one more year.

Shit. They're both has-beens, except that maybe Tad Thomas is a never-was. Lisa's over the hill, too. What is she?—thirty-eight, thirty-nine, something like that. People are tired of her, nice tits or not. She'll be finished in another year or two. I don't see getting into a fight with her. Her voice was never all that much hot shit. I got all the time in the world. Neither of those two have much time left. So, what the fuck, I figure I can wait.

But no, Tad insists. We have to face Lisa down in Chicago and straighten things out. Besides, he thinks we both can get an extra featured number in this year's program. "Lisa's vulnerable," he says to me, those little faggot eyes of his glittering at the sight of gold. "Her tiff with George at Morton's didn't help her one bit. She has to be extra gracious to me this year if she wants to polish up her image. I'm going to insist that she be extra gracious to you."

That's a lot of horseshit. Thomas is lucky if he has any clout for himself, much less me. Besides, this new flick of Lisa's will create so much attention that everybody is going to forget poor Georgie-Porgie popping her in the chops in the restaurant. All anyone will remember is that she has good boobs for an old woman. What the hell, she could even play the part of Sweet Little Lisa, the Sweet Little Martyr.

My parents? Sure they're still alive. They're as bad as Lisa, trying to run my life. They're proud of me, they tell me, but why can't I be more like Lisa? Can you imagine that? My own parents want me to be like her? They tell me I should clean up my language and talk like her. What kind of a family is that? When I go home after the Christmas special, they complain that I don't look like her or dress like her or sing like her.

I hate them.

A Christmas special next year? Who the fuck knows? Well,

now it doesn't look like Lisa's going to be around next year, does it? Even before that, this flick is a big success if it wins a couple of Academy Awards. Shit, Lisa can sing all night on ABC and nobody'll complain, and she'll need us even less than she'll need somebody to brush makeup off her dress. On the other hand, by next year she could be washed up. Either way it doesn't make a goddamn bit of difference to me. It's my career that's still ahead of me.

Yeah, I hear the flick is pretty good. Well, I'm glad she finally has learned how to act because she sure as hell can't sing worth a shit. I mean, you know, it's a nice voice, huh, I mean sweet and pretty and that sort of thing and okay, people like it and she makes a bundle, so fine—more power to her, says I. She's made her bundle. Some one of these days it's going to be time for her to get out of the way and make room so that somebody that's younger than her and has a hell of a lot more talent than she does can also make a bundle.

Yeah, a bundle of bread. That's the name of the game. Lisa's in it, she says, because of professional standards and because it's God's will, and that kinda shit. I don't believe it for a minute. She's in it for the same reason that we're all in it—bread. What else?

At first I thought it was my big break, getting hooked up to her. It hasn't been bad. I'm taking in a lot more cash than I did with that fuckin' rock group. Lisa heard the record somewhere. Can you imagine an old broad like that listening to punk? She kinda liked my voice. The old bag that used to sing with her at Christmas stormed out in a rage when Lisa insisted on a ninth time around rehearsing "O Holy Night." Yeah, that's her big number, I don't know why. Anyway, this old bitch walked out, and they didn't have anybody to sing with her. So somehow Lisa remembers my voice from the record, tells her people to hunt me down and the next day, whaddaya know, I'm on stage with her. Real Cinderella shit, huh?

Well, I don't mind it, ya know. It's a lot more bread than I've been earning before, and while it's not exactly my kind of music, I figure that she's right, it fits my voice a lot better than the punk rock shit that I've been singing. So I don't have to listen to myself, so why the fuck not become Lisa Malone's background music?

Yeah, sure she's generous. She pays plenty. More than she has to. That's part of the sweet, generous Lisa bit: it's image, ya know, all image. When you get into that kind of shit, you can't get out of it. After a while you don't know your ass from a hole in the ground—you confuse who you are with what your image is. Shit, Lisa hasn't had an unselfconscious thought since she was my age. I piss on all that stuff. No way I'm going to work on the sweet little Dina public image. People will buy my records and listen to me because they like the shit I sing and not because I'm some kind of plaster statue saint. Ya understand?

Besides, she should pay me a lot of money for putting up with the fucking big sister advice she gives me. Hey, who is she to tell me about what life means? She fucked up her marriage, didn't she? Where I come from, any guy that hits his wife in public needs to be straightened out, and let me tell ya, I know some people who know some people who could straighten out the dumb bastard.

Not that George is all that bad a guy. Kinda sexy in a laid-back, dirty sort of way. Yeah, a complete nerd, even with the pocket protector for all his pencils and pens. But, ya know, not bad-lookin' and probably real good in bed. Yeah, sure, I gave him the eye, and I can tell he's interested, but what the fuck, I still depend on Her Nibs for my bread, so I'm not gonna mess around with her Georgie-Porgie. Besides, he's gone most of the time.

So, here we are in Chicago, waiting for our big confrontation with Lisa, and what happens? She gets herself pushed around again, this time kinda bad. So they think that we might've done it. I don't know about Tad Thomas, he's crazy enough to do anything, but I'm sure as hell not gonna do her in. She's my bread, man. If anything happens to Lisa, I go back to hangin' around with those piss-drunk punk rockers. Yeah, it's a lot freer life, maybe. When you're workin' for Lisa you gotta be real careful when you sniff your coke because she sure is uptight on the drug business.

It's just the opposite with my punk friends: if you're not on coke, they don't want you around. So I kinda miss 'em, but they don't have much bread to give me, and Lady Bountiful has a lot. So I do my coke sniffin' on the side and hang around with her. If she cashes in, then I'm nobody. I never quite thought of it that way before because, while she's old, look, man, I figure she's not that old. If I knew somethin' like this was gonna happen, I woulda leaned on her last year, maybe, to build me up a bit in the program, so if anything happens to her maybe they'd think about goin' with me this year or next year. But right now? I got no chance at all, I'm not worth shit.

So why the hell would I push her around?

Okay, so you know what happened in high school. Look, man, it wasn't my fault, see? This stuck-up bitch was really givin' me a hard time. I warned her off. I go: "Hey, nigger bitch, stop fuckin' me over," and she doesn't pay any attention. So one day I lose my temper and scratch her up a little bit. So I get thrown out of high school. Shit, I didn't like the school anyway. Stuck-up bitches and bull dike nuns. I'm glad to be outta there. All right, I've got a temper. What's wrong with that? It's a lot better than tying everything up inside yourself, the way Lady Bountiful does. Let it all hang out, I say. Get it out in the open and deal with it. It's better to be a savage than a wimp.

There were times when I would've liked to scratch Lisa's eyes out, too. Like every day. So goddamn much piety. Shit, you're not in the business we're in unless you're a whore at heart. I'm sure she didn't get where she is without screwin' half the kike executives in the industry. So what? That doesn't bother me, but I can't put up with the fuckin' piety.

And voice lessons, can you believe it? Voice lessons for me? I'm not gonna be no fuckin' operatic diva. I'm good, I'm better'n she is, and I'm about as good as I'm going to be. Why work your ass off to get a little better? Lady Bountiful says just about every cliché in the book, except maybe "What's worth doing at all is worth doing well." Fuck, what's worth doing is what you have to do to earn the bread and nothing more.

Shit, she's paying the freight, so if I want my bread, I gotta go off to the fuckin' freak that teaches voice lessons and learn how to breathe deeply while he's lookin' down my tits and search for the real high notes that don't make any difference anyway. It's not enough that I go to the sawed-off little bastard, she has to come by every coupla weeks, sway her sweet little boobs at the freak, and listen to me like I'm her fuckin' daughter or something.

The kids? I don't even notice them. I don't go for kids. They're harmless little brats anyway. I leave them alone and they leave me alone.

Don't get me wrong though—hey, you want another gin and tonic, it's on Lisa Malone Productions, so why not? Oh, that's right, you were drinkin' Perrier. Okay. Well, where was I? Oh, yeah.

Like I say, I don't fool myself none about Lisa. She is what she is. She's had her run, and it's time for her to step aside and let me have mine. Like I'm entitled to it. Shit, I don't hate the fuckin' little bitch. I just can't stand her. But I'm not gonna beat up on her. Hey, man, she's my meal ticket, my breadbasket. If she cashes in, I don't know what happens to me. I suppose poor Georgie-Porgie comes back and takes over alla Lisa's bread. While he thinks I'm cute and sexy, that kinda shit, hey, man, there's no way Georgie's not gonna throw me off the side of the ship with all the other rats that're deserting it.

So I hope she don't die, not this year anyway. That's what I tell the fuzz when they come to ask their polite little questions. I mean, I don't give 'em any shit like Lisa's my second mother or she's the one that gave me my break in show business, that sorta shit isn't worth diddley. I give it to 'em straight on. I go, "Fuzz, that fuckin' bitch was my breadbasket. There's no way I'm gonna beat up on her."

Yeah, the fuzz are impressed. Because they know I'm telling the truth. Still, it looks bad, and it wouldn't even look bad if that wimpy little queen Tad Thomas hadn't dragged me into this fuckin' stupid scene. I don't need it. Believe me, I don't need it.

So, I don't know, I tell myself, "Hey, Dina kid, you should

get your ass over to the hospital and pretend to stand sympathetically at her bedside. That way people will think you
really care about her, insteada figgerin' that maybe you went
after her like you did after that stupid bitch in high school."
I haven't been over there yet. I don't like to hang around
dead people.

27
BLACKIE

I was dragged away from the rich delights of Ms.
King's vocabulary to take a phone call from Mike Casey. She
had been on a roll of abusive language, as out of control as
a pilot in a plane whose hydraulic systems have failed. She
was a prisoner of her own tough little bitch mask, just as
Sister Winnie was a prisoner of her revolutionary rhetoric.

Mike provided the answer I had expected. Trying not to
look too much like the cat who had ingested the canary, I
returned to Ms. King's table, noting that the pollution from
her cigarettes had banished the fresh, lemony smell of the
Mayfair Regent's lobby. Surely when she left, a black-tied
employee would rush about with a deodorizer.

Poor Dina King. When she talked about her family, there
were tears forming in eyes softened with memories. She may
have hated them. She also loved them and wanted from them
the approval she would never get. The "tough broad" act that
she so carefully cultivated was a mask, a persona to protect
her from pain. She didn't quite believe it yet. In a few years
the persona and the personality would be the same.

No wonder she hated Lisa—the good little second grader
to whom all the naughty little second graders were compared.

"Geez, I'm sorry for all the bad language I used, Father,"
she said with a shy smile, one that was almost appealing.

"My mother would die if she knew I was talking that way with a priest." Then the mask fell back into place. "My mother doesn't know the world has changed since she was a kid in the early sixties."

"If I understand you correctly, Ms. King," I said as I seated myself once more at the table and folded my hands like the polite and formal cleric I sometimes try to be with foul-mouthed women, "you're saying that you came to Chicago at Mr. Thomas's instigation to make certain that you and he would have a part in the *Lisa!* special at Christmastime. Is that correct?"

"Yeah, that's what I been saying." She lit a new cigarette from the butt of her old one.

"You were to see Ms. Malone the morning after she was assaulted?"

"Yeah, I think we were supposed to have breakfast with her. Isn't that a crock of shit? Business at breakfast. What the fuck, I'm not even thinking straight until eleven o'clock in the morning, and that's LA time."

"You and Mr. Thomas were out walking . . . let me see" —I removed the chart from my jacket pocket and studied it carefully— "toward the lake, I believe, on Delaware, walking right by the Westin Hotel at the time the police assume the assault on Ms. Malone was taking place."

"What can I tell ya? Sure, we were out enjoying the Chicago fog. Even worse here than in LA. The scene in this burg is really a piss-off." She blew out a cloud of cigarette smoke. "I was going bonkers sitting in my room in this creep-show hotel, so I called Tad on the phone and said, 'Get me the fuck out of this place.' So we go for a walk."

"You did not, of course, stop in to visit Ms. Malone during your walk?"

"No way." Her eyes darted dangerously. "Nobody's going to pin that shit on me."

"You're absolutely certain."

"Yeah, sure I'm absolutely certain. I oughta know what I was doing that night, shouldn't I? Besides, ask Tad Thomas. He'll tell you the same thing."

"Then how do you explain the fact that the Chicago police

have found staff members at the Westin Hotel who distinctly remember you and Mr. Thomas going to Ms. Malone's room sometime between eight and nine o'clock on the night of the assault?"

Her shrewd Sicilian mouth tightened in a thin line, and her black eyes hardened fiercely. Dina was trying to make up her mind whether I was bluffing. A crafty animal expression came over her face. She snubbed out the mostly unsmoked cigarette and reached for the pack. It was empty.

"I told the fucking bastard to level with the fuzz. 'No way the fuzz aren't going to get around to showing our pictures to that little twerp at the registration desk who wouldn't tell us her room number but called up to see if she would talk to us.' He goes, 'The young man sees so many people every day, he won't remember us.'"

"Indeed."

"Yeah." A hood descended over her eyes as she considered the remnants of her gin and tonic. "Yeah. What the fuck, I may as well tell you the whole truth. It was a bad scene up there. The faggot boy, you see, couldn't stand the suspense, so he has to go over and check on the dragon in her den. Well, dragon lady, I suppose. Anyway, Lisa's in a robe, getting ready to take a shower, and looks all dragged out. She doesn't tell us that Georgie-Porgie's coming back, but you can tell by looking at her face that she wants to be left alone. So the faggot goes, 'We really have to know about the special, Lisa. If Ms. King and I are not going to appear or be given the proper billing, then we should withdraw now in order not to lose other potential bookings.'

"How the fuck do you like that? Other potential bookings? That shithead hasn't had another potential booking in five years.

"Anyway, Lisa goes that no way is she going to drop us." Her fingers were twisting the empty cigarette package into tatters. "What she has in mind is even worse. She wants the fucking kids to sing with her. Yeah, the two little girls. Shit, they don't even have tits yet. Well, they didn't the last time I saw them anyway. They're supposed to do 'O Holy Night' with her and, can you believe it? they're going to get equal billing with us. Yeah, after us, but with names in the same letters. Can you see it? All that family shit at Christmastime and everybody farting around over how cute Lisa's daughters are. Who the hell is going to notice us!"

"So you had an altercation with Ms. Malone?"

"Me? Fuck, no. I told you she was my breadbasket, didn't I? No, I just sat there and steamed. I told myself I'd get even someday but I didn't want to be walking down the streets of LA next week looking for a job, so I just sat there and listened while pisshead ranted and raved and foamed at the mouth. Yeah, literally. Poor little faggot foamed at the mouth and made all kinds of wild threats about dire consequences, called her an 'ungrateful little whore,' which I thought was pretty funny, coming from a cocksucker like him. Man, it was a great big laugh, but I wasn't sitting there laughing."

"How did Ms. Malone react to his anger?"

"You know." She shrugged listlessly and discarded into the soiled ashtray the shreds of her cigarette package. "The sainted Lisa bit, patient, forbearing, gentle. Lady Bountiful being tolerant of one of her crazy serfs. How else does Lisa react? After a while though, I could tell she was getting tired of all his shit. Anyway, she goes, 'I think that will do for the evening, Tad. We're all tired. None of us is in any condition to try to find a solution to this problem. Why don't you go back to your hotel? Where are you staying? The Mayfair? Why don't you go back there, have yourself a glass of your favorite Napoleon Courvoisier, and get a good night's sleep? I'm sure tomorrow morning this problem won't look nearly so bad.'

"Well, the faggot wants to keep the argument going. I say, 'No way. If Lady Bountiful wants us to go home and sleep it off, we'll go home and sleep it off.' So I practically have to drag him out of the hotel room. But we leave."

"About what time?"

"Uh . . ." She held her hands out toward me, a streetwise person's classic protestation of innocence. "What can I tell ya? Nine-twenty, maybe even nine-thirty. I don't know. Shit, we might have been riding down the elevator when the other guy was riding up."

"And the two of you then returned to the Mayfair."

"We walked back, and I went up to my room. Taddy boy dragged his lard ass into the bar. Probably looking for some young stuff, I tell myself, but I don't know what he did after he left me."

"He might have walked back to the Westin then?"

"You better believe it. He was furious enough that night to do almost anything to her. He's a fuckup, always has been. That's why he's never made it big in the industry. Always fucking up. Why the hell would you push a woman around when there's witnesses who sent you up to her room an hour before? That's the kind of fuckup that Taddy boy is. Yeah, if you ask me, I wouldn't be at all surprised if he went back there and beat the shit out of her. You know how faggots hate women, and goddamnit, he hated her, clumsy old asshole."

"Do I understand you correctly, Ms. King? Are you suggesting that Tad Thomas is the one who assaulted Ms. Malone?"

"Naw." Her face looked like that of a fox being pursued by hounds. "Naw, I didn't say that at all. What I said was, I wouldn't be surprised that he did it. I was his alibi. I'll be goddamned if I'll alibi anymore for that fuckup."

Then she broke down and began to weep again. "Will you call my parents, Father, and tell them I'm all right? They won't believe me. Please! They think I'm shit, but they will still worry."

It sounded like an obvious trick, but when I did call her parents, it developed that they did indeed think she was shit—not their word—and they were indeed worried. If her tears were fake and her solicitude about her mother and father a ploy, they were nonetheless very clever tactics.

She had offered me a solution to the crime on a silver platter. But it was not a satisfying solution to a puzzle—a nasty young woman (regardless of her concern for her mother and father) caught in the prison of her own pretense at toughness, snidely implying that a man who had been her ally until a few moments ago might have been the killer.

She could feel pain at how far she had drifted from her parents, but none for either Lisa or Tad Thomas.

Could she not easily be the kind of sociopath who, in a fit of temper, had determined to rid herself of the only obstacle to a successful career? There was a strain of viciousness in Dina King's personality that seemed to fit the killer perfectly.

We had to keep a close watch on her. If Dina King was the would-be killer, she would surely try to strike again.

28

BLACKIE

After my usual simple, light supper of steak, mashed potatoes, carrots, and zucchini, preceded by scotch broth and followed by two helpings of raspberry pie à la mode, my staff tried to provide an occasion for relaxation by ganging up on me in a conversation about the Chicago Bears. It was a virtuous if vain enterprise on their part. After routing them completely with my superior knowledge of football, past and present, I retired to the musty serenity of my room to consider the mystery again.

I liked the King/Thomas duo as suspects in the assault on Lisa. But, on the other hand, I didn't like them at all. There were too many pieces missing in the puzzle. Too many parts of Lisa's life and personality that I didn't understand. Too many half-formed images tripping around in the back rooms of my memory. I could count on the Chicago police to check every detail of the perambulations of Dina King and Tad Thomas a couple of nights ago. I could also expect those two con artists to turn savagely on one another. Such proceedings would doubtless facilitate the release of George the Bean Counter and his reunion with his traumatized kids. That was all to the good. I wasn't sure that it would give us our would-be killer.

My problem was that I couldn't, at the moment, see either

King or Thomas as the brilliantly resourceful improviser that the assailant seemed to be. Lisa's attacker was vicious and cruel and reckless. Also quick and ingenious in time of crisis. I assumed that patrol officers at the hospital would be vigilant. The killer was determined, and perhaps patient enough to wait until the police guard was relaxed or withdrawn. I had to assume that Lisa's life was in danger, despite the guards. The killer might strike again. Especially if there were hints that Lisa was recovering.

I studied my charts yet one more time, listing the motivations of each of the possible suspects and their physical locations at the time of the killing. Almost anybody could have done it, and almost everybody had some reason to do it. *Crime passionnel*, as the old fella had suggested? Lisa had surrounded herself with people who could be called passionate, even though their passions were sometimes shallow and kinky. Almost everyone might have done it.

I thought of the Jameson's bottle and virtuously declined my own invitation. I still had ahead of me the unpleasant task of facing Francis A. (for Assisi) Leonard.

So I glanced at the day's newspapers. Rick Sutcliffe, it was said, would win the Cy Young Award. Jim McMahon's throwing hand no longer needed injections before he played. Jerry Faust might or might not be replaced as the coach of Notre Dame. Mondale and Reagan were busy preparing for Sunday night's debate. Bill Murray was trying to blot out our memory of Tyrone Power in *The Razor's Edge*. The Bishop of New York continued to make a fool out of himself.

So what else is new?

Mike Casey phoned to say that the police were questioning, "informally," King and Thomas, and that they had admitted their visit to Lisa, and that they were trying to implicate one another in the crime. "Nasty people, Blackwood," said my cousin. "What was your friend Lisa doing with people like that around her?"

"Mistaken generosity, I suppose," I replied, realizing that this was yet another aspect of the mystery of Lisa that I did not understand.

"Either one of them could have done it, but we need more

evidence that one or the other or both of them did do it before we can make an arrest," Mike observed tersely. "I can't see either one of them donning nun's garb and sneaking into the hospital, however."

"Who can you see doing it?"

I went back to my newspapers but didn't read much. That picture in my brain, which cried out to be finished, teased and tantalized, taunted and tempted me, but it continued to escape my grasp like a madcap little boy running from his mother on the beach.

The receptionist phoned my room to announce that Mr. Francis Leonard was at the door to see me. I told her I would be down, thought about it for a second, and then said no, ask Mr. Leonard to come to my room.

He might be at a little more of a psychological disadvantage sitting across my coffee table with a drink in his hand. It would be no mean trick, however, to obtain any kind of psychological advantage over Francis A. Leonard.

He is the kind of Irish Catholic that I despise.

As Ms. Dina King would have put it, in her colorful and pungent if unimaginative vocabulary, Frank Leonard is shit.

29

BLACKIE

"Well, Monsignor." Frank Leonard's hands were placed casually in the pockets of his formal dinner jacket, a jaunty male model posing alongside a woman in the most fashionable evening dress, for a picture in *Vogue* magazine. Or maybe a Dewar's ad. "You live quite simply for a man of your importance."

There was no woman with him, but Frank Leonard had such a knack of looking as though he were in a fashion magazine photograph at almost all times that you found your-self looking for the beautiful woman who ought to be standing next to him.

He was a few years older than Lisa and I and, like us, a graduate of St. Praxides, two years ahead of my sister Eileen Kane. He was tall, almost unbelievably handsome, with finely chiseled, ruddy face and dark red hair turning silver at the edges—carefully crafted with a razor cut, one suspected, twice a week—broad-shouldered, slim-hipped, flat-bellied, athletic. Crisp of voice and manner. Incisive in gestures and movements, with twinkling blue eyes that radiated sincerity, Frank Leonard was the kind of bank vice-president to whom you would cheerfully entrust your life savings.

Unless you were extremely fortunate, you might never see them again.

"The pleasures of the monks are few and simple," I said. "Might I offer you a wee drop?"

"My normal drink is J and B and water." He smiled briefly, revealing twin rows of neatly constructed glowing teeth—probably the best reconstructionist in the city had worked on them; no Irishman has ever been born with teeth that perfect.

"Well, this rectory has a reputation of giving every man his drink, if not necessarily his due."

"I remember the story about Cardinal Kroll demanding a twenty-year-old bourbon and getting it." His hands remained in his jacket pocket, jaunty pose prolonged just a bit too much.

"Does anything go on in this city, Frank, that you don't know about?" I poured the Scotch into a Waterford tumbler of the second grade—not the Powerscourt, which I reserve for Sean Cronin and the old fella.

"I try to keep informed." He moved his lips in a pattern that said, "Really, Blackwood, knowing gossip about what goes on in the cathedral rectory is no great achievement for a man of my importance."

I don't hold with Scotch. As you've probably guessed, I think it a vulgar drink. Nonetheless, it was suitable for a man like Frank Leonard, and I was personally delighted that my duties as a host did not constrain me to waste any of my precious Jameson's on him.

As I noted, Francis A. Leonard (the A. for Assisi) could conveniently be described as shit. Not a shit, but shit.

Or, if you prefer, a scumbag.

You must understand that many Chicago banks have a senior vice-president whose principal function is to be the bank's liaison with the Outfit. The Mob. The Syndicate. Organized Crime. The Mafia.

Choose your own name.

Even the most respectable and honest and upright and staid and staunch of the WASP banks can be tempted by one thing. Money. The Outfit has lots of it. Thus it is necessary for someone in the bank administration to become a specialist in the intricate task of laundering the Outfit's money. He must keep one step ahead of the various pursuing federal agencies, developing ever new leaks in the dike as the Feds plug up the old ones. It is an interesting task, and a rewarding one, so long as you limit yourself to a strictly financial relationship with the West Side (as we Chicagoans call the Mob in our more euphemistic moments—"your friends on the West Side" is a most discreet reference to cold-blooded killers).

The president, the chairman of the board, the trustees prefer not to know either the quantity or the methods by which Mob money flows into and out of the bank. They presume that it will be done with sufficient cleverness that should the government investigators, rarely as clever as either Mob or bank executives, be able to trace such flows, the bank will not be implicated in any indictments that may be handed up. The bank takes for granted, as a matter of course, that there will be nothing illegal in its own activities. Nothing, that is, which can be pinned on it. Or, in matters of last resort, it assumes that the most responsible figures in the bank can find a convenient scapegoat if proof is discovered that there were not only improprieties and immoralities, but also illegalities in such exchanges of funds with pimps, panderers, thieves, loansharks, drug pushers, and killers.

Thus it is necessary that the senior vice-president in charge of "our friends on the West Side" maintain all the appearances of probity. If, beneath these appearances, he is troubled very little by conscience, so much the better. Indeed, if he has certain psychopathic propensities, they might make him admirably qualified to be a major bank's ambassador extraordinary and plenipotentiary to the crime syndicate. Woe unto him, however, if he finds the Mob and its amusements attractive. Then he will slip gradually into the highly dangerous role of being not an ambassador to the West Side but an ambassador from the West Side.

His chances of ending up in the trunk of a stolen car then increase dramatically.

Francis A. (for Assisi) Leonard, smelling of top-of-the-line Pierre Cardin cologne, relaxed, casual, content, soon to be joined at some intimate establishment dinner party by a gorgeously gowned and attractive woman who was most likely not his wife, was one of the first Irish Catholics to occupy such an ambassadorial role. In manner and, up to a point, in appearance, he could have passed for Lake Forest WASP. Though, in fact, he was a second generation crook, the son of the most corrupt police captain in the history of the south side of Chicago. A heroic statement, I admit, but Captain Flannery Leonard achieved heights of excellence in his kinkiness that most experts in such matters say will go unsurpassed in the Chicago Police Department for the rest of this century.

Mike Casey admitted to me once that he could never understand why the First Illinois had taken the risk of giving the job to an Irishman. "You don't want a man with flair dealing with the Mob," Mike said, dabbing at a painting of pre-fire houses on a tree-lined street on the north side of Chicago. "And certainly not a man who shows up on the society pages of the paper with a different beautiful woman—not his wife— a couple of days every week. That's asking for trouble."

"What do our friends out on the West Side think of him?"

"Who knows what they think?" Mike flipped the brush against the gray stone outer wall of the house and miraculously produced a stained glass window. "They understand us better than they understand WASPs. We're all Catholics, aren't we? I suspect Frannie Leonard makes them jumpy. They must get a little uneasy about a banker who uses the company credit card for his limo bills—and includes in the charge payment for the hooker who is waiting for him when he climbs into the limo—a different one each time, I hear. I'm sure that offends our friends' sense of decorum. But it's kind of against the rules of the game to put down a bank vice-president."

Doubtless both our friends on the West Side and their counterparts at the First Illinois were nervous about Frannie Leonard. With his yacht, his gambling forays to Vegas, his beautiful women, and his carefully burnished public image, Leonard was the sort of man whom neither side could be completely confident it controlled. Exactly, in other words, the sort of man you didn't want in the job he had.

"I suppose you want to talk to me about the Lisa Malone business?" He continued to stand, doubtless looking for a fireplace against which he could lean as the floodlights reflected off his clean-shaven face, his ruffled shirt, his impeccable dinner jacket, and the sparkling crystal whiskey tumbler.

"Why don't you sit down?" I said mischievously, spoiling the effect.

"Oh, I'm sitting most of the day, Monsignor." He shrugged his broad shoulders in a motion which, I'm sure, would have increased the heartbeat of a substantial number of members of the opposite sex, should any have been present. "Don't mind me. You sit down, please."

A point for Frannie.

"Why don't you tell me whatever there is to tell about the Lisa Malone Foundation?" I did indeed sit down, and filled my matching Waterford tumbler with Perrier water.

"What's to tell? Lisa's been putting in money every year for the last, oh, ten years, between half a million and a million dollars a year, so we have a net worth now somewhere between seven and eight million and a payout of about eight hundred K per annum. That makes it a nice solid little foundation. Lisa and George and I are the board of trustees, and I am the treasurer and executive director. I get paid a small stipend for the record; it doesn't make much difference in my life-style, to be candid. I manage the investment disburse-

ments—ordinarily to Catholic schools and hospitals and char-
itable institutions in Chicago and in mission countries served
by priests and religious from Chicago. I make the recom-
mendations for the grants, and Lisa and George routinely
approve them. We have the annual meeting either here or in
Los Angeles, usually just a week or two before our fiscal
year expires. The books are all in order, Monsignor. You can
ask the government accountants who have been looking over
them. You really don't think I would steal from the Church,
do you?"

"Eight hundred thousand dollars a year is not nothing,
Frank."

"In my world, Monsignor, it is next to nothing. Come to
think of it, we may even have made a small grant to the
cathedral grammar school this year. I didn't have time to
check the disbursements before I came over."

"I am impressed and grateful to Lisa."

He nodded his gracious acceptance of my gratitude. "I hope
she's able to accept your gratitude soon," he said smoothly.

"Indeed. You do not disburse money, however, to Sister
Winifred's Liberation Commune."

"Lisa did raise the question with me a couple of years ago.
I told her that I thought it would be pretty difficult for us to
justify such grants to the IRS. The Liberation Commune or
Collective or whatever they call it does not, in principle, seek
tax-exempt status. Moreover, I was not altogether sure it
would be appropriate for the image of the Lisa Malone Foundation. So I advised against it. Lisa apparently chose to make
personal contributions on her own, in addition to and beyond
her contributions to the foundation."

"I see. What proportion of the monies from the foundation
are spent inside the Chicago area?"

"About a third, I should say." His eyes flickered warily.
"The rest, to anticipate your question, is dispersed to overseas
missionaries, notably in Latin America."

"And especially, if I might venture the guess, in Colom-
bia?"

"And Brazil."

"Indeed."

"You won't be able to prove a thing, Monsignor." He grinned genially. "Neither you nor your friend Mike Casey. That nun's outrageous charges were a defensive smoke screen in response to my warning to Lisa that the money she was giving to the Liberation Commune was going to Marxist guerrillas, particularly in El Salvador. It would have been devastating to the image of the foundation and to the image of Lisa personally should it have been revealed to the public that her money was supporting terrorism."

"As devastating as if it were revealed that her money was being used to facilitate the international cocaine trade?"

"The difference between the two sets of charges," he said as he emptied the whiskey tumbler and looked once more for the fireplace on which he might elegantly deposit it, "is that the charges against Sister Winifred can be readily proved. The charges about my disbursement of monies to South America are totally unfounded."

"Why don't you put the Waterford glass on my desk? We don't have a fireplace in this room. There's one in the Cardinal's suite, however. By 'unfounded,' you mean, of course, unprovable?"

"Curious old rolltop you have here, Monsignor. I should think it would be quite valuable." He caressed my precious desk with his slimy paw. "Yes indeed, unprovable," he said with just barely a moment's hesitation, "because untrue. When Lisa asked me about the accusations, I told her that the best IRS accountants had carefully examined our books and found no substance to the charges. I offered—indeed, I recommended—that she hire a top-flight accounting firm of her own choice and have them investigate the books. I said that perhaps even George should run the numbers through one of his—what does he call it? Early warning system? No, smoke detector?—programs. I'm absolutely confident that no one would find the slightest impropriety in my management of the funds of the Lisa Malone Foundation, which, by the way, I would add, is an almost trivial part of my responsibilities at the bank."

The Malones and the Leonards had been friends in the old neighborhood. May Malone's respectability did not extend so far as to exclude a crooked police captain from her personal circle. I was certain that if Lisa had asked George the Bean Counter about the wisdom of putting the Malone Foundation in the charge of Fran Leonard at the First Illinois, he would have demurred. Their noninterference pact, wise in so many respects, perhaps, precluded such discussion. Lisa, the pure-minded and clean of heart, had given her funds and her trust to a devious, dangerous crook.

"The foundation might have changed its disbursement policy to avoid not only the fact of impropriety." I pointed toward the giant J&B Bottle on the coffee table. Fran Leonard shook his head with an implication that there were many other drinks to be consumed before the evening was over. "A woman in her position must follow the Caesar's wife rule, must she not?"

"Of course. In Lisa's position it surely would not do merely to say that there was not the slightest possible evidence of impropriety. A charge, even a reckless charge like that of Sister Winifred, might well be grounds for changing our grant policy."

"Did you suggest such a change to her?"

"I would have," he said incisively, "at the next meeting. Lisa herself phoned me and said she was going to be in Chicago this week and wished to discuss the matter in anticipation of the meeting. I told her I was in complete sympathy with her request for such a discussion."

"Your recommendation would have been?"

"I would have suggested a change in policy. Sister Winifred has done an enormous amount of harm to the missionaries who have been benefiting from Lisa's largesse."

"Indeed."

There was a moment of silence, Leonard leaning casually against my bookcase. I hunched over the Perrier glass, considering the patterns that its base was making on my coffee table. I had learned very little from him. He was a smooth enough operator to tell a good deal more of the truth than you might expect and to be substantially more forthcoming than a less clever man in his position would be. He was under the Mob's gun for some reason but would give not the slightest hint of it in a conversation with me. I didn't doubt that Lisa would want to modify the foundation's guidelines for grant-making. Nor did I doubt that he would recommend such modifications, even without being asked, as a response to Sister Winifred's charges and the rumors of government investigations. Frank Leonard was shit, but he was not stupid shit. I did not particularly believe his plea that $800,000 a year was too trivial an amount for him to engage in crook-edness with it, or, as the old fella had said of his father, "Flannery Leonard took everything in sight, even the stationery from your desk."

"Lisa's conversation with you was not heated or angry?"

"Not in the least." He dismissed my question with a wave of his hand, a wave that was just a little bit too quick.

"Nonetheless, Frank, is it not true that you told her you thought it would be better if the matter was permitted to wait until the next meeting of the trustees—which, if I'm not mistaken, is in June?"

I was making it all up out of whole cloth, the poor, be-fuddled cathedral rector who didn't even know where the grants to his grammar school originated.

"George tell you that?" his body tensed ever so slightly, and his eyes hardened.

I nodded, which wasn't altogether a lie. My shot in the dark had found a target.

"Well, as a matter of fact, yes, I did suggest that the matter should be held in abeyance for some months. Our meetings are in April, by the way, not June. You see." His agile mind had doubtless prepared this cover-up for Lisa. "A change in our guidelines now might attract some attention, which is precisely what we do not want to have happen. A routine shift in policy at the annual meeting of the trustees? That sort of thing happens in foundations every year. Lisa seemed agreeable to the suggestion, although she said she still wanted to speak with me when she was in Chicago. I was only too happy to do so." He smiled briefly. "One does not have all that much opportunity to walk into the Mid-America Club at noontime with a woman like Lisa on one's arm."

"Indeed."

"I had no idea that she'd spoken to George about the matter. I had been given to understand . . ."—he hesitated for a fraction of a second, looking for the precise word—". . . that there was a certain estrangement between them."

"I have been given to understand that the estrangement was coming to an end."

"I see."

Francis A. (for Assisi) Leonard knew that he'd been bluffed by a poker player who wasn't even holding a pair of deuces.

"I can understand the reason for your advice, of course." I plodded on, still the awkward, incompetent stumblebum. "As I said to my friend Mike Casey, when he and my father and Rich Daley were discussing the matter, it's six of one and half a dozen of the other. I think most of us, if we were in Lisa's position and understood that there might be media publicity about an IRS investigation, would take the risk of the minor disturbance that a change in foundation policies, oh, say, next week, might produce."

I was sure that Fran's quick mind had been calculating the probability that I had mentioned George's imaginary conversation with Lisa about Frank's stupid advice to her to anyone else. You could, in a pinch, put out a contract on George Quinn, who was scarcely known outside the accounting profession, and on an innocuous disciple of Alfred North Whitehead and William James, who happened to be rector of Holy Name Cathedral. But a former acting superintendent of police and the hero of the battle of Samar Island and the State's attorney of the County of Cook who was the son of the city's late mayor? Ah, no, the friends on the West Side wouldn't like that at all.

"Well, that's a matter of opinion." He shrugged again, easily, lightly, casually, a man unworried, and reached for his carefully tailored cashmere topcoat. "That would be a judgment call. It is hardly necessary to say that I would have abided by Lisa's wishes. Now, I suppose, the matter will have to wait until she recovers. I presume, of course, she will recover?"

"So do we all. Her injury does take some pressure off, doesn't it, Frank?"

He laughed softly as he put on his double-breasted coat. "There is no pressure, Monsignor. No wrongdoing, no evidence of wrongdoing, no hint of wrongdoing: I have nothing to be afraid of, the books are open. Anyone can come in and investigate them. I will abide by Lisa's wishes, and by George's, if, God forbid, Lisa does not recover. I am terribly upset by Lisa's accident, if we may call it that, and I hope and pray for her speedy and complete recovery. Satisfied?"

I permitted a solemn silence to pervade the room. When I spoke again, I gave a fair imitation of the old fella at his most icy.

"Remind your friends on the West Side that some of their predecessors learned a long time ago to leave Ned Ryan and his family alone. It would be a shame to have to repeat the lesson for them. We are defining Lisa as a member of the family. Understand?"

Francis A. (for Assisi) Leonard stared at me coldly, the veils of civilization having been ripped away. "Neither I nor any friends of mine on the West Side had anything to do with what happened to Lisa," he snapped at me. "It's embarrassing to them; they have enough troubles as it is. They don't like any more public attention. If they find out who the criminal is, they will be only too happy to deliver him or her to Rich Daley dead or alive, your choice. Is that clear?"

"Quite clear, Frank," I murmured softly. "But not necessarily credible. We could bring a copy of the Gutenberg Bible into this room and have you stand on it, and I still wouldn't believe a word you said."

Our eyes locked in a staring contest. Frank flinched first, turned without a word, and strode out of my room.

Symbolically I cleansed the premises with a deodorizing spray. (I do not believe in opening the window since fresh air might harm the carefully cultivated Dickensian atmosphere of my suite.)

Our messages had been duly exchanged. I, in my way, and he, in his, knew not where we stood, but where we both were saying we stood.

On the whole, it was rather more likely than not, I thought, that he was telling the truth.

I had been relying on Mike Casey's information that Leonard was in trouble with his friends on the West Side. I was bluffing in my hint that he could easily survive a change in the foundation's policies in a few months, but would be acutely embarrassed by a change now. Indeed, so embarrassed that murder might seem like a reasonable alternative. The assault on Lisa was certainly a convenient event for Frank Leonard and his friends out on the West Side. However, because it was convenient for them in one respect did not mean that it was not also embarrassing, at least potentially, from the perspective of the deeply conservative elder wise men of the Outfit. "Don't mess with that broad, Frankie boy," I could hear one of those gentle, slightly accented voices saying. "We don't need it. Let's wait and see what happens."

The voice might well have added, "You're the one who's in trouble, Frankie boy, not that woman. You get yourself outta trouble without hurting her."

Yet Frank, always one to play the long shot, might have tried to silence Lisa on his own, without the Mob knowing about it and without using one of their official or semiofficial hit men. I could imagine him vigorously denying, in some Melrose Park restaurant, that he had had anything to do with the assault on her.

A reasonable hunch, and totally unprovable. Unlike the other suspects, Frank Leonard wouldn't give much away. I had tricked him once, perhaps; I would not do so again. The men seated at the rear of the Melrose Park restaurant, with their hats on and their backs to the wall, would tip their hats respectfully to me and cheerfully make contributions to the cathedral school fund, but they would also deny that they'd ever heard of Francis A. (for Assisi) Leonard. "Didn't he play for the White Sox a coupla years ago, Fadder?"

I couldn't see Frank himself bursting into Lisa's hotel room and trying to shatter her skull. His face was too well known and he was, in any event, several inches taller than the alleged nun who had visited the Olson Pavilion. A professional killer, even an independent operator about whom the Outfit might not know, would work quickly and efficiently, omitting the preliminary sadism.

However, the preliminary sadism might also be a blind. Frank might point at it and say to the man across the table from him in the restaurant, "No pro does anything like that. It's some kook. You guys know what the crime rate is like in Chicago. It was some crazy rapist, not a gun with a contract."

The hats might believe him, and then again they might not. They would deplore the violent crime rate in Chicago and buy Frankie boy another drink. They would go along with him for the time being. Despite his serenely unwrinkled forehead, Frank Leonard's days might be numbered. You don't hit the vice-president of the First Illinois Bank. Not unless he provokes you. It would not be surprising, however, if there were somber voices on the West Side saying, "That poor Frankie, he sure is provoking, isn't he?"

I considered the advisability of strolling down the corridor, ascending wearily to the third floor, and reporting the situation to my Lord Cronin. Before I could stir up enough energy for a session with himself—always an exhausting affair—the phone rang.

"Blackie? Mary Kate. Rodriquez is going to have to do surgery again. You'd better come over to the hospital. Now."

30

BLACKIE

"Lord God," I began my dialogue with the deity. "Look graciously upon your servant Lisa, lying here on her bed in intensive care, perilously poised between life and death. Consider her husband, her children, her friends, those who admire and respect her. It is not nearly the appropriate time for her to return to you. You doubtless feel enormous passion for her, more exuberant and more determined and more loving than any of which we are capable. Moreover, while, in the final analysis, she may be much happier with you than she is with us, I would, nonetheless, respectfully submit that it would be exceedingly wise policy on your part to leave her in this world for the time being and to restore her to full health. There is much that she is yet capable of doing. Through your nefarious—excuse me, I didn't mean that word—ingenious and brilliant plans in this world, a substantial amount of time and energy and effort have gone into making this poor woman into the perfect instrument of your service that she presently is. While I would be the last one in the world to want to interfere with your carefully refined plans, I nonetheless respectfully observe that it doesn't make all that much sense to bring her to the height of her career and the most important and most potentially useful crisis in her relationship with your good servant George the Bean Counter and then waste all the potential that she possesses."

I could picture the Lord God staring at me in disbelief. "Since when does John Blackwood Ryan, Ph.D., speak with such diffidence and respect? Usually he gives me my instructions in the form of marching orders, more abrupt and more authoritarian than he would dare risk with one of his associate pastors at the cathedral. God, do this, God, take care of that, God, straighten out this mess, God, why did you permit this stupidity to occur? Now Blackie Ryan turns humble and even servile; he must love this woman. That was part of my plan, but I wasn't prepared—or was I? After all, I'm prepared for everything—for his loving her so much. Perhaps I ought to listen to him, merely out of curiosity."

You must be very shrewd, you see, in dealing with the Lord God.

There had been more hemorrhaging, more pressure on the brain, more surgery to relieve the pressure, more dangerous moments on the operating table, another narrow brush with death; and Lisa, now a fragile alabaster statue, was surrounded with the elaborate machines of intensive care and seemed terrifyingly like a corpse in her casket. Rodriquez had merely shrugged his shoulders, no sermon this time. "We need not yet abandon all hope."

Too much like a quote from Dante for me.

A nurse and a resident watched grimly on one side of the bed. A woman patrol officer, blonde, Slavic, delicate and frightened, stood at the end of the bed, looking like she wished that she had the power to work miracles in order to restore this woman, whom she was supposed to be protecting, to life and health. Behind me, Kerry Ann Randall was sobbing inconsolably, the arm of my stepmother Helen reassuringly around her waist. Leaning against the door, his face in incomprehensible anguish, was her brother. Was he worried about himself? Worried about his family? Or finally, perhaps, somehow or the other touched by the drama, worried about Lisa?

I returned to my dialogue with the Lord God.

"No, it is not at all fair of you to suggest that I order you around the way my Lord Cronin orders me around. It is a singularly inappropriate metaphor. The big difference, as I'm sure you perceive, is that the Cardinal can claim some legitimate authority over me and I can claim no legitimate authority over you, save that of a beloved over a lover. We both know how much power there is in that!

"Not to waste any more of your precious time, I will be direct. We've all known that this poor woman is special, but none of us, not her husband, not her children, not her family, not her friends, not those of us from the old neighborhood who love her, none of us knew how special she was. If your intent in this sad business is to convince us that she is a very special woman to whom we should have paid more attention and for whom we should have exercised much more care and concern, then your plan has been brilliantly successful. It is time to bring the affair to its proper conclusion. Restore her to us. I think I can promise you that we've learned our lesson. We will take good care of Lisa for the rest of her life.

"'How comes it,' you say, 'that she was permitted in a hotel room in Chicago, unprotected, alone?'

"A fair question. After all, the Westin Hotel is part of my parish. I am in charge here, am I not? Should I not have insisted with full vigor that she did not belong in that room and that I would summon forth a limo to carry her off to the safety of St. Praxides? My only answer is that I never thought of it. None of us ever thought of anything to protect Lisa because she seemed fragile but nonetheless indestructible.

"Now that we realize that she is both fragile and destructible, I think I can guarantee you that she will be much more appropriately cared for in the future.

"All right. All right. I know all you hear is promises, promises. What more do you expect of us, however? Have you not yourself indicated on many occasions that all you really expect of us is that we promise to try?

"Consider her husband, who will go through life with the terrible guilt that comes from realizing that if he were but a few minutes earlier at the hotel, or a day earlier in flying back from Australia, none of this would have happened. Consider her fey, winsome little children. You surely don't desire that the rest of their lives be blighted by this tragedy?

"I concede my own vested interest in a moderately happy ending to the story. You need not feel called upon to make that point. The fact that Lisa waited until I was ordained to marry establishes beyond any doubt that I didn't have to be a priest because no one would marry someone as quaint and unusual as Blackie Ryan. She loved me as much as I loved her; that, I will confess, is both flattering and moderately incredible. With George the Bean Counter I share an inability to believe that someone like Lisa could possibly love someone like me. The difference between us, as I am sure you are well aware, is that poor George would admit his lack of faith in himself as Lisa's lover and I would admit it to no one save your esteemed Self, and then only under the duress of the present moments. A world without Lisa would be a hollow world for me, too.

"She is a mystery to all of us. She approaches her fortieth birthday. One of the clean of heart, the purely motivated, the single-minded. Transparent, but, bizarrely enough, no one of us, yet, has been able to see through the transparent veils to find out who the real Lisa is, mostly because we thought we knew already. That, I suppose, is our worst sin of all. You sent us a woman of magic and mystery, and we thought we'd solved the mystery and understood the magic. Now, too late

perhaps, we discover our error. Whatever the message you
intended to convey to us through your servant lying here close
to death, the message hasn't been perceived yet. So it is
certainly in your vested interest to see that she remains with
us until we comprehend, at least a little better, the reality for
which she seems to be a special sacrament.

"In truth—and I am too much of a philosopher to pretend
I don't understand the point—you might be using one of your
more crooked lines with which you intend to draw straight
in Lisa's story. It would be a neat twist to the story if we
understand that which you are trying to reveal to us through
Lisa only after she has been taken from us. I fully appreciate
the irony of such a story line, and I'm in no position to argue
with you if you've made up your mind to play out that scenario. But I want to make strong representations that other
scenarios seem, to our poor, limited human understanding,
at any rate, to be far more desirable.

"Amen.

"P.S. Please, please, give us Lisa back."

The response to such contribution to the dialogue is always
the same: "You do what you're supposed to do and find out
who the lunatic is who tried to kill her so there'll be no
repetition, and let me do the worrying about her recovery."

"Fair enough."

You say that I anthropomorphize outrageously. Of course.
It is of the essence of the Catholic imagination that we are
not afraid of anthropomorphisms. Neither, be it noted, were
the people who wrote the Scriptures—your man David, for
example. How else can we dialogue at all with the Ultimate,
the Absolute, the Ground of Being, the Totally Other, unless
we assume that She is also a Thou, and indeed, a loving
Thou who, as one philosopher remarks, weeps every time
the little child weeps. If all of us were close to tears or,
indeed, crying around Lisa's bedside, I have to believe, good
process philosopher that I am, that God somehow was weeping with us and that He desired Lisa's recovery even more
than I did.

"Kevin and I are here now, Uncle Punk." Caitlin slipped
silently into the room with her giant redheaded fiancé law

school teacher and gentleman farmer in tow. "You go back to the cathedral and get some sleep. The sun is coming up already. I'll call you the moment there's any change."

As I was leaving the room, Kerry Randall threw her arms around me and sobbed on my shoulder. "Oh, Blackie, don't let her die, don't let her die, don't let her die!"

"It's in God's hands now, I'm afraid, Kerry," I said, fully conscious that my resignation to God's will was no better than hers. "Pray for her, that's about all we can do."

"I know," she sobbed. "I didn't believe in prayer up until three days ago. Now I think I'll pray every day for the rest of my life."

"We've all learned something from this disaster, Kerry," I said softly and slipped away.

Dr. Rodriquez stopped me at the elevator. "Still here, doctor?"

"I've just come out of surgery from another emergency case." He waved his graceful brown hands expressively. "This seems to be a month when humans are doing bad things to one another's skulls."

"How is Lisa really doing, Doctor?"

"With you, *Padrecito*, I will be honest. There is not much hope. A little bit, perhaps, but not much. Even if she lives a couple more days, the chances of her ever emerging from the coma are very slight."

"When do they become virtually impossible?"

His thick expressive lips moved dubiously. "I would not want to be held to a specific day, but, well, after November first, I would be very surprised if there were a substantial recovery; indeed, any recovery at all."

"But there still could be a surprise, couldn't there?"

"Oh, yes," he agreed. "There's always room for surprises."

"Then we will pray for a surprise, won't we?"

31
BLACKIE

The telephone in my room jarred me unceremoniously out of my sleep. I cursed the associate pastor (in the old days he would have been doomed forever to Coal City) for putting the night bell in my room. It wasn't my turn, and besides, I was the rector, wasn't I?

And why had he arranged for the sunlight to be peeking around the corner of Wabash Avenue and prying its way through my drapes?

"Father Ryan," I told the telephone dyspeptically.

My throat was dry from sustained anxiety, my muscles sore from all-night tension, and my mouth tasted of bile—an unusual phenomenon in one with such a placid gastrointestinal tract as mine.

"Sorry to disturb you, Blackie," said the youngest of the young priests in the rectory, a mere child of twenty-four. "Mr. Quinn is down here. Your father left him off."

"Ah, bless the old fella. Give me five minutes and send up Mr. Quinn."

"I'll send up breakfast, too."

"Ah, Steven, perhaps a little more than the usual breakfast this morning . . ."

"Naturally."

I had stumbled home down Superior Street just as the sun was rising once more over the lake. At last Indian summer had arrived. An appropriate day, I had told myself, for solving a mystery.

If only I had even the beginning of a clue toward a solution.

Fran Leonard, acting through a semiprofessional hit person, to protect his standing with the Mob and perhaps his life? Dina King or Tad Thomas, who were both in a fit of rage at a threat to their dubious careers? Roddy Malone, hungry for his inheritance and fed up with the embarrassment he thought Lisa was causing for his family? Kerry Randall, a lifelong second fiddle to Lisa? Sister Winifred, quite possibly with the help of one of her commune sister's, executing revolutionary justice? Ken Woods, a frustrated and humiliated Pygmalion, incurably in love with the woman he thought of as his own creature?

All had motive; all had opportunity; all might have been sufficiently captured by the green-eyed monster of envy to be able no longer to tolerate Lisa's existence. Who might play Antonio Salieri to her Mozart? As I collapsed into my bed in the cathedral rectory, I told myself that Lisa was no Mozart.

But then, no one among the suspects was Antonio Salieri, either.

Then it was obvious to me, overwhelmingly obvious, that it had been out of the question from the very beginning to suspect George Quinn of the crime. How stupid of me not to have understood that! Then, just before I fell asleep, the reason that it was stupid, the image that had been scurrying through the corridors in the subbasements of my brain, finally came up in the express elevators to full consciousness. Yes, of course!

By the time I remembered that experience, as I opened the door to my study for George Quinn, the image was gone again.

"I didn't even recognize her, Blackie," he said, a hurt little boy. "I didn't even know it was Lisa."

Almost anyone but an Irishman would have wept. George sat down dutifully by my coffee table and accepted the mug of black coffee I offered him. "I can't believe it, I just can't believe it."

"There are two things you must believe at the very beginning, George the Bean Counter," I insisted, after draining one of the two glasses of grapefruit juice that the thoughtful cook had sent up to me. "The first of these is that you saved her life."

"Me?" He peered up at me quizzically. "What do you mean?"

"Everyone has been preoccupied with your guilt or innocence. It has occurred to no one, apparently not even you, that if your innocence is once granted, then your opportune arrival prevented the would-be assassin from torturing Lisa to death. If she's still alive, she owes her life completely to you."

"It might be better, Blackie, if she were not alive, than to be in the condition she is now." He shook his head sadly. "I didn't even know it was her. . . ."

"Be that as it may, she is still alive and Doctor Rodriquez assured me himself, earlier this morning, that there are still some slight grounds for hope. You did all that you could to save her."

"I suppose so." He put the coffee cup aside. "Somehow that doesn't mean much to me now. Maybe it will. And your second point, Blackwood?" He managed a faint smile; indeed, the same old George the Bean Counter, whimsical, resilient, finally, implacable.

"The second thing to remember is that your marriage did not go through a dissolution, it merely went through a crisis, a crisis that was at least as much your wife's fault as it was your own, and a crisis the like of which is inevitable in any marriage after a certain number of years."

"Oh." He reached for the coffee cup again, his square solid shoulders sagging hopelessly. "I know that, Blackie."

"You do?"

"Sure, I know that."

"Indeed?"

"I came to Chicago, Blackie, to celebrate a reconciliation, not to find my wife dying in a hospital bed."

32
GEORGE

You see, what I did—and it was absolutely outrageous—was send her those three chapters I had written as background for Kerry's "study," as she calls it, of Lisa. I admit it took a lot of what our Jewish friends call chutzpah, but I couldn't think of any other way to start us negotiating again.

It took me a long time to figure out what to do. I'm slow, Blackie. Too slow by about ten minutes, I guess.

Anyway, I sent it air courier at that—so she had it almost as soon as the Qantas plane landed in Los Angeles.

The next morning there was a phone call from LA. "You have the job if you still want it." It was a woman's voice, but so brisk and efficient, I didn't recognize it.

"What job?"

"You know what job: president, chairman of the board, chief executive officer, head accountant, and senior programmer for Lisa Malone Productions."

My vocal cords froze. There were so many things I wanted to say, and nothing seemed to come out of my mouth.

"I'll give you a hundred and twenty-five percent of your present salary," she rushed on wildly, "not a penny more. . . . Well, maybe a hundred and fifty percent, but that's the absolute limit. . . ."

Inarticulate animal noises came out of my mouth.

"Do you want the job?" She spoke with a mixture of impatience and terror.

"Of course I want the job," I managed to croak.

"*Well*, it took you long enough to make up your mind. I'll

have a computer terminal put in every room in your house, even the bedroom."

"I could think of something I'd much prefer in the bedroom to a computer terminal."

A laugh of happy relief. "No law says you can't have both."

Then we both began to laugh because we knew we were beginning again. We knew nothing could occur in the future that we would not be able to negotiate. Even if the future, too, has another crisis as bad as this one.

"I miss you terribly, George the Bean Counter. It was all my fault. I'm sorry I neglected you." I could tell she was crying, and I wanted to cry, too, but you know what we Irishmen are like.

"I miss you more, Lisa, than I'll ever be able to tell you," I replied. "I miss you the way a man dying of thirst in the outback misses water."

"Not bad for spontaneous metaphor," she said between her sobs. "If you want, George, I'll retire. I've had enough of a career. Maybe we should move back to Chicago. The kids want to do that. They say they know they'll like Chicago better than Los Angeles."

"I don't want you to give up your career, Lisa; that isn't necessary and that never was the problem."

Well, not much anyway.

"I know you don't want me to give up the career." She was now weeping like a little child. "But I'll give it up rather than go through anything like this again. What about Chicago?"

"You want to move home, Lisa?"

"If you do. One of the nice things about having your own company is that it travels with you."

"Let's talk about it. Maybe a summer home at Grand Beach with all the crazy Ryans around us."

"Including Blackie, your archrival?"

"I can take care of him."

"The first production will be the story you sent me. Okay?"

"What story?" I asked, baffled.

"You know the story—the one about the woman you loved. The singer."

"You mean the sexy one."

"Right. Whom do you think we could get to play her?"

"Kathleen Turner? Kelly McGillis?"

"You're fired!" She laughed merrily. "Hurry home."

So we agreed that we would meet on Monday, three days away, in Chicago. Lisa would be there on her way to New York. I would wind up my business in Australia, inform them I was taking a month off and would return for a few more weeks if necessary to finish the work before I began my new career as the head of a small but potentially very affluent film production company, then fly to Los Angeles and on to Chicago where Lisa and I would, perhaps, begin house hunting, or at least, summer-home hunting. Lisa and I were going home together.

And we would be going home together now if I wasn't too slow.

33

BLACKIE

It would be a terrible day to have to die, I reflected, as I walked with George the Bean Counter out onto Wabash Avenue, to Kevin Maher's waiting Dodge Ram pickup (every law school teacher/gentleman farmer *needs* a Dodge Ram pickup). It was an incredibly soft, golden, luminous Indian summer day, as though the Lord God Herself had descended to earth and was trailing some of His splendor across the land.

But then, there were no good days on which to die.

In my office on the first floor, there was a stack of mail, yesterday's and today's. Somehow, I never quite made it into the office yesterday. I called the hospital to check, once again, on her condition. It was described to me as "serious." I phoned the old fella who said that it seemed very unlikely that Mr. Daley would go to the grand jury to seek an indictment. I checked with Mike Casey the Cop, who reported that the police had grave doubts about the explanations being provided by Tad Thomas and Dina King but could find precious little evidence that would suggest that either of them was, in fact, the killer. Yes, of course, there was no reason to doubt that they were both sufficiently skilled in the use of drugs to be able to work a hypodermic needle. He added that the rumor "out on the West Side" was that some of the oldest of the Outfit wise men wanted to put out a contract on Frank Leonard. "They think he might be involved. Preventive action."

How thoughtful of them.

I went back up to my room, collected my map and charts, brought them down to the office, and laid them on the desk as I prepared to open the mail. There was nothing much to add to what I'd put on the chart yesterday. I followed the Indian paths through my parish, down Superior Street to the Olson Pavilion, then over Fairbanks Court, Chicago Avenue, and Seneca Court to Delaware Street, the John Hancock on the left, the Westin on the right, back up to the corner of Delaware and Michigan. Straight ahead, half a block down, behind the Fourth Presbyterian Church was the Whitehall, and right behind it, on Chestnut, across from Quigley Seminary, the Tremont. Around on my left, across Chestnut Street, was the Carlton. On my right, down Michigan Avenue, on the other side of the Playboy (ugh, I said that word) building, was the good, gray Drake. And around the corner, a few steps down east Lake Shore Drive, the chic Mayfair. Everyone literally within a stone's throw of the Westin. A five-minute walk or, at the most, a two- or three-minute run. Sister Winnie up Lake Shore Drive in Rogers Park in her commune, but at 9:30 at night, no more than a fifteen-minute drive down Lake Shore and onto Michigan, stopping right in front of the Westin. Fran Leonard in his office at the First Illinois building on La Salle Street, ten minutes by cab from Michigan and Delaware. Any and all of these people could have been out on the fog-crowded streets that trail away like lesser canyons from the Magnificent Mile.

I stared dully at the map. Somehow, somewhere on that map or on the chart that lay next to it were the beginnings of a solution. I still couldn't see it. Faith and works, as Michael Polyani would have put it, but as yet, no grace, no blinding illumination, no impish image leaping out of the express elevator.

I began to open the mail. The second letter, obviously delivered yesterday, was postmarked last week in Los Angeles. It was from Lisa.

34
LISA

Blackie, darling,

I think I need a priest.

I mean a real priest, a priest priest, not one of the smooth-talking flannel-mouthed Irishmen at my parish church or one of the Jesuits trying to figure out, after their first visit to my house, where the checkbook is locked up. I'm spooked, Blackie. Not by ghosts or anything like that. I'm scared stiff, and I don't know why.

Or maybe I do know why: I've finally broken all the rules. I feel very much alone, very frightened, very much like I want to quit. It's as if I'm standing in a cemetery in the middle of the night and there is a grave open and I'm at the edge of the grave and I see the headstone says: Lisa Malone 1945–1984.

It's all silly, but I still want to talk to a priest about it, and that's why I want to see you when I'm in Chicago next week. I'll call you as soon as I get in, since I hope this letter gets there before I do, to make an appointment. I think George will be with me. He will have read the enclosure the night before. Then the three of us will be able to have a good talk about it.

Won't that be fun: Lisa and her two lovers talking about the favorite subject of all three of them? What's that?

Why, Lisa, of course!

I know all this sounds crazy, Blackie, dear. I have probably worked too hard on my new film, and it's too long since George has been in bed with me. By the way, don't believe all the things you might read in the newspaper about me and George. Although I've really let him down badly, things are on the mend, and we'll have lots of good news to talk about next Tuesday as well as the "worrying" news that's in the accompanying memo (I won't say it's bad news because I don't know whether it is or not. It's scary though).

Where was I?

I suppose the best place to start is to tell you why I wrote this memo. You remember that Kerry Ann Randall is writing a "study" about me, don't you?

No, of course you don't remember. Why should you remember? I haven't told you. Anyway, George sent me, from Sydney, a copy of three long chapters in a "memoir" that he wrote about me. Blackie, they were the most beautiful thing I've ever read. He is such a strong, solid, determined man. In addition to being cute. I love him desperately. They gave me a wonderful idea for a film. George understands me so well and loves me so much. More than I deserve to be loved, but that's beside the point.

Kerry Ann has been after me to do a "little memo" for her about my religious faith. I've avoided doing it on the excuse that the final work on the new film had to be done first. I think I was also afraid even to look at my faith and my religious motivations, and not because I have failed so badly to live up to my faith—we all do that. I knew that once I began to think seriously about religion, I would realize that this new film (it's called The Friendship Factor, *and I hope you love it), which I really began for kind of religious reasons, has been interfering with a lot of the other things that are really valuable in my life. I wouldn't have thought that one aspect of my religion could interfere with the rest. However,*

I think there was another and deeper reason that I didn't want to do Kerry Ann's memo.

I knew, deep down inside, that fear has been gnawing at me, oh, really since my mother died, but especially since I decided I wanted to try to turn The Friendship Factor *into a film and that I would produce it and direct it and even write some of it if necessary. Ever since I made that decision, there's been a secret little terror eating away at me. I didn't want to give it a name, I didn't want to acknowledge the risk involved in* The Friendship Factor. *I thought that if I had realized how dangerous making the film would be, I wouldn't have tried it or I would have quit halfway through. I have broken all the rules, Blackie. You know what happens to people who break the rules.*

Then I was so moved by George's recollections about me that I knew now I had to talk about what I believe and how I have failed, for so many years, to live up to my faith and why I was so afraid and why I began on The Friendship Factor *and why there is so much terror in me now.*

A lot of "whys," aren't there, Blackie, dear?

Maybe this doesn't make any sense at all. Maybe I'm just a worn-out, crazy, lovesick, man-hungry woman. Forgive me if it sounds weird. Just read my little memo and think about it. We can talk next Tuesday.

I'm terrified, frightened out of my mind, and the funny thing is, I don't know exactly what I'm afraid of.

My mother's ghost. Maybe.

I love you, Blackie, darling. See you soon.

Pray for me.

Lisa.

P.S. I haven't showed this to anyone but you, though of course George will have seen it before we come over to the cathedral rectory.

35
LISA

      I don't want to write this, but I know that I have to.

    First of all, I'll write about what I believe, and then I'll write about how I haven't lived up to my faith, and then I'll do a section on why I made The Friendship Factor *and, finally, a couple of paragraphs on why I think I'm so afraid.*

    I. WHAT I BELIEVE.

    I never thought of myself as a very devout Catholic. I go to Mass and Communion every Sunday and confession at Christmas and Easter, contribute to the support of the Church, send my children to Catholic schools, remain faithful to my husband (which doesn't take much virtue on my part because I love him so much, despite some of the stupid things I have done lately), carry a rosary in my purse and say it occasionally, recite my morning and evening prayers almost every day, teach my children to say grace before and after meals, pay all my income tax, try to keep my terrible temper under control, and manage to be patient with my colleagues and to avoid as much uncharitable conversation as I can.

    That doesn't exactly make me a saint. It only means that I'm an ordinary Catholic. I probably ought to go to church every day. There's no reason, now that Ned is four, why I shouldn't. And I ought to read more religious books (I ought to read more books of every sort), and I desperately need a day of recollection or even a retreat, maybe a week-long retreat. I'm worldly and often selfish and self-centered. I could be much more generous, particularly to my husband and children, generous not with my money (I think I'm pretty generous with that), but with myself.

241

*I am a Catholic for the same reasons that I'm a Democrat:
I was born that way, and none of the alternatives look any
better or even equally attractive. Moreover, I'm a typical
American Irish Catholic matron, pushing forty. Maybe I do
some unusual things like making films and singing in Christmas specials and recording an album every year or so. (I
thought the last one,* Lisa Sings Sacred Songs, *was really
very nice, and very hypocritical because I wasn't feeling
sacred when I sang them. How do you sing sacred songs and
mean them when you've driven your husband to a public
confrontation with you? Poor, dear man. He loses his temper
only once in fifteen years, doesn't even hurt me, and gets
caught by a camera. And it was all my fault, too. I was too
busy being a great producer to be a great wife. Lisa Malone,
who always said "both," didn't say it at the most important
time in her life.) I do practice birth control, but I guess
everybody does that nowadays, and I've never really been
convinced it's wrong. The Pope is a wonderful man and I'm
terribly impressed by him and he really is quite cute, but the
poor dear doesn't know what he's talking about when the
subject is sex in marriage. The problem between me and
George right now is not that we have too much sex, with
each other or anyone else, but that we haven't had nearly
enough sex, especially really good sex, in a long, long time.*

*This memo is about my faith and not about my marriage—
if my faith had been stronger though, my marriage would be
in a lot better condition than it is.*

Now *we come to the serious part.*

*I also believe that I have a vocation from God. I realize
that everyone has vocations, but I think my vocation is special. I'm not called to the religious life, as poor old Sister
Winifred used to tell me. I'm called by God to be an actress
and a singer. When I sing a song well or when I turn in a
competent performance in a film, then I'm revealing God to
people, if only in a small way. Anything that's good or true
or beautiful or nice or helpful or kind or generous or sweet
or loving tells us something about God. I don't know why
God would want to use me as His representative, kind of
maybe a little bit like a priest, on a Christmas TV program*

or in a song that makes people happy or a film that entertains them and instructs them maybe a little bit. But God gave me the talent to do those things, and I would be failing in my vocation if I didn't do them.

Also, because I am doing them for God, I have to do them well, I have to sing and act and be beautiful for people as best I possibly can so that they may see a little bit of God when they see or hear Lisa Malone.

I hope that doesn't sound too arrogant. I can deceive myself as well as anybody else. There are times when I am a terribly proud and ambitious woman. After a while, to tell the truth, the acclaim and the adulation and the fan letters and people recognizing you in the streets or restaurants, don't make that much difference. Not to me anyway. I think I would have retired when Georgia Anne was born if those things were all I was seeking. I wanted to retire. I wanted to spend more time with my babies. I wanted to be closer to my husband, who drives me out of my mind with desire almost every time I see him, even when I'm mad at him. A voice inside me—I suppose you could call it conscience—kept saying: Lisa, you can't quit. You haven't done yet the things God wants you to do. You have more to give to the world than you've given already.

II. MY RELIGIOUS FAILURES

All my life I've known that I was special. My mother and father treated me like I was special (which hurt my poor brother terribly, but there was nothing I could do about that), and I suppose that's where I started thinking that I was not quite like other people. As I grew up, even in the early years of grammar school, I knew, aside from anything my parents said or did, that I was very special and that that gave me a terribly heavy responsibility. Maybe that's why I like Blackie Ryan so much. He was such a cute little boy, and so wise and so kind and so funny and the smartest boy in the class. In the whole school actually. He knew that he was a special little boy, just as I knew that I was a special little girl. He knew that God had called him to be a priest, and I knew that God had called me to be an actress.

I didn't tell anybody this because being an actress didn't

seem all that good an idea in St. Praxides back in the 1950s. My poor mother and father would have been horrified, as they were when I finally went off to my own seminary after Blackie went to Mundelein. Not that I wanted to be an actress. If I had had my own way, I wouldn't have wanted to be an actress at all, I would have gone to St. Mary's of Notre Dame and seduced poor George Quinn the Bean Counter in a little more leisurely fashion than I did. I was called to be an actress. I had to be an actress. God wanted me to be an actress. That was all there was to it.

I knew more about acting in high school than a hundred Sister Winifreds. I pretended not to know anything because I was afraid of what might happen if I was too good in the high school play. When poor Ken Woods sent me to that acting coach, as though he were doing me a great favor by teaching me how to get inside a character and understand that character and play that role to the limit, I secretly laughed to myself. I knew a lot more about acting than the acting coach. After the first couple of films, I knew more about filmmaking than did most of the directors I worked with. I was sweet and cooperative and did what they told me, but I knew when they were right and when they were wrong. I'm sorry that I never had an opportunity to work with the really great directors: Bresson, Rohmer, Bergman, Buñuel (those last two men, poor dears, so haunted by God. I could have explained to them who God was), or even some of the Americans, even the younger Americans like De Palma or Coppola. No, Lisa Malone was the sweet, chaste, pale-skinned, black-haired Irish Catholic colleen from Chicago.

I was an actress, wasn't I? I was influencing people with my songs and my films, wasn't I? When they saw how pretty I was, didn't it make at least some of them think about how beautiful God was?

So why should I have to do anything more? Sometimes I've gone for years at a time without thinking about these things, then something happens, like my mother's death, for instance, and I realize that I'm doing the perfect "Hound of Heaven" sequence. (What a marvelous film you could make about that poem!) Till The Friendship Factor *I was able to drive those thoughts out of my mind. When my mother died and I realized that I was going to die someday, I also saw that the values she stood for, poor, well-meaning woman, were winning out over what I stood for in my own life.*

Ned was born a little less than ten months after my mother's death. I suppose, in a way, he is a hedge against my own mortality. Maybe I wanted to give George a son. However, the months of carrying the poor little guy gave me the time I needed, the time I had to force upon myself, to think about what I was going to do with the rest of my life.

Neddie is such an adorable little boy. If it works out and he should read this someday, he'll realize the wonderful gift he was to me even before he was born.

If things don't work out, then I'll make sure this "memoir" is torn up.

Almost as soon as I knew I was special, I realized that it was bad to be special. People disliked you and punished you and hated you and wanted to hurt you because you were special. I've never been able to understand that. Many of my friends, including, I think, even George and Blackie, think that I'm oblivious to the hatred people feel toward me. I'm not. I don't understand it and I don't know what to do about it, but from the very first moments I knew that I was special, I was frightened because I understood that people would hurt me when they found out.

I had to leave the theater halfway through the film Amadeus *because I could not stand what they were doing to poor Mozart. I'm not Mozart, I'm only Lisa. If they hate me as much as they do when I'm only Lisa, what must it have been like to have been the greatest musician who ever lived?*

They call it envy, but, as Mary Kate Murphy said, when she and Joe visited us last autumn, "A label isn't a diagnosis."

The people hate me because I have a little bit of acting talent and a nice voice and look pretty, in a way even prettier now than when I was eighteen, would be insane with rage if they knew how good I really am, not at singing (I can't pretend my voice is poorer than it is), but at acting. You can pretend, with enough talent and skill, to be a sweet little chastely erotic Irish Catholic girl from Chicago and nothing more. That's what I've done for almost twenty years. I've known, deep down inside my personality, with absolute certainty, that I have the potential to be a great actress and a great filmmaker, and I haven't done it because I have been afraid of being hurt even more than I have been hurt through the years.

I've hidden my light under a bushel, like Jesus warned us not to do. I've hidden the light that Jesus gave me because I'm scared.

Not that I've been all that great a martyr. Still, I don't care how successful you are and how much you pretend you don't mind what people say, it hurts when a gossip columnist or a critic or a reviewer says vicious things about you. So I compromised with them and with God. Then my mother died.

III. WHY I MADE The Friendship Factor.

When I decided to try to turn The Friendship Factor *into a film and at the same time demonstrate to everybody that the erotic attractiveness of a woman's body could be an integral part of a great film performance, for the first time in my life, I was responding to God's call. It took a lot of nerve. I was afraid I'd fail and be humiliated. I was even more afraid that I would succeed and maybe be destroyed completely because I had succeeded.*

Perhaps I was just a little too old to throw myself into something so new and different and terrifying, and at the same time avoid all the personal mistakes that I've made in the last couple of years.

A young woman with the same kind of feeling about her vocation might have the energy and the self-confidence (or only the naiveté) to try what I tried and be true to her responsibilities to her family and her friends. I let myself be overwhelmed. While God may be pleased with me that I'm finally responding to His vocation, I think He (or, as Blackie might say, She) is terribly upset at my imprudence in forgetting about my kids and especially not paying any attention to how badly poor George was hurting.

Ironically, if I had thought of how much poor George was suffering, I wouldn't be alone now and wouldn't be so fright-

ened. I'm the one who always said "both." Why didn't I say, "Both the film and George"? No. Why didn't I say, "Both George and the film"?

I made the film, just the way I knew it ought to be made and had to be made. I'm glad I did it. I'm sorry I hurt George. I'm also terrified about what will happen.

Not terrified that the film won't succeed. It will make a lot of money because I'm in it and because there will be a lot of controversy and because many people, missing the point, will come to see if it's really true that I have my clothes off for part of the film (if I've done it right, they'll be disappointed, and no director will ever again use an actress's body as a prop, only as an integral part of her acting craft—unless he's making porno). Nor am I afraid I won't win the Academy Award. I probably will win it. I'm certainly not afraid that a critic ten years from now might say, "Well, The Friendship Factor isn't a classic." It will be a classic.

No, my fear now is not that the film will fail, but that it will succeed, even more, perhaps, than I expect. If it does succeed, then those who hate me may try to kill me.

IV. WHY I AM AFRAID

I am afraid, as much as I hate to admit it, mostly because I don't trust God enough. If I really trusted God, I wouldn't care what happened to me when I had done what I know He wants me to do. Since my faith is weak, I'm terrified that they will kill me.

Who are they?

I know who some of them are. All the people out there who are so angry at me and wrote such terribly hateful letters when George and I had our fight (poor George got the blame, and it was about ninety-eight percent my fault). Oh, there's lots of people who like me, too. Somehow they don't count because they can't protect you from those who hate you and want to hurt you. Blackie and George and Mary Kate and Joe Murphy and Ned Ryan and Caitlin and all my friends were never able to protect me from the pain my mother inflicted upon me. She didn't intend to inflict it upon me, but she did, right up to the very end of her life. "Who do you *think you are, Lisa? What right do you have to reach for the stars?"*

I never had the nerve to say it to her, "I have to reach for the stars, Mom, because God wants me to reach for the stars."

I will hurt all my life because my mother didn't approve of me. She didn't kill me, not physically, but she tried to kill me emotionally by pretending for most of those years that I didn't exist and by ignoring my husband and my poor kids.

They are all the people out there like my mother. All the people like Antonio Salieri, who will be absolutely furious that Lisa Malone dared to reach for the stars and even more hateful because she succeeded in touching the stars.

I don't mean that they'll physically murder me. I'm not John Kennedy or Martin Luther King or President Reagan or the Pope. I don't know exactly what they will do to me. After a while, I suppose, they'll be tired of being hateful and will go away and leave me alone. I do know, when The Friendship Factor is released and stirs up all the controversy, makes enormous amounts of money, and is hailed—by some critics anyway—as a classic and probably wins the Academy Award, that the sky is going to fall in on me.

I've been trying to hide from that for at least thirty years, maybe even a little longer. Because I'm a Catholic and because I know that I'm doing what God wants me to do when I reach for the stars, I must take the risk that there'll be people around me to protect me when the sky falls in and to help me put the pieces back together

What if there aren't any people to help me? What if they can't put the pieces back together again? What if there's no Easter Sunday in my life? What if I can't win George back? My wonderful, glorious Bean Counter in shining armor, the kindest and strongest man in the world. Have I lost him because I was so dense? He has been my epiphany, firm and loyal and generous and tough, with enough flair and wit to be always a surprise, like I imagine God to be. God came with him that February afternoon when he waited in my driveway with a glint in his eye, a determined grin on his wonderful face, and irresistible power in his arms. What if

I've lost him forever? What if I have to face alone those who hate me?

I'm not a good enough Catholic to say that it doesn't make any difference. I hope I have enough faith to say that I'll do what I have to do anyway.

Well, none of this sounds much like Lisa Malone, sweetheart of Irish Catholic Americans, does it?

I don't think I'll show this to Kerry Ann for a long time.

In this last section I've tried to give a name to my fear, hoping, if I could name it and put the name down on paper, that maybe a little bit of it would go away. I really haven't been able to be precise, so I'm still terrified.

There's one sentence that keeps echoing and echoing over and over in my poor, weary brain: They're going to try to kill me.

36

BLACKIE

Lisa slipped on her plain beige negligee with a vigorous tug. She walked over to the Gothic-shaped window and glanced out to the lawn bathed in golden sunlight. Then she turned back toward us, a whimsical smile flitting across her lips, suggesting a quick, light melody.

"I'll begin again, what else is there to do?" She picked up the Coca-Cola bottle. "I'd begin again even if I knew I was going to die tomorrow." Her eyes widened thoughtfully. "The difference between us and the other animals is that they're programmed to keep trying and we can choose not to. Tomorrow will be different."

"Better or worse?"

"After what's happened to me, different is bound to be better. No, that's not true." She sipped the Coke and grinned impishly. "For everybody different is better . . . if we want it to be."

The camera closed on her mischievous face and, accompanied by the music of "Shenandoah" (nice touch that) seemed to pass through her hazel eyes, leaving her transparent as it absorbed the radiance of the sunlight outside her window.

The story of a singer who came out of the slums of Chicago in the 1920s in search of wealth and love, found them, became an alcoholic, lost everything, rediscovered a forgotten love, and climbed out of the grave she had constructed for herself. Not an original story line perhaps, but executed perfectly. You loved the poor, flawed woman from her first appearance as an adolescent on Oak Street Beach. You knew she was headed for disaster. You also knew that she had the resources to survive the disaster. But did she have the courage and faith to put the pieces of herself and her life and her love back together again?

The suspense of the story then was whether there was enough courage and faith. Remarkably ingenious to make that theme so explicit and yet so natural. Film as epiphany.

The girl in the movie was not Lisa, but enough like her to appeal to the nation's multitude of Lisa fans. You draw the audience into the film, again very clever.

The credits came up; the film was over.

"Like, wow!" Reardon waved his massive arm in the air and dramatically flicked the ash off the end of his cigar into my wastebasket (he never misses). "She really did it! Sensational!"

"Academy Award," Roger Ebert exhaled softly. "Maybe a Cannes prize, too. A ready-made classic. Even Siskel will like it."

Being prejudiced, I said nothing.

"I can't think of a single false move, Roger." Reardon leaned forward, staring at Sean Cronin's large-screen television as though the tape were still rolling. The Cardinal himself was immobile and silent in his easy chair.

"There'll never be a nude scene in a film again," said Ebert as he continued his ecstatic praise, "that doesn't have to take what she did into account. She turned the erotic away from

pornography and converted it into drama. Physical beauty as
a grace—you'd say sacrament, wouldn't you, Father
Blackie?—of spiritual redemption. I wouldn't have believed
that a woman could convey so much tragedy and hope with
a few subtle movements of her body."

Reardon, the burly, brilliant, black Irish giant glanced at
me. "Wouldn't you say, Blackwood, that Rohmer and Bresson
and Fellini are her heroes? She has them all in it, and a good
deal of John Ford besides."

"As American as hamburgers, frankfurters, and pizza," I
murmured.

"The pathos of that lovely body, aging but still wonderful,
yet hinting of the inevitable further deterioration. Heartrending hints of a death to be defied till the bitter end."

"We will all be young again, we will all laugh again." I
scraped out the last tiny bits of popcorn.

"Do you really believe that?" The Cardinal's eyes were
always anguished when the subject was death. As he himself
once remarked, a good Cardinal these days is ninety-five
percent agnostic and five percent mystic. Sometimes the mystic needs reassurance.

"As Professor Haught has recently remarked," I said, shov-
ing the popcorn into my mouth, "there are only two religious
truths: we are in the embrace of mystery, and that mystery
is gracious. He might have added a third: mystery is revealed
to us mostly by other humans, especially by people like Lisa."

"She *has* to recover," Ebert accepted one of Reardon's
cigars. "There's so much left for her to do."

"Maybe she's done enough," I observed cautiously.

"Nonsense!" Lord Cardinal announced. "Again I say to
you gentlemen, nonsense! Pay no attention to Blackwood
here, he is in one of his melancholy moods. Of course Lisa
is going to recover."

The Cardinal's fine, handsome features, attractively haggard from time and suffering, assumed their characteristic
now-it's-time-for-a-fight expression. "It is unacceptable that
the woman should be taken from us. What's the report today,
Blackie?"

"Vital signs normal, coma still deep, some improvement

in movement and reflex activity in her limbs. Dr. Rodriquez
continues to propound agnosticism about how the brain works.
She may never awaken. She may come out of the coma a
vegetable. She may regain consciousness notably impaired
but with a long-term prognosis for almost complete recovery.
Or she could open her eyes one day and, with minor kinks—
double vision, headaches, trouble with vocabulary—be the
same old Lisa. That's still not impossible, though with each
passing day the probabilities diminish."

"That can't be permitted to continue." The Cardinal rose
from his easy chair. "I have a confirmation somewhere, I'm
sure. Lisa must recover. See to it, Blackie." He reached for
his deftly tailored jacket, jabbed the Roman collar back into
his clerical collar, and departed, an Irish warrior prince riding
into battle.

"'See to it, Blackie'?" Roger Ebert eyed me quizzically.
"Does Cronin expect a miracle from you?"

"Every day." I strove to sound appropriately melancholy.
"Needless to say, when they happen, I claim credit."

After my guests had left and I had rewound the tape,
thinking that perhaps I would view the film again, I contem-
plated the fact that far from working any miracles, I had not
even accomplished what is in my province rather than that
of the Lord God. I had yet to figure out who had twice tried
to kill her. Who was the lunatic who had fractured her skull
and then later torn the oxygen cord off the ventilator? Who
was the lunatic who would, unless I was completely wrong,
soon try again?

In a weary ritual, like an elderly bishop going through an
ordination ceremony, I pulled out my charts, my diagrams,
and my map—exactly the names I had four days ago—
George Quinn (now substantially exonerated), Kenneth Woods,
Kerry Ann Randall, Tad Thomas, Dina King, Sister Winifred,
Francis Leonard, Roderick Malone.

Some of them it was possible to exclude with reasonable
confidence. I pondered the list. Five of them were wandering
about the fog-blanketed canyons of Streeterville (as no one
but the papers calls the area north and east of the Water Tower)
that night. Woods, Randall, King, Malone, Thomas. Two of

them, King and and Thomas, had seen her. Woods and Malone had spoken with her on the phone, at least. Perhaps they had seen her, too. George and I were clearly innocent, I by definition, since I was the detective (this was real life, not Mary Roberts Rinehart), and George by empirical evidence.

Leonard and Sister Winnie had alibis, but how good were they? They, too, could easily have been picking their way through the gloomy darkness of the Magnificent Mile.

With a dull pencil—the only kind that survives in my rooms—I ticked off the names of three of the suspects. The odds were heavily against any one of them being the criminal. Too difficult to pull off the logistics.

If the alibis were valid . . . that left two possibilities, both of them reasonable and for the same reason. . . .

But maybe the alibis were invalid. And maybe, logistics or not, one of the others might have been able to work it out, perhaps with the help of an ally.

I threw my pencil away. The fog was still murky, only now it was inside my sinuses.

I had hoped there would be something in the film that would supplement Lisa's message to me in her brief memoir, a message somehow from the depths of her coma. While the film might well be assumed a classic in the making, its message was one of death and rebirth. It pointed no fingers in the direction of would-be murderers.

Yet the film was involved somehow. It had to be more than a coincidence that the assaults on Lisa occurred shortly after the completion of the final touches on *The Friendship Factor*.

I loved her now more than ever. The self-description in the letter was perfectly confirmed by the film. Lisa was indeed a genius. My sweetheart the genius! My sweetheart the gorgeous genius! Roderick Malone, M.D., had lied about his sister. She was not falling apart. Her own evaluation was correct. She was even more appealing now.

Although she would lose some prudish Catholic fans because of the nude scenes in *The Friendship Factor*, I was willing to wager that the subtle and nuanced implication of those scenes would be grasped by most of those who would see the film. The Catholic tradition was slowly coming around to realize that the erotic, properly presented, could be not salacious but sacramental. Lisa had given us a strong shove in the direction of full realization of that instinct.

George Quinn, who had more reason to know than anyone else, had been quite correct in his analysis: Lisa's beauty sneaks up on you, delicately and gradually, and then takes possession of you before you know what's happening.

I shoved my diagrams and charts away impatiently. They were of no use, not in this case. It was, after all, Indian summer, the most beautiful day of the year, whether it be a day of life or a day of death. It deserved a toast of John Jameson's.

I poured a modest amount of that precious liquid into a Lismore tumbler, set it on the coffee table, and removed the cassette of *The Friendship Factor* from Cardinal Cronin's video player.

The Cardinal maintains a supply of Jameson's in his suite to accommodate me when I happen to be discussing grave matters of ecclesiastical policy in his quarters. (He maintains such a supply, of course, by borrowing it from my liquor cabinet.)

I gathered my papers and stuffed them into the pocket of my Aran Island knit sweater, which I wear in the cathedral rectory from October 1st to April 15th, regardless of the weather (unless I affect my maroon smoking jacket, which is one of the better sartorial products of the late nineteenth century) and, Jameson's in one hand, *The Friendship Factor* in the other, I walked down the corridor and descended from the third floor to my own suite on the second floor, noting that at one end I could hear Vivaldi music from the young associate's room and at the other end Prince from the senior associate's room. Such are the times.

The light of Indian summer did not penetrate the dreariness of the cathedral rectory.

Inside my own parlor I placed both the cassette and my Jameson's tumbler on my rolltop desk and collapsed wearily into the venerable judge's chair that my father had claimed for me from the ruins of the old federal building.

Poor George. I would have to give him Lisa's autobiographical note and play for him the tape. The anguish of losing such a woman could deprive a man of his sanity. For the rest of his life he would reproach himself for his slowness.

I picked up my Jameson's glass and began my toast to Indian summer, slowly and meditatively. While the creature never helped me solve a puzzle, it made the solution marginally more enjoyable.

It was stupid of them to charge George in the first place. Obviously he had saved Lisa's life. Moreover, I had known from the beginning that George was not the killer.

I frowned. Yes, I did know that three mornings ago when Mike Casey and I discussed his arrest. Why did I know it? What was the tip-off, the hint, the clue, the quick, unnoted insight that exonerated George the Bean Counter?

The express elevator opened, and my formless image emerged, full-grown, mature, challenging.

A beautiful image, how could I have missed it for so long?

With trembling fingers I replaced the Lismore crystal on my desk. Could it possibly be?

The image now raced across my mind, like a comet illuminating a darkened city. It fit every detail perfectly. Of course. The film had been the final straw, the decisive turning point. If the initial reactions had indicated that it would be a disastrous, even a ludicrous failure, there would have been no assault on Lisa. Her own instincts that "they" would try to kill her because of the film were absolutely correct.

I reached into the pocket of my sweater and pulled out my rumpled pile of charts and diagrams. Next to the names of each of the subjects I made a new entry. Yes, of course, that was it. How obvious! And how stupid of me not to notice it. Indeed, how stupid of me not to notice it when I was mentally recording the evidence all along!

The killer's work was not yet finished. There would be an enormous compulsion to strike again and end that which had been begun. Whether the killer was truly insane or not was problematic; however, there was a certain reckless genius, a brilliance of improvisation, that made the killer deadly dangerous. A police guard would not deter such a person indefinitely.

I knew who it was now, but I didn't have enough proof to justify an arrest, much less to incarcerate the killer so that there would not be a lifelong threat to Lisa, however long her life might be.

So it was necessary to find evidence and find it quickly. See to it, Blackie!

Yeah, but how?

Then I knew how. Oh, yes, indeed, very satisfactory.

I reached for my phone and punched in the first five digits of Mike Casey's number. Then I paused. No, there was a more appropriate organizer of this delightful little caper.

I punched in another number.

"Ned Ryan." The old fella always answers his own phone.

"DE-DIV 39, follow me!"

37

ALIQUIS

I stared at the television screen in stunned disbelief. Recovering? Out of danger? Regaining consciousness? A near miracle?

Outrageous!

How did she dare to recover?

There were now two reasons to strike. Lisa must be finished to assuage my raw hunger for her destruction. She also must be killed and killed quickly because her recovery put me in mortal danger.

Turning off the television set, I removed from the closet a new disguise, the best one yet. Dull green garments of the operating room—loose jacket, floppy trousers, tight-fitting skullcap, surgical mask hanging just beneath the chin, thick glasses, even a badge with a real staff member's name on it.

One could, in such a uniform, wander almost at will through the corridors of any hospital. I had used the disguise before in certain other adventures and, moreover, had tested it this time by strolling through the Olson Pavilion, serene, relaxed, and self-confident. No one had noticed, no one had challenged, no one had objected. I had actually walked by Lisa's bed in the neurosurgical intensive care section of the hospital without protest from anyone.

Stupid fools. They ought to have known that they couldn't protect her from what she deserved.

The next time I would slip into the room, nod to the police officer sitting listlessly in the corner, lean over Lisa's body, and, shielded temporarily from the cop's eyes, plunge a sharp little dagger that was carried inside the elastic waistband of the surgical pants into Lisa's belly or chest.

Then there would be a few moments of terrible danger for me. Perhaps the arrangement of intensive care equipment would hide what had happened from the cop for almost ten seconds, and I would have an opportunity to duck into the corridor. Then, changing physical appearance by standing up straight and discarding the surgical cap and mask, with a bit of good fortune I could become lost in the bustle of a busy hospital floor. It would require speed and luck, but it might be possible to escape without being recognized. In any event, it would be hard for the cop to prove who had plunged the knife into Lisa because I would make quite certain that the cop saw no face to recognize.

The odds were that I would be captured. If Lisa should live, however, the probability of capture became a certainty. This way, while I might go to prison, though more likely to a mental institution for a couple of years, Lisa would be dead.

That was what mattered. Lisa must be destroyed. Forever. The time to destroy her was now.

38
ALIQUIS

It was absurdly simple. The police and the hospital security forces were incredibly stupid. How could they expect to protect someone in an intensive care area? Men and women walked to and fro in that area with surgical masks pulled up over their faces, their eyes hidden behind thick glasses. I counted four such persons in the slow, agonizing, and enormously pleasurable stroll from the elevator to the door of Lisa's room.

Once more I gritted teeth savagely. Orgasmic pleasure, this time, as last time, should take place after the act, not before. Appetizers should not spoil dinner; foreplay should not ruin ecstasy.

Approaching Lisa's bed I was again filled with the same warm, absorbing love that had characterized the initial moments in Lisa's suite at the Westin. Poor, dear, wonderful Lisa. I love you so much. It is a shame you must die. It's more of a shame this time that you're not going to see the pleasure on my face as I rid the earth of your offensive presence. I love you, I hate you, I want you, I will kill you.

You do look so tired and so vulnerable lying there on your hospital bed. Your face is like an ivory mask, a death mask. I'm just putting you out of your misery, Lisa. You don't want to spend the rest of your life a withered vegetable in a hospital ward.

I leaned over her and fumbled with the dagger underneath the surgical jacket. Everything was going exactly according to plan. The police officer, a young Hispanic woman, was working a crossword puzzle and had nodded in response to

*my respectful bow. Can you kill silently? How much noise
does a knife going into a human body make? Perhaps there
was hardly any sound at all. If I struck with a cool hand and
steady nerve, one quick, savage thrust might be no more
noisy than a spring breeze against a windowpane. It might
be minutes before the cop looked up and saw the knife handle
jutting from Lisa's body.*

*I held the dagger at eye level. Where to strike? The ribs
were a dangerous target. The knife could be bent or broken
on impact. Aim for her stomach, not for her heart.*

*What am I waiting for? Now! Do it now! My nerves failed:
there was too much heartbeat, too much throbbing temple,
too much trembling fingers. I am going to blunder. I will
blow this. Lisa will live, I'll be locked up, perhaps forever,
in a mental institution. I should run now, escape, fly out of
the country, hide.*

*It is too late. I can see the police officer's eyes on my back.
She will be suspicious. She will look more closely at my face.
She will speak with me and ask what I am doing in the room.
I will never be able to slide this knife back under my belt. I
have no choice. I must kill!*

*Savagely I struck. It was surprisingly easy, astonishingly
quiet. The razor-sharp blade plunged quickly and cleanly
into Lisa's stomach.*

39

BLACKIE

The killer struck again and again and again, scream-
ing and laughing hysterically. Then the savage thrusts stopped
as she stared in hypnotized horror at what was beneath her
on the bed.

The old fella entered the room and gestured to the police

officer to close in on her. Three more cops moved in behind him.

"Having fun, Kay Kay?" he asked. "It's not Lisa, you know. This time we outsmarted you."

Four policewomen swarmed over her. Quickly they pried the knife out of her hand. Kerry Ann Randall was difficult to subdue. It required all four of the policewomen and two male officers who followed them in from the corridor to pin her on the bed, next to the tattered dummy with which we had trapped her, and affix handcuffs.

"It was all a trick, you see, Kerry Ann," my father went on implacably, his ice-blue eyes glowing with the fire of the midnight sun. "We moved Lisa to another room. We knew that when you heard the false announcement on television, you would come back to try to finish what you'd begun. We didn't have enough evidence for arrest until now, Kerry Ann. You've given us enough to put you behind bars for the rest of your life."

"Where you'll never be able to hurt her again," I added tonelessly.

It wasn't true. A few months or years at the most in a mental hospital, and she'd be free to try again. We would stop her the next time.

She screamed terrible obscenities at us, exhausting herself with murderous hatred. My father ignored her. "I think, officer, you can call the superintendent and Mr. Daley and tell them they can come up now."

"You've always hated her, haven't you, Kerry Ann?" I said, now feeling some sadness for this demented woman. "You've been second fiddle to her all your life. You consoled yourself through the years with the argument that while she was popular and successful and beautiful, you were the intelligent one—sophisticated, aware, well informed, ideologically correct. Lisa might be the star, but she was a shallow, superficial, naive woman. You loved her and you hated her. You could not tolerate her existence, but you were not driven to kill her as long as you could tell yourself that poor, dumb Lisa was economically and socially irrelevant. Then she made *The Friendship Factor*. You watched over her shoulder as it emerged. You were the only one of her friends who realized how good it was and that Lisa's conviction that she could be a great actress and a great filmmaker was not an illusion. Your rival was not merely a stupid little actress who starred in foolish popular entertainments, she was one of the greats. That offense cried to heaven for vengeance. All the other things she had done to you throughout your life paled by comparison. Her beauty, her talent, her happy marriage you could tolerate, although just barely. You could not tolerate her achieving what you knew by right was yours, to be acclaimed as a genius.

"That's what you think you are, isn't it, Kerry Ann? An unrecognized genius. How dare an insignificant little child receive acclaim for what is rightly yours? She had deprived you of your rightful recognition, so you had to deprive her of her life."

"I loved her! I loved her!" shouted the red-eyed, hysterically twisting woman. "Don't you understand? I loved her!"

"Of course you loved her, Kerry Ann. That's why her crime was so terrible that it could only be expiated by death."

The police led her away, and the State's attorney and the police superintendent entered the hospital room, Mike Casey prudently staying away to permit his successor a few moments of press attention.

"How did you know, Father?" Rich Daley's strong, boyish face turned toward me, dark eyes sparkling with curiosity.

"Oh *that*. Once I saw the clue that was staring me in the face from day one, it was easy.

"First of all, you could list some of them as questionable starters, like Jim McMahon next Sunday, if you consider opportunity. I didn't see how those who had come in from out of town could have brought the blackjack and the hypodermic syringe through airport security. Moreover, King and Thomas and Woods discovered their reasons for wanting Lisa dead late in the day, too late, I thought, for them to obtain the syringe, the drug, and the sap. Perhaps they were thinking about murder before they left LA and had made contact before they came with a confederate in Chicago, who provided them with the equipment. But that was only a possibility.

"A doctor, of course, could bring medical equipment. He had the largest potential profit to gain from Lisa's death. And Kerry, a native of Chicago and a sometime radical journalist, surely had contacts who could supply her with what she needed. My guess is that she made plans long ago. While the crime was furious, it did not seem to be hasty.

"Leonard and Winnie? Both were Chicagoans, both with more than enough contacts to find all the equipment they needed. Both, however, had alibis. Maybe we could break the alibis, but maybe they were honest. If I presumed for the sake of the argument that their friends were telling the truth, that seemed to leave us with Kerry and Roderick."

The old fella cocked a quizzical white eyebrow. "This was all clear before your mysterious *big* clue?"

"The thought process I've just described was taking place in my head when I finally saw the clue. Maybe it helped me to see it. Professor James would say that the congruence and luminosity—"

"Johnny." The old fella sighed just like I do. "Mr. Daley here can read your article on Professor James some other time."

Score one for the old fella.

"I'll send you a reprint, Rich. Anyway, if you looked at it from the point of view of motives, you came up with the same two names. As the old fella here said, it was a crime of passion and not of reason. Actually, since the old fella likes to show off how much he knows, he used the French words, not *rationnel* but *passionnel*. Most of the suspects had reason to want to be rid of Lisa, but not for reasons that were compatible with the violence and the anger of the crime. Ken Woods, it seemed to me, would not risk his comfortable old age to punish a lost love. Anyway, he still adores Lisa. Kill her? Maybe. Brutalize her? No way.

"Thomas and King were in career jeopardy, but you don't maim, then kill a woman merely because she wants to put her kids on TV with you. So the goose has other eggs. She's still given you the golden one. Kill her and you kill it.

"Sister Winnie talks a good line, but she'd probably lose her nerve when it came to real violence. Besides, she probably thought she could still get money out of Lisa, if not for the Sandinistas, then for someone else.

"Frank Leonard wouldn't lose his nerve, but I was pretty sure that the men with their hats on would warn him that they wanted no more trouble from him.

"Her brother? He hated her enough, but he's not the S and M type. Who did that leave? Kerry Ann had hardly any rational motive for killing Lisa. If we were simply looking for a man or a woman who could profit in some way or another from Lisa's death, Kerry was the least likely of suspects.

"If, on the other hand, we were looking for somebody whose passions would drive him or her to need and demand and revel in a violent and brutal destruction of Lisa, then Kerry Ann became the prime suspect. Her mixture of love and hate, an early adolescent, envious crush that turned sour instead of maturing, could easily have led to what the rest of us might call senseless violence. For her it would be obligation, a necessity.

"I knew that the film, somehow or the other, was the cause of the killer's hatred, especially after I saw it. Lisa had hit a home run with the bases loaded the first time she came to bat in the major leagues. To the killer this was absolutely intolerable, God's final exultation of Lisa at the killer's expense, Salieri's fury at Mozart. Kerry was the one who had seen the film develop from the beginning.

"I suspect that her original plan was to use Lisa's friendship as a pretext for worming her way into Lisa's life so that she could write a savage exposé. What's the point of doing a savage exposé of a woman who's going to pick up every film prize for 1984 and '85? Not very many people will bother to read your book. Those who read it will say, quite accurately, that it's sour grapes. You can't kill Lisa with words, so now it becomes essential to kill her with a blackjack or a knife, and as brutally as possible." I shrugged helplessly. "Kerry was the only one who might have had that kind of motivation."

"You figured it out that way?" The State's attorney's forehead wrinkled. "Maybe I ought to hire some philosophers for my staff."

"No," I admitted, "that came later. As I just told counsel here, my thought processes were finally beginning to work again. My head had been stuffed with confusion and worry and self-pity about losing Lisa. Besides, I knew that the most I could do with the game of eliminating people on grounds of motive and opportunity was to produce a case for you filled with holes. I kept waiting for the clue I knew was there if only I could see it."

"And that was?" Admiral Ryan could on occasion show some signs of impatience. I had kept him waiting long enough.

"The real tip-off was the drinks."

"The drinks?" The old fella, perhaps for the second or third time in his life, seemed surprised at me. "What drinks?"

"One of Lisa's courtesies was remembering what her guests' favorite foods and drinks were. When you came to visit her, she had the drink already prepared for you and the food on the stove. Without realizing it, I knew the Bean Counter was innocent because, like me and"—I nodded at the old fella—"like himself here, George has the good taste to enjoy John Jameson's Irish whiskey. Right?"

"Right." The State's attorney laughed his generous, contagious laugh. "Maybe Lisa can make her next film about you."

"Come now, Rich, you're being excessive. In any event, it couldn't be George the Bean Counter because the bottles in her suite at the Westin were vodka. Subconsciously I realized that fact and made a careful note of the favorite drinks of all the other suspects. I was innocent, of course, not only because I was innocent, but also because, like George the Bean Counter, I indulge in Irish whiskey. Tad Thomas drinks white wine; Dina King consumes—in truth at a prodigious rate—gin and tonics; our good friend Francis A. for Assisi Leonard is given, somewhat vulgarly, to J and B and water; Sister Winifred ostentatiously and self-righteously does not drink; similarly, Roderick Malone will not permit his steady surgeon's hand to be corrupted by John Barleycorn. Ken Woods, I fear, is addicted to old-fashioneds."

"And Kerry Randall drinks vodka?" The State's attorney considered me in goggle-eyed disbelief. I imagined what his father might have said under similar circumstances.

"Indeed."

"I wouldn't want to have to tell that to a jury."

"The point, Rich," I said, blinking my nearsighted eyes at him, "is that you don't have to."

The State's attorney exploded again with the famed Rich Daley laugh. We all laughed with him.

"I assume, Mr. Daley, that you're prepared to have all charges against my client dismissed?" the old fella asked.

Rich reached for the telephone.

None of which revived Lisa from the coma.

40

BLACKIE

On the eve of the Feast of all the Saints, the Lord God dealt us a trick card, doubtless from the bottom of Her stacked deck.

The Lord God made the rules and created the deck and the rest of the cosmos, too, for that matter. Thus She can cheat whenever She wants to, understandably enough in the Roman (though not Anglo-Saxon) law adage that the lawgiver is above the laws.

The Lord God, He cheats outrageously.

All the time.

George Quinn and I were in Lisa's room, watching her silently in her long sleep, which now seemed likely to last forever. He had been appointed conservator of her finances and was about to fly back to California to supervise arrangements for the premier of *The Friendship Factor*. A *Time* magazine cover had been guaranteed for two weeks after the presidential election.

The Chicago Bears had routed the Buccaneers, the Vikings, and the sometime Oakland Raiders and were four games ahead of the pack, something that my father contended had not happened since 1932. Ronald Reagan, having been declared the winner in his last fitful debate with poor Walter Mondale, was now a lead pipe cinch to be reelected President of the United States. Indira Gandhi had been murdered. The Dubuffet "Monument with Standing Beast" had been hauled to the front of the State of Illinois Building. Stevie Wonder was on top of the charts with "I Just Called to Say I Love You."

Michael Jackson had agreed to replace Lisa on her Christmas special if she did not recover, with fervent and obviously sincere prayers that she would recover. Kerry Randall was undergoing psychiatric testing with no guarantee that in a few years she would not be free to walk the streets again, the blackjack and a knife in her purse. Beth and Georgia Anne had proclaimed themselves enthusiastic Chicagoans with no desire to leave St. Praxides Grammar School. Beth was already telling everyone that she intended to go to St. Ignatius High School.

I prayed for Lisa each morning at Mass with sustained fervor but sinking hope.

The fortieth anniversary of the Battle of Leyte Gulf, the greatest naval engagement in history, went unnoticed. Save for a party in honor of one of the survivors at the house of my sister Eileen, near Lincoln Park.

On the day before All Hallows' Eve, the Democrats staged an enthusiastic torchlight parade for Mondale and Ferraro through the streets of my parish. Our day would come again.

That same night I attended the opening of a Swiss milk chocolate store on the Magnificent Mile—marked by the presence of a large and very contented bovine chewing thoughtfully on her cud along the parade route on Michigan Avenue. Perhaps the cow was taken in by the enthusiasm for Walter Mondale.

I considered buying some dark chocolate for Lisa. I decided against it and walked out of the shop quickly. She would never be able to eat it.

Outside I hesitated in the pleasant, humid autumn evening and listened to the bands.

Hope is still hope.

I returned to the store. "Dark chocolate," I informed the young person behind the counter.

"Two pounds, Monsignor Blackie?"

"Huh?" I was thinking of a black-haired tyke on a tricycle.

"Two pounds of dark chocolate?"

"No." If you're going to hope, hope big. "Five pounds."

When the young person passed the package across the counter, I felt constrained to add, "It's a gift."

A gift with fingers crossed.

We knew, as the November first deadline approached, that we had lost Lisa, that the Lord God, for reasons of His own, was not going to give us the second chance for which I had so persuasively argued.

"I suppose I'd better get to the airport," George whispered in a tone usually reserved for wakes. That was what the hospital room was, a wake with a still-breathing corpse.

"We'll stay in touch and let you know immediately if something happens," I said, feeling powerless to respond to George's now completely hidden grief.

"I've given up hoping for anything like that, Blackie." We both walked toward the door. "We were lucky to have her as long as we did."

George preceded me into the corridor. As I walked after him, I glanced back at Lisa's bed. She had turned her head in our direction and was watching us with a faint, quizzical smile.

"George." I clutched at his arm. "Her eyes are open."

"They can't be." He wheeled around. "Good God, Lisa!"

"If you two are here," she struggled with a dry, cracked voice, "and I'm dead, I must be in heaven."

George threw himself to his knees at the side of her bed, grasped her hand, and kissed it fervently.

Rather demonstrative, I thought, for an Irishman.

"What time?" Lisa's eyes seemed to drift out of focus, and then back, firmly, into focus.

"About five-thirty in the afternoon," I said hoarsely.

"Afternoon?" She touched her throat painfully. "Sore arm." She shook her head patiently. "No, sore *throat*."

"It'll be all right, Lisa, don't worry."

"Be all right. What day?"

She had yet to ask where she was. Apparently she didn't know the script for this scene.

"All Hallow's Eve, Halloween."

Her eyes widened. "Halloween! Oh, my!" She closed her eyes lightly and then opened them again. "Treat or trick!" She made a wry face. "No." And she beamed happily. "*Trick or treat!*"

Both, Lisa darling, both.

As I left the room, George was weeping into her hand and kissing it. Lisa's fingers were complacently tapping his cheek. She saw my quick glance and winked.

I raced down the corridor of the Olson Pavilion to the nursing station to summon Dr. Rodriquez and fetch my offering of five pounds of dark chocolate. The lights were still on in the skyscrapers of Chicago, firm, implacable, like stars in the heavens. The lights never really had gone out.

It was not Halloween, it was Christmas.

Both.

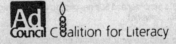